"For some inexplicable reason I like you."

She had once more managed to startle him. "You *like* me?" he repeated in astonishment.

"Yes—but much against my will," she warned him mischievously.

"For God's sake, why?"

"Good God, I don't know! Because you look like a man and not a painted popinjay, and because you are not in the least interested in my fortune," she said, still in amusement.

When his lips twitched, despite himself, she added cheerfully, "And that is another reason why I like you, I suppose. However disagreeable and disapproving you may be, at least you have a sense of humor. But you needn't worry, my lord! It is merely one of those odd quirks of taste for which there is no accounting." She added thoughtfully, "And, I daresay that were I to get to know you better, I would soon find you as tedious and predictable as everyone else."

He burst out laughing. "Oh undoubtably, ma'am! And I can at least return the compliment so far as this: I still am wholly undecided whether I like you or not, but you at least have the novelty of being the most outrageous female I have ever met, and I thought I knew your sex."

Her eyes twinkled responsively. "Yes, so I have frequently been told. But most people don't mean it as a compliment, I fear."

"I am not at all sure I do either, Miss Cantrell!" he told her frankly. . . .

Coming next month

SAVED BY SCANDAL
by Barbara Metzger
"One of the genre's wittiest pens."–*Romantic Times*

Abandoned at the altar, Lord Galen Woodbridge decides to stir up a scandal–by wedding the London songstress Margot Montclaire. But in saving his pride, he never planned on losing his heart....

0-451-20038-1/$4.99

MISS TIBBLES INVESTIGATES
by April Kihlstrom

Pamela Kendall is in love with her childhood friend Julian, who pines for an altogether different girl. But as luck would have it, her mother's former governess, Miss Tibbles, is visiting–and she knows the best way to avert a disaster of the heart....

0-451-20040-3/$4.99

CASSANDRA'S DECEPTION
by Gayle Buck

While pretending to be her twin sister, Cassandra Weatherstone finds passion in the arms of a refined young suitor. But being true to her heart means being exposed as an imposter. And is any love strong enough to survive such a scandal?

0-451-20037-3/$4.99

The Nabob's Daughter

Dawn Lindsey

A SIGNET BOOK

SIGNET
Published by New American Library, a division of
Penguin Putnam Inc., 375 Hudson Street,
New York, New York 10014, U.S.A.
Penguin Books Ltd, 27 Wrights Lane,
London W8 5TZ, England
Penguin Books Australia Ltd, Ringwood,
Victoria, Australia
Penguin Books Canada Ltd, 10 Alcorn Avenue,
Toronto, Ontario, Canada M4V 3B2
Penguin Books (N.Z.) Ltd, 182–190 Wairau Road,
Auckland 10, New Zealand

Penguin Books Ltd, Registered Offices:
Harmondsworth, Middlesex, England

First published by Signet, an imprint of New American Library,
a division of Penguin Putnam Inc.

First Printing, May 2000
10 9 8 7 6 5 4 3 2 1

PUBLISHER'S NOTE
This is a work of fiction. Names, characters, places, and incidents either are
the product of the author's imagination or are used fictitiously, and any
resemblance to actual persons, living or dead, business establishments, events
or locales is entirely coincidental.

BOOKS ARE AVAILABLE AT QUANTITY DISCOUNTS WHEN USED TO PROMOTE
PRODUCTS OR SERVICES. FOR INFORMATION PLEASE WRITE TO PREMIUM
MARKETING DIVISION, PENGUIN PUTNAM INC., 375 HUDSON STREET, NEW YORK,
NEW YORK 10014.

Chapter 1

"**I** am going to marry Guy and there is nothing you can do to stop me!" declared Miss Georgiana Hughendon in an intractable tone, as if daring her brother to deny it.

Lord Chance turned his head to regard his young sister in the pale light afforded by the carriage lamps of his elegant town chaise. "I have not said otherwise," he reminded her rather impatiently. "Nor do I mean to discuss it on the way to a ball, especially one I've not the least desire to attend."

Miss Hughendon, a petite brunette with a lively countenance, pounced on that. "Yes, but if you let me marry my dearest Guy," she pointed out triumphantly, "you need not escort me at all, but might return to your own fusty, dusty pastimes."

His lordship did not much resemble his half sister, for he was a dark, somewhat harsh-featured individual, considerably above the average height, and with a powerful build that showed to best advantage in the riding dress he habitually preferred, even in town. "And has it occurred to you that if you were as in love with this Ludlow as you say, you would not care to be attending balls every night, and flirting outrageously?" he asked dryly.

She cast a darkling glance at him. "What else is there to do, besides mope at home with Mama?" she complained. "And I warn you I have every intention of getting my way in the end."

"And I have told you that if you are of the same mind when Ludlow returns—which I doubt!—we will speak of it again."

"But that is eighteen months away!"

"Yes, and by then you just might—notice I say might—be able to persuade me you are old enough to be married. I consider I am showing quite remarkable restraint towards a man who made up to you when I was not by to keep an eye on you, and made no attempt to request my permission to pay his addresses to you."

Georgy's eyes snapped becomingly. "I knew you would say that! Just because *you* think every female is after you for your money, Stone, you think it's the same with me. But as a matter of fact, Guy didn't even know I was an heiress when he fell in love with me!"

His lordship managed to refrain, with admirable restraint, from revealing the very real nausea this naive declaration inspired in him. "I confess I would be more inclined to believe you had his own relations not packed him off to the West Indies in disgrace."

"I told you about that!" Georgy retorted angrily. "He wished to go, for he—he feels the difference in our fortunes as much as you do, and went out there to try to establish himself, which just *proves* that he is not merely an odious fortune hunter after nothing but my money. And far from waiting eighteen months for him to come back, I mean to join him as soon as possible and be married. So there!"

This defiant declaration, however, had not quite the desired effect. His lordship remarked sardonically in the darkness, "Which wild statement merely proves to me exactly how far you are from being old enough to be married. Good God, Georgy, aside from every other consideration, what do you know of Jamaica? Believe me, if I were such a fool as to countenance so absurd a plan, you would soon be heartily sick of your bargain—if the voyage alone did not kill you. Why, you can scarcely travel five miles without being carriage-sick, and yet you calmly propose to set off on a voyage of two or three months, I daresay, only to find yourself at the end of it in a barbarous country full of dangerous fevers and I know not what else besides. Jamaica! This from a chit who has been pampered and spoilt from the hour of her birth, and would soon find herself at a stand even in England without a host of servants to do her every bidding."

Her eyes kindled. "Oh, I hate you!" she cried passionately. "I *will* marry Guy, and I *will* go to Jamaica, if I have to run away to do it! Just because y-you h-hate women and er mean to marry, you think I sh-should not either."

"Good God, what nonsense is this?" he demanded impatiently. "I don't hate women!"

"Y-yes you do. You are as hard as your name, and I only hope that someday you are made as m-miserable as I am!'

His expression hardened, but before he could retort in kind, the chaise slowed, and he saw that they had reached their destination. He handed her down with a certain grimness, for to escort a damsel to a ball who was in the throes of a temper tantrum held not the least appeal to him. But though Georgy's expression remained stormy, and she turned a cold shoulder on him, once inside Lady Ravenhurst's overheated ballroom, she showed faint signs of returning to normal.

They were soon joined by the Honorable Beverley Mac-Corquodale, one of his lordship's oldest friends, who made her an elaborate bow, which lessened the storm clouds still further. She even giggled when the Honorable Beverley exclaimed in mock astonishment to her brother, "Good Gad, dear boy, thought I must be foxed when I looked across the room and saw you."

"Hallo, Bev," remarked his lordship mildly. "I am here strictly in the role of chaperon, I assure you."

"He means to prop up the wall and scowl at anyone who has the temerity to approach him," said Georgy darkly. "But if he thinks he is going to spoil my evening, he is very much mistaken!"

The Honorable Beverley did not miss these signs of familial discord, but was far too tactful to comment upon them. He was famed for both the elegance of his dress and the grace of his manners, and was, besides, a general favorite with the ladies, which made a sufficient contrast to his old friend to make a great many people wonder at the friendship. Lord Chance possessed a barbed tongue and a pronounced dislike for all such *ton* parties, and far from being a general favorite with the ladies, had a brutal way of discouraging all but the most determined of matchmaking females.

The Honorable Beverley added now, even more tactfully, "It seems to be a night for surprises. Just saw your cousin here as well, dear boy, which gave me almost as great a shock, I can tell you."

Georgy looked faintly interested in this, and his lordship frowned and responded with the bluntness for which he was famous, "Good God, you *must* be foxed, Bev. Darcy would never abandon one of his hells to grace so insipid a party as this."

"Surprised me too," murmured Mr. MacCorquodale, taking a pinch of snuff with a great air, "until he explained to me that since you are so disobliging as to refuse to pop off, dear boy, and leave your title and vast fortune to him to play ducks and drakes with, he has no choice but to reform his way of life."

Georgy giggled again, but Lord Chance said resignedly, "I suppose that means he is under the hatches again. I can only shudder to think what his idea of reforming his life might mean."

He was not left long in doubt, for Mr. Darcy Hughendon, his cousin and heir, himself soon wandered up. He was an engaging scamp who belonged to a set of wild young bucks whose favorite pastimes included drinking a great deal too much, gaming for ruinous stakes at one of the discreet hells in Pall Mall and then ending up the evening by rubbing elbows with far from genteel companions in one of the sluiceries in the east, drinking blue ruin, or else boxing the watch, both of which activities almost inevitably ended in the round house in the early hours of the morning. His tastes were expensive, and his ill luck legendary, and he was always more or less in dun territory, a fact of life he accepted as cheerfully as he did everything else. He cared very little more for fashionable life than did his noble cousin, and seldom graced such harmless affairs with his presence.

He said now, in his careless way, "Good Gad, Chance, never thought to see you at such a devilish dull event as this! Georgy, you're obedient! Only heiress I know that ain't an antidote—though mind, ten years ago when you was in a torn apron and had lost your front teeth, I never thought you'd turn out half so well. You wouldn't consider marrying yours truly, and rescuing me from my current embarrassments? I daresay we would contrive to rub along tolerably well together. In fact, never even need see each other if we didn't want to, and at least I can promise I'd be a damn—dashed sight more tolerant than Chance here."

"No," said Georgy, unembarrassed by either the reminiscence of her past or this exceedingly unromantic proposal. "I am going to marry someone else. Besides, Stone would never permit me to marry you."

Mr. Hughendon evolved faint interest in this news. "Are you? If it will annoy Chance I will reluctantly subordinate my claims. But only think what a public service you'd be performing. My creditors would fall on your neck in tears of joy."

"Tipstaffs after you, Darcy?" inquired his lordship resignedly.

"Lord yes, but there's nothing new in that," replied his cousin with his engaging frankness. "In fact, another night or two like the last one, and you'll be relieved of me at last, coz, for I shall either be clapped up in jail, or forced to go drown myself. If you possessed the least compassion, Chance, you'd long ago have decently broken your neck on one of those damned brutes you ride, or overturned your curricle, or been murdered by footpads on your way home one dark night. I've nothing against you, mind—in fact, devilish fond of you! But what good is that when I'm about to be clapped up for debt? Besides, it ain't even as if you enjoyed your wealth, for you've no expensive vices. I could have a vast deal more enjoyment out of it, give you my word!"

Georgy merely giggled again, and his lordship remarked dryly, "Never fear: Georgy may yet drive me to an apoplexy."

"Yes, but will it be in time to do me any good?" objected Mr. Hughendon reasonably. "Besides, you may be a confirmed misogynist, but who's to say you won't yet marry and beget a pack of brats in your own image, if only to spite me? Which is why I've come to the conclusion it's time to reform my ways."

This impressive announcement did not achieve quite the desired effect, for Georgy fell into helpless giggles, and even Lord Beverley merely inquired with mild interest, "Does that mean you intend to give up faro and French hazard, and getting drunk six nights out of the seven?"

"Good Gad, are you mad?" exclaimed Darcy, profoundly shocked. "Might as well shoot myself at once and be done with it! The thing is, even if I were to apply to Chance to relieve me of my most pressing obligations, there's no getting around it that in six months' time I'd be back in the same state."

"From past experience I suspect it would be rather less than six months," observed his lordship dryly. "But you have us all waiting with baited breath, Darcy."

"Mind, I don't say it's what I like," warned his cousin. "I ain't a misogynist like you, but never had much of a taste for being petticoat-led. In fact," he added gloomily, "I don't say that of the two, debtor's prison don't sometimes seem preferable to me than a lifetime of being leg-shackled. But since there's precious little hope you'll obligingly go off in an infectious complaint, Chance, I'm left with little choice in the matter."

"Good God," said his lordship, "can't it be you hope to repair your fortunes by marrying an heiress?"

"Aye, that's it! I don't say it's an ideal solution, and aside from Georgy, here, never knew an heiress yet that didn't squint like a bag of nails. But I tell you, it's either that or put a bullet through my brain, for I never knew the cards to run so much against me. That's why when I heard there was a new heiress in town, some nabob's daughter or other, I made up my mind there's no help for it but to make a push to meet her. Which is why you find me here tonight at this damned-devilish dull affair."

"Good God!" said his lordship again. "The only thing that would surprise me more than this sudden resolution of yours, Darcy, would be if you were allowed anywhere near this or any other heiress. You must rank high on the list of the town's most ineligible bachelors."

"No, no, you're forgetting that I'm your heir," Darcy remarked, unoffended. "*I* may set precious little store by that, for you'll live to be a hundred if only to spite me; but don't I keep on telling you she's some dashed Indian merchant's daughter? As vulgar as bedamned, I make no doubt, but said to be as rich as Croesus, and with any luck *she's* not to know how little hope I have of ever stepping into the title."

"Who is she?" inquired the Honorable Beverley, interested. "I thought I knew all the latest *on-dits,* but it's the first I've heard of some new heiress in town."

"Oh, she's staying with Lady Fernhurst, who's her aunt,

or some such. *That* ain't so bad, but her father's said to have come out of some back slum in Bristol, or was it Birmingham? I forget, not that it matters, but he's as vulgar as bedamned. Ran away to sea when he was twelve, or so the story goes, and made his fortune in trade. Eventually managed to marry above his station, and is no doubt ambitious now to see his only daughter suitably established. She's held to be a thought more genteel—not that I put much stock in that, for she comes from some devilish outlandish place in the West Indies. But the father's said to own half of Jamaica, and she inherits everything when he cocks up his toes. And as long as the dibs are in tune, Lord knows I'm in no position to be too choosy. *Now* what's to do?"

For Georgy had given a sudden screech, causing several matrons nearby to turn to regard her with disapproval. "Did you say he owns half of *Jamaica*?" she gasped.

Darcy was looking at her with mild interest. "That's right. Why? What's there in that to set you screeching?"

"Merely that the man I am going to marry has gone out to Jamaica, and I am *determined* to join him there," Georgy informed him. "Oh, where is she? I must make her acquaintance immediately, for she may actually have met Guy, and at the very least, she will be able to tell me all about Jamaica. Oh, could anything be more fortunate?"

"Good God, that's torn it!" exclaimed her brother resignedly.

"Who's Guy, and why the devil should you want to go to such a dashed uncomfortable place?" demanded Darcy curiously.

"Guy is the man I'm going to marry, as you'd know very well if you ever listened to a word anyone said to you!" exclaimed Georgy impatiently. "He's been sent out to Jamaica by his horribly disapproving family, which is why I not only want to go there, I am *determined* to go, whatever Stone may say!"

"You don't say! What *does* Stone say, by the way?"

"Everything of the most disagreeable, but only because he is fusty and dusty and as hard as his name, and thinks I am still a child. Oh, where is Lady Fernhurst? Do you know her? Has she arrived yet?"

Darcy obligingly began to look around the crowded ballroom. "Damme if I see why you're so set on going out to such a devilish uncomfortable place, but if you were to get upon terms with this heiress, I don't know but what you might be in a position to do me a good turn, coz," he added hopefully.

"What, to help you marry an ugly heiress?" Georgy demanded with equal frankness. "Why should I? Oh, there! Isn't that Lady Fernhurst in the purple turban and the plumes?"

Mr MacCorquodale, something of an arbiter, winced at this description, but Georgy had already darted off in her usual impetuous fashion, leaving her cousin Darcy to stare after her in some disapproval. "Come to think of it, she ain't changed so very much after all," he complained. "Always was a dashed unrestful chit! She really going to marry some fellow in Jamaica?" he inquired skeptically of his lordship.

"No," answered Chance, not mincing matters.

"Didn't think so," said Darcy, evidently happy to have that mystery cleared up. "Sounds like a dashed loose screw to me, and you're devilish high in the instep, especially where she's concerned."

"I am," agreed his lordship. "And has it occurred to you, Darcy, that if you were to step into my shoes, as you so ardently desire, you would inherit the responsibility for my sister along with my fortune?"

It was plain, from his arrested expression, that it had not, but Chance had already gone in pursuit of his sister. Darcy stared after them and remarked somewhat resentfully, "Dash it, and they say *I'm* ramshackle. Never knew such a pair! All the same," he added thoughtfully, "I don't know but what Chance ain't right, for once. No wish to say a word against Georgy—fond of her, in fact. But that don't mean I wish to have to keep an eye on her, or be obliged to keep her out of mischief."

"No, I'd stick to your heiress, if I were you," recommended Mr. MacCorquodale in some amusement, also prepared to saunter off. "It's likely to be far more peaceful in the long run."

Chapter 2

Lady Fernhurst was a raddled widow of uncertain age, unknown to Chance except by sight, but reputedly with four daughters to dispose of on an always inadequate jointure. His lordship, annoyed with the coincidence that had led her to sponsor her provincial niece at that precise moment, was yet honest enough to acknowledge that if the niece was indeed rich, the temptation must have been almost irresistible. He was vaguely aware that her long-deceased spouse was said to have run rapidly through a respectable fortune and then capped an already ruinous career by dropping dead of an apparent apoplexy at the races, on which he had staked a considerable wager. It went without saying that the horse he had backed had been unplaced.

Lady Fernhurst was attired respectably, if not particularly becomingly, in an elaborate gown of puce satin, with a purple turban with several nodding plumes, making her readily identifiable even in that crowd. His lordship, with his superior height, had no trouble in singling her out, and also in discovering that she was accompanied by two much younger females.

The first, a pale blond child in a white muslin gown, Chance dismissed after the most cursory of glances, his eyes going instinctively to her far more striking companion. This was, without a doubt, the West Indian heiress, and his lordship, looking her over extremely critically, nevertheless found his first impression was not unfavorable. He had been prepared for ostentation and vulgarity, but in appearance, at least, he found nothing to object to. In an age when young girls traditionally decked themselves out in only the palest of blues or pinks or ambers, she was almost as colorfully attired as her aunt, in a gown of vibrant green silk with a gauze overdress. But it bore the unmistakable stamp of being both expensive, and indefinably not English in origin, and even his lordship, wholly uninterested in feminine fashions, could tell at a glance that it had not been fashioned by any provincial dressmaker. His sister, along with every other female in the room, could have informed him, with considerable envy, that it came straight from Paris, for since the long war with France French fashions had been almost wholly unattainable in England.

For so reputedly wealthy an heiress she boasted few jewels, which also surprised him, though the pearls around her neck were large and extremely well matched, and her emerald and pearl eardrops looked equally expensive. Her hair, of a rich mahogany color, was simply dressed, and he was forced to admit that she had an indefinable air of self-possession that belied both her age and her allegedly humble origins.

Her complexion was certainly unfashionably brown, particularly in a country where females habitually protected themselves from exposure to even the mildest of English suns; and she was taller than was strictly fashionable, though her figure was both slender and elegant. Her face was too strong for conventional beauty, for it was marked by a generous mouth that looked to be unexpectedly passionate, and she had a slight cleft in a decidedly willful chin. Her eyes were her best feature, for they were of an indeterminate hazel, now turned a vivid green by the color of her gown, and of considerable size and brilliance. In fact, it occurred to Chance that she looked decidedly out of place in that well-bred assembly, but only because she made every other female in the room look suddenly pale and bloodless, like a peacock let loose in a room full of wrens. His lordship's eyebrows rose despite himself.

His sister had already darted up to them with her usual impetuosity, and he arrived somewhat grimly just in time to hear her exclaim, "Oh, is it true you're from Jamaica? Dear Lady Fernhurst, how do you do? Pray don't be offended! I am Georgiana Hughendon, you know, and—and I just *had* to speak to your niece, for there are particular reasons why I wish to know *all* about Jamaica."

Lady Fernhurst was looking understandably taken aback, and the heiress somewhat amused. His lordship drawled as he joined them, "You must forgive my sister, ma'am! She is a minx, as you have no doubt already discovered for yourself."

But Lady Fernhurst, certainly not blind to the unexpected good fortune that had brought two such notable figures into her orbit, had already recovered herself and hurried into speech. "Oh, pray do not apologize, my lord! Indeed, you must allow me to introduce my daughter Anne to you and your dear sister. And of course my niece, Miss Cantrell. Lord Chance and his sister, Miss Hughendon."

The shy blond blushed hotly and bobbed a schoolgirl's curtsy, but the heiress looked him over almost as coolly as he had done her. Under any other circumstances his lordship might have been diverted by so unusual a female, and would certainly have followed her assault upon London with mild interest. As it was, however, he wished her at Jericho, and so favored her with only the coldest of bows.

Georgy was saying cheerfully, "Pray do not mind my brother, Miss Cantrell, for he is fusty and dusty and always preaching propriety, but he never succeeds in stopping me from what I *really* wish to do. Please, will you tell me about Jamaica?"

Miss Cantrell spoke in a slow, attractive voice that gave no hint of her supposedly humble origins. "Of course I will be happy to tell you all I can, Miss Hughendon."

"Thank you! I have a particular reason for asking, as I said. My—my fiancé just went out there, and I mean to join him as soon as may be possible!" Again she shot a defiant glare at her brother, and tossed her head. "Perhaps you know him. His name is Guy Ludlow, and he only arrived a few months ago."

Miss Cantrell furrowed her brow in a thoughtful manner Chance also found unexpectedly appealing. "Ludlow . . . ?" she repeated, "I'm sorry, but I can't seem to recall—no, wait, I may have met him just before I sailed. Is he a tall, fair man?"

"Yes, that's him! I knew if you had met him you could not forget him, for he is the most charming creature imaginable," said Georgy enthusiastically. "Indeed, I have little doubt all the Jamaican beauties will be setting their caps at him, which is one of the reasons I am *determined* not to wait eighteen months before we can be married. It is all very well to talk about absence making the heart grow fonder, but I have always thought that the greatest piece of nonsense imaginable, haven't you? *Especially* with any number of females no doubt perfectly willing to console him."

Miss Cantrell seemed amused by this naive revelation, but said merely, "We must hope your Mr. Ludlow will prove more constant. But if you are really interested in hearing about Jamaica, you may call upon me almost any morning. I ride in the park at an early hour, but I am usually free after that. Do you know my aunt's house, in Hill Street?"

Georgy promised eagerly to call at the first opportunity. His lordship, cynically used to having females use every artifice in their arsenal to try and engage his interest, was obliged to own he also liked Miss Cantrell's poise and the disinterested way she received this promise. It was her aunt who exclaimed with flattering deference, "Oh, pray, Miss Hughendon, come any day, for we have very few engagements just at present—this early in the Season, I mean. Indeed, I am sure my niece will be delighted to receive you, for she has but little acquaintance in London just yet, of course, and I declare you will be conferring a positive favor upon her to call."

Chance thought Miss Cantrell looked far from pleased by this eagerness, which also surprised him. She must have known she was unlikely to be accepted in London with open arms, however wealthy her father might be. Indeed, she and her aunt and cousin had been standing in a little circle of isolation in that crowded throng, the object of many surreptitious glances and much whispering; and she would have had to be very stupid not to realize—as he was himself annoyingly aware—that the advent of his sister and himself upon the scene had greatly intensified those stares and whispers.

It played no part in his schemes to encourage false hopes in so provincial a female's breast, but Miss Cantrell betrayed no awareness of the signal honor being shown her. Her manner was friendly, but held a good deal of reserve, and if it had not been so ridiculous, Chance would almost have said she seemed oddly detached from the proceedings as if willing to be amused by the quaint practices she saw around her.

If so, she was soon to be richly rewarded, for at that point they were interrupted. A veritable tulip of the ton

minced up, instantly recognizable from his exquisitely wind-
swept hair to his rigidly starched shirt points, so exaggerated in height that he could not turn his head more than a
few inches in any direction. The spotless cravat about his
neck was quite a foot wide, and arranged in so elaborate a
style that he looked as if he were perpetually suffering from
a sore throat, and his black coat was clearly the product of
a master tailor's art, and fitted his somewhat willowy form
so tightly it must have required the services of two stout
menservants to help him into it. He carried an ornate gold
quizzing glass in one white hand, which magnified his eye
quite hideously whenever he looked through it, and boasted
so many fobs and seals that they proclaimed him without
doubt a very pink of the pinks, slap up to the echo.

Sir Winsley Fawnhope was, as Chance well knew, peren-
nially on the lookout for a wealthy bride, for he was almost
as expensive as Darcy, and his estates provided an inadequate income. An addiction to dandyism, not gaming, was
his vice, and he spent a fortune on his wardrobe. He had
an exaggerated air of pride, which sprang from his unflag-
ging belief in his own unquestioned superiority to every
other mortal, and only the direst of necessities had led him
to consider matrimony, for his interest, first, last, and always, was centered firmly upon his own scented person.

He made an elaborate bow to the general company, but
his quizzing glass was directed unfailingly at the heiress,
and his brows rose as he pronounced in a voice that held
something of a lisp, " 'Pon my word! Your servant, Lady
Fernhurst. Miss Hughendon! Miss Fernhurst. I declare, I
never thought to see *you* at such a crush, Chance. But I
protest you have stolen a march on me! Positively you have
stolen a march. I hope, dear Lady Fernhurst, that you mean
to introduce me to your so-charming niece, for I have already heard her praises sung so highly that I have been
positively agog to meet her. And now I find report has
vastly understated the case, for I declare she is charming!
Positively charming!'' Once more the quizzing glass swept
appreciatively over her. He pointedly ignored the presence
of that other notable heiress in the party, for Chance had
been exceedingly blunt on the subject the one time he had
attempted to make up to Georgy.

His lordship found his ridiculous airs nauseating and seldom troubled to hide the fact, but Lady Fernhurst was looking even more gratified at so much flattering attention. His lordship glanced curiously at the heiress to see how she was taking the newcomer, and discovered that her glance seemed far from admiring. But even as he looked she had lowered her long lashes and he could no longer read her expression.

Lady Fernhurst delightedly performed the requested introduction, and Sir Winsley swept another magnificent leg. "Enchanted, Miss Cantrell," he exclaimed gallantly. " 'Pon my word, I declare I am positively enchanted! I beg that you will do me the honor of standing up with me for the next pair of dances."

Georgy observed this byplay with considerable interest, but the heiress responded at once, in her low, attractive voice, "I fear you must hold me excused, sir. As you can see, I am otherwise engaged at the moment."

Sir Winsley Fawnhope was not to be so easily deterred, however. "No, no, my dear Miss Cantrell, I declare I will not be so refused," he insisted. "Surely you cannot mean to be so cruel as to deny me the chance to be the first to lead out such a goddess? Lady Fernhurst, I beg you to add your entreaties to mine."

Lord Chance, his distaste of so much affected nonsense at the fore, and with ulterior motives of his own, surprised the assembled company very much by intervening at this point. "I am afraid you are doomed to be disappointed, Fawnhope," he remarked blandly. "Miss Cantrell is already promised to me for the next set."

Georgy fairly goggled at him, and even Lady Fernhurst looked astonished, for it was well known that he almost never danced. Lord Chance was grimly aware that he was laying himself open to precisely the sort of gossip he most deplored—let alone rousing ambitions in the heiress's breast he had no intention of fulfilling. But it might pay him to get upon terms with her; and besides, so far she had managed to surprise him, which was not a thing that happened very often.

Miss Cantrell was regarding him with a certain speculation, but it was again impossible to read the thoughts going on behind those long lashes of hers. But she did not repudiate his words. "His lordship has indeed already engaged me for the next set. Perhaps another time, sir."

Sir Winsley had nothing to do but bow himself away with what grace he could muster, but as Chance escorted her to the dance floor, his companion surprised him still more by saying in apparent amusement, "It appears I must thank you, my lord, for rescuing me. Who is that coxcomb?"

"You are severe, ma'am. I assure you Fawnhope is a veritable pink of the *ton*. Unfortunately he possesses neither wealth nor wit, but the sheer audacity of his dress and manners generally assure his acceptance by the uncritical majority."

"Well, he would be very much laughed at at home," she said frankly.

He was obliged to wait until the movements of the dance brought them together again. "That I can well believe, but I fear you will never get Fawnhope to credit it. His utter conviction of his own superiority is the only thing that sustains him."

This time she did not trouble to hide the amused contempt in her eyes. "Good God! But then, from what I have observed so far, London seems to be full of such absurd creatures."

His brows rose. "I hope you do not include me in that category, ma'am?" he observed politely.

She looked startled, and then unexpectedly laughed. It transformed her face, softening its strength and making her look slightly mischievous. "Well, you may very well be a coxcomb, my lord," she told him even more frankly, "but at least you have the good sense not to look like one."

He was slightly taken aback, despite himself. He certainly was not used to receiving veiled insults from strange young ladies, especially provincial nobodies, and scarcely knew whether to be amused or affronted. She surprised him still more by performing her part in the dance with considerable grace. She had all the assurance of a young matron with several Seasons at her back, not a young unmarried female of questionable origins visiting London for the first time from one of the more uncivilized colonies. Had it not been for his sister, he might have found himself considerably intrigued by so unusual a female.

She promptly increased his curiosity by asking in a way that showed she gave little more credence to his gallantries than she had Fawnhope's, "Why did you ask me to dance, my lord?"

He wondered if she could really be trying to put him at a disadvantage. It seemed unlikely, but it was the second remark she had made with a distinct edge to it, and he could not make up his mind whether she merely had not the least conception of how to behave in polite company, or was being deliberately provoking. The latter seemed unlikely, for he could not imagine what she had to gain by it, but he could not forget the impression he had earlier received that she was secretly amused by them all. "And how am I supposed to answer that?" he demanded, hoping to turn the tables on her.

It did not succeed. "Truthfully, I hope," she told him in amusement. "I am grateful for the rescue, but I had gained the distinct impression that you did not approve of me."

There was unmistakable provocation in her tone by then. Well, he thought grimly, if she was deliberately trying to put him out of countenance, she would soon find that two could play at that game. "Come, come, Miss Cantrell!" he countered. "Such modesty no doubt does you credit, but you must have known that the success of so great an heiress was virtually guaranteed in London. To be sure, there may be some old-fashioned sticklers who will turn a cold shoulder, but you need not regard them. I feel sure Fawnhope is but the first to attempt to make an assault on so—rich a prize, and you may expect shortly to find yourself positively besieged. But then I can only suppose you came to England for no other purpose."

He thought she stiffened, but then she had lowered those deceptive lashes of hers again. But if he thought he had managed to disconcert her, he was to discover he was mistaken. "Why, this is excellent, my lord!" she exclaimed with every appearance of delight. "You encourage me to think England is not so very different from home as I had begun to fear. My aunt has warned me that although few people will be in any doubt as to why I have come, I must on no account speak of it. But your frankness encourages me to hope the English are not quite so hypocritical as she had led me to believe. After all, London is known as the marriage mart, is it not?"

She was indeed outrageous. "Why, certainly, ma'am," he agreed affably. "And if there are still some who prefer to cloak such frank business transactions in polite euphemisms, I feel sure you are to be applauded for your rejection of such hypocrisy, as you call it."

"Why, so I think, my lord. My aunt also warns me that although my papa's fortune should ensure that I have not the least difficulty in achieving an advantageous marriage, I must take care not to remind people of his connection to trade, which seems to me the height of absurdity. You may be sure we are not so squeamish about that particular subject at home."

His first, slightly favorable opinion of her had been swiftly overborne, and he could not resist retorting a trifle grimly, "I wouldn't worry, ma'am. You may find a few who are unprepared to overlook your—er—origins—for the sake of your fortune, but I am sure their number will be far overshadowed by those who, like Sir Winsley Fawnhope, care not a jot who your father may be, or even the source of his income, so long as the marriage settlements are generous enough!"

Her eyes were again concealed from him. "Why, you do indeed relieve my mind, my lord!" she said lightly. "Even Papa, who grew up in England, you know—though in very different circles, of course—warned me that although the English may be known abroad as a nation of shopkeepers, the upper classes are quick to disavow any connection to so sordid a subject. But I see no reason to indulge such snobbery."

"Why should you?" he inquired sardonically, having himself well in hand again. "In the terms of sordid trade so much deplored by the more hypocritical among us, it is undoubtedly a seller's market. And that being the case, you would certainly seem to hold all the cards, Miss Cantrell."

She seemed once more amused. "Why, I am glad to hear you say so. My aunt assures me that in these expensive times, I may look almost as high as I please. Indeed, I think I should be selling myself very short not to hold out for an earl at the very least. What do you think, my lord?"

"You are ambitious, ma'am!" he could not resist saying

even more grimly. "You must be very sure of your— attractions."

"Why, not at all. I am merely very sure of the attraction of my papa's fortune."

"In that case, why stop there?" he demanded. "After all, there are at least two royal dukes unattached at the moment."

She laughed. "Now I fear you are roasting me, my lord. I hope I am not unreasonable, and Papa has always taught me that in business one must be realistic. But I do not despair of finding exactly what I am looking for. In general, you know, I am quite as determined as my papa, and he began life in a back slum and ended by being one of the richest men in Jamaica."

He was once more slightly taken aback by her frankness. "He must be very proud of you, ma'am."

If she recognized his sarcasm, she did not give any sign of it. "Why, I hope so." Her brow furrowed, and she outraged him even more by adding ingenuously, "As yet, of course, I am almost wholly ignorant of London society, which I confess is a decided disadvantage. What is your own title, for instance, my lord?"

But that, at least, failed to pierce his armor. "Oh, I fear I am quite beneath your touch, Miss Cantrell," he informed her sardonically. "With your—ambitions, you would be positively throwing yourself away on a mere viscount."

She frowned, as if disappointed, then shrugged. "Oh, well, I don't mean to do anything too hastily, of course. It is always fatal in any business arrangement to limit one's options, you know."

"Then I can only wish you good hunting, Miss Cantrell. Though after getting to know you slightly better, you might reconsider your rejection of Sir Winsley. I feel sure so hard-headed a businesswoman as yourself realizes it is well not to take anything for granted."

He thought that he had at last succeeded in getting a spark out of her, but he could not be sure. Before he could pursue this promising new possibility, the music came to an end. All in all, he was not sorry to restore her to her aunt, where he bowed and remarked with only thinly veiled sarcasm, "I must thank you for a—most informative interlude,

Miss Cantrell, and can only wish you good luck in your current enterprise."

"Why, thank you," she returned with seeming indifference. "But I believe that luck has very little to do with it."

His lip curled, and he bowed again and took his leave.

When he returned to his own party, he found both Georgy and his cousin inclined to be indignant with him. "Dash it, coz, if it ain't just like you to try to queer my pitch," complained Darcy. "*You've* no need to dangle after an heiress, and it's dashed unsporting of you to raise expectations in her breast that you've no intention of fulfilling! First heiress too, since Georgy here, who ain't an antidote!"

Georgy giggled at this reference to herself, but said severely, "And if your object in standing up with her was to convince her not to talk to me, it won't do you a particle of good, and so I should warn you!"

"Aye, pretty paltry behavior, I call it," agreed Darcy. "Especially when you've been after me forever to reform my way of life. And when I decide to do just that, dashed if you don't spoil sport."

Georgy eyed her brother rather assessingly. "Still, it *is* unlike him, you must admit. Do you think he could really be attracted to her?" she demanded of her cousin.

"Of course he ain't!" retorted Darcy. "If you ask me, he did it just to be disagreeable. After all, she ain't at all in his line, besides being a dashed cit, or as near as makes no odds. He's too devilish proud for that."

"Yes, but she's not at all what I expected," pointed out Georgy thoughtfully. "She wasn't in the least vulgar, and dressed in a Paris gown, too!" she added somewhat enviously. "And you said yourself she's *very* pretty."

"She's not in the least pretty," corrected her brother rather grimly. "She is also exceedingly vulgar, and wholly outrageous. And you might at least wait to discuss me until I'm no longer present."

Georgy gaped at him, but Darcy was still nursing his grievance, and said severely, "That's all very well for you to say, but beggars can't be choosers, and in any event you've no right to go putting ideas in her head you ain't the least intention of fulfilling, and spoiling it for the rest of us."

"You needn't worry," put in his lordship more grimly

still. "Miss Cantrell assures me she means to hold out for an earl at the very least."

"Hold out for— Dash it, cousin, she can never have told you so!" insisted Darcy indignantly.

"On the contrary, she was quite frank on the subject."

"Good God!" said Darcy. "Yes, but—dash it all, *which* earl?"

"I've no idea. Nor does she, I imagine."

"Well, if that don't beat all!" Then Darcy brightened slightly. "Though it would almost be worth it if I thought she'd given you a set-down. Do you a world of good, in fact."

"Yes, but what is so odious is that females never do give him a set-down," complained Georgy. "He never makes pretty speeches, or does the least thing to encourage them, and yet even I have to admit he is so disgustingly wealthy he could have almost anyone by the mere lifting of a finger. You would be amazed at the number of females who cast out lures to him, when he is downright rude to them in return. It's enough to make me almost believe he's right, and everyone in the world is as mercenary and cynical as he is himself."

"Then it should reassure you to remember that my fortune can be of very little interest to Miss Cantrell, at least, who informs me that her father is one of the richest men in Jamaica," pointed out his lordship sardonically.

"No, dash it, coz, she can't have said so!" gasped Darcy.

"On the contrary. In fact, I would put very little past Miss Cantrell. I can't make up my mind whether she is wholly contemptible, or very clever indeed! You should be grateful, Darcy, that she has her sights set on bigger game, for I cannot imagine a worse fate than to be married to her, whatever her father's fortune! Whether she will succeed in her ambition is another matter entirely, however," remarked his lordship, not without considerable satisfaction.

Chapter 3

Despite his words, Chance was riding in the park at an early hour the next morning, even though it had been long past midnight by the time he had been able to drag his sister away from the ball. She had stood up for every dance, flirting outrageously and betraying very little sign, in her cynical brother's eyes, that her heart was indeed broken. He had very little doubt that she would soon forget her current obsession—unless, that is, she were to be encouraged in her present folly by romantic tales of the West Indies. But he meant to take whatever steps necessary to mitigate that particular danger, even if it meant further contact with the outrageous new heiress.

Intimate familiarity with his own young sister's matutinal habits did not lead him to place any great reliance on Miss Cantrell's assertion that she rode in the park early each morning, but he was himself an early riser, and had already ridden his gray once around the park when he saw her riding toward him at a clipping pace. She was dressed, that morning, in a scarlet habit, severe in cut, and with a daring mannish beaver set on her mahogany curls, two scarlet plumes curling down becomingly beside her vivid face, which would have made Georgy even more envious; but his lordship had very little interest in French fashions. He was, however, considered no mean judge of horseflesh, and his brows rose at sight of the black she rode. He thought it far too strong a horse for a female, but he couldn't help wondering curiously where she had found it. It certainly had not come out of Lady Fernhurst's stables, whose only son was a slowtop and scarcely noted for his prowess in any field of sport, let alone his judgment in horseflesh.

He pulled his own rat-tailed gray up to watch her approach, half in reluctant admiration, half in disapproval. She rode at a reckless speed for the conditions, and either she had left her groom well behind, or had come out without one, which no well-bred English female would dream

of doing. He thought it well for her that some unsuspecting
fool did not cross her path, or that black of hers did not
run away with her. Nor was he a particular admirer of hard-
riding females. But even so, he was forced to admit he
had never seen a female with a better seat or lighter hands.

She must have seen him in turn, but she made no attempt
to pull up. For a moment he feared the black had indeed
gotten away with her; but there was unmistakable mischief
in her face as she passed him at a full gallop. His lips
tightened at this deliberate provocation, but after a moment
he spurred his gray to go after her.

Still she did not stop. She turned her laughing face back
and instead urged her black to even greater speed, lying
along his back as if she had been born in the saddle, so
that his lordship knew another reluctant twinge of admiration. He had very little hope of catching her, for she was
a lighter weight on a faster horse, and had had a good
length's head start to boot. But still he grimly pursued her,
his own innate dislike of being beaten—and that by an
outrageous and badly behaved female!—spurring him on.

Somewhat to his surprise, she pulled up when they began
to penetrate into a more populous part of the park. When
he brought his own gray up beside her, she exclaimed impetuously, "Oh, that was marvelous! I have not enjoyed
anything half so much since I left home. I made sure your
gray could not give me a race, but I see I underestimated
him."

He said dryly, "We were never in any danger of catching
you, I fear. I thought I knew every horse in the south of
England. Where did you get him?"

"In Ireland, of course," she returned promptly, bending
to pat the black's steaming neck. "Papa and I stopped there
on our way here, for I have heard the praises of Irish horses
sung all my life, even in the West Indies. I found this fellow
in a stable you would not have said could have produced
a coach horse."

His brows rose, but he merely remarked politely, "Then
I congratulate you, for you have succeeded in stealing a
march on all of us, ma'am. I hadn't realized your father
was over here with you."

She laughed, and he again saw how it completely altered

her face. He thought inconsequently that in the ballroom she had undoubtedly been striking, but here, with her cheeks flushed and in her vivid habit, she was almost as magnificent as her horse. He had not thought her beautiful, and still did not; but he was forced to acknowledge that she had a vitality and a strength of personality that made a mockery of what passed for beauty in London. Next to the demure, colorless, curiously passive females who were generally regarded as toasts, he thought her an exotic flower next to an English rose.

"Oh, no, for he hates England, and spends as little time here as possible. He accompanied me on the voyage, but has gone back home now. And I think I have indeed found a bargain in Erin here, for I have yet to see his equal, especially in the showy and overfed bits of blood that are daily paraded in the park." She stooped to pat the sweating black neck once again. "In fact, I have every hope that I have found—"

When she broke off abruptly, and did not complete her sentence, he repeated curiously, "You have every hope that you have found—?"

The mischief was back in her eyes, but she said quickly, "An animal that will put everyone's nose out of joint, of course! It seems Englishmen care for nothing so much as their cattle, and spend enormous sums on creatures that would not last a week at home."

He frowned, still regarding her curiously. "Perhaps, but I have a feeling that was not what you were going to say."

When she merely laughed and shook her head, he added disapprovingly, "Do you always ride unattended, Miss Cantrell?"

"Are you offended, my lord?" she demanded in amusement. "My aunt is certainly convinced she is in constant danger in the middle of London, and none of my female cousins will stir out-of-doors without a maid or a footman to attend them, but I must warn you I have little sympathy for such restrictions. Besides, I cannot conceive of what danger I could possibly encounter in such tame surroundings as this, where I am never out of sight—or sound, more's the pity!—of half a dozen nursemaids and their charges at the very least. I am used to go off into the bush

on my own at home, so that the wilds of Hyde Park in full
daylight hold very few terrors for me."

He said repressively, "If concerns about propriety do not
persuade you, ma'am, and Lady Fernhurst is satisfied with
your somewhat—unusual conduct, who am I to quibble at
it? But if you mean to career through the park in that neck-
or-nothing style, you may be in more danger than you
know."

She gave an attractive peal of laughter. "Well, if I allow
myself to be thrown in such a place as this, I will undoubtedly deserve my fate. But I am well aware you mean to
remind me that it is considered very improper ever to go
above a strict trot in the park. I am well aware of it, I
thank you! Why else do you think I ride at such an early
hour, where I can be assured of some privacy and no tab-
bies to stare disapprovingly down their noses at me?"

After a moment he shrugged. "As I said, if Lady Fernhurst does not object—and you consider such conduct ac-
cords with your stated objectives of attracting a noble
husband—who am I to quibble, Miss Cantrell?"

"Exactly!" she returned cordially. "Which reminds me
that I met yet another member of your family last night,
my lord. A cousin of yours, I believe."

His mouth twitched at this deliberate set-down, but he
thought her more outrageous than ever. "So I am given to
understand, ma'am," he answered. "But I fear he is wholly
beneath your interest, for he has no title, after all."

"Yes, but he assures me that he is your heir, and that
you are almost certain to go off in an apoplexy before very
long," she countered. "And from what I have seen of you
so far, my lord, I would think he's very right."

"But then I thought we were agreed that a mere viscount
is scarcely worth your notice? But marry him by all means.
Did you imagine I would object? Quite the contrary. In
fact, you would be doing both me and his many creditors
a positive favor, ma'am!"

She laughed. "Oh, as I told you last night, I do not mean
to make up my mind too hastily, my lord." She added even
more outrageously, "I confess I wondered for a while
whether you meant to add your name to the list of possible
suitors—though your approach is certainly a unique one.
Men desirous of making a good impression upon me for

the sake of my fortune usually do not go out of their way to be rude and insult me, as you did last night. It had me in a considerable puzzle, until my aunt, and indeed your own cousin, rectified my ignorance. It seems that we are even in something of the same position, my lord, which explains a great deal to me. *You* are clearly so sought after yourself that you feel not the least need to be conciliating, let alone even ordinarily pleasant."

"Then we are indeed in the same position, Miss Cantrell!" he retorted. "I will admit you also had me fooled last night; but in the cold light of day I find your own tactics somewhat more understandable. In fact, despite your delightful frankness on the subject of your matrimonial ambitions, I would almost suspect you, like me, of being intent upon driving prospective suitors away, ma'am, not attracting them, for your own manners are—decidedly unusual, to say the least."

She had bent rather hurriedly to fiddle with her stirrup leather, but when she sat up again she could not quite hide the laughter in her eyes. But it seemed she was still not ready to concede defeat yet. "On the contrary! But I hope I am a realist, my lord! I merely have no intention of wasting my time on those who will not be able to overlook the peculiar drawbacks of my situation, as you call them. Any good businessman would tell you he sizes up his market with a practical eye, and eliminates all the false prospects."

"Oh, is that what you are doing?" he inquired politely. "And do you find so novel an approach answers, ma'am?"

"Not so far," she replied, with more bitterness than perhaps she meant to reveal. "Indeed, most of the men I met last night—including your cousin, my lord!—would be prepared to marry me for the sake of my fortune if I had three heads and a Hottentot for a father."

"Oh, undoubtedly, ma'am—provided the Hottentot were safely three thousand miles away, and your fortune were sufficiently large enough," he agreed cynically.

She was obliged to laugh. "So it would seem. But it will certainly make my task easier, for it would seem I have merely to choose which is the least object—I mean, of course," she corrected herself hastily, "which has the most to offer for my investment."

"You are always so delightfully frank, Miss Cantrell, that

I do not scruple to inform you that I believe you to be a shocking liar!" he told her calmly. "Confess, you have not the least intention of marrying while you are in England, and indeed seem bent on playing an elaborate May game upon us all."

She showed him an innocent face, though there was the betraying mischief in her eyes he was now coming to know. "Why, how can that be, my lord, when you and all the world—even my own aunt—are convinced I could have come for no other purpose?"

He gave the lopsided grin he reserved for a select few, and was very different from the cynical smile he generally showed the world. "I am beginning to think, Miss Cantrell," he told her even more frankly, "that you are an even greater minx than my sister, which I had not thought possible. I will confess, however, that the temptation must have been almost irresistible. Did you come to England with the express intention of making fools of us all, or could you merely not resist seeing just exactly how outrageous you could be and still not drive the worst of the fortune hunters away, once you had discovered which way the wind blew? In either case, I can supply the answer from my own vast experience on the subject: be your father's fortune but large enough, I can assure you there is nothing you could do to give men like Fawnhope a disgust of you!"

She laughed, and capitulated. "Is that why you behave so rudely yourself?" she inquired curiously. "If so, I confess *I* cannot blame *you*. But I certainly did not come here with the intention of pulling the wool over everyone's eyes. It was only when I discovered that even my own aunt believed I had come to make an advantageous marriage—though why anyone should think I would be willing to give up my home to come and live in this overcrowded, damp climate is more than I can understand!" she added roundly. "Or why, for that matter, I should consider it a privilege to rescue some impecunious fool from his embarrassments in exchange for a lifetime of condescension and a title I've not the least use or desire for!"

He was amused despite himself. "I see. So you take good care at every opportunity to flaunt your father's humble origins, and his connection with trade, in hopes of giving potential fortune hunters a disgust of you? You are certainly an original, Miss Cantrell."

She laughed. "My aunt was very careful to warn me, you see, that however large my fortune might be, I must take care not to give people cause to remember the source of that income, or do anything to make them say I am bad *ton*. I merely thought I would see if she were right. Unfortunately she was not, as you undoubtedly know from your own experience, my lord."

His brows rose, but he merely asked curiously, "Why did you come to England then, Miss Cantrell?"

"Oh, my mama wished it, and I will admit I have always been curious about England and my English relations. Papa does not care for it, as I told you before, and though I have seen most of the other great countries of the world, I had never been here."

She had once more managed to startle him. "Seen most of the other great countries of the world?" he repeated in astonishment.

"Yes, for I take at least one trip each year with Papa. His first love was the sea, and he is never so happy as when aboard one of his ships. India is even more crowded than London, of course, and far filthier. Peking is the cleanest city, and most remarkably civilized as well—though that, of course, is because they keep all the thousands of destitute out of sight, for fear of offending the emperor's sensibilities. Paris is very well, though since the war it is sadly altered, I fear, and I have seen Rome, and Athens, and Constantinople, as well," she informed him blithely, apparently unaware that such experiences were in any way out of the ordinary.

"Good God! You are indeed most intrepid, Miss Cantrell. It is no wonder you find England tame in that case."

"Oh, I have seldom been in any danger," she told him even more blithely, "except once or twice, when we hit a bad storm, of course. And that time in Zanzibar—but we were able to escape from the mob in time, so that it hardly signifies!"

He could not help it. He burst out laughing, startling both of their horses, now contentedly cropping at the grass. "You are indeed a most unusual female, Miss Cantrell. I would like to hear of your adventures sometime. But in the meantime, do you intend to carry on this absurd masquerade of yours, or will you soon grow tired of it?"

"Oh, I daresay I shall grow tired of it. Though I'll admit I can seldom resist the temptation to depress pretensions. Papa warned me before I came that the English were all pride and hypocrisy, but I little understood what he meant until I saw it for myself."

You speak of the English as if they were another race," he remarked curiously. "Do you not consider yourself English, then?"

"Good God, no! My parents were both born in England, but I am Jamaican through and through. It is true that many who come to Jamaica do so for the purpose of making as much money as possible and returning home again to so-called civilization, but Papa told me he decided the first time he arrived there, as a cabin boy on one of his first voyages, that he would someday make it his home. And I was born there, of course."

He was interested in her unexpected view of the world, and commented, "You seem to be very attached to your father, Miss Cantrell."

"Oh, yes," she said matter-of-factly, as if unaware that others might not share her view. "He is the wisest man I know. My mama died when I was very young, so I can scarcely remember her, but I have never felt the lack, for Papa became both parents to me. He himself was an orphan, you know, and grew up in the back slums of Bristol, as I told you, and so made doubly sure I should never feel abandoned. I suppose it is his experiences that initially gave me such a bad impression of England, for it has always seemed incredible to me that no one in all this so-called civilized and Christian country cared one iota what became of a young orphan cast alone upon a wicked city. Even the females, Papa tells me, were far more likely to abuse him or drive him away, which gives me a very odd idea of the enlightenment Britain claims to bring to the rest of the world," she added scornfully, her eyes flashing becomingly.

He was still watching her curiously. "I—er—did hear something of the sort," he conceded.

"Yes, I'll be bound you have, and that's another reason I couldn't resist trying to make a May game of everyone here, as you put it. It quickly became more than apparent to me that I was expected to be little better than a barbarian, coming from such a place and with such a background. The only thing that would make me even marginally acceptable was my papa's fortune—but then only if I showed myself properly ashamed of him, and spent my time apologizing for his humble origins! It is such hypocrisy that I have no patience with!"

"So I can see," he said dryly. "He would seem to be a remarkable man."

"Indeed he is," she said warmly. "He ran away to sea when he was only twelve, if you can imagine, and from what little he will tell me, conditions must have been unspeakable. The discipline too—and aboard an English ship, mind you!—was incredibly barbaric. Even the food was so scarce, and what there was so inedible, that he tells me he often feared he would starve to death. It was worse even than his earlier hand-to-mouth days in England. But he fell in love with the sea, and was exceedingly shrewd besides, and he says himself that if he had not received such ill treatment, very likely he would not have discovered his passion for adventure, or ever seen Jamaica, which he tells me was the true date of his birth. Even as a boy he could see the immense possibilities of trade to the West Indies, which then was still in its infancy."

Chance had little interest in the West Indies, or even in her father, if the truth be known, but she amused him, and he was obliged to admit she was the most unusual female he had yet come across. "He is indeed remarkable," he said politely.

It was a tone that most females trying to attract his interest would have picked up on immediately, and obligingly changed the subject; but this unusual female seemed impervious to the faint boredom to be heard in his voice. "Yes, but he was lucky as well. If he had been born to position and wealth, I suspect he would not have had nearly as satisfactory a life, for he would undoubtedly have been as bored with everything as you are yourself, my lord!" she said even more frankly.

It was so unexpected he was startled. "How do you know I'm bored?" he demanded involuntarily.

"Good God, how could you not be? You have had everything you could ever want handed to you on a silver platter," she said, the mischievous twinkle back in her eyes. "It is no wonder you are so rude!"

He made a swift recovery. "And how are you any different, ma'am?" he countered. "It seems to me you have had everything handed to you as well."

"Yes, but I don't live in a place where everything is so rigid and settled, and there is almost no scope for ingenuity or ambition," she told him with unexpected seriousness. "I daresay I would be bored to death in England as well! But in the New World there is still so much to be done that there is no room for boredom."

"Still so much to be done in the New World—" he repeated slowly, an arrested expression on his face.

"Yes, though not everyone finds it so, of course," she admitted. "My aunt can scarce recall her sojourn in Jamaica without a shudder, and my cousins look upon me with the greatest imaginable pity, as if they cannot conceive of living a life of such deprivation as I have been forced to lead. They would be shocked indeed to discover that I pity them even more than they do me, and would consider it a far worse fate to be condemned to spend the rest of my days in this overcrowded, overcivilized place."

"Do you know, Miss Cantrell, I am beginning to think you are indeed the most unusual female I have ever met," he said, still slowly. "You find the comforts and entertainments of a sophisticated city boring, and prefer the dangers and discomforts of a raw new colony."

"Infinitely!" she agreed cheerfully. "And little though you may think it, my lord, I suspect you are exactly the type to succeed in the New World yourself," she added even more surprisingly.

That brought his eyes swiftly back to her face, wondering what this outrageous female would say next. "Good God! How can you possibly know that?" he demanded.

"Oh, I don't, of course, except that you don't seem to be as easily shocked as everyone else I have met here so far. In fact, you remind me a little of my father. The difference is you *were* born to wealth and position, with the result that you have nothing to do but be rude to fools and repulse matchmaking females. It is little wonder you are so bored!"

"Even so, I somehow doubt the solution is to abandon all my responsibilities and set sail for the West Indies," he informed her dryly. "Besides, what makes you think I'm not as disapproving and hypocritical as every other Englishman you so much despise?"

"You may be, of course. But somehow I think you are nearly as out of place here in London as I am. And besides, for some inexplicable reason I like you."

She had once more managed to startled him. "You *like* me?" he repeated in astonishment.

"Yes—but much against my will," she warned him mischievously.

"For God's sake, why?"

"Good God, I don't' know! Because you look like a man and not a painted popinjay, and because you are not in the least interested in my fortune," she said, still in amusement. "And when I am with you I don't have to guard my tongue, which is a considerable relief. My aunt and cousins tend to be shocked by most of the things I say, and have not the least vestige of a sense of humor. Besides, do you always know why you like someone?"

"No, but then I find I like very few people, Miss Cantrell," he retorted cynically.

"You had no need to tell me that, my lord! My aunt informs me you have a reputation for being the rudest man in England, and spend as little time in London as is possible. She also says most matchmaking mamas have long since abandoned any hope of your ever tossing out your handkerchief, for you are a hopeless misogynist and are now considered unlikely ever to marry, even for the sake of an heir."

"I am *not* a misogynist!" he exclaimed involuntarily, stung for some reason.

Her eyes twinkled up into his, and she said frankly, "Well, if all you have to choose among are the overcorrect, exceedingly well-brought-up young ladies I saw at the ball last night, I don't know that I blame you. It is as if I were forced to choose between Sir Winsley Fawnhope and— forgive me!—your cousin, though I liked your cousin the better, of course. But I cannot imagine either of them at home in Jamaica. We have our share of fortune hunters there, of course, but very few gamesters, and still fewer dandies. Life is too hard, and men who have earned their fortunes themselves seldom care to game it away to idle wastrels like your cousin."

When his lips twitched, despite himself, she added cheerfully, "And that is another reason why I like you, I suppose. However disagreeable and disapproving you may be, at least you have a sense of humor. But you needn't worry, my lord! It is merely one of those odd quirks of taste for which there is no accounting. And I daresay," she added thoughtfully, "that were I to get to know you better I would soon find you as tedious and predictable as everyone else."

He burst out laughing again. "Oh, undoubtably, ma'am! And I can at least return the compliment so far as this: I still am wholly undecided whether I like you or not, but you at least have the novelty of being the most outrageous female I have ever met, and I thought I knew your sex."

Her eyes twinkled responsively. "Yes, so I have frequently been told. But most people don't mean it as a compliment, I fear."

"I am not at all sure I do either, Miss Cantrell!" he told her frankly.

Chapter 4

That made her laugh, but she said merely, "Yes, but you didn't seek me out this morning just to tell me that! Now let me guess. Since I doubt it has to do with my *beaux yeux,* and since you hate women and have not the least need to hang out for a rich wife, I suspect it has something to do with your young sister and her fiancé. Am I right?"

"He is not her fiancé!" he retorted irritably.

"Then I was right! But unless you object to marriage for everyone, not just yourself, which I do not suppose, I can only guess you fear he is also a fortune hunter?" she demanded in her abrupt way.

She was certainly outrageous, of course, but he found himself unexpectedly thinking how restful it was not to have to deal with a female who, like the majority of her sex, saw everything in terms of her own vanity. She sounded merely curious, instead of being offended at so unflattering a reason for his presence. "It seems very likely," he answered rather grimly. "But you have the advantage of me in that, at least, for I have never met him. He took good care to make up to my sister in Bath, when I was not there to interfere, and since my stepmother is as sentimental as she is foolish, I count her opinion as worth very little."

"Ah, now I begin to understand why you hate women," she murmured provocatively.

He pointedly ignored that. "What did you think of him, ma'am? For I am beginning to suspect you are a pretty shrewd judge of character."

"No, no, such belated flattery will get you nowhere, my lord," she teased him. "Especially since I already know what your real opinion of me is. Besides, I have scarcely exchanged a dozen words with him. Tell me, is that your only reason for thinking him a fortune hunter?"

"That, and the fact that his own family shipped him off to the West Indies in disgrace, which is scarcely a recommendation in my eyes."

"Yes, but that is hardly likely to weigh with me," she pointed out frankly. "Half of our richest men could say the same. For all you know he may do very well there."

"I hope he may!" he retorted. "But you will forgive me for not wishing to stake my sister's future upon the chance! But I notice you have been careful not to answer my first question, which tells its own tale. Confess, you did not like him, did you?"

"I didn't say that. Nor does it matter in the least what I—or indeed you, for that matter, my lord!—think of him!" she reminded him. "Perhaps I should warn you that I am far from being in sympathy with arranged marriages, especially since my own parents made just such an unequal marriage. If the only reason you have to disapprove of the match is because of their disparate fortunes, I fear you will get little help from me."

He said frostily, "I disapprove of the marriage, ma'am, because my sister is no more fit to be married at this moment than she is of knowing her own heart. She is a minx, and has been spoilt from the hour of her birth, but were Ludlow still in England, I am not such a tyrant, as I can see you have labeled me, to forbid her to see him. I would also be in a position to judge for myself what are his intentions and how lasting the attachment might be. Unhappily, however, that is not the case, and since my sister is as romantic as she is foolish, and has formed an absurd notion of going out to Jamaica to join him, you may perhaps understand why I have considerable reservations."

"Ah, now I see why you have sought me out!" she said in amusement. "But if you wish for someone to discourage your sister from going out to Jamaica, I fear you should have approached my aunt. From what little I have seen of her, I think your sister might do very well there."

He was in danger of forgetting all of his earlier good impressions of her. "Good God, you cannot be serious!" he exclaimed in some annoyance. "My sister is incapable of surviving for a day in England on her own, let alone in such a benighted—in such a very different place!" he corrected himself hastily. "At the moment she is inclined to think it highly romantic, but she has no conception of the heat, or the diseases, or the hundred other dangers she is likely to meet with there. Surely even your affection for your home cannot blind you to its differences, or how ill-suited a gently bred female like my sister is to cope there? Tell me honestly, ma'am, how many English ever adapt as well as you have, especially the women? As you yourself pointed out, you have only to look to your aunt for the truth of that!"

"Yes, but that is because most people, like my aunt, expect to live in the tropics exactly as they lived at home," she pointed out. "They dress the same, and build their homes the same, and bring their absurd prejudices against fresh air and exposure to the sun with them, so that it is little wonder they complain of the heat and succumb to diseases. Though it is at least better now, in this age of light muslins," she added thoughtfully. "I sometimes wonder how fashionable females do not die of pneumonia by the droves in this frigid climate, especially in the winter, but nothing could be better suited to the tropics. Indeed, Papa told me that when he first came to the West Indies it was much worse, for women *would* bring their heavy brocades and velvets with them, however ludicrous it might be to dress in such garb in so hot a climate. And when you add to that their habit of tight lacing and whale-boned corsets, it is easy to see why it must have been well nigh unbearable for them. He said many women literally did die rather than be considered unfashionable! Ugh!"

He forgot the main thread of his argument for the moment. "Good God, is there *nothing* you will not say?" he demanded involuntarily.

She showed him an innocent face. "Oh, are you offended by my speaking of corsets, my lord? And you such an advocate of plain speaking yourself! Should I have pretended you can have no knowledge of such things—when I suspect that nothing could be further from the truth? How very hard it must be to keep up a conversation in mixed company in England, since there are so very many prohibitions to remember! According to my aunt, one must not speak of business, or religion, or politics, or, I gather, anything having to do with birth, or death, or indeed any normal human function. And now it seems I must not even allude to garments you must be almost as familiar with as I am myself."

"Your aunt has all my sympathy," he told her grimly. "And we are straying rather far afield, don't you think?"

"On the contrary, I begin to think we are getting to the very crux of the matter, my lord!" she retorted. "You say your sister is no more fitted to be married than a baby, or to go out to such a primitive place, when the truth is you have kept her in cotton wool all her life, so what else can you expect? Since I don't know your sister, you may be right on all counts. Young Ludlow may be the most gazetted of fortune hunters, and your sister might dislike Jamaica as much as my aunt did, all those years ago. But you don't know that, any more than I do."

He was disliking her now quite as much as she had interested him earlier. "Are you seriously suggesting that I should allow my sister to journey halfway round the world in pursuit of a man I have not even met, and who has shown himself so unsteady that even his own relatives have shipped him off in disgrace?" he demanded in considerable annoyance.

Her eyes began to twinkle. "No, what I am suggesting, if you had a grain of sense, my lord, is that you should take her out there yourself. I wonder it has not long since occurred to you as the only possible solution."

"Good God, are you mad? I should take her there myself—a trip that would take six months from start to finish, at the least computation, to meet a man I have reason to believe is a loose fish? That is if the journey itself did not kill her, of course, or she did not succumb to some deadly fever the moment we arrived."

"Oh, Good God!" she retorted impatiently. "How insular all you English are. Die on the way indeed! From what I have seen of your sister so far, she would enjoy the journey very much. What you mean is that it would be vastly inconvenient to *you*."

"It would, especially since I should undoubtedly find at the end of it that she had fallen out of love, and it had all been for nothing," he returned acidly. "Perhaps I have not made it sufficiently clear to you that my sister is a minx, ma'am, and will likely be in love a dozen more times before she is ready to settle down."

She laughed. "Why then, you would have nothing more to worry about. But I warned you that you were unlikely to find me at all sympathetic, my lord. She may well do so, but don't pretend your decision was made for her sake, instead of your own convenience. Indeed it seems to me you have everything to gain and little to lose by taking her out there and letting her discover for herself if her feelings should turn out to be mere infatuation."

"I thank you for the advice, but I have not the least intention of doing anything so foolish!" he retorted in one of his comprehensive snubs. "She will undoubtedly do the same remaining safely in England, without putting me to such unnecessary inconvenience and expense. Which is, as you so correctly point out, my first consideration."

Far from heeding the snub, her eyes twinkled responsively, but she shook her head more seriously. "You can know little of females if you think that, my lord. All your opposition is likely to do is to make her the more determined—or drive her into open rebellion. Only think! She is probably already imagining herself a Juliet, for I don't imagine you have refrained from behaving exactly like a Capulet and forbidding her even to think of such a marriage. Add to that the fact that Ludlow is both young and charming, and, thanks to you, now invested with all the additional romance of the forbidden, and is even safely out of the way as well, so that she has no chance to become disillusioned with him. Indeed, I can only wonder at your folly, for if you had been determined to drive her into his arms, you could not have set about it more directly."

He made no attempt to hide his annoyance. "And what would you have me do instead? Give my consent to as ill-matched and foolish a pair of young lovers as could well nigh be imagined and allow my young sister to go halfway around the world to a barbaric place she would soon be heartily sick of? I don't know whether you actually believe what you are saying, ma'am, or merely hope to annoy me, but I fear I have no taste for such romantical rodomontade. Nor have I requested your advice in the handling of my sister. And I do not scruple to tell you to your face, Miss Cantrell, that if you mean to encourage her in this folly, you will be doing her the worst turn imaginable!"

"I have no intention of interfering at all. But nor do I mean to do your dirty work for you, my lord, if you hope I will try to discourage her," she countered. "Remember, my mother married my father in the teeth of just such opposition, and by all accounts it was a most happy marriage."

"Your mother was already in Jamaica at the time, as I have been led to understand, and no heiress, as my sister is," he retorted coldly. "Nor do I think she was just seventeen."

"No, but she was not a great deal older. And it is no use our brangling, for it is clear we are never likely to agree on this particular subject. I have given you my advice for what it is worth, but the remedy is still in your hands, you know. You have only to forbid your sister to have anything to do with me, thus avoiding the danger of my contaminating influence."

"I would, if I were such a fool as you so obviously think me!" he returned frigidly. "Bu you are right that we are never likely to agree on this subject, ma'am. After all, what is it to you if my sister ruins her life?"

"And I thought you said you were not romantic? That is in the best tradition of a novel straight from the lending library, my lord! I have no desire to see her ruin her life, but nor have I any desire to help you in controlling it for her. I will tell her anything she wishes to know about Jamaica, but I will certainly be honest with her, and not sug-

arcoat the difficulties. They are not as great as you make
out, for most of us lead remarkably comfortable lives, I
assure you, and are not in the least barbarians. But plainly
you will never be convinced of that. And since the only
thing you have yet told me to young Ludlow's discredit is
that he lacks a fortune, and his ancestors did not come
over with the Conqueror, I find your arguments less than
compelling. But then I must confess I have never seen why
the mere possessing of a fortune that he had neither the
wits nor courage to make for himself should be a recommendation for a man, or justify his being everywhere toad-
eaten," she added thoughtfully.

"Thank you, Miss Cantrell!" he returned acidly. "I now
may assume to know precisely what you think of me! Pray
allow me to apologize for having taken up so much of your
valuable time."

But she merely laughed. "Oh, now you are on your high
ropes, again, and disliking me quite amazingly, no doubt.
But you would do as well to follow my advice, my lord, or
you may very likely drive your sister into doing something
outrageous. I am quite certain you believe you have only
to forbid her to think of this young man, in the best tyrannical male fashion, and that will be the end of it; but you
may find to your cost that it is not quite that easy. And
you need not tell me you have not the least intention of
taking my advice on the subject, for I am well aware of it!"

"I am glad you find the subject so amusing, Miss Cantrell," he retorted frostily. "I can only repeat: if you encourage her in this folly, just to spite me, it will be the worst
turn you could do her. Whether or not that matters to
you, of course, I have no idea. You must search you own
conscience for the answer to that." He gave her a cold bow,
and left her.

Anjalie Cantrell returned in some amusement to her
aunt's house in Hill Street. From the first she had found
England an inexplicable place, full of snobbery and hypocrisy and vastly convinced of its own superiority to every
other place on earth, on no grounds at all that she could
discover. It had not taken her father's warnings to know
that she would meet with but grudging acceptance there,
despite his wealth, for her mother's own family had cast

her off after her unequal marriage, and only her father's unexpected success had done anything to heal the breach. Nor were the West Indies entirely devoid of snobbery, for name and rank still meant an exaggerated amount there, and who one's ancestors were was still considered more important by far too many than a man's worth in his own right.

Well, she had come out of curiosity, and did not think it would be many weeks before she was pining for the freedom and warmth of her native land again. But in the meantime, there were several amusements to be had, not the least of which was seeing how far she could push the fools pursuing her for no other reason than her wealth, and who would be the first to turn up their noses were she suddenly to announce herself penniless. And there were several mysteries to ponder.

There was his lordship, for one. She might have taken an unexpected liking to him, because they were in much the same circumstances, and because of a certain blunt way he had of speaking that reminded her of her father, and even because he looked more her idea of a man than the willowy, overdressed fops generally to be found in London. But that did not mean that she was blind to his faults. She strongly suspected, in fact, that Miss Hughendon would not be paying her a morning visit—at least if her brother could contrive to prevent it—which would be a shame, for she suspected even more strongly that, left to his own devices, Lord Chance would do everything in his power to drive his young sister into open rebellion.

It had nothing to do with her, of course, as Chance had pointed out. But she thought she had never met so many unhappy, misguided people as she had since coming to England. Her aunt's household, for instance, seemed to her to be a hotbed of discontents and unhappiness. Her cousin Sir Frederick Fernhurst, was a pompous nodcock, forever lecturing to his mother and younger sisters on matters of decorum and the correct behavior to be expected in a gentleman's household, and frequently reducing his mother to tears by his complaints of her extravagance and lack of management. Anjalie, used to a very different type of male, found him insufferable, but since he disapproved of her quite as much as she did him, and had strongly counseled his mother not to accept her unknown niece into her household in the first place, it was fortunate that they saw very little of each other.

Her female cousins she profoundly pitied, and could only render up thanks that she herself had not been reared in such a stifling atmosphere. Even her eldest cousin, Anne, in her first Season and thus emancipated from the schoolroom, lived a rigidly circumscribed life that Anjalie could not have tolerated even for one day. She never went out except when escorted by her mama or her maid or a footman, and seemed to spend her days, when she was not attending some social event—and the number of parties and balls and breakfasts that could be packed into a single day left Anjalie gasping—either shopping with her mama, walking sedately in the park with her younger sisters and their very correct governess, or sitting over her stitchery. As for the younger children, still under the tutelage of Miss Fieldstone, a most stern moralist, their lives centered wholly around schoolwork, lessons in deportment, and genteel walks around the square or in the park, always in the company of their governess.

Anjalie, reared in a very different environment and used to a far more adventurous life, found it all extremely stifling. Left without a mama at an early age, and with a papa who fortunately had no ambitions toward gentility, she had largely wandered unaccompanied wherever she chose on their own land, usually returning only at sunset with her dress torn and her face filthy. When Juba, her black nurse, would complain that she was growing up more boy than girl, Papa would only laugh, for missishness ranked high on his list of dislikes, and say that they lived in the New World, thank God, where even females could dispense with such outmoded shibboleths.

She had also accompanied her father on his voyages, with only the disapproving Juba for chaperon, and in the far-flung worlds they visited had been allowed to mingle freely with all classes and types of people. After such a life, to sit yawning over her stitchery, as her cousins did, and for exercise plod once or twice around the park at the snail's pace dictated by fashion, would soon have driven Anjalie mad. Indeed, she had lost no time in making it plain to her bewildered and disapproving aunt that such restrictions would not suit her at all; and subsequently scandalized that poor woman by wandering far and wide in her excursions to explore London, scorning to be burdened with the maid her aunt tried to foist upon her, and riding in the park each morning at an unfashionable hour without even a groom to accompany her.

Anjalie thought her aunt an object of both compassion and wonder. She was a weak, rather foolish woman, who seemed to exist in equal dread and annoyance of her pompous son, and lived such an idle, frivolous life that Anjalie had been frankly shocked. Nor had it taken her long to realize that her aunt was quite amazingly selfish, and her first and last consideration was always her own comfort. She seldom saw the younger of her children, especially those still in the schoolroom, and the sum of her ambitions seemed to be centered around maintaining her position in the *ton,* and achieving respectable marriages for her son and all four of her daughters. By respectability it was clearly meant a marriage that would enhance her own social standing, and help the remaining to find equally advantageous partners.

She had been kind enough to her niece, in her easygoing way, and even wept a little over her resemblance to her poor dead sister, whom she had not seen in more than twenty years. But she did little to hide the fact that she could not sufficiently deplore her sister's inexplicable marriage, however well it had turned out. Money and respectability were her twin gods, and Anjalie was left in little doubt that had her sister's disgraceful marriage not ended so successfully, she herself would not have been accepted into her aunt's household, however much like her dead mother she might look.

Her aunt's reaction, in fact, had been Anjalie's first intimation of the construction all of London would likely place upon her arrival. Lady Fernhurst took it sublimely for granted that she had come to England with no other purpose in mind than to make a successful marriage, and not only thoroughly approved of such a plan, but thought the better of her niece for it. Indeed, her only concern was that her independent niece would give potential suitors a disgust of her that not even her fortune would be able to overcome.

"Pray do not mistake me, my dear," she had told her niece forthrightly in one of their earliest conversations. "For in these hurly-burly times, even the highest sticklers would scarcely care to turn up their noses at so large a fortune, *however* obtained. Your father's background is certainly unfortunate, but luckily not many people know of it, for you may be sure *I* have not set it about. And on my poor sister's side, of course, you have nothing at all to apologize for, my dear. It was certainly thought very odd of her to marry so far beneath her and remain in that dreadful place, but that was all a long time ago, thank God, and not many people remember it. There is no disguising your papa's connection with trade, of course, but I am sure if you will but curb your unfortunate tendency to prattle on about your home, and will but be brought to see that it will be positively *fatal* to give people the least cause to say you are fast, or not quite the thing, I do not at all despair of you making an eligible match."

Anjalie, half amused, half annoyed, forbore to assure her aunt that she had nothing to apologize for on either side of her parentage; but her aunt was already going on, blissfully unaware of having offended her niece in any way. "How lucky it is that you have no brothers, for you must inherit all your papa's fortune, which would be a sufficient attraction, you may be sure, even if you were the plainest girl alive, which you are very far from being, my dear. To be sure, I can never sufficiently deplore that no one had the good sense to warn you that in that climate, the sun can be positively *fatal* to one's complexion. You are dreadfully brown, but I am sure no one could find any other fault in your appearance, and indeed you look almost exactly as my poor dear sister did at that age. Oh, dear, how it takes me back! But where was I? Oh, yes. And that is particularly why it is so important that you should do nothing that will set up people's backs, or make them say you are dreadfully provincial. I am sure you will not object to my speaking so frankly, my dear, for I can see you are a sensible girl, and will not take anything I've said amiss. And it would be folly indeed to allow you to ruin all your chances merely for the lack of a little plain-speaking!"

Anjalie had done her best to disabuse her aunt of her misapprehension that she had come to England with the intention of catching a titled husband, but with only limited success. Lady Fernhurst had received her increasingly urgent denials with polite disbelief, and said merely, with approval, "It is very right of you to say so, my dear, for I'm sure nothing could be more unbecoming than a female perceived to be on the catch, as the saying is, especially in your situation. Such modesty does you extreme credit, and you may be sure that nothing so vulgar or ill bred as an open declaration of your intentions will be at all necessary, for no one will be in the least doubt as to why you have come. In fact, I have already received *several* invitations from ladies with expensive sons to dispose of."

So Anjalie had obligingly held her peace, and taken her own steps to deter the most determined of the fortune hunters, which had the added advantage of promising to be most amusing. But her aunt would no doubt have been profoundly shocked to learn that, far from wishing to marry and settle down in England, her niece was already wondering how soon she could decently draw her visit to a close and return home.

Chapter 5

Somewhat to Anjalie's surprise, however, and her aunt's considerable gratification, Miss Georgiana Hughendon paid them a morning call that very day, and even more unexpectedly, came escorted by her formidable brother.

Anjalie's one brief meeting with Miss Hughendon had not led her to suppose that that enterprising damsel would submit docilely to her brother's decree, but she certainly had not expected him to accompany his sister. She wondered if he hoped to contain the damage she might do, and if so how he proposed to accomplish it, and it was thus in a spirit of considerable mischief that she greeted their entrance. She also wondered fleetingly if Lord Chance had informed his sister of their earlier meeting, but quickly saw that Miss Hughendon betrayed no awareness of it.

She danced in in her usual impetuous fashion, most becomingly attired that morning in a dashing walking dress of lemon yellow, with lemon kids gloves on her hands and an even more dashing bonnet with a high poke front, all of which seemed to argue that however strict her brother might be, he did not begrudge any expense on her behalf. She said immediately, in justified triumph, "See, I told you I should come at the first opportunity, Miss Cantrell! Oh, how do you do, dear Lady Fernhurst? I hope you don't mind, but I am so eager to hear all about the West Indies that I couldn't wait. Chance *would* come, though I'm sure I don't need an escort merely to pay a morning visit. Is your brother antiquated, and a fussbudget, and never believes you are in the least grown up and *quite* capable of handling your own affairs, Miss Fernhurst?" she asked, with a darkling look at her brother.

Poor Anne looked taken aback, and murmured something incoherent, and Lord Chance, civilly shaking hands with Lady Fernhurst, said dryly, "Do at least try for a little conduct, Georgy. How do you do, Miss Fernhurst? Pray ignore my sister. Miss Cantrell, your obedient servant!" Nothing in his demeanor revealed that they had met once already that morning, and for her own reasons Anjalie had not revealed it either. She sat back now, waiting to see what would transpire.

Miss Hughendon, wholly unchastened, sat down by Anjalie, saying in her lively way, "Now you must tell me everything! Only first tell me how Guy looked. Did you like him? Did he flirt with you? I am sure he did, and if every female in Jamaica looks like you, I fear he will soon forget all about me. Especially if everyone in the West Indies wears Paris gowns," she added a trifle enviously. "Where on earth did you get them? Because of the war no one has seen Paris fashions here since before I can remember."

Anjalie, casting a mischievous glance at Lord Chance, could not resist saying cheerfully, "Pirates, of course."

Her aunt's eyes showed signs of starting from their sockets, and Georgy almost screeched, "*Pirates*? Oh, you are teasing me! You can't be serious!"

"No, but they prefer to be called buccaneers, you know. We are under blockade too, of course, since we are still an English colony, but France controls several islands in the West Indies, besides supplying the United States with all sorts of luxuries. The buccaneers find it very profitable to capture French merchant ships and sell their cargos at a profit, which fortunately gives us a steady supply of all manner of French goods."

"But—but—you really mean actual *pirates*?" demanded Georgy, still half inclined to believe she was being roasted.

"Oh, they are not nearly as murderous as their reputation. Papa says when he first came to Jamaica they were still a force to be reckoned with on the island, preying on shipping and from time to time even raiding plantations and murdering the inhabitants. But they have grown sadly tame of late, I fear. They now have letters of marque from the English Crown to prey on enemy shipping, and sell their prize like any merchant, which would no doubt make their notorious predecessors turn in their graves could they but know of it."

But if she had thought to shock Miss Hughendon, she was soon to learn her mistake. "Oh, please, tell me all about it!" Georgy breathed, her eyes as big as saucers. "Only first tell me about my adored Guy. Was he in good health when you last saw him? Did he seem happy?"

Anjalie laughed and tried to answer all her eager questions. "Why, as I told you last night, I fear my acquaintance with your—with Mr. Ludlow was of the briefest. I met him at a formal reception, which precluded anything but the exchange of the merest commonplaces. He certainly seemed to be in excellent health some two months ago, and happy enough. I gathered that he was already very well liked, but more than that I fear I cannot tell you, Miss Hughendon."

"Oh, pray call me Georgy! Everyone does. You needn't tell me he was well liked, for I expected no different. He is the most delightful creature! And that is why I am *determined*," she added, with a glowering look at her brother, "to go out there before some West Indian heiress snaps him up."

Anjalie could not help laughing again, but said teasingly, "Why, do you think him so inconstant, then?"

Miss Hughendon did not seem to resent the question. "No, but it would be naive not to acknowledge that men are far more susceptible than females, don't you agree?" she said frankly. "Of course I know he loves me, but separated by so many miles, and not seeing me for years and *years,* at least if my brother has his way, it would be remarkable if he did not fall victim to some other lures cast out to him. No, I am very practical, whatever my odious brother might say, and that is why I do not mean to sit docilely at home, waiting for something to happen. Would *you,*" she demanded of Anjalie, "if you knew exactly what it was you wanted and it was only stodgy rules of propriety that stood in your way?"

"Well, no," Anjalie acknowledged truthfully, trying not to meet his lordship's eyes. "But you are still very young, you know. And Jamaica is not for everyone, as my aunt will no doubt tell you."

Lady Fernhurst practically shuddered. "Do not speak to me of that place!" she exclaimed. "I was only a girl at the time, of course, not much older than you are now, Miss Hughendon—but I will never forget that dreadful year. Papa went out as vice-governor, you know, and Mama felt obliged to accompany him, but we were none of us prepared for the reality. In the first place, even after all these years I cannot recall that dreadful voyage without horror, for we were all dreadfully ill, and although it was not supposed to be the stormy season, I am sure you could not have proved it by me, for we saw more foul weather than fair, and the wretched boat pitched so much that I still sometimes have nightmares about it. Never was I so glad to see land—any land!—but *that* was before I had understood the horrors still in store for us, of course."

Even Miss Hughendon looked slightly daunted at this recital, and glanced to Anjalie for rescue. "My aunt is clearly a very bad sailor," she said in amusement, "but I must admit her experiences are not uncommon. On the other hand, I am never so happy as when I am at sea."

"My sister," put in his lordship dryly, "is inevitably carriage sick on even the shortest journeys."

"There you are, then!" put in Lady Fernhurst triumphantly. "Do not listen to Anjalie, my dear Miss Hughendon, for she is by no means typical, I assure you. The ships are cramped, the crew in general foul-mouthed and smell so bad that if one had the strength to venture up on deck, if only for a breath of fresh air, you were soon driven below again by the incredible stench, and the food is monotonous and very bad—not that *that* signified, for I'm sure I was far too unwell to eat anything. And the worst of it is knowing that once you have at last landed, and the torment is over, you still must face it all again on the return journey!"

Miss Hughendon ignored the better part of this to ask interestedly, "Is your name Anjalie? I have never heard that before."

"It's Arabic," said Anjalie, knowing how her aunt disliked so barbarous a name. "My mother thought it pretty, and as her own name was Anne—my cousin here is named after her—she thought it very fitting."

"It's unusual. I like it," said Georgy decidedly. "And that proves that Jamaica cannot be so very bad, for your mother chose to remain there, did she not?"

"Yes, but I'm bound to own that her experience was not at all typical," Anjalie warned her. "Most of the English there are like my aunt, and cannot wait to get back to so-called civilization."

"But—but, isn't it at all pretty?" Georgy demanded uncertainly.

"I think it beautiful, but it is not anything like England, you know. It is very green too, but not the cool green you are used to. The sea is so blue it almost blinds you, and the flowers—for it is a tropical island, of course—make you doubt that such vivid colors could really exist outside of your imagination. But it is not a tame country, Miss Hughendon, and many, like my aunt, find it too wild to be beautiful. It is not a large island, but the roads are very bad, and to travel an hour in any direction is to find yourself in untamed wilderness, without a human being for miles. But I must confess that having grown up there, England seems almost too congested to breathe, for here you seem never to be out of sight of some sign of civilization."

Georgy looked intrigued by that, but Lady Fernhurst shuddered again. "Pray do not talk to me of the wilderness, for I am sure I lived in abject terror the whole time I was there, and found very little beautiful about it. You cannot imagine the heat, my dear Miss Hughendon, not to mention the mosquitoes and the flies, and the dirt! I can scarcely bear to think of it even now. The roads are all but impassable, as my niece says, but that is of little consequence, for there is nowhere to go, and no genteel society to be found when you get there. The people, though kind enough, I'm sure, were all dreadfully provincial, and nothing but the shabbiest of entertainments were offered—and even then, the talk was all of sugar and rum and the state of trade, until one felt like screaming. And as if all that weren't bad enough, there was the constant threat of fevers, for I'm sure it is the most unhealthy place on earth. You have only to add to that the hurricanes and earthquakes, both of which were commonplace, and capable of leveling whole towns without warning, and you will get some idea of what I suffered. And I have not even mentioned the threat of pirates, who are by no means as tame as my niece would have you believe, and even slave rebellions—and people may say what they wish about the inhumanity of slavery, but I have always deplored it on far more practical grounds, for I never saw a slave that was not lazy and surly, and delivered such bad service it was frequently easier to do it yourself. And what is worse, I could never understand one word in ten that they uttered, so that it is little wonder nothing ever got done. Indeed, there is nothing bad enough I can say about such a place, Miss Hughendon, and I urge you most strongly to reconsider any desire to go there, for nothing could be more injurious to your health and happiness, I can assure you."

Then as Miss Hughendon glanced wonderingly at Anjalie, Lady Fernhurst added with dignity, "I make no apologies to my niece, for she knows exactly how I feel on the subject. Besides, I am sure there can be no need for you to undertake so hazardous a journey, for this young man you speak of is unlikely to find the place any more to his liking than we did, and you may be sure will not remain a day longer than he has to."

Anjalie was obliged to laugh at Georgiana's disappointed expression. "I must warn you that my aunt's views are by no means unusual, Miss Hughendon. But on the other hand, I love it very much, and cannot imagine living anywhere else for the rest of my life."

"But—are there indeed earthquakes and hurricanes?" Georgy demanded doubtfully.

"Yes, but they are hardly daily—or even yearly occurrences," Anjalie assured her.

"And slave rebellions?"

"On occasion," Anjalie conceded, her eyes beginning to twinkle.

"As well as *pirates*?"

"Yes, but their threat is not in the least what it used to be."

Georgiana gave an ecstatic sigh. "I can't *wait* to get there," she breathed, her eyes alight.

Lady Fernhurst gasped at this unexpected reaction, and her brother exclaimed involuntarily, "God give me patience!"

But the twinkle in Anjalie's eyes became even more pronounced. "You are not daunted by my aunt's descriptions?" she demanded curiously.

Georgy was scornful. "Of course not! You can't conceive of how boring my life is here, Miss—oh, may I call you Anjalie? I do like that name," she added approvingly. "My brother is disapproving, and strict, and won't let me have the least little adventure, simply because he is far too stuffy to wish for any adventures himself. But he knows that when I have really set my heart upon something, I always get it," she ended, with a challenging look at her brother. "Oh, do tell me about the pirates, for I used to love to read about the Spanish Main, but I never *ever* dreamt I might actually meet one."

Lady Fernhurst tried somewhat desperately to catch her niece's eye, but Anjalie said merely, in some amusement, "Well, if you do go to Jamaica you will almost certainly meet one or two, but I am afraid you will find them rather disappointing. Papa complains that one may as well be living in England now, things have grown so sadly flat. In their heyday, of course, the pirates—or as I said, the buccaneers, as they prefer to be called—were a continuous threat to life and property for the early settlers. They formed a community, called the Brethren, and made their headquarters at Port Royal, which quickly became known as the most wicked city in the New World. They would menace ships and even raid towns sometimes, and were said to be amazingly brutal, torturing their victims until they revealed where their treasure was hidden, and murdering without compunction. But of late years they have become deplorably respectable, though I suspect few of the island residents would agree with me. They are happy enough to take advantage of them in times of threat, for you must know the French have been trying to retake Jamaica for years, and England will not send out enough ships to protect us. In former times the Brethren have been used almost like a regular army, marching on cities in South America and conquering them for England, taking fabulous prizes as their reward, and dividing it up equally among their numbers, as is their custom. The most famous of these, Henry Morgan, even ended up being knighted by the Crown for his services, and made vice governor of Jamaica. But all that was long before my time, of course, and whenever their protection is no longer needed, and they begin to interfere with trade, they quickly fall into disfavor again. At present the Brethren are reduced to raiding French ships—which the English government again finds useful— and selling their ill-gotten gains to colonists starved for French luxuries. We get most of our brandy, perfumes, and indeed fashions, from them and they drive extremely hard bargains, I can tell you."

Lady Fernhurst moaned again, but his lordship's lips twitched, as if he were reluctantly amused.

"Yes, but it seems all the excitement was in the past," Georgy complained. "Are all the pirates—I beg your pardon—the Brethren—become so tame?"

"Most of them, I'm afraid. They are still considered a menace by many of the residents, who would like to see them eradicated from the island completely, and now and again they will commit some atrocity, of course, which keeps their reputation for evil alive."

"Do you speak from personal experience, Miss Cantrell?" inquired his lordship skeptically.

"Well, a drunken pirate once broke into the house, when Papa was away," she answered him in amusement. "'There were no men in the house, except for a very young houseboy, for it was broad daylight and they were all out in the fields, so we were naturally alarmed. The man was vilely drunk, too, and had great black whiskers and a cutlass thrust in his belt, and—what was a great deal more to the point—two loaded pistols as well. He threatened to ransack the place, and hold us all to ransom. We had no notion what to do and were starting to give ourselves up for lost, but then he made the mistake of beginning to smash up the room. Well! Juba, who is my old nurse, and the closest thing I have to a mother now, was so affronted that she began to berate him, and this great, hulking pirate, who had committed who knows how many heinous deeds in his day, was so taken aback that he just stood there and took it. It was all I could do to keep from laughing, and I almost expected at any moment to hear him begin to apologize."

"What happened?" breathed Georgy, entranced.

"Oh, it ended most tamely, fortunately for us. I keep a pistol for just such emergencies, but before I was obliged to use it, he began to back down, and at last retreated, with a bee in his ear from Juba, who told him he ought to be ashamed of himself for terrorizing helpless women and children, and ought to take a bath once in a while as well! I think in the end he was glad to get away."

His lordship, far less impressionable than his sister, demanded cynically, "Did this tale really happen, or is it merely a farrago of nonsense to entertain my sister?"

Anjalie laughed. "Oh, it really happened, but I am not the heroine of the piece. Juba has led a far more adventurous life than I have, but she can never be brought to tell me more than bits and pieces of it, alas."

"And you expect me to believe you keep pistols in the house for just such emergencies?"

"There is nothing remarkable in that, for most of the estates are isolated, you know, and have to be prepared to maintain their own defense. Papa taught me to shoot when I was still a little girl, and I always take my pistol with me when I go out riding, especially when I am alone."

Georgy heaved a heartfelt sigh. "Oh, how I envy you, Miss Cantrell! Nothing in the least exciting ever happens to me. We were held up by highwaymen, once, but all that happened was that Mama fell into strong hysterics, and I lost my pearl necklet."

"And if a drunken pirate—or anyone else!—were to break into the house, you would be the first to hide under your bed, my girl!" pointed out her brother somewhat brutally.

"I would not!" she cried indignantly.

"Well, I would!" confessed Lady Fernhurst frankly. "And it only confirms me in my detestation of the place. But thank goodness at least we never had drunken pirates to contend with!"

"But do you dare to ride alone in such country?" asked Georgy, ignoring this weak-minded response. "Aren't you frightened to be held up, or even murdered?"

"On our own property I am usually quite safe. In Kingston, of course, or even Spanish Town, which is the capitol you know, I must often burden myself with an escort, for the port cities in particular are full of all the scaff and raff of Europe, most of whom have been at sea for weeks, and mean to enjoy themselves while in port. There are areas that I would not venture into without a strong guard."

"You amaze me, Miss Cantrell!" put in his lordship sardonically.

She ignored his sarcasm. "Not at all, for I am not a fool. But you must not think that all Englishwomen live as I do, Miss Hughendon. The majority of them live quite as restricted lives as females do here. It is only that I made up my mind long ago that I was not going to go in fear for my life, and luckily my papa grew up in a very different class of society, and has no absurd notions about women being helpless beings to be sheltered from the world at all costs. He was an orphan himself you know, and was forced to learn from a shockingly early age to be self-reliant, and taught me to be the same."

Georgy goggled at this frank admission, and Lady Fernhurst closed her eyes, and pronounced with conviction, "I can only think he must be mad! Indeed, I shudder when I think of you growing up in such a place, and it is *not* to be laid at my door, whatever people may say, for when my poor dear sister died, I wrote to him, begging him to send you to me—though with five daughters of my own it would have been—but never mind that! But he would not, and so it all came to nothing."

"I know you did, ma'am, and it was very kind of you," said Anjalie consolingly. "But I fear growing up in England would not have suited me nearly so well, you know, and Papa would never have consented to be parted from me—or I him."

"Well," said Georgy frankly, beginning with some reluctance to draw on her gloves, "you cannot know how glad I am to have met you, and everything you have told me has only made me even more anxious to go out to such a place. It is *exactly* like a novel, only even better, for I never dreamed people actually lived such stirring lives. You cannot imagine how much I envy you, and how I have always longed for excitement and adventure myself. I must go now, for I have taken up too much of your time, but I hope I may come again? Nothing would please me more, and I am sure I still have a great deal to learn about Jamaica before I go out there."

Her brother refrained from making any comment, but his expression left Anjalie in no doubt that he was most seriously displeased. She thought him absurd, and could not resist, when he formally shook hands with her in farewell, to cast him a glance that was as provocative as it was mischievous. He scowled at her, and escorted his sister out.

Chapter 6

Georgiana and his lordship were not their only visitors. A gratifying number of people called that day, among them Sir Winsley Fawnhope, who brought Anjalie a tight little posy, and paid her many extravagant compliments. He seemed torn between the necessity of puffing off his own consequence so that Anjalie would be made fully aware of the depths of his condescension in singling her out in so flattering a way, and the need to fix his interest with so great an heiress before someone else should get in before him. She thought him more ridiculous than ever, and when he gracefully begged to be allowed to take her driving in the park the next afternoon, had no hesitation in declining.

Lady Fernhurst did her best to soften this blunt refusal, but he stiffened, and went away at last, clearly inclined to be offended.

Lady Fernhurst took her niece to task as soon as he was gone, saying in some alarm, "My dear, what were you about to offend him so? I'm sure he is of the very first consequence, and what is more to the point, he is related to half the families in England. I only hope he may not begin to tell people you are not quite the thing, for he can be very spiteful."

"That I can well believe," said Anjalie frankly. "Indeed, I am sorry to disappoint you, dearest ma'am, but I would far liefer die an old maid than to be wed to such a ridiculous creature! Good God, he is so puffed up in his own conceit there is no bearing it, and if that is truly what the so-called *ton* considers of first consequence, then I am very glad to be thought unfashionable. How I wish Papa could have met him, for he would have laughed very much."

This did not seem promising. Lady Fernhurst had already dimly begun to perceive that introducing her niece to the *ton* and seeing her advantageously married might prove more difficult than she had anticipated.

Another caller was almost as ridiculous, but he was so lively and amusing, and Anjalie was interested enough in the family by then, that she forbore to snub him. Mr. Darcy Hughendon had contrived to dance with both her and her cousin Anne the evening before, and set out that morning to further ingratiate himself, paying both ladies several audacious compliments and even making the shy Anne laugh. He too invited Anjalie out to drive the next afternoon, and had the wit to include her cousin as well. Anjalie was nevertheless about to refuse this offer when she caught sight of her cousin, who had blushed fierily. After a moment she thoughtfully accepted.

Lady Fernhurst gave her consent to the projected expedition, but once he had taken his leave, felt herself obliged to warn her niece that *that* connection was scarcely to be encouraged. "Indeed, my dear, I was a little taken aback to see you accept Mr. Hughendon's invitation, when you had rejected Sir Winsley, who is far more eligible," she said earnestly. "I grant you he is an amusing rattle, but he hasn't a penny to scratch himself with, and is very wild, besides. And if you are thinking that he is Chance's heir, I must warn you that it is very unlikely he will ever step into his cousin's shoes. People have begun to say that Chance will never marry, but that is absurd, of course. You may take my word for it he will do so in the end, if only to secure the succession."

"Believe me, ma'am, I have not the least expectation of his stepping into his cousin's shoes," said Anjalie promptly.

"It is just as well, for Chance will never let that rattlepate loose to game away his fortune!" said her aunt almost tartly. "I don't know what he can be thinking of not to have married long since, for however rude he may be, there is no denying he is one of the biggest prizes on the Marriage Mart. Indeed, I must warn you, my dear, that if you are looking to bigger game there is very little hope that you will be able to attach Chance himself. He is quite dreadfully proud, and has not the least need to marry a fortune, and it would not do to get your hopes up in *that* direction, I fear."

"You may be sure I do not, ma'am!" said Anjalie dryly.

"Well, it is just as well, for I daresay in the end he will marry some dreadfully starched-up female who is every bit as disagreeable as he is himself," said her aunt regretfully. "Though I was extremely astonished to learn that his sister has taken this absurd notion into her head to go out to Jamaica and marry some nameless adventurer. The sooner Chance nips *that* in the bud and marries her safely off the better, for you must know she is a great heiress as well. I am afraid the Dowager Lady Chance—you will not have met her, my dear, for she is always imagining herself a great invalid and is far too selfish to bestir herself even to take care of her own daughter—is clearly a great deal too lax in her chaperonage. But where was I? Oh, yes, Darcy Hughendon! You must do as you please, of course, and the family is certainly excellent, but to my mind you would positively be throwing yourself away on such a match. It is certainly not one I would countenance for one of my own daughters, for he is all to pieces, and quite dreadfully expensive. Chance gives him an allowance, of course, but I daresay he games that away. Indeed, if he is starting to hang about him for a rich wife, it is the most intelligent thing I have yet known him to do!"

"Indeed, ma'am, I have no intention of marrying either of them," said Anjalie even more dryly. "Must every man I find amusing be regarded as a matrimonial prospect?"

"No," said her aunt frankly. "In fact it has often seemed to me that the more amusing a man is, the less eligible he will prove to be. Why that should be I don't know, unless those with nothing else to recommend them must rely upon their charm to get by. Unfortunately, one looks for a great deal more in a marriage partner. Naturally I do not mean that one should positively *dislike* one's husband, for I'm sure that would be most uncomfortable. But—"

Then she broke off, for her undutiful niece had given way to her pent-up amusement. "Oh, pray don't be offended, ma'am," said Anjalie, laughing. "But I gather that if a prospective candidate be but well-born enough, then it little matters whether we can abide each other's company."

But as Lady Fernhurst began to look a little affronted, she begged pardon and allowed the subject to drop.

Since it was plain that she was still in Lord Chance's black books as well, Anjalie was surprised to find him waiting for her in the same spot when she went for her usual ride the next morning.

She was tempted to again give him the go-by, if only to annoy him, but after a struggle with her conscience, reined in, and said merely, "Good morning, my lord! If you have come to vent your bad temper on me because of yesterday, I warn you I am not your sister, and thus obliged to endure it. You had rather thank me, for you have considerable reason to be grateful to me, you know."

He ignored her greeting, and said disagreeably, "Grateful to you? For filling my sister's head with romantic nonsense, and encouraging her in the greatest possible folly?"

"Dear me," she said in amusement. "Can you find no one else to quarrel with my lord? What a dull life you must lead! But in point of fact, I told your sister the truth, and made no attempt to whitewash anything. And certainly no one could accuse my aunt of romanticizing it."

"And did not my sister's reactions to your highly colorful revelations prove to you just how incapable she is of being married and going out to such a place? You heard her! To her it is no more real than an exciting novel. But she would soon be singing another tune if I were so irresponsible as to let her risk her life and health on such an absurd journey."

"On the contrary. Has it occurred to *you,* my lord, that the fact she still finds such tales romantic reveals a great deal about your sister?" she countered. "My cousin Anne, for instance, is quite as horrified as my aunt, and cannot pity me enough for the life I have led. Your sister may merely be in love with romance. But you will certainly not cure her of her romantic notions by forbidding her to think of them!"

"And nor will you by filling her full of romantic tales of pirates and the Spanish Main. But it will be as well if you understand me, Miss Cantrell! If you encourage her to take matters into her own hands—or even aid her to do so, which I would not in the least put past you!—you will have gone your length, and may discover what it is to cross swords with me," he pronounced grimly.

But she was unimpressed by his threats. "Oh, pooh! You don't frighten me, my lord—why should you? I am neither in awe of your title nor one of the females you so much despise who pursue you for your fortune, and it takes a great deal more to impress me than mere words. That may work with your sister—though I take leave to doubt it!—but I am not some mealymouthed Englishwoman, taught to know her place. Why, it has seemed to me since I came that the men in England are all vastly impressed by their own superiority, on very little grounds that I can discover. My cousin Frederick, for instance, is the poorest creature, and scarcely possesses even common sense, and yet he expects my aunt and my cousins to knuckle under to his slightest utterances"

"He has all my sympathy!" said his lordship even more grimly. "I had previously thought *my* lot a hard one, but I now see I should be profoundly thankful that I have not been saddled with the care of you. But do not think to meddle in *my* household, Miss Cantrell."

Her eyes began to dance. "Yes, so say all despots—before they are inevitably overthrown!"

"Thank you! I know how to take that, I suppose?"

Her twinkle grew more pronounced. "Well, I imagine you might, though if you would trouble to use the intelligence I believe you to possess in your dealings with your sister, you would be a great deal better off."

"If this is the way you show your liking, Miss Cantrell, I shudder to think how you behave toward anyone you positively dislike!" he retorted.

She laughed. "Well, I warned you that my opinion might change the better I got to know you. You are certainly rude and overbearing, and far too set up in your own conceit, but in your defense, I daresay that is the result of having females positively throw themselves at you all the time, which is enough to turn anyone's head. And at least you are not a fop, or a dandy, and—except on the subject of your sister—talk and look like a reasonable man, which is more than I can say for anyone else I have yet met in London."

Unexpectedly his lips twitched, and then he burst out laughing. "No, no, my dear Miss Cantrell, I fear such praise will only add to my already overweening conceit. Besides, you will forgive me for pointing out that you are as great a matrimonial prize as I am. I will leave you to draw the obvious inference."

"You mean to imply, no doubt, that I am every bit as conceited and overbearing as you are. But at least I do not ride roughshod over people." She added thoughtfully, "My father was always wishful he might have had a son, to succeed him in the business, but I am glad now that he never did so. Based upon my acquaintance with you and my cousin Frederick, I begin to think I should not have liked it at all."

"No, for you might then have had to learn to ride under a curb rein, which it is more than obvious your father never troubled to apply!" he retorted swiftly.

She chuckled again. "Well, if he did not, you at least will never succeed in repairing that omission, my lord! Besides, talk is cheap. Instead of bandying useless words, do you care to put your much-vaunted male superiority to the test? Or do you fear that that rat-tailed gray of yours can never keep pace with my Erin here?"

His eyes began to gleam, but he said disagreeably, "Talk is indeed cheap, Miss Cantrell, especially when you know well you have the clear advantage. I ride a good deal heavier than you and you have the better horse."

"True, but then I am hampered by this ridiculous sidesaddle. Now if we were at home, and I could ride astride as I usually do there, you would not stand a chance of keeping within a hundred yards of me. But a hundred pounds says I can beat you over any distance you'd care to name. Or are you afraid to risk being beaten by a mere woman?" she added with deliberate provocation.

"We shall see that, my girl!" he responded immediately. "To the Serpentine and back, and if you beat me, I will double the stakes."

She needed no other prompting, but said even more provocatively, "What, don't you mean to remind me that it is very improper to race in the park, and that you would never allow your sister to engage in anything so ill-bred?"

"I thank God you are not my sister, Miss Cantrell! And as for shocking people, I begin to think you came to England with no other intention."

Mischief peeped through again. "No, but I confess the temptation is almost irresistible. But I believe you are stalling, my lord!"

"Do you, my girl? Do you indeed?" he demanded in a goaded voice.

She laughed, and in another moment they were off. This time she didn't have the advantage of surprise, and he gave her a good race, but her lighter weight on a faster horse in the end gave her the edge, and when they at last pulled up, she was breathless and laughing. "Oh, capital! You gave me a better race than I had thought, my lord! I will even handsomely own that you were indeed at a disadvantage, and forego the forfeit."

He too had leaned forward to pat the sweating neck of his gray, but she had to own that he took his loss to a woman in better part than she had expected. "Thank you, but the wager stands. I begin to think you were born in the saddle, Miss Cantrell, for you are the best female rider I have ever seen."

She laughed at that. "Why that is a compliment indeed, and what is more, one that perhaps cost you something to own, which makes it all the more valuable. I admit I was tossed up on my first pony before I could scarcely walk, but many of the roads are still so bad in Jamaica, that that is nothing remarkable. Riding remains the most comfortable mode of transportation. And Erin deserves most of the credit. I begin to think nothing can touch him, even here in England."

He asked curiously, "You once started to tell me of your plans for him, and then broke off short. Do you mean to set up your own colors and race him here? Is that it?"

"Good God! In England?" she pretended astonishment. "You must be aware I would never be permitted to join the Jockey Club, or race him under my name here, my lord. But fortunately racing is still in its infancy at home, and I have long had the ambition to set up a stud, and see if bloodstock from Europe cannot be bred to adapt to the climate. I hope in Erin to have the first of my breeding stock."

His brows rose, but all he said was, "Remarkable! Is this some new enterprise of your father's?"

"Good gracious, no! Papa would be perfectly happy if he could go everywhere by boat, and considers horses only an inferior way to get from one place to another. As a matter of fact, he is by no means enthusiastic about this latest venture of mine, for he thinks I will never succeed in making it profitable, which is his only measure of success. I fear my motives are often too impractical for him."

"What are your motives?"

"Oh, I welcome the challenge," she said lightly. "Besides, if I succeed it will be good for the country as a whole, I think. And I do not wholly despair of making a profit in the end, you know."

"You called it your 'latest venture.' What did you mean by that?" he inquired still more curiously.

"Oh, I have started a coffee farm up in the Blue Mountains, which Papa also thinks is a complete waste of time and money," she said airily. "But then Papa has very little interest in land, and although he owns a good deal of it, bought cheap over the years when land prices were depressed, he is by no means an agriculturist."

"You have set up an experimental coffee farm?" he repeated incredulously.

She put up her brows at his surprise. "Yes, why not? Are you surprised because you disapprove of my engaging in so ungenteel a profession, or merely because you think women have no head for business? I assure you I am almost as hardheaded a businessman as my papa, and little though he may be brought to acknowledge it, I am convinced coffee will one day be as profitable to export as sugar is today."

He said dryly, "Your tales are all so fantastic, Miss Cantrell, that I can never tell whether you are telling me the truth, or this is merely another of your Banbury stories."

She laughed. "Why, what an unhandsome thing to say! I don't tell Banbury stories. Indeed, I've no need to, for you are so very easily shocked that the barest truth will suffice. But all this talk of business reminds me that there is something I have been meaning to ask you, my lord!"

"I am filled with misgiving, Miss Cantrell," he said frankly. "What is it?"

"Nothing to alarm you, I promise. Merely, I wondered if you were acquainted with a certain Lord Sedgeburrow, and if so, could you tell me where I might find him? My aunt disavows all knowledge of him, and my cousin Frederick would only prim up his mouth, in that disagreeable way he has, when I asked him. But it occurred to me that you might be the very one to help me."

"And that is the worst insult you have yet directed at me," he retorted. "I can also see that my misgivings were well founded. What the devil do you want with that old squeeze-crab?"

She laughed. "Is he very bad? I am not surprised, for his reputation at home is of the very worst. But it cannot be helped, and I am determined to talk to him before I leave England."

"You will be wasting your time. Whatever it is you want of him, you are unlikely to get," he told her frankly.

"Yes, that is what the last agent Papa employed to speak to him reported. But I thought there was a slim chance I might succeed in person where others have failed. He owns a plantation near to ours, and is the worst absentee landlord on the island. The absentee system must always breed abuses," she added severely, "for the absentee owners care for nothing but wringing the last groat out of the land, and the overseers and agents have little incentive to be honest. But Lord Sedgeburrow's agents are even more notorious than most. They overwork and mistreat their slaves disgracefully, and advocate such cruel punishment that even the most zealous advocates of slavery are appalled. We—Papa and I!—have been trying for years to get him to sell to us, but he returns all Papa's letters unopened, and even refuses to admit his English agents when they try to call on him. But I am determined to speak to him before I leave, if I have to camp on his doorstep to do it!"

He said with a finality that put up her back at once, "Nothing I could learn of him would surprise me, but I still say you will be wasting your time. He is the most notorious skinflint in England, and if his Jamaican estates are profitable, you may be sure that is the only factor that will weigh with him. The last I heard, he resided in one wing of a drafty mansion in Grosvenor Square, being too miserly to employ the servants—or indeed the coal to heat it—to open the rest of the house. But if you take my advice, Miss Cantrell, you will save yourself a most unpleasant encounter. And," he added resignedly, "you need not bother to tell me you have no intention of doing so, for I am well aware of it!"

She merely laughed, and soon afterward took her leave of him.

He sat watching her go, an unreadable expression in his eyes, then shrugged and returned home himself.

He found his sister Georgy on the point of going out, but she unexpectedly followed him into the library, asking curiously, "Where have you been so early?"

"Out riding," he told her briefly, turning through the mail on his desk. "Where are you off to, brat? Shopping, or merely lionizing in the park?"

"Oh, shopping. There is nothing else to do," she said discontentedly.

He lifted his eyes to regard her suspiciously, but all he said was, "Poor mistreated girl! You have all my sympathy."

Her lips tightened, but then she said abruptly, "No! I am determined to go at least one whole day without quarreling with you, and so you won't succeed in goading me, *however* unpleasant you may be!"

"Good God! And to what do I owe this admirable resolution—or can I guess?"

"Well, I should expect you might, for you may be fusty and dusty, and think you always know best, but at least you never have to have things explained to you," she said frankly. "What did you think of Miss Cantrell, by the way?"

"I thought you were determined not to quarrel with me this morning?" he retorted.

She giggled at that, but said somewhat defiantly, "Well, I liked her! Didn't you?"

"*Like* her? No, I did not," he stated positively.

"I knew you would say that, if only to be disagreeable. But she was not at all what I was expecting. I have never met a West Indian nabob's daughter before, but she was not in the least vulgar, as I expected her to be."

"No, she is not vulgar," he conceded. "Merely out-rageous."

"Well, I may as well tell you now, Stone, that I have every intention of seeing her again. Such stuffy prejudices are what I have no patience with!"

"I have not forbidden you to see her," he pointed out mildly.

She looked a little surprised at that, but added even more defiantly, "And what's more, I hope Darcy does succeed in marrying her."

"He won't."

She bristled at once. "Why? Because her papa made his fortune in trade, and is not sufficiently blue-blooded to suit the high and mighty Hughendons?"

"No, because she is not such a fool as to take him."

That succeeded in deflating her. "Oh!" she said, a little uncertainly. "Well—well, I am telling you now that I don't mean to regard such things when *I* marry."

"Careful! I thought you were determined not to quarrel with me today, brat. And such things as what? Birth and breeding? It is all very well to talk in that romantical fash-ion," he added a little impatiently. "But you owe something to your name, little though you may like to admit it. I care very little whether you make a so-called advantageous marriage, and I don't even greatly care if your prospective husband should possess an unequal fortune, so long as he is a man of birth and character. Does that surprise you? But that is a very different thing from allowing you to throw yourself away upon a man interested only in your fortune—nor can I think you would wish to be wed for such a reason! And old-fashioned and stuffy as it may sound to you, it is only asking for trouble to marry totally out of one's own social sphere. Take Miss Cantrell, for instance. She may have a thousand amiable qualities—which I am very far from conceding—but she is as incapable of entering our world as you are of entering hers. I have no objection to your making a friend of her. Good God, Georgy, when did I ever interfere in your friendships?" he demanded rather irritably. "You and Miss Cantrell between you seem determined to make me out to be some kind of gaoler, but I have never tried to restrict you in any way. But when she fills you full of her romantic tales of the West Indies, you might at least try to remember that she has led a very different life from your own, and that what suits her would not suit you at all."

Georgy forbore for once to pick up that gauntlet, for she was regarding her brother in wide-eyed amazement. She said tentatively, still watching him closely. "You've never talked to me like this before. But at least you must own she is exceedingly beautiful."

"She is not in the least beautiful," he retorted, "Her eyes are very fine, and she is certainly striking, besides possessing an admittedly elegant figure. But her mouth is too generous, her complexion too brown, and her face far too strong for beauty. She is also stubborn, opinionated, outrageous, and badly brought up, and the man who is fool enough to marry her, despite her much-vaunted fortune, will never know a moment's peace! She would make mincemeat of Darcy within a week of the wedding."

"Oh!" said Georgy again, in a very different tone. "Considering that you have only met her twice, how do you know so much about her?"

"To have met her twice is to know far too much about her!" he retorted scathingly. "In fact, I begin to think your Miss Cantrell has come to England with no other intention than to annoy me."

His sister cast him another wide-eyed look, and for once wisely made no answer.

Chapter 7

At about the same time, Mr. Darcy Hughendon arrived in Green Street to squire the two young ladies for a drive. He was soon handing the two ladies into his dashing phaeton, and inquired good-naturedly where they wished to go.

He clearly envisioned Hyde Park, where all the fashionable world wended in the afternoon to see and be seen, but Anjalie surprised him very much by asking, "Grosvenor Square is not far, is it? Would you mind very much driving

me there? I have a call I must make, and I don't imagine
it will take me very long. Indeed, I may not be admitted
at all. But if I am, you may drive my cousin around for
twenty minutes or so. With your groom up behind, I imagine there can not be the least impropriety, could there?"

Mr. Hughendon looked a little startled, but for a gentleman there could be but one answer to either question. "Not
the least impropriety in the world," he assured her. "Happy
to be of service, ma'am—especially when duty coincides
so much with pleasure." He reflected on that, and added
insouciantly, and with engaging honesty, "Not that I've ever
gone in much for duty, mind you! Too dashed fatiguing."

Anjalie, who had not missed her cousin Anne's faint
blush at this compliment, began to wonder if she were not
doing her a disservice by encouraging the attentions of this
engaging rattle. She was by no means in sympathy with the
general expectation that females should sell themselves to
the highest bidder in order to mend the fortunes of the
entire family. But nor could she imagine that either her
aunt or her cousin Frederick would welcome the advent
of such an expensive fribble into the family, whatever his
connections. She salved her conscience by telling herself
she was unlikely to gain admittance into Lord Sedgeburrow's house, so that the danger of throwing her two companions into a dangerous tête-à-tête would be safely
averted. But she could not resist asking Mr. Hughendon
curiously, "What do you go in for, Mr. Hughendon?"

He grinned, in no way abashed at the question. "Pleasure, ma'am. Life's too short for anything else."

"Well, it seems very strange," she reflected. "And more
than a little tame, I must confess."

"Why, what do people do where you come from?" he
inquired, slightly startled.

Anjalie was amused. "They work. Oh, don't look so horrified, not in the fields! But they work at their business, or
manage their estates. Very few people are idle."

"What, even the gentlemen?" Mr. Hughendon gasped,
quite shocked.

"Yes, indeed, though fortunately we have fewer of those
than you have here, for they seem to me to be nothing but
a drain upon the economy. But remember, people have

come out to Jamaica in hopes of making their fortune, you know."

Mr. Hughendon blinked at this greatest of all heresies, and exclaimed, "Well, if that don't beat all! Sounds devilish fatiguing! In fact, always thought the tropics wouldn't suit me, and now I dashed well know it."

"Well," said Anjalie, even more amused, "a great many people there would find your lives here almost as fatiguing, I fear. Indeed, I have never been quite able to understand what a gentleman of fashion finds to do with his time, Mr. Hughendon."

"Good lord, nothing in the world mysterious about that, ma'am," he told her promptly. "For one thing, never rise before noon, of course—that goes without saying. Then, if my head is clear enough—which I'll confess it ain't often!—I'll toddle round to one of my clubs for lunch. Then, as often as not, I'll have a look-in at Tatt's, to place a bet or two, and it's Carlton House to a Charley's shelter I'll bump into one or another of my friends there, and we'll go off to spar with Jackson, or attend a cockfight, or some such thing. Then it's on to one of the hotels for a tight little dinner, followed by an evening spent at the Great Go—Watier's, you know." He grinned disarmingly. "After that, as often as not we'll finish up the night in one of the Tot Hill sluiceries, drinking blue ruin. Then, always assuming I don't end up in the round house, which unfortunately ain't in the least uncommon, it's home to bed, only to do the whole thing over again the next day."

"Good God!" This account was almost as alien to Anjalie as her life would seem to him. "And that actually amuses you?" she inquired curiously. "Speaking for myself, I can't imagine anything more boring."

"What else is there to do?" he inquired simply. "I daresay it's amusing enough, as long as the dibs are in tune. Of course, they very seldom are, but a man may always get by, you know. A run of luck—though I'll confess the cards have been damme—dashed unaccommodating of late!—or a lucky bet on a nag, and I'm full of juice again. Besides, a fellow gets used to being in dun territory, after a while," he added with his frank grin. "And in a real pinch, of course, I can always apply to Chance. Though I confess that's a thing I don't like to do until the tipstaffs are at the door, for he can be devilish unpleasant."

"And does he agree to pay your debts?" asked Anjalie curiously.

"Oh, Lord yes! It don't suit his pride to have his heir clapped up in jail for debt! Not that I escape wholly unscathed, you understand, for I've said he can be damn—dashed unpleasant. And what's almost worst, he always insists upon frittering away good money on paying tradesmen's bills. Where's the sense in that, I ask you?"

Anjalie had to laugh. "I pity your poor tradesmen! What do you usually do with their bills?"

"Put 'em on the fire!" he retorted promptly. "No sense in pitying tradesmen, ma'am, give you my word! Damme—demmed rascally bloodsuckers, the lot of 'em!"

"And does that answer?" she asked curiously.

"Lord, yes! Most of 'em anyway. Dash it, it's their own fault, for why did they accept my custom when they must know my pockets are almost permanently to let?"

"Good heavens. One wonders indeed why they continue to accept your custom," Anjalie said a little unsteadily.

"Aye, most of 'em are little better than highway robbers! After all, a fellow's got to eat, and dress, and present a certain appearance to the world. It's not my fault I was born without a feather to fly with."

Anjalie was even more amused, but her cousin Anne did not seem to find these unusual views at all out of the ordinary. "Oh, yes," she said, "even Mama says tradesmen don't expect to be paid at once. Unfortunately my brother is so unreasonable that he demands she settle all her bills every quarter, which always leaves her very cross."

"Aye, that's it, Miss Fernhurst!" Darcy grinned. "Devilish waste of good money!"

"Well, I myself would not care to have debts all over town and be forever on the brink of ruin," said Anjalie frankly. "I would find it far less exhausting to get a job."

He almost goggled at her. "Good God! As what?"

"Well, gentlemen do have jobs, I know—even in England! They join the army, or enter the church, or government service."

"Good God!" said Darcy again. "What, toddle off to work like some damned cit—" He broke off, then grinned disarmingly. "Beg your pardon, ma'am, but you see what I mean." Then a thought seemed to occur to him, and he added suspiciously, "My cousin Chance been talking to you?"

"No, of course not. Is that what he recommends?" inquired Anjalie still more curiously.

"Lord, yes! Always lecturing me about something. It's all very well for him, for he's so rich he could never hope to spend all his money! Why, I daresay he hasn't an unpaid bill in the house!"

"It's no wonder you resent him," said Anjalie, teasing him.

He grinned, but said strongly, "I daresay I wouldn't mind so much if he himself spent even the half of his fortune, or occasionally went in for some excess. But I've only seen him half sprung once or twice in his life, and he's no taste for gaming, which is the biggest sin of all, in my book. His only extravagance is his horses, and though he does spend a fortune on *them,* he's no taste for fashionable life—well, nor have I, come to that, for there are far better ways to spend one's time than doing the pretty to the dowagers, and being forced to dance with a lot of simpering females at a ball, or making formal calls in the afternoon. But the thing is, he prefers country life to town, and though I'll admit he's a devil to go in the field, and devilish handy with his fives, too, and I don't know anyone who handles the ribbons better than he does, come to that, his immense fortune is positively wasted on him. I could find a great deal more amusement out of it, give you my word, ma'am."

Anjalie was listening thoughtfully, but she said now, "Clearly he is a perfect fiend of selfishness not to step out of the way and give it to you, Mr. Hughendon."

Darcy grinned again. "Why, so I think! But the devil's in it he refuses to obligingly break his neck over a regular rasper, and leave his fortune and his title to yours truly to play ducks and drakes with. I don't mean to say that I ain't fond of him, and in his defense he's had a good deal to bear from that stepmother of his, and now Georgy. But the fact is, he can be devilish autocratic."

"That I can well believe," agreed Anjalie.

"Still, for all he can possess a dashed bitter tongue, I must confess there's no one I'd liefer go to in a fix," he confessed. "The truth is, for all my complaining, he's a dashed good fellow, I suppose. Don't tell him I said so!"

Anjalie found his artless revelations about his noble cousin extremely interesting, and could only conclude that Lord Chance did indeed betray more tolerance toward his eccentric heir than she would have credited. She couldn't help wondering in some amusement how her own papa would react if she ever dared to bring such a ne'er-do-well home on her arm, and did not have much trouble in picturing the scene. Papa had retained all the working-class contempt for the idle gentry, and far from wishing for her to marry a title, would very likely disinherit her completely if she showed what he would consider so little sense.

When they reached Grovesnor Square and Mr. Hughendon discovered the name of the person Anjalie meant to call on, he was quite as shocked as one of his indolent disposition could be. "Lord Sedgeburrow?" he repeated in astonishment. "No, no, must have the wrong name, ma'am! Good God, Sedgeburrow's nothing but a dashed mushroom! Made his fortune manufacturing bootblack, or some such thing, and then purchased himself a title and set up in the best part of town to lord it over everybody. Said to be as rich as Croesus, but that don't mean he's succeeded in buying himself the entree into polite society, for he's a curst rum touch, besides being dashed unpleasant and still smelling inevitably of the—"

Then he seemed to remember whom he was talking to and broke off, but Anjalie cheerfully finished his sentence for him. "Smelling of the shop. Well, I naturally care nothing for that but he is also said to be abominably close-fisted, which I consider a far less excusable sin."

Darcy begged her pardon. "Forgot who I was speaking to," he explained. "But you're right, ma'am, rumor has it he don't spend a groat he don't have to, even on his own comfort. Never knew such a bad-tempered old screw. Not that I do know him, of course, for he's not the sort of person I seek out, and besides, been a recluse for years. In fact, waste of time visiting him, for he won't see you. Never sees anybody but his man of business," he added simply.

"Well, he may not see me either," said Anjalie cheerfully, "but I have some business with him, and at least I mean to make the attempt."

Mr. Hughendon scratched his head in bewilderment. "Well, he's apt to be dashed unpleasant, and—did you say you have *business with him*?" he repeated in astonishment, slewing around to look at her.

Anjalie laughed at the shock on his face and prepared to alight from his phaeton. "Yes, I am aware that no young lady of fashion is supposed to know anything about such vulgar matters, but you must recollect my sordid background, sir. You may return for me in half an hour or so, if you please, for if he refuses me admittance I may easily stroll through those attractive gardens until you return."

Mr. Hughendon was clearly at a loss, but in the end consented to do as she bid. He drove off reluctantly, with an uncomfortable feeling he should not have let her confront such an old devil by herself, but an even stronger feeling that to accompany her would have been even more uncomfortable. And since he had a lifetime habit of eschewing responsibility, he turned to his far gentler companion with considerable relief, though he did ask her, thoughtfully, "Your cousin often do such dashed unusual things, Miss Fernhurst?"

Anne blushed and stammered, "No! Oh, no! That is—she has once or twice—but her upbringing has been very different, you know, and from what Mama tells me of that dreadful place, I'm sure it is not to be wondered at if—if she should at first find our ways strange, and we hers."

Mr. Hughendon was still looking unnaturally thoughtful, but he returned a polite answer, and since his manners were lively and he was at base kindhearted, he soon had drawn his shy companion out, so the half hour passed quite agreeably for both of them.

In the meantime, Anjalie had contrived to be admitted into Lord Sedgeburrow's house, if only by dint of putting her frivolous parasol in the door when the elderly butler showed signs of shutting it in her face.

He was clearly offended by this, and repeated frigidly, "His lordship is not at home to visitors. His lordship sees no one."

"I have come all the way from Jamaica to see his lordship," Anjalie said briskly, "and have not the least intention of going away until I do. Have the goodness to carry my card to him, if you please!"

The butler grudgingly agreed to do so, and left her standing in the hall instead of showing her into one of the drawing rooms. This proved to be well swept and polished, contrary to what Anjalie had been led to expect, if somewhat Spartan in nature. She took a seat on an extremely hard bench to wait. Apparently her threat not to leave until she had seen his lordship had been effective, for the butler at last returned and announced ungraciously, "His lordship will give you ten minutes, miss. This way, if you please."

She was led up one pair of uncarpeted stairs, and saw everywhere the same attempt to arrest the general decline. It looked as if an army of cleaning maids had been recently employed there, and Anjalie was puzzled, for it accorded ill with the decay and parsimony she otherwise saw around her.

The chamber she was at last shown into was at least distinguished from the rest of the house by being amazingly cluttered, as if his lordship had everything of value placed in his own rooms. Lord Sedgeburrow huddled in a wing chair before an enormous fire, though it was a mild day outside, a blanket over his thin legs and a permanently peevish expression on his face. A dirty fringe of white hair curled around a freckled, bald scalp, and his chin was sunk deeply onto his chest. A stick propped against his chair attested to some disability, and certainly he made no attempt to rise when Anjalie was shown in. His mouth was dry and desiccated, his cheeks stained with snuff, and his dress extremely old-fashioned, and he barked shrilly the moment she entered, "Well? What do you want? You have ten minutes! I don't know why I agreed to see you, for I don't see anybody!"

"So I was informed, my lord," replied Anjalie coolly. "My business will not take up much of your valuable time. I have come to see you about your Jamaican property, as you must be well aware. We—that is, my father and I, have made repeated attempts to buy that property—"

"Ha!" he interrupted rudely. "Waste of your time to come here, my girl! And what is much more to the point, a waste of mine! Been throwing the letters from your father and that agent of his in the fire for years, and when some other fool dared to show up here, told him to his face that I had no intention of selling! And if they think that by sending you, I'll be influenced by a pretty face, they're fair and far out!" he added with a cackle. "Never let myself be out jockeyed yet, especially by a woman!"

"That I can well believe," said Anjalie, taking little trouble to hide her contempt for the outlandish figure before her. "But my father didn't send me. I came myself because however unpleasant your reputation may be, my lord, I was sure you could not be aware of how your property was being mismanaged, or what goes on behind your back."

"What do I care how the property's being managed?" he demanded impatiently. "Shows a profit, which is more than I can say for a great many other of my investments these days. I daresay that rascally agent of mine, and my attorneys as well—bloodsuckers, the lot of 'em!—are stealing me blind, if the truth be known, but there's nothing new in that. Can't trust anybody these days."

Anjalie strove to hold on to her temper. "Your agent is, in fact, one of the most ruthless and unscrupulous men in the island, my lord," she informed him steadily. "He does indeed cheat you, but he also manages the plantation in the most brutal way possible. Believe me, it is a byword at home and so are you."

"What do you think I care for that?" he retorted. "Never set foot in the place and never wanted to. Damned unhealthy, uncivilized place, if the half of what I hear is true. What the devil do I care what a parcel of provincial rustics may say about me?"

"That I can also believe, sir, but you should at least care that a great deal of waste is being committed, and at the present rate your land will soon be worthless. It is in bad heart already, and though I have no doubt you care nothing for the plight of slaves you own, you might consider that they have cost good money, and it is foolhardy to work them to death, as your present overseer is doing."

But even that failed to reach him. "You're quite right, young lady!" he cackled again. "What do I care for a passel of savages? And don't give me any sanctimonious nonsense about having sympathy for the masses! I daresay you think your father and I have a lot in common, for it's said we both clawed our way up from the gutter! But the difference is, I scorn to try to gammon the world after the fact by setting myself up as a philanthropist. Freed all his slaves in a fine grand gesture, didn't he? I notice no one else in that damned primitive place was quick to follow his lead! Now he's sent you to London to make a fine marriage, has he? Well, I've achieved a title, and set up in the best part of town, too, but much good it's done me! Still look down their noses at me, though I could buy and sell the lot of 'em! I ain't one of 'em, and I never will be, and nor will you be, my girl, for all your fine airs and graces. So don't come lecturing me about my duty!"

Anjalie was almost rigid with disgust. "My father has not the least wish to purchase himself a title, nor do I!" she told him contemptuously. "As for looking down their noses, everyone does who has had the misfortune to know anything about you—and it is not because you began life in the slums or pulled yourself up by your own bootstraps. It is because you are a miserable human being. Well, I was warned it would do no good to come here, for you clearly possess no better nature to appeal to. But seeing the miserable way you live, I confess myself at a loss to understand why you are so bent upon wresting every groat you can make. You clearly do not enjoy the fruits of your fortune, and I cannot believe you are doing it all for the sake of your heirs."

That seemed to enrage him further, for he raised the cane beside his chair menacingly, and half rose from the welter of shawls that enveloped him. "My heirs? Don't dare to talk to me of my heirs," he shrilled. "My only heir is a wastrel and a spendthrift, and I shall leave nothing to him! Nothing, do you hear? And you may tell him so with my compliments! Lives on post-obit bonds, I make no doubt, and is counting the days until he can squander my fortune when I am safely underground, but he'll not get the opportunity!"

She began to be curious about this dreadful old man, despite herself. "What then? I cannot believe you mean to leave all your fortune to charity."

"Charity!" he cried even more shrilly. "I leave that to fools like your father. What do I care for the plight of a pack of fools I don't know and probably wouldn't like if I met 'em?"

"Then unless you have succeeded in finding a way of taking it with you, what do you mean to do with all the money that has caused so much misery and seems to afford you so little comfort?"

"Ha!" he exclaimed in some triumph. "I mean to build a monument to myself, and endow the funds to perpetually maintain it! Set it up in the square here, so future generations of blue bloods will have to acknowledge me. That way I'll have the last laugh after all!"

She found him despicable, but oddly pitiable as well. "Good God! Well, I suppose that is as close a way as any of being able to take it with you, but what a pathetic ambition it is."

But he was untouched by either her contempt or her pity. "Only thing I regret is that I shan't be able to see my nevvy's face when he realizes how I've diddled him," he cackled. "His mother—my sister—married above herself, and never let me forget it, though that wastrel husband of hers was glad for enough me to bail him out often enough. Not that he ever got so much as a farthing from me, mind you, and nor will his son. Lives like a king, and dares to look down on me for being socially beneath him. Never done a day's work in his life, and yet thinks to live high on the hog on *my* money after I've cocked up my toes! What's worse, gave some fancy-piece a slip on the shoulder, and then dared to send her to *me* to take care of! Well, I don't support another man's by-blows, and so I told her! But even there I outjockeyed him, for I hired her to keep house for me. Now what do you think of *that*?"

"I expect I had better not tell you," said Anjalie even more contemptuously, remembering her surprise at the evidence of recent hard work on the house, and profoundly pitying anyone caught in this despicable creature's toils.

"Best piece of work I ever did too!" he boasted. "*She'll* not be giving her notice the moment the work grows too hard for her, or she gets it into her head I've hurt her precious feelings, as every other servant I've ever had did. Made her sign a contract, but she knows that nobody else will take her in with her curst brat. There's philanthropy for you!" he cackled. "Especially since her own family kicked her out, for which I don't blame 'em!"

Anjalie rose without another word, her expression compounded of disgust and revulsion. "I had thought reports must lie about you, my lord, for I didn't believe anyone could really be as despicable as you were painted," she said scathingly. "But I see now that the rumors grossly underestimate the case. Pray forgive me for having wasted your time and mine." She did not even accord him a curtsy, but swept out of the room without another word.

Chapter 8

Anjalie was so angry that she was tempted to instantly sweep the unknown housekeeper out with her and away from the house. But a moment's reflection made her realize that that would be premature. She thought it would be as well to be on surer ground, and make some plan for what to do with the unfortunate woman and her child before she acted.

Fortunately she had not many minutes to wait before Mr. Hughendon's phaeton bowled into view. She had time to note that he and her cousin seemed to be getting on excellent terms, for she had never seen Anne look so animated. That was likely to prove a further difficulty, but she hailed the phaeton, unaware that her eyes were still sparkling dangerously and her cheeks becomingly red.

Mr. Hughendon, regarding these telltale signs, said sympathetically, "Warned you you was unlikely to get anything out of the old maw worm, ma'am. I take it your—er—business didn't prosper?"

"Oh, that! To be honest, I have forgotten my own business for the moment," said Anjalie, still too angry to mind her tongue, and impetuously poured out a history of her interview with Lord Sedgeburrow. But if she had been expecting the same indignation from them, she was speedily brought to the realization that she had misjudged her audience.

Mr. Hughendon said with easy sympathy when she had finished, "No, you don't mean it! Well, I knew old Sedgeburrow was a dashed loose screw, but I never thought he was as bad as that. Told you you ought not to call on him, ma'am!"

But her cousin was blushing furiously, and said urgently,

"Oh, pray, *pray,* cousin, you mustn't speak of such things! Why, Mama has never even discussed such a subject with me, let alone in mixed company!"

Mr. Hughendon added, "Dashed unpleasant story, mind you, but not a subject for delicately nurtured females. I warned you the fellow was a curst rum touch."

Anjalie stared at them both, her eyes still alarmingly bright. "I don't believe it! I tell you of a—a dreadful injustice, and the most you can find to say is that it is not a subject for *delicately nurtured females* to discuss?"

"No point in anyone's discussing it," Mr. Hughendon assured her practically. "Devilish shocking, and all that, but nothing you can do about it. Best thing is to put it out of your mind."

"Put it out of my mind!" repeated Anjalie. "I have no intention of putting it out of my mind! I intend to do something about it!"

Anne gasped and even Mr. Hughendon began to look a trifle uneasy. "Nothing you can do, ma'am!" he repeated. "I don't say such sentiments don't do you honor, but not your affair. Besides, no laws broken that I know of. Perfectly free country, you know."

"Not my affair, when he admitted to me—no, he *boasted*!—that his nephew had seduced a girl and then refused all responsibility toward her? I can only think you do not fully understand the true circumstances, for this is not some lightskirt, you know, but a poor, misguided soul, whose own family has now even disowned her."

"C-cousin!" gasped Anne, more scarlet than ever. "Oh, pray hush! It is most improper—I dare not guess what Mr. Hughendon must be thinking of you!"

"No, no, no need to fear that," responded Mr. Hughendon gallantly. "Thing is, though, don't know any of the circumstances. No proof even whose the child is. What I mean is, some of those women will say anything, you know, ma'am. Why, dash it, the more I think of it, not sure old Sedgeburrow ain't a public benefactor for taking her in."

"A *benefactor*? You can't be serious!"

"You said her own family had disowned her, didn't you? Ain't at all easy for such females to find work, especially with a baby in tow. In fact, she's dashed lucky not to end up in a—" then Mr. Hughendon broke off in confusion, remembering belatedly whom he was talking to.

But Anjalie grimly finished the sentence for him. "In a magdalen? Is that what you mean?"

Anne could only protest faintly by then, but Anjalie ignored her. "I am not as naive as you seem to think, sir, for I thank God I was not reared in England. But if so, that is her only piece of good fortune. He has deliberately taken advantage of her misfortune to force her to become little better than a slave to him, at the complete mercy of his tyranny, and forced to be grateful merely for a roof over her and her baby's head, and what few miserable shillings he doles out to her. But he may yet learn he has *me* to reckon with."

Anne protested again, and even Mr. Hughendon was looking slightly alarmed. "No, no," he said hastily, trying to retrieve his position. "Whatever her folly, she don't deserve such a fate as that. But the thing is, you called her little better than a slave, ma'am, and that's surely an exaggeration. I mean, she has only to leave if she's unhappy."

"To end up in the magdalen you already spoke of?" demanded Anjalie bitterly. "Besides, he told me he made her sign a contract. And even if he had not, I don't imagine in all this cruel city there is anything else for her to do but to end up in outright prostitution, as no doubt thousands have done before her."

"*C-Cousin*! Oh, no, pray—! Oh, you mustn't—!" cried Anne, hardly knowing where to look.

"No, no," said Mr. Hughendon, still toiling manfully. "Dashed shocking story. But you must be practical. Don't need a housekeeper yourself. Besides, you have only that old—I mean, Sedgeburrow's side of the tale. No notion what this woman's past may be, or anything else about her, for that matter. Never even laid eyes on her. I'm sure your aunt would advise you to forget the whole matter."

"She may, but I have no intention of doing so," said Anjalie somewhat contemptuously.

"Oh, pray—*pray* do not take this tale to my mother!" begged Anne, faced with a fresh horror. "Besides, M-Mr. Hughendon is right! What on earth can you hope to do?"

"Well, for a start I mean to confront this nephew!" retorted Anjalie. "If he has indeed seduced her, he must be made to take responsibility for his actions. I don't say he should marry her, for from the sound of it, that would scarcely prove a rescue for her, poor creature. But if the child is his, he should certainly be required to set them up in a modest way, and pay for their support. Do either of you know who this nephew is?"

Both could not have been more appalled if she had announced her intention of plunging into a magdalen herself. It would have been amusing if Anjalie were not so angry. Mr. Hughendon gave every appearance of a man profoundly relieved to disavow any knowledge of the ramifications of Lord Sedgeburrow's family tree. "*On-dit* is the old makebate's sister married above her station, and this nephew is no doubt the product. But don't ever think I heard what his name was, and you must admit he's hardly likely to go around bragging of the connection," he pointed out with some truth. "Besides, can't confront him! Dash it, delicate matter. Nobody's business but his own. I don't say I approve of what he's done, but you can hardly call on him and lecture him on his failure to support his mistress and her by-blo— I mean, baby. Extremely likely to take it in very bad part and be dashed unpleasant to you." He added reflectively, "In fact, don't know but what I wouldn't be myself, under the same circumstances."

"He may be as unpleasant as he cares to, but he is at least going to hear a few home truths from me," said Anjalie belligerently. "Why, what a poor creature I would be to let a little thing like that stop me!"

But they had reached Hill Street by then, and Mr. Hughendon was clearly glad to be able to wash his hands of the whole affair. "The more I think of it, Miss Cantrell, the more I think you're right," he said ingenuously. "Thing to do is to talk the whole thing over with your aunt. She'll be able to advise you far better than I can."

Anjalie regarded this craven behavior with some contempt, but attempted no more argument, for it was clearly a waste of her breath. Nor did she have the least doubt that her aunt's opinion would be the same as theirs. She therefore maintained a disdainful silence until Mr. Hughendon had set them down. It was left to Anne to thank him for the drive, adding in a trembling voice and with a beseeching look, "Mr. Hughendon, you will—I know you will not betray—that is—my cousin is new to England and does not understand— Oh, pray—!''

Mr. Hughendon bowed gallantly and made haste to reassure her. "No need to fear me, Miss Fernhurst! Wouldn't dream of spreading such a tale." He reflected and added truthfully, "In fact, ain't the sort of story I'd be likely to blab if I was the worst tattlemonger in London, so you may set your mind at rest." He then bowed with even more gallantry and gave every appearance of a man who could not escape rapidly enough.

Lady Fernhurst, when duly applied to by her niece, seemed uncertain whether to be more horrified at the news that her niece was on calling terms with every cit in London, or that she calmly proposed to rescue some man's abandoned mistress and child. In fact, she was so alarmed that she had to have recourse to her vinaigrette. "Oh, dear, oh, dear, I scarcely know what—surely you must know it is *fatal* for a gently bred female to reveal she knows anything about—about a certain class of female! Perhaps I should have warned you, but it never occurred to me—but I dare not guess what Mr. Hughendon must be thinking of you! I can only pray he will not spread the tale, though men are all so odious I have no doubt he will!"

"He may pass on the tale with my good will!" retorted Anjalie. "I keep telling you this is not some lightskirt cast off when her charms began to pall. Even if it were, I hope I would still find it in my heart to pity her,"

But her poor aunt almost shrieked and covered her ears. "Dearest, you must *never* dare to soil your lips with such a word! For a delicately nurtured young girl to speak of such things—even to acknowledge she knows they exist!— is considered *most* unbecoming! I can only pray you have not already ruined yourself, and Anne as well, for there is no depending on such a rattlepate to be discreet."

"Ruin me?" demanded Anjalie in a hard voice. "Surely such an heiress as myself may be allowed to be as eccentric as she pleases? And it would make no difference if I thought no one in London would ever speak to me again. However, if you are worried that my sins will reflect badly on my cousin, she made it very clear she was every bit as shocked as you are."

"Oh, heavens!" moaned her distracted aunt. "And what

is worse, I daresay Frederick will blame me for the whole. Dearest, I don't mean to sound hardhearted, but for you to talk of rescuing that young woman is absurd. You cannot know all the details, and you must be as well aware as I am that there is a certain class of female who—oh, dear, to think I should ever be discussing this with you, and in front of my own daughter as well! The thing is, my dear, that my own mama—your grandmama, of course!—warned me long ago that a wise woman pretends to know nothing of such things."

"I am very well aware men frequently have mistresses," interrupted Anjalie somewhat impatiently, "but that is a very different thing from seducing and then abandoning a young girl, and refusing all responsibility for the child. Good God, it is his child too! Does he care nothing for that? And then for Lord Sedgeburrow to compound the sin by taking advantage of her plight is more than I can stomach. And with all due respect to my grandmama—who, incidentally, cast off her own daughter when she made a disadvantageous marriage, and thus hardly can appear as a model to me—it is that sort of hypocrisy that I most despise. Women are pilloried and shunned, and driven into the most desperate of lives, while their seducers are accepted everywhere, and even decent women like you and I close our eyes to the whole."

"But dearest—!"

"No, Aunt, pray say no more, for I don't wish to be disrespectful, and I fear I shall be. It has been made more than plain to me that fashionable London is almost wholly without a heart, and that no one else will lift a finger to help this poor creature. But I assure you I am not so squeamish."

A dreadful possibility occurred to Lady Fernhurst. She exclaimed with even greater alarm, "Surely you cannot mean to bring her *here*? No, no, Frederick would never allow it!"

"Rest easy, ma'am!" said Anjalie rather scornfully. "Under the circumstances, this is the last place I would bring her. I don't know what I mean to do yet, for I must discover the legal ramifications of the contract she has signed. I daresay you are right, and no respectable employer would hire her now, and with the baby she should not be working anyway. I suppose I could install her in some comfortable house, perhaps in the country, but—"

Lady Fernhurst seemed to lose sight of the larger considerations for the moment. "Install her in some comfortable house—?" she almost gasped. "Are you *mad*? A female you have never seen? And do you equally propose to make her your pensioner for the rest of your life?"

"It may be necessary," retorted Anjalie coolly, "but first I must confront the true author of her troubles, and try to make him assume responsibility."

Lady Fernhurst was almost past being shocked. "Oh, I am sure my nerves will never recover! Dearest, you cannot confront—oh, I shudder even to think of such a scene! Besides, you do not even know who he is!" She seemed to gain some slight relief from this reminder.

"Good God, do you imagine I am afraid of him?" demanded her niece. "As for not knowing who he is, that should not be overly difficult to discover. Surely there is someone in this dreadful city not so terrified of what people might think to tell me—" She was the one to break off this time as a thought occurred to her. "In fact I think I know exactly where to get the information I need."

Her aunt moaned, but failed to convince her to abandon the unknown female to her fate, and at last tottered away, apparently a broken woman. She would have been even more appalled to know that Anjalie rode out the next morning with even more anticipation than usual, and was delighted to overtake Lord Chance before she had ridden once around the park.

She pulled up, and exclaimed, "If you have come to quarrel with me this morning, my lord, you will find me very willing to oblige you! But let us get the kinks out first, for I refuse to have my ride spoiled by one of us losing our tempers, as will inevitably happen."

His brows rose, but he obediently turned his gray to ride beside her. Anjalie let Erin lengthen his stride, and they thundered along for a good distance, Erin always a pace or two ahead. Anjalie at last regretfully pulled up, the worst of her crotchets galloped away.

"There, that's better!" she exclaimed unguardedly. "Don't you feel sometimes as if you cannot *breathe* here, with so many people and so little space?"

He was stroking his gray's neck with the handle of his whip, watching her with an unreadable expression, but said merely, "Frequently! But when that happens I go to Chance, or to Leicesterhire to hunt."

"Good God! Are you a Melton man?" she demanded with exaggerated respect. "I had no idea!"

"I am," he conceded. "And do not try to pretend you either know or care what that means."

She laughed. "At least I am aware it is considered the most difficult and demanding of the hunts. That is one thing you must be able to do better than I can, for there is very little hunting at home, and no natural foxes, of course. Someone once tried to import them, but they all died, and most of the bush is too inhospitable anyway."

"Yes, but then you far outstrip even me in setting everyone by the ears, Miss Cantrell," he countered smoothly. "Did you really lead my cousin to believe you intended to adopt some fallen woman and her child, or was that merely another attempt to frighten away a fortune hunter? If so, it certainly worked, for I have seldom seen him so alarmed."

She laughed again, despite herself. "That was probably because I advised him to find a useful profession."

"Ah, then no wonder he was alarmed. It was a waste of breath besides, I fear, for I have been doing the same for years."

"Yes, so he told me. What alarmed him was the fear I might actually expect him to bestir himself for something beyond his own selfish pleasure! But I have given up expecting anyone in this heartless city to care a rap for anything beyond themselves."

His brows rose. "Good God! Don't tell me the tale was true?"

"Of course it was true! Why else did you think I was so glad to see you this morning? You are the very person I need."

"Then God help me! I seem also to recall that when I requested a favor of you, Miss Cantrell, you were in no hurry to do so," he pointed out disagreeably. "Besides, what makes you think I am any less selfish than anyone else in this heartless city?"

"I don't, of course! I have not the least doubt you are quite as odiously selfish as all the rest!" she retorted frankly. "The difference is, you care very little more for propriety than I do—at least where anything else but your own sister is concerned!—and know better than to believe me some ignorant, naive creature to be protected from all knowledge of the world like the typical English miss. Besides, you needn't worry! I don't expect you to bestir yourself anymore than your cousin would have."

"No, I possess few delusions about you, Miss Cantrell," he told her in amusement. "I gather at least that you did call upon Lord Sedgeburrow? Did you succeed in your aim?"

She cast him a darkling look. "No, he is wholly contemptible, far worse even than I had been led to believe—as I expect you anticipated."

But when she had poured out the whole sordid tale once more, he at least showed no signs of being shocked. He merely said somewhat impatiently at the end of it, "My instincts for danger are seldom at fault! What, you impossible girl, do you expect me to do in all this Cheltenham tragedy? Confront Sedgeburrow? I assure you I will have no more success than you did—probably far less. And what the devil is this poor wretched woman to you anyway?"

She bristled immediately at that. "I expect nothing more of you than I might expect of someone who possesses the least modicum of Christian charity, which I am beginning to think is not to be found in this dreadful country! As for what this poor wretched woman is to me, there is no answer I could give you that you would understand."

He was regarding her with a slight frown, but at that his face hardened slightly. "Cut bait, you little virago! A word of friendly warning: do not be quite so ready to sport your canvas, especially with me, for you should know by now I will give as good as I get! I repeat, what is this woman to you?"

"Nothing!" she retorted somewhat bitterly. "But my father was once abandoned in a great, heartless city, and my mother was cast off by her own relations, so I know a little of what it must be like. And I can promise you that however unfashionable it may be, however many eyebrows I may raise, I do not mean to turn my back on this poor unfortunate creature."

He was still regarding her with an odd frown, but he said, "And what do you want from me?"

"Merely a little information, my lord!" she told him scornfully. "If you will tell me who Lord Sedgeburrow's nephew is, I won't bother you further!"

He took the wind out of her sails most effectively by saying calmly. "Very well. His name is Lord Purfleet, and he lives in the Albany, I believe."

Chapter 9

"Oh—! Thank you," she said with a diminution of her former antagonism.

He smiled faintly. "What do you mean to do? Confront the nephew and shame him into providing for the woman? You won't succeed, I promise you."

She bristled again. "Why? Because he, like men the world over, believes he has every right to take his pleasure and owes not the least responsibility to the poor female or the child that may result? I am fully aware of it!"

"I warned you to lay your hackles, my girl! And little though you may want to believe it, it is not the—er—invariable custom of every man to behave so. But you are unlikely to get anything out of the nephew for the simple reason that he is under the hatches himself, and would be hard-pressed to do so even if he wanted to. I don't say he would have provided for the creature in any case, but it is well known that he has been living on the strength of his expectations for years, and has not a feather to fly with."

"At this point I would have been surprised if you had told me anything else," she said irritably. "Good God, does everyone in England live above his income? I have already learned from your cousin the peculiar economy practiced by the upper classes, and have no doubt your Lord Purfleet manages to live in luxury, but somehow cannot spare even the few shillings a week that would suffice to support his cast-off mistress and his child. And all the while he, like your scapegrace cousin, looks down on anyone in trade, or who performs any useful labor for hire, while thinking nothing of accumulating debts he has no intention of repaying! Gaming debts I understand are the one exception, of course. I gather they must be paid immediately, for that touches a man's *honor,* while honest merchants can whistle for their money and poor females they may have ruined and abandoned do not reflect upon their honor at all."

He was still regarding her curiously, but he said, "Do not confuse my cousin—who is admittedly a sad case—with more hardened rakes like Purfleet, for Darcy at least is perfectly harmless. As for touching a man's honor, I will admit the world is a cynical place, but few would condone such behavior, believe me."

"You are mistaken! Mr. Hughendon assures me it happens all the time, and my cousin and my aunt were not in the least shocked that such things occur, but merely that I should dare to speak of them!" she told him bitterly.

He smiled again at her indignation. "Yes, that is true enough. But I daresay you might find a thousand women in London at this moment in the same plight. Even you cannot hope to save them all."

"That is the usual response of people wishing to salve their consciences for turning away their eyes!" she said scornfully. "No, I cannot hope to rescue every orphaned child, or wronged female, but that is no excuse for doing nothing when one of them is thrust upon me."

He said as if reluctantly, "No, I don't suppose it is. Purfleet will be bound to resent your interference, and is likely to be rude to you—and you need not waste your breath in telling me that that is unlikely to deter you either, for I am beginning to know you by now, Miss Cantrell. Very well. If you are determined to see him, you had better let me go with you."

He had once again managed to surprise her. "You!" she repeated in astonishment, then demanded suspiciously, "Why? Do not pretend you care anything for this poor woman, for I wouldn't believe you."

"Not very much, I confess," he conceded dryly. "But you will only get in more trouble if I don't. And if Purfleet calls me out for daring to stick my nose into his affairs, as I myself would be strongly tempted to do in his place, I will expect you to contribute a handsome wreath to my obsequies, for I understand he is an excellent shot."

Anjalie would have gone at once, but Lord Chance warned her that their quarry was unlikely to emerge from his bedchamber before noon, and promised to call for her at that hour. He was as good as his word, and seemed resigned, though he continued to regard her as if she were a curious puzzle he had not yet found the key to. On the short drive to Piccadilly, he again remarked dryly, "I warn you he is apt to be unpleasant, ma'am. You would do much better to let me see him on my own."

Her lip curled. "So can I be unpleasant, I promise you! I am not afraid of him."

He turned his head to regard her. "Tell me, is there anything you're afraid of, Miss Cantrell?" he asked.

Her brows rose. "Good God, what a question! I don't know. Not much, perhaps. But you may be sure I am not afraid to confront a despicable creature like that. And you need not tell me, my lord, that you don't mean to flatter me by the question. I am very well aware the world would like me better if I simpered and fawned and shrieked at the sight of a mouse."

He smiled reluctantly. "No, I was not going to tell you that. But what do you intend to do when—if he refuses? Or have you thought that far?"

She did not miss the correction, but said merely, "The same as if he had agreed, I daresay. The poor woman must certainly be rescued from that dreadful man, and some long-term arrangement made for her. I consulted with an attorney yesterday, and he advises—"

"You consulted with an attorney?"

Her brows rose again at the surprise in his voice. "Yes, why not? He works for Papa's London office, and he informed me that if she had signed a contract, it will unfortunately be more difficult to remove her. But I assure you I don't mean to let that deter me. I shall have no compunction in spiriting her away, if need be."

He regarded her as if she were a rara avis that had unexpectedly come in his way. "I doubt your father's attorney approved of that," was all he remarked. "And then what?"

She shrugged. "That will be up to her. I would like to send her home, for—"

"Send her *home*?" he again interrupted, even more startled.

"Don't keep repeating everything I say," she complained impatiently. "I know you believe life in the colonies to be little short of barbaric, but it would be by far the best solution. She may start anew there, and even pass herself off as a widow if she chooses. No one will ask many questions, for she will hardly be the first to come to the West Indies with the hope of leaving her past behind and starting over."

Such practical arrangements and dispassionate discussion of so delicate a topic from a young, unmarried female was certainly unusual, but his lordship was not particularly shocked. He tried, however, to picture his own young sister in just such a situation, and speaking with such crisp authority, and wholly failed. He was not at all sure he approved of such license in young females—and he was perfectly sure that most men of his acquaintance would not hesitate to roundly condemn it. He was certainly very far from approving of this wretched chit's likely influence on his young sister, and still meant to do everything in his power to foil any action she might take in that regard. And yet he could not deny that Miss Cantrell was at least unlikely ever to bore him, as most females did sooner or later. "Do you really think people are more tolerant there of such—er—peccadilloes?" he inquired skeptically. "I somehow find that hard to believe."

She appeared to give it some thought, and he was obliged to own that he liked as well her simple straightforwardness. She said what she thought, and if that was usually outrageous, at least she didn't shrink from controversy, or try to flatter him by agreeing with everything he said, as did females trying to capture his interest.

Now she conceded, as if only with extreme reluctance, "Perhaps not. A great deal of gossip goes on there, of course. But too many people have gone out with the hope of escaping their past, and so we do not tend to ask too many questions. Most people, like my papa, have reason to wish to make a new start, and for the most part we let them. The poor woman may even marry if she chooses, for there are still a great many more men than women, and wives are at a premium. But this is all the merest speculation, for she may not wish to go at all—especially since people here seem to regard the colonies as they would the darkest Antipodes."

His lips twitched despite himself. "Whereas you would have us believe that a trip across six thousand miles of dangerous ocean is of little more consequence than a drive into the country."

She laughed. "Well, not much more, at any rate. But I have not tried to discuss the matter with her at all yet. And were she extremely eager to make such a journey, there must be some delay. Papa has a ship due in London any day now, but it will not make the return voyage for several weeks, and something must be done with her in the meantime. I had thought of installing her in some comfortable inn, for my aunt—or I *should* say my cousin Frederick!— will not think of taking such a fallen creature into the house! But luckily a friend of mine, the widow of one of Papa's oldest business associates, has retired to England and lives in Chelsea. My aunt disapproves of her as well, for evidently Chelsea is considered the back of beyond, and she has not the least pretensions to gentility. But Mrs. Tixall possesses a kinder heart than any I have yet found here, and she has promised to take the poor woman in and look after her as if she had been her own daughter."

"You have been busy! And all of this is for a female you have never even met? Remarkable," was all he found to say.

She lifted her chin. "Perhaps in England, but not at home. We are still used to helping each other there, for you never know when it may be your turn to need help next."

"Don't try to convince me that all colonists are like you, Miss Cantrell," he said dryly. "Especially the females, for I warn you I don't in the least believe you."

When she merely laughed, it occurred to him how refreshing it was never to have to explain his meaning, or guard his tongue in her presence. Most females of his acquaintance pretended to be shocked by the more acerbic things he said, or worse, interpreted the most idle remark through the distorting lens of their own vanity. She shrugged and said, with an indifference he also liked, "I am not quite as unusual as you suppose, my lord. Females do enjoy a great deal more latitude in the colonies, and I have an added advantage. For far from being ashamed of my father's humble origins, I have always been particularly grateful for them, Since it means he has never had the least ambition to turn me into a lady."

"One advantage to your company, Miss Cantrell," he told her truthfully, "is that I never have the slightest idea what outrageous thing you will say next. But you begin to inspire me with as a considerable curiosity about your remarkable father."

"He would almost certainly surprise you," she told him readily. "I have always thought him living proof of how misguided the English class system is, for I believe he has scarcely changed at all from the day he first saw Jamaica. He has no pretensions to gentility, and unlike Lord Sedgeburrow—who I must say gives all self-made men a bad name!—has no desire for a title for himself or his grandchildren. Indeed, he told me once that making a fortune had been purely accidental. He bought his first ship because it was going for a song, and he wished to be his own master. He is now one of the richest men in Jamaica, and yet I do believe, if it were not for me, he would spend all of his life at sea, aboard one or another of his ships, and be perfectly content."

"You paint an admirable picture indeed. I would like to meet him one day."

She appeared to consider that. "I suppose you *might* get along together," she said cautiously, "for he is even more blunt than you are, and has less sympathy for fools. But I must warn you that he also has no sympathy for a pride based on nothing more than a fortune someone else had the trouble of making, and the ability to know who your great-grandfather was."

"If that is to my address, Miss Cantrell, I must warn you that my withers are still unwrung. I can assure you I pride myself on neither of those things."

She was regarding him assessingly, and retorted, "You do, perhaps without noticing! You are admittedly contemptuous of those who toad-eat you, but you are so used to being sought after and deferred to that you take it completely for granted. I will even admit that there may be at least some slight justification for your misogyny. But the remedy is easily in your hands, and I am surprised you have not taken it long since."

He regarded her in resignation. "I have not the least intention of gratifying you by inquiring what that may be, Miss Cantrell."

She went on, looking mischievous. "Instead of avoiding women, you should have married long since, of course! I cannot believe that in all of England there is not some female able to meet even your exacting requirements, and if she weds you for the sake of your fortune, why you are so unromantic yourself that it can scarcely matter! In your world such a practical arrangement is taken entirely for granted, and besides gaining a conciliatory wife, as well as a chaperon for your sister, such a marriage would have the advantage of saving you from any further matchmaking females. Besides, what good is an hereditary title without an heir? Sooner or later you are going to have to swallow your pride and marry, and all the advantage seems to be with making it sooner."

"Not quite *all* the advantage, ma'am!" he countered promptly.

Her eyes laughingly acknowledged the hit, but she said merely, "Why, the way marriage seems to be conducted in England, you need scarcely meet each other after she has duly presented you with a son, my lord. From what I can tell, most fashionable husbands and wives can go days without ever spending more than five minutes in each other's company."

"Let me tell you, Miss Cantrell, that the things you do *not* scruple to say have almost lost the power to any further surprise me," he said acidly, "and would give me a far odder notion of the West Indies than any you have accused me of holding if I believed you were in any way typical. But may I remind you that your arguments might equally be applied to yourself? Why have you never married? Or is there not a man alive who can measure up to your exaggerated ideal of your father?" he added unkindly.

But that dart glanced off her armor. "You mean that as a dig, I know." She chuckled. "But I have not the least intention of marrying a man like my father. I fear we would soon murder each other, for we are both far too strong-willed. By the same token, you should certainly marry some meek little female, my lord, willing to regard your least pronouncement as law, and unlikely to dare to cross you. But with your temper I am sure you are already well aware of that."

He ignored that, but inquired with reluctant curiosity, "Is that what your mother was like?"

She appeared to consider that, and it occurred to him,

even more unwillingly, that as a result of her odd upbringing she was in many ways more like a man than a woman. "I don't think so, but I can't really remember. And after having met my aunt and my cousins, I can't help but wonder even more what she was like, for it must have taken great courage for her to defy her family and marry a man everyone looked down upon, and remain in a strange new land."

"How did she die?" he asked.

"Not of some West Indian fever, as you are obviously imagining! She died in childbed, which is a thing that could happen anywhere. And do not seize upon that as yet another reason to prevent your sister from going out there," she warned him, "for she was in Kingstown at the time, and under a most able physician's care."

His face hardened a little at the reminder. "We were not discussing my sister," he answered frigidly.

"No, and you were not in the least disapproving until I mentioned her," she acknowledged. "But on that particular subject you are every bit as bad as my cousin Frederick!"

"And I gather worse you could not say of anyone!" he retorted. "Thank you! I am much obliged to you. But since you are the one to keep bringing the subject up, it leads me to conclude you only do it to annoy me. Indeed, I strongly suspect you care not a jot whether my sister marries Ludlow or not, and only choose to interfere in what should be my private affairs from the malicious desire to annoy me. Deny it if you dare!"

She laughed. "Nonsense! I dislike seeing any female forced into a marriage she does not desire. I notice you reserve the right to choose your own partner, and even remain single if your capricious requirements are not met, but you clearly mean her to make the advantageous marriage you yourself reject."

He said even more grimly, "You have made your opinion of me very plain, Miss Cantrell. Now let me be equally plain! I do not dislike you—except when you are bent on meddling in my affairs, for what reason only you know best! There are even times when, very much against my better judgment, I find you amusing. But it would have been as well for all of us if your father had ever taken his attention off his ships long enough to break you to bridle!

Since he did not, I give you fair warning: the day you encourage my sister to run off to Jamaica to marry Ludlow is the day you will find how dangerous it may be to thwart my will!"

"Oh, pooh!" she said, unimpressed. "I am not your sister, my lord, to be frightened into compliance by such threats. And since you are in some sense doing me a favor by coming with me today, I will even refrain from reminding you that when you get upon your high ropes it is sometimes hard for me to remember exactly why it is I like you. But then if you are astonished that my father never broke me to bridle, as you call it, I am astonished that your female relations should have let you become such a domestic tyrant. Indeed, it seems to be a peculiarly English trait, and one I cannot admire."

But that, for some reason, merely amused him. "You have no need to tell me so, ma'am," he said mockingly. "Only two things continue to astound me about you. The first is that you speak of the *English* as if we were an alien species, and both your parents were not born and bred here. And the second, Miss Cantrell, is that someone has not strangled you long since."

Chapter 10

Lord Purfleet's rooms in the Albany proved to be indescribably untidy, littered with old newspapers and empty wine bottles and glasses, as well as several items of carelessly discarded clothing. A desk, left open and cluttered with what looked to be months' worth of bills and duns, all crumpled and stuffed into every available cubbyhole, gave Anjalie a tolerable notion of his way of life. They were admitted by a slovenly manservant, who did not take it upon himself to say whether his lordship was in a fit state to receive visitors or not, but at a sharp word from Chance, ultimately went away to inform his master of their presence.

Chance, looking around the room with an expression of

disgust, said grimly, "I should not have let you come. You had best go and let me handle this. Wheeling will take you back to your aunt's house, and I will call upon you to let you know the outcome."

She was merely amused. "Nonsense! We are here on *my* business, not yours, and I assure you I am not to be deterred by a little untidiness."

"No, but your presence is unlikely to soften him, if that's what you hope. Nor, by the look of it, does rumor lie when it says he is perpetually under the hatches. He is a gamester, by all reports, and though a gentleman by birth, at least on his father's side, I am afraid he is unlikely to remember that fact—especially when he learns why we have come."

She was still more amused. "The gentleman side is the one I should like least, I promise you. But I am curious, my lord. Is he accepted in society?"

"Not by me," he retorted.

"A waste of time telling me so! I have yet to find anyone you approve of, my lord. But you have told me he is a gamester, and heavily in debt, and I have every reason to believe his character less than admirable. I am merely curious to know if all that is overridden by the fact that his father was a gentleman?"

"Not by people of discernment! Do not try to force me to defend a way of life that I deplore every bit as much as you do, Miss Cantrell, for that is also a waste of breath."

She laughed, but there was no time for more, for Lord Purfleet lounged in then, looking both surprised and slightly wary. He was younger than Anjalie had expected, but an unhealthy pallor and lines of dissipation around his eyes and mouth made him look older than his years. He was almost as untidy as his room, and looked heavy-eyed, as if he had just gotten out of bed or had not slept long enough.

He knew Chance by sight, of course, and seemed surprised to see him there. But when he learned why they had come, he was at first astounded, and then incensed. "Good God, what do I care for some slattern and her by-blow?" he demanded unpleasantly. "And if I *did,* I still wouldn't appreciate the pair of you meddling in my affairs, rousing me out of my bed at an ungodly hour, and lecturing me like a Methodist! Damme, it's the outside of enough, especially coming from *you*, Chance, for you can't bamboozle me into thinking you ain't had any number of mistresses in keeping over the years! Why, I never heard of anything so shabby!"

"At least you never heard that I gave any of them a slip on the shoulder, and then left then destitute," replied Chance contemptuously.

"Aye, if I had the half your money I don't doubt I could say the same! It's easy enough for you to look down your nose at others, for you're as rich as Croesus and don't care how you waste the ready. It's otherwise with me, and I'm damned if I'll tip over the possibles for some little ladybird and a brat that I don't even know for sure is mine."

"I will request you to remember there is a lady present! And you should be thankful that there is, for otherwise I would be strongly inclined to teach you your manners," said Lord Chance grimly.

But their host was as proof against threats as he was shame. "Well, who *asked* her to come, I'd like to know? As for *ladies*," he added with a nasty laugh, "that's another matter entirely, if the half of what I hear is true. I may have to put up with that kind of thing from my uncle, with his vulgar notions, but I'm damned if I'll—"

He did not finish, for Chance had moved with unexpected speed, and now grasped his neckcloth with one hand and had twisted it in a way that made it impossible for Purfleet to breathe, let alone speak. "Perhaps I did not make myself clear," he said steadily. "You will at all times behave to Miss Cantrell with all the respect she deserves! Is that perfectly understood?"

Lord Purfleet was scrabbling ineffectually at his throat, and making faint noises of strangulation. His eyes had begun to start from his head and his face had assumed an alarmingly purple hue, so that he did not look to be capable of understanding anything at the moment. Anjalie, while not unappreciative of the unexpected speed and strength of this assault, nevertheless thought it time to intervene. "Let him go," she said calmly. "Do you suppose I care what he thinks of me? And much as he deserves to be strangled, I have no need for you to defend my honor, I thank you. I said let him go!"

After a moment Chance did so. "Very well, ma'am, but

I fear the only thing that will manage to get through to him is the toe of my boot."

Lord Purfleet had fallen back against the wall, trying to get his breath back, but he cowered a little at that and exclaimed shrilly, "If you touch me again, I'll have the law on you, by God I will! Damme if it ain't the outside of enough when a man can be assaulted in his own home!"

Chance looked wholly disgusted, and Anjalie said impatiently, "Good God, what a contemptible creature he is! You might thrash him with my good will if I thought it would do any good, but I doubt anything could."

Lord Purfleet, still nursing his bruised throat, cried resentfully, "Aye, it's all very fine for both of you to sneer at me, for you've never known what it's like to be obliged to make and scrape, and what's worse, be forced to truckle under to that despicable old man for fear he'll cut me off without a penny! How d'you think it feels to have everyone know that old cheese-paring mushroom is my uncle, sitting there as he does in that damned mausoleum of his while I live in rented rooms, crowing like a cock on its own dunghill, boasting of his purchased title, and refusing to spend a spare groat, even where his own comfort is concerned! It's enough to drive a fellow to drink if he weren't there already. And now you come, prosing to me of some lightskirt I can scarcely remember, and her muffin-faced brat, and expect me to do the decent thing? I tell you, with the best will in the world to do the right thing by her— which God knows I haven't—I'd be damned puzzled to know how, without knocking myself into horse nails. I told her the same, when she dared to come whining around here, threatening to go to my uncle if I didn't help her. My uncle! What a laugh that gave me! By God, if anyone has gotten so much as the time of day from him in the last thirty years, it's more than I ever heard of. I only wish I could've been a fly on the wall to observe *that* encounter!"

Anjalie was regarding him rather as she would have some insect she had never encountered before. "Well, she did go to your uncle, but you're right that far from trying to help her, he has merely taken further advantage of the poor creature. Are you aware he has taken her in and turned her into his housekeeper, knowing full well that she dare not complain or leave his service no matter how much he ill-treats her."

Lord Purfleet gave a rather wild laugh. "Lord, you don't mean it! That's hell's own jest, that is! I'll say one thing for the old purseleech, he don't miss a trick that can save him a penny or two! But if that's the case, you can have nothing more to say to me, for it appears she's amply taken care of!"

"And your child?" she demanded evenly. "Are you really content to have it brought up under such circumstances?"

"Good God! Next you will be saying you expect me to adopt the brat and raise it as my own! Chance knows better, I'll wager," he sneered. "Ask him how many by-blows he's had come in through the side door!"

She ignored that. "I don't expect you to adopt it. Indeed, the poor child has enough to bear having you for its father," she said contemptuously.

"If you care so much for the woman and her brat, I wonder you don't rescue her yourself," he said, obviously as untouched by her scorn as he had been by Chance's physical threats. "By all accounts you can afford it, instead of coming preaching round to me!"

"I intend to, if you refuse to do your duty by her. But I suspect she would prefer the help to come as her due, not as charity from a stranger."

"Ha! What right has she to be so proud?" he demanded. "She may count herself lucky to have a roof over her head and useful employment."

Chance had been leaning his shoulders against the wall, taking no part in the conversation, but his face was eloquent of his contempt. But now he straightened and said grimly, "Come, Miss Cantrell! You will get nothing from him that might be expected of a man of honor or breeding. Unless you would like me to deal with him in the only way he is likely to understand—and I would be very willing to do so!—we are wasting our time here."

"Why, so I told you from the start!" retorted Lord Purfleet peevishly. "You might have saved us all a damned unpleasant interview."

But Anjalie was not finished yet. "You are mistaken. I know exactly how to pay him back in his own coin, and it does not involve violence. Did you know your uncle means to leave his fortune to erect and maintain a statue of himself to perpetuate an ego even greater than your own, and leave not one penny to you? Yes, I thought that would get you, as nothing else could."

For Lord Purfleet had turned first red, then very white. "That old *devil*!" he cried viciously. "I might have known he'd find some way to take it with him in the end. He can't enjoy it himself, and yet he means to see that no one else gets the chance either. I hope he rots in hell with it, is all I can say!"

Lord Chance determinedly drew her out of the room, saying appreciatively as they went down the stairs, "You were right: you did manage to wound him far more than a mere thrashing could have. How did you know his uncle meant to leave his fortune like that? Or did you make it up, just to punish him?"

"He boasted of it to me," she said. "I thought the uncle was wholly despicable, but I believe the nephew even manages to outdo him. At least he earned his fortune, and so may do with it as he wishes, but I can find no redeeming features in that parasite abovestairs."

"Oh, he is wholly contemptible," agreed Chance. "But I apologize: I should have more strongly insisted you leave him to me, for I knew what he was."

"Good God, when will you learn that I am not your sister, my lord, to be sheltered and protected?" she demanded impatiently. "As for that poor female, there is not a penny to choose between the nephew and the uncle as far as a total lack of charity and common human compassion are concerned, and I have come to the conclusion the child will be lucky never to learn what his father was like."

"You mean to send her to Jamaica, then, if she will go?" he inquired with interest.

"Yes, indeed, for she will be very much better off there."

He helped her into his chaise, and said even more dryly, as he took his place beside her, "So she becomes your pensioner instead of Purfleet's?"

"Perhaps, but she may become independent sooner than you might think, which most people outside the idle privileged class usually much prefer."

"No, idleness is certainly not your besetting sin, Miss Cantrell. I imagine a great many people—myself and your aunt included!—might wish it were. But I confess I'm growing increasingly curious about your life. What do you do at home to keep yourself busy—besides running an experimental coffee farm, of course, and meaning to set up a racing stable?"

"Oh, a thousand and one things, none of which would interest you in the least, my lord."

"Try me."

She cast him a quick look, then said in amusement, "Remember, I warned you I am not at all genteel! Papa has acquired a great deal of land over the years, which he was letting go to shocking waste, until I grew old enough to take it over from him. I—*he* owns several sugar plantations and a rum distillery which are beginning to show a profit again, or they were until this unfortunate war. It has affected all shipping to a certain extent, and especially now that England is blockading American ports, the price of sugar has gone sky-high, which would be excellent news if most of it was not forced to sit idle in the warehouses. The same is unfortunately true of rum. I told you I possess none of the English upper-class objections to trade, and engage in it quite happily."

"Good God! Do either of you happen to remember that Jamaica is an English colony?"

"What do you think we care for such a foolish war—except that it interferes with our profits, and deprives us of many luxuries obtained from America? The truth is, our sentiments are closer to America's than England wishes to believe, and I understand it was a close-run thing, when America declared her independence, whether we would not join her. The war with France is more popular, since everyone in the West Indies hates the French probably even more than you do here. In England people merely complaint that French fashions are no longer obtainable, and taxes to support the war are grown iniquitous. But since the French have coveted Jamaica ever since it was wrested from the Spanish, and have invaded and conquered several nearby islands, we are under constant threat at home. Unfortunately England will do nothing to provide for our defense, but has merely increased our taxes to help pay for its costly wars in Europe, so that we have little enough cause to be grateful to her."

"I see. And it is to this you would have me take my sister?" he demanded disagreeably. "Never mind! I have not the least intention of discussing politics with you. But do you seriously expect me to believe you run these plantations by yourself?"

"Of course I do! Why should I not? I have overseers, of course, but you must know from your own estates that no overseer, however honest and hardworking, can be wholly relied upon."

"Do you run them with slave labor?" he inquired dryly.

"Good God, no! You mean to sneer, I know, but Papa once served on a slaver, when he was only a boy, and the horrors he saw there convinced him never to own any slaves himself. That is one of the reasons it is so important that I should succeed with my plans, for I hope to prove that slave labor is not economically necessary, as many people in Jamaica still believe. We use freed blacks, of course—indeed, my own housekeeper, and the closest thing I have to a mother is one—and though I have mostly white overseers now, I mean to try to move more of the blacks into positions of authority. That requires educating them, of course, and I have schools set up on all my—I mean Papa's—estates."

He could only shake his head. "I seldom know whether to give any credence to the remarkable things you say, Miss Cantrell," he told her frankly. "But loath as I am to bring the conversation back to more unpleasant matters, what do you propose to do next about your protégée?"

She shrugged. "My first step must be to contrive a meeting with the poor woman and then if she is agreeable, I begin to think the best thing may be for her to disappear without a trace."

"That's what I was afraid of," he said resignedly. "It will do no good, I suppose, to point out to you that what you propose is illegal, not to mention likely to cause you a good deal of trouble and expense? No, I feared it would not. Very well, you had better let me—"

But he was never to finish what he had meant to say, for they had reached Hill Street by then and as they pulled up before her aunt's house, Anjalie started up at the sight of a slim figure on the doorstep. "Good God! *Adam*!" she cried. Then she added with irrepressible mischief, "I thank you for your kind if reluctant offer, my lord, but here is someone very used to helping me out of scrapes at home, so I shan't need your help after all. And I suspect that is news you will be very relieved to hear!''

Chapter 11

Anjalie then tumbled out of the chaise almost before it had stopped completely, to the astonishment of his lordship's well-trained servants, and launched herself onto the bosom of the newcomer.

Chance, descending more leisurely from his carriage, watched this touching reunion with a cynical eye. The newcomer turned and received her with aplomb, laughing and protesting. He seemed to be a well-set-up young man of some thirty years, well if not fashionably dressed, and with the telltale tan his lordship was coming to recognize. After a moment his lordship, realizing he had been forgotten, shrugged and climbed back into his chaise and signaled his coachman to drive on.

Anjalie, in the meantime, was again ruthlessly hugging the newcomer. He stood it very well, merely grinning and remarking, "Well, at least London has not succeeded in changing you so far. I suspect it is the other way round, and you have by now taught them all how they should go on."

"Oh, Adam! When did you arrive, and why didn't you tell me you were coming? How *brown* you look!" Anjalie ended foolishly. "I am so tired of seeing nothing but pale London faces."

Adam Trelawney, like her father, was of humble origins, and had come out to Jamaica at an early age to relieve his mother, an impoverished widow, of the expense of his care. He had soon fallen into her father's orbit, and since he was as shrewd as he was honest, from that point his future had been assured. Anjalie had known him from the age of eight, and looked upon him as the big brother she had never had.

"Now that I come to think of it," he teased with a brother's candor, looking her over critically, "perhaps you have changed a little. I certainly am unused to seeing you without your hair falling down your back and a smear of mud on your face. Does London please you? How do you manage to go on? I wondered if you would find enough to occupy you in this tame setting."

She sighed. "I wondered, too, and it is true that everyone is dreadfully idle and frivolous. Why, if my aunt and cousin do no more than some shopping in the afternoon, and attend a ball in the evening, they think themselves exhausted and must take the next day to recuperate!"

"No, that would never do for you. But are you sure they aren't merely exhausted from having you under their roof for some weeks?" he asked in amusement. "What do you think of your English relations? Is your aunt kind to you?"

"Oh, yes," she said quickly. "That is—she is very good-natured, and would like to stand to me in place of a mother, if only I would let her. I fear I shock her a great deal, and though we are at outs at present, for reasons I will explain later, in general she is very kind. But let us not talk about that now. Only tell me *once* how Papa is doing, and Juba and—oh, and everyone!—and then you can tell me why you have come, and how long you can stay." She added with another sigh, "It seems like very much more than three months since I left home, and I never believed I would miss it all so much."

"They are well, of course, though your father is going around like a bear with a sore paw. He will not own that he misses you, and has compensated by a surge of new energy. He prowls restlessly around, looking for things to criticize and thinking up new tasks for everyone, so that you can imagine how much the rest of us are longing for your return. Juba put up with it for a few weeks, and then forbade him to sit up late in his study drinking rum and smoking, a habit he had taken to, on the grounds that it stank up the room and made him unbearable to live with the next morning. She will soon have him in hand, I predict."

Anjalie laughed, but ruefully. "Indeed she will. She and my mother are the only women who have ever been able to manage him, I think."

"You do fairly well," he pointed out dryly. "As we have all learned to our costs these last few months."

She sighed again, and resolutely changed the subject. "Is that why you have come? To escape Papa's moods?"

But he had come, as she suspected, on a double mission. Mr. Cantrell, on his brief visit to England escorting his daughter, had developed an interest in a canal being dug in the north, and wished his second in command to look further into it. "But I think that was merely window dressing, to give me an excuse to come," Adam confessed. "The truth is, my mother is in increasingly indifferent health, and one of my younger sisters is getting married, and since I suspect he also hoped I could keep an eye on you at the same time, here I am. His hopes are misplaced, of course, for I have never yet been able to talk you out of any mischief. But I was glad enough of the excuse."

"Your poor mother! I was so glad to finally meet her after all these years. And all your brothers and sisters, too!"

"Yes, she wrote me of your kindness in calling. And that is another reason for my trip. It seems your father, in his inimitable way, discovered that one of my younger brothers is keen to come out to the West Indies, and offered him a position on the spot. I am to escort him out when he comes."

She laughed. "Yes, he can never resist anyone who shares his enthusiasm for business and for Jamaica as well. That is how you first came to his notice, as I recall. But your poor mother indeed, to lose another of her sons. She was being very brave about the whole thing, but I knew she felt it. Pray give her my love when you see her."

"I will," he said gratefully. "She does feel it, of course, but I have done so well, with your father's patronage, that she would never dream of restricting Robert. But enough of my family affairs. How do you go on in London? And more important still, what does London make of you? It is still standing, I was thankful to see, so there cannot have been any major volcanic disturbances—at least so far. But I fully expect that by the end of your visit you will have set them all to rights, and showed them how they can conduct themselves a great deal better."

She made a face. "I only wish it might be so, for there

is much I find to disapprove of. But so far I fear my influence has been negligible. My birth, you understand, is to be deplored, and my manners are not in the least what is expected of a properly brought-up young lady. That would suit me very well, of course, for you know I have not the least interest in wasting my time attending a lot of boring balls and such! But unfortunately, the size of Papa's fortune apparently more than makes up for that and since everyone—including my aunt!—seems to take it for granted I came with no other purpose in mind than to buy myself a title, I am at present the target of every gazetted fortune hunter in London, and every expensive younger son who thinks Papa might very well pay for his excesses."

He laughed. "If they knew you as well as I do, they would soon realize their error! But something tells me you do not like the English very much," he added even more teasingly.

She paused to consider it. "Here the only thing that seems to matter is *what people might think* and they are all so fearful of being thought bad *ton* that they scarcely dare have a thought on their own. Add to that the fact that females are reared to be perfect *pattern cards* of respectability, and you will begin to see that fashionable life in London does not particularly suit me."

"No, it would not, of course. I naturally never moved in such exalted circles, but you must remember that few females have been given the latitude you have, even at home. I fear you would find even my sisters far too docile by your standards, for they do not career all over the countryside unattended as you do, or take joy in putting up people's backs."

"Well, I liked them both, and at least they do not see marriage as their only option," she retorted. "Your sister Beth is employed as a governess, and your sister Meg means to become a teacher, both of which are useful and worthwhile professions, and do not depend upon a man to rescue them. But I don't know what I am thinking of to keep you standing on the doorstep in this ill-bred way— except that my provincial upbringing has obviously taught me no better! Oh, dear, and I must make you known to Lord Chance as well, for your arrival knocked me so cock-a-hoop, that I completely forgot about him. Good heavens!

I guess he has already gone," she added, looking guiltily around.

"If you mean the tall, powerfully built man you arrived with, he drove off sometime ago. Who is he? Lord Chance, did you say?" Adam asked curiously. "Is he one of the fortune hunters you mentioned?"

She went off into a peal of laughter. "Good God, no—though I did think he was at one time! Never mind! He is very wealthy himself, and it will do him good to receive a set-down. Now I fear we had better go in, though I should warn you that my aunt is unlikely to approve of your arrival, for she is already afraid I mean to fill her house with rustics and cits! My cousin Frederick, too—my eldest cousin—is the most odious, self-righteous prig imaginable. But don't let him condescend to you."

"I am quaking in my boots already," confessed Adam. But he withstood the introduction to Lady Fernhurst with admirable fortitude.

That lady, already reeling from the introduction of a fallen woman and her child into her previously calm world, did look a little taken aback at learning who Adam was, and acknowledged the introduction with a certain chilly hauteur. But she was seldom proof against a personable young man, and since Adam's manners were excellent, if a trifle staid, and he seemed to be perfectly genteel, she soon thawed somewhat, even going so far as to graciously invite him to dine one evening with them.

Anjalie mischievously did not inform her aunt of the one fact that would have made Adam instantly acceptable to her: that he was her father's right-hand man, and heir apparent, and was already extremely rich in his own right. She affected an escape as quickly as possible, saying mendaciously that Adam had offered to escort her on a shopping expedition to purchase a wedding present for his youngest sister.

Adam, who beneath his sober appearance possessed a wry sense of humor, said with twinkling eyes as they took their leave, "I almost find it in me to feel considerable pity for her, for it is obvious she little knows the firebrand she has taken within her midst. Should I decline her invitation to dine?"

"By no means! If that is the worst she ever need bear,

she will be fortunate, indeed. Besides, if she knew how wealthy you were she would sing a very different tune. Of course, to really impress her you would have to appear intolerably bored, and mince a little, and dress outrageously, and make it clear to the meanest intelligence that you consider yourself vastly superior to your fellow creatures. Then she would fall upon you with open arms."

He laughed and demanded an explanation, and so she entertained him with a description of Sir Winsley Fawnhope, and then Mr. Darcy Hughendon. He was amused, but remarked in some surprise, "You would seem to be on considerable terms with all of that family. Is Lord Chance promoting the match between you and his cousin?"

But her eyes had taken on a mischievous twinkle as she saw two familiar figures walking toward them down Bond Street. "By no means. But hush, for here he comes with his sister. I will tell you all about it later, but I should perhaps warn you that Miss Hughendon is almost singular in London for being interested in Jamaica, and will no doubt bombard you with questions. Lord Chance is very far from sharing that particular enthusiasm, for reasons that will soon become clear to you. I wonder what the two of you will make of one another?" she added curiously, a small smile hovering about her lips. "He may be upon his high ropes, of course, for he disapproves of me quite amazingly. But he is not a snob, and at least has the distinction of being the most sensible man I have yet met in England."

If Lord Chance disliked the introduction, at least he did not betray it. Georgy had hailed Anjalie with enthusiasm, and seemed to accept Adam unquestioningly, though her brother looked rather narrowly at him before shaking hands.

Georgy was saying in her usual impetuous way, "It is famous to meet you again, Miss Cantrell, for I have been longing to call on you, only that my brother said it would be rude to monopolize your time. Pray let us walk a little way together, at least until the end of the street. Stone is driving me to Kensington Park this afternoon, only I suddenly remembered an errand I must run. So he was obliged to escort me—with no very good grace, I might add—particularly since that entailed leaving his horses standing, which apparently is the greatest crime one can commit. I have never understood why that should be so, especially when he has no such compunction about keeping *me* waiting above an hour for him, as he did this very day! But that is a very different matter, I collect, for I am merely his sister, after all, and so cannot hope to rank in his esteem with his horses."

Anjalie glanced rather quizzically at his lordship, gathering that he had not sullied his sister's ears with an explanation of what had detained him that morning. But she merely said in amusement, "An unpardonable crime, Miss Hughendon. It is no wonder you are vexed with him."

"Yes, indeed, though I should certainly be used to it by now. I am sure my brother never shows me half the solicitude he does for his wretched horses, and I can only pity his poor wife, if he should every marry, for she will clearly find herself playing second fiddle to them all her life!"

Anjalie laughed, and Adam looked rather surprised at such vivacity, but her brother observed dryly, "I fear you are addressing the wrong audience, Georgy, for Miss Cantrell is almost as addicted to horses as I am."

She pouted and cast Anjalie a reproachful look. "Oh, sad work! Are *you* addicted to horses as well, Mr. Trelawney?" she inquired saucily of Adam.

Adam smiled faintly. "No, Miss Hughendon. I fear I have long since earned Miss Cantrell's contempt by regarding them merely as a means of getting from one place to another."

"Excellent! Then *you* shall walk beside me, for I have heard enough reproaches for one morning," she decided. She cast her brother a teasing look, as if she dared him to object, and took Adam's arm, beginning to chatter to him in her usual disarming style. Anjalie had little doubt she would soon be quizzing him about her fiancé, but since her brother had made no attempt to prevent the pairing, she herself accepted Chance's escort.

As soon as the other couple had gotten a little ahead, she said teasingly to him, "You did not care to avoid your sister's displeasure by informing her what had detained you today, my lord?"

"You must be well aware by now that from my sister to the world is a very short step, Miss Cantrell," he retorted. "Is Trelawney on a long visit?" he added abruptly.

"Oh, no! I was sorry you left before I could make him known to you earlier," she said tranquilly. "He is my father's right-hand man, and came because his mother is not well, and one of his sisters is getting married."

"Oh, is that the reason?" he inquired rather mockingly. "I had thought it might have been some other."

"I don't think so. But you have every cause to be grateful to him, my lord. He has arrived just in time to help me with this unfortunate affair, so that you need not be dragged into it any further against your will.

"In that case he has all my sympathy. Have you yet informed him of his fate?"

She chuckled. "No, but I have known him since I was a child, and so he is quite used to coming to my aid."

"That is what I supposed," he said dryly.

They had reached the top of the street by then, and Georgy and Adam were coming back toward them. "Would you believe it," Georgy announced buoyantly, "Mr. Trelawney actually saw Guy in the week before he sailed!"

"You are to be felicitated," remarked her brother. "You now know that some eight weeks ago he was apparently alive and in excellent health, a circumstance I never doubted for a moment, and can therefore have no further excuses for keeping my horses waiting."

Georgy laughed, and submitted, but it was Mr. Trelawney who helped her into her brother's curricle, though he did it in his usual efficient way that robbed the gesture of any particular gallantry. Georgy, as if she did not quite know what to make of him, thanked him more demurely than was her wont, and then, with a slightly more saucy smile cast at her brother, promised to call upon Anjalie again at the first opportunity.

Once she was bowling along beside her brother, she eyed him rather provocatively and remarked naively, "Well! I must say I would never have guessed he could be engaged in trade, for his manners were very gentlemanlike! So perhaps Miss Cantrell's papa is not so bad either."

Her brother glanced cynically down at her, then said briefly, "No, but I imagine his origins are rather more middle-class than Cantrell's. Poor devil! He has all my sympathy!"

"Why, what on earth can you mean?" demanded Georgy, wide-eyed.

He shrugged. "Unless I am much mistaken, your Mr. Trelawney is the inevitable *prétendant* to your Miss Cantrell's hand. He will be able to run the business when her father is gone, and the alliance is no doubt an imminently practical one. But he will pay dearly for the privilege, poor devil, for he is decidedly *not* the man to handle her. But that is none of my affair, I thank God!"

Chapter 12

Georgy stared at him, astounded. *"What?"* she almost shrieked "You mean you think Miss Cantrell is going to *marry* him? Well! I would never have guessed it! But perhaps they are in love."

"I seriously doubt that love has anything to do with it," remarked her brother cynically.

She was still staring at him in some astonishment. "Why do I get the feeling you know Miss Cantrell much better than you are letting on?" she demanded severely. Then, as her quick suspicions were aroused, she added, "And if you have been plotting with her against me, it would be the outside of enough, for she is my friend, not yours! Besides, it won't do you any good, and so I warn you, for I mean to marry Guy, whatever you say!"

"Calm yourself, brat. Miss Cantrell has certainly not betrayed you. In fact, she thinks I should take you out to Jamaica myself." Then as Georgy's face lit up, he added dampeningly, "Which is a piece of foolish advice I need not tell you I have not the least intention of following."

She was for once too taken up with Anjalie's affairs to bristle up, as she would normally have done. Instead she said in a dissatisfied voice, "Well! If you are right, I must say I'm disappointed in her. I have nothing against him, except that he seemed a trifle respectable and dull, but I certainly thought that *she* of all people would never consent to make a practical marriage! I have no doubt that you disliked him merely because he is in trade, but I am not such a snob, I assure you."

"I did not dislike him," he returned shortly, "and if I am right, he shall one day be a great deal richer than I am. Though whether he can call his soul his own is another matter entirely!"

She ignored that. "Well, if she does marry him, I warn you I shall visit her as much as I like when *I* am married and living in Jamaica," she informed him. Then she experienced one of her lightning changes of mood, and added suspiciously, "But I still have the oddest feeling you know more about Miss Cantrell than you are admitting."

His lordship hesitated, then considerably to his young sister's astonishment, reluctantly gave her an expurgated version of Anjalie's story. Far from appearing to be shocked, however, Georgy exclaimed indignantly at the end of it. "How odious men are! I hope the poor woman will go to Jamaica, and when I am out there, I shall do everything in my power to help her."

His brows rose, but he said merely, "And what do you know about such affairs, brat? More than your mother or I ever guessed, obviously."

She tossed her head. "I keep telling you that I am grown up, and know more about the world than you will believe. Of course I am aware such things go on, and that even you have doubtless had many mistresses in your keeping. Mama at least had the sense to explain *that* to me, though I must say it gave me the most dismal view of men, for it all seems so sordid, and not romantic at all."

"Cordelia explained to you that I had had *many mistresses in keeping*?" he repeated in far from gratified accents.

She giggled. "No, no, stupid! That was my own conjecture, for although you are not in the least romantic, I don't doubt you are just as odious as every other man! No, she explained that men, even poor Papa, don't regard these things in the same light that respectable females do, and warned me against ever seeming to notice what she called a certain class of female. She had to, for I asked her about one of them once, in Bath. Mama primmed up her mouth, in the way she does, and would only read me a lecture about the dangers of any female's losing her virtue, which she said is her most precious commodity, and once lost, ultimately must lead to poverty and degradation. But I must say I might have believed her more if the female in question had not been quite so dashing, as well as being *very* beautiful, and driving in an expensive chaise with cream-colored horses to draw it. In fact, she did not look to me to be suffering in the *least* from poverty or degradation for she wore a diamond necklace that must have cost the *earth*."

While her brother was grimly digesting this remarkable speech she added belligerently "Besides, it seems to me that such women have a good deal more fun than respectable women do, for at least they need never worry about chaperones, and being thought fast! And that is another reason why I mean to be married as soon as possible, for I hate being treated as if I were only a silly chit of a girl and never being allowed to go anywhere on my own, or do anything *I* want to do, but only what Mama or you think proper."

He retorted grimly, "Oh, do you? I wonder how many other notions you have in your head that neither your mother nor I have any clue about?"

She tossed her head again. "I daresay a great many, for you neither of you pay any attention to who I really am. That is why you won't take me seriously about Guy, though I must confess," she added handsomely, "that lately you have managed to surprise me occasionally, like just now, telling me about that poor woman. So perhaps you, at least, are finally beginning to realize I am grown up, and not the little girl you used to give sweetmeats to and take for a ride on your horse."

Then something seemed to occur to her, and she added accusingly, "Though I have a strong suspicion you still have not give me the whole story, and that there is something going on between you and Miss Cantrell that I know nothing about!"

But since he prudently declined to take up this gauntlet, she could get no more out of him. The subsequent drive, however, was accomplished in more accord than they had enjoyed in some years.

Adam, in the meantime, was regarding his old friend with something of the same curiosity. "What an unusual girl," he remarked, as soon as Lord Chance and his sister had driven off.

Anjalie laughed. "Yes, isn't she? I confess I like her better than anyone else I have yet met in London. Did she tell you she is engaged to this Guy Ludlow, and that her brother has forbidden the banns? I told you she is the only person I have met in England who does not regard the West Indies as they would the furthest reaches of darkest Africa. In fact, she is determined to go out there to join him, but her brother is equally determined, of course, that she do no such thing. Are you any better acquainted with Ludlow than I am?" she asked curiously. "I only met him once or twice, and though I did not particularly take to him, that does not mean he is in fact the fortune hunter Lord Chance firmly believes him to be."

Adam's brows had risen at the news, but he said merely, "I know even less than you, but I gathered he was generally well liked."

Something in his tone made her say quickly, "Ah, that means you didn't like him either!"

"No, but then we exchanged only a very few words."

She had a good deal of respect for his judgment, and so said in a dissatisfied voice, "Well, mere disparity of fortune does not weigh with me, of course, nor do I at all care to encourage Lord Chance in his outmoded and tyrannical notions! Aside from everything else, he is firmly convinced that she would scarcely survive the voyage, let alone the dangers of so backward a colony! Where *do* they get their Gothic notions from, I wonder? But what a nuisance that you didn't like Ludlow either, for I confess I would love to encourage her, if only to spite her odious brother."

"I hope you will do nothing of the kind," he replied in his measured way. "Miss Hughendon is very young, and to encourage her to defy her brother, and on such a matter, must surely be very wrong."

"How like a man!" she retorted, teasing him. "I assure you I wouldn't let *that* weigh with me if only I could be convinced that the marriage would work out. Oh, well! I daresay her brother is right and it will all come to nothing, for she is very young, as you say. But I can't help suspecting that Miss Hughendon would do very well in Jamaica, whatever he might think!!"

"Do you like him?" he asked curiously.

She colored a little, for some reason, then laughed. "I do when I am not disliking him amazingly! He is odious and opinionated, and quite dreadfully proud, besides being arrogant and supremely convinced of his own infallibility on any subject, based on no more, I take it, than his title and wealth and sex. Worse, he has been so spoilt all his life, and has been so hounded by ambitious females that he is even more cynical about matrimony than I am. The truth is, it would do *him* a world of good to go out to Jamaica for a few short months, though he would never own it, of course. But at least he can be amusing, and is more open-minded than the average Englishman, besides more nearly *resembling* a real man than the rest of the man-milliners I have met so far in England."

"Yes, I thought he would strip to advantage," observed Adam thoughtfully.

She was surprised. "Strip? You mean you think he *boxes*? Oh, I don't think you can be right, for I am sure he is far too idle to do anything so exhausting."

"Well, I understand it is quite the fashionable thing for members of the *ton* to take boxing lessons from the great Jackson."

"Good God!" she said, impressed despite herself. "If it were so, I would think a great deal the better of him, I confess. But you heard his sister! All he cares about are his horses."

"Well, that should certainly recommend him to you, at least!" said Adam, teasing her in turn.

"Yes, but alas! He disapproves of me quite amazingly, besides disliking my independent ways, and the outspoken things I say. And since he also is angry with me for not filling his sister full of horror stories about Jamaica as he wished me to do, there is plainly little future in our relationship."

"I see," answered Adam a little dryly, very much in the tone his lordship had used not too many minutes before about him.

She knew him too well to be deceived. "Good God, he might like me well enough, if he would let himself, and I'll confess he amuses me. But if you are imagining anything more, believe me nothing could be further from the truth.

He is too great a snob ever to ally himself with so unworthy a candidate, and *I* have not the least intention of remaining here, to be condescended to and forced to conform to a style of living I find ridiculous. So I am afraid there is not the least scope for your teasing!"

If he was not fully convinced, like Georgy he wisely said no more. He listened instead to the tale of Anjalie's latest protegée, and accepted his own role in the forthcoming rescue with resignation if not enthusiasm. Even the news that he might be called upon to escort an unknown woman and her infant on a voyage lasting several months did not seem to unduly faze him, though he said ruefully, "I seem to recall that you told me you were not in a scrape!"

"Oh, Adam, I do love you!" said Anjalie truthfully. "I don't even know if the poor woman wishes to go yet, but it is as well to be prepared. In the meantime you may help me to rescue her from that dreadful man. Even if her own plight failed to move me, nothing could please me more than to be able to thrust a spoke in Lord Sedgeburrow's wheels in any way that I can! He is far worse even than I had thought possible, and his nephew is little better."

Mr. Trelawney agreed to it in his calm way, but he was secretly a little dismayed at how often Lord Chance's name had come up in Anjalie's story. He stole another look at her face, but once more wisely held his peace.

Chapter 13

Anjalie would have been astonished to learn that she had somehow succeeded in disturbing Lord Chance's well-ordered life far more than he liked, even without her outrageous and unwarranted interference in his sister's affairs.

The appearance of Adam Trelawney on the scene had done much to set his mind at rest, for he thought cynically that he should indeed have guessed that there would be a provincial swain somewhere lurking in the wings, ready to marry the heiress and take over her papa's business in one fell swoop. If so, Adam Trelawney was welcome to her, poor devil!

His lordship did not accept the accusation that he was a misogynist, but he certainly had a reputation for being a rational, even a hardheaded man. He was well aware he must ultimately marry in the end, for the sake of an heir, but he was in no particular hurry to shackle himself with a wife. And when he did, he had long made up his mind that his would be the most practical of marriages, undertaken in cold blood to a woman of superior sense and breeding. His wife must, after all, become mistress of his considerable properties, not to mention undertaking the guidance of his sister, if Georgy should happen to still be unmarried. Even more important, her conduct would inevitably reflect upon his own name and reputation, and materially add to or detract from his domestic tranquility to a degree that had so far kept him from being in the least tempted to plunge into the married state.

He supposed he demanded a certain degree of beauty in a prospective bride, but that was not his main consideration; and in truth he cared less that she be of equal wealth than Miss Cantrell, or even his own sister, were likely to credit. He would prefer not to be married simply for the sake of his fortune, but even that he could have borne, so long as the female of his choosing possessed not only superior understanding and sense, but an evenness of temperament and maturity of character that would prevent the sort of domestic scenes that had rendered his youth hideous, and still led both his stepmother and his sister into such folly and caprice. He had had more than enough of domestic turmoil to last him a lifetime, and a wife who enacted him jealous scenes over the breakfast cups and indulged in endless megrims, or expected him to dance constant attendance on her would soon drive him to blow his brains out—or, at least to seek speedy consolation elsewhere.

He had never yet found such a woman, which explained his continued single state. Indeed, he strongly suspected such a paragon did not exist, for he had been the object for far too many years of females with an ambition to acquire his title and fortune to have many illusions left. Anjalie might amuse him, and at least had no interest in his fortune, but that was about the only things to be said in her favor. In fact, he could have searched the world over and hardly found anyone *less* qualified in every way to fill the exalted position as his wife. She was opinionated, hot at hand, stubborn, and always convinced that she was right, and the man fool enough to saddle himself with her would never know from one moment to the next what she might take it in her head to do. He cared less for her inferior connections than that she seemed to delight in setting everyone by the ears, and nothing was more certain than that her future unfortunate spouse would never know a moment's peace. It was very much open to doubt whether he would even be master in his own home. In short, she possessed every quality that must render her wholly unacceptable to a man of sense and breeding.

That conclusion drawn, Chance was at a loss to understand why he sometimes liked her far more than was good for his peace of mind—let alone casting serious doubts upon his sanity—or why she intrigued and amused him as much as she frequently did. She was undeniably unusual—inexcusable might be the better word!—but he had to admit that in an age of mealymouthed damsels brought up to flatter and fawn, he could not help but find her outspokenness occasionally refreshing. He was certainly not shocked by the unusual things she said, and while having no intention of encouraging his own sister to follow her example, he had from the first been reluctantly drawn to her, for she possessed a degree of shrewdness and determination most unusual in one of her sex. Perhaps she was the model of the modern female in the New World, but he somehow doubted there were many like her, even there. Undoubtedly that was a blessing, for he could not envision a country peopled with such unusual females, any more than he could imagine her in his own home. But that did not prevent him from admiring the courage with which she stood up to him and everyone else, and how little she cared for the whisperings and condescension of a set of people she so obviously despised.

He supposed she was unwomanly; but since he had little taste for the more usual feminine coyness and megrims, that was scarcely a mark against her in his own book. Still less did he care for the hypocritical notion that females, especially unmarried ones, were expected to disavow all knowledge of the more unpleasant side of life. Well, Miss Cantrell certainly paid no lip service to that outworn shibboleth, and snapped her fingers in the face of anyone who dared to disapprove of what she did. Her intent to rescue that unfortunate female was an excellent case in point. Chance might know it to be both futile and quixotic in the extreme, for she could hardly hope to rescue all such women, and he guessed she little reckoned on the difficulties and risks she was likely to encounter. But he had to smile a little at the mere notion that that would in anyway deter her. She obviously made nothing of the prospect of spiriting away a woman and her baby and transporting them thousands of miles, and more than likely assuming total financial responsibility for them for the rest of their lives. He had not the least notion whether the poor unfortunate woman had any desire to go out to Jamaica, and suspected she was more likely to be appalled at the very suggestion. But he thought he knew enough of Anjalie by then to guess that she would find herself sent out there, willy-nilly, and scarcely knew whether to congratulate or pity the poor creature.

What was more, if Anjalie thought she would even be grateful for such extraordinary help, she undoubtedly would soon discover her mistake. Chance cynically knew from his own long experience that she was far more likely to batten on her benefactress for the rest of her days, and even the infant would become a millstone round her neck, giving Anjalie ample time in which to regret such ill-judged generosity.

But at least Anjalie betrayed a warmer heart than was commonly to be found even in the so-called sentimental sex, especially in England. The majority of the females of his acquaintance would not only have averted their eyes from what they saw as so unsavory a situation, but would not have hesitated to condemn the victim herself, and self-righteously wash their hands of the fate of either mother or child. Well, Chance might think it foolish himself, and extremely likely to backfire on her, but he could not help but be amused by a will that ignored obstacles and even personal disadvantage in the pursuit of what she thought to be right.

Safe in the knowledge that she was the last woman in

the world to make him happy, and undoubtedly had every intention of returning to her provincial island and marrying her rustic swain, his lordship was free to admit, if only to himself, that he also liked the straightforward and efficient way she went about it, and her unblushingly frank discussion of the whole. Well, perhaps that was not quite so admirable, for she undoubtedly delighted in shocking the unwary. But he could not help appreciating her unexpected and unabashed head for business, and her refusal to make any apologies for her birth or upbringing. She talked coolly of running farms and starting schools, and seemed to take it for granted that every female did the same, as if blithely unaware that the majority of her sex took care to secrete their intelligence behind an air of featherheaded and helpless femininity, for fear of being thought a bluestocking, that most unflattering of feminine descriptions.

Unconsciously seeking to further justify his unexpected liking for Anjalie, Chance could not deny that her intrepid spirit in the saddle was certainly part of it, as well as her undoubted sense of humor, and the intelligence clearly to be read in her eyes. The tales she told of her life in Jamaica might astonish him—which was no doubt the purpose—but if even the half of them were true, spoke of a degree of capability and courage, not to mention passion, that in his experience were almost unprecedented in either sex. She had said, almost at their first meeting, that the New World demanded much of its citizens because there was still so much to be done, and she could not possibly guess what unexpected chord that had struck in him. It was absurd, but he had found himself almost envying her, for she was at least right that he often found life more than a trifle flat. He had duties and responsibilities, of course, but the thought of a new world to conquer, with all the dangers and adventures that implied, appealed to him at some basic level in a way even he would never have expected. He would never act upon it, of course, but that did not prevent him from reluctantly admiring Anjalie's spirit, and the careless courage that let her speak so casually of the terrors of pirates and runaway slaves, and journey fearlessly all over the world with her father.

As for her looks, she was certainly no beauty. He had heard her spoken of by the disapproving as being hideously

sallow, and aside from an admittedly good figure, had little
to recommend her. As for her French fashions, even that
found no favor, for not only did they consider it to be
flaunting her wealth in an unbecoming manner, but unpatri-
otic as well, for even in the colonies they must be aware
that England was still at war with France and that mon-
ster, Bonaparte.

Chance could not deny any of it, and certainly no one
would ever mistake her for a demure English damsel. But
he had been conscious, on first setting eyes on her, that she
stood out like an exotic tropical bird in a roomful of wrens,
and the impression recurred forcibly every time he saw her.
Her face was too strong, her mouth too generous, and everything she did spoke of a confidence and a zest for life
that had nothing to do with the self-conscious and often
hideously arch females of his acquaintance. In her company
he found every other woman faded into obscurity, like a
dainty watercolor was likely to be totally eclipsed by the
stronger colors of an oil painting. The latter might be more
primitive in technique, the colors even garish; but set side
by side, the one was apt to appear hopelessly insipid and
mannered next to the glorious passion of the other.

Undoubtedly he would be glad by the time she returned
to the West Indies, for her novelty was bound to grow less,
and he would in time become disgusted by her outrageous
conduct. But he found himself, in the meantime, even less
inclined than ever to throw out his handkerchief to any of
the more acceptable females of his acquaintance. Their docility and eagerness to please seemed more grating than
ever, their modest disavowals of any claim to an opinion
on complex matters so much sycophancy.

Chance was surprised to discover, as a matter of fact,
that before meeting Anjalie he had simply accepted that
females were incapable of interesting themselves in any
matters much more serious than what gown to wear or the
latest *on-dits*. They certainly did not boast of their business
acumen, or talk with such passion about the future of their
country, much less see themselves as actively helping to
shape that future. Such a wife would undoubtedly be exceedingly uncomfortable, of course; but on the other hand
a wife with no opinions, and no intentions of setting up her

will in defiance of her husband's, was likely to bore him within a month—nay week!—of the wedding.

That he required some spice in his partner had never before occurred to him, but he saw now that it was of paramount importance. The woman he ultimately married must possess both passion and conviction, as well as at least some concern for those less fortunate than herself. And with all that, she must still conduct herself with decorum and dignity, of course, as befitted her position, and run his house smoothly, as well as controlling the starts of his minx of a sister, and raising as paragons any children the marriage might produce.

The last was added savagely, for he was well aware that no such female existed. It annoyed him to think that Anjalie could have had such a profound effect upon him, somehow making him alter his very definition of what an eligible wife should be. But then, it was perhaps the very fact of her being so ineligible in every way that had done the mischief. Secure in believing she had no intention of marrying in England, and firmly aware that she was the last wife for him, he had allowed himself to become intrigued by her, and had not troubled to keep her at a safe distance. In general he was careful not to encourage any female to imagine an interest he was far from feeling, for he had learned long ago, through bitter experience, that a man of his wealth was endlessly vulnerable.

He told himself firmly that once Miss Cantrell was safely back in Jamaica, and Georgy had recovered from her current romantic folly, he would forget all about her and return gratefully to his former comfortable, untrammeled existence. And if it reluctantly occurred to him that for some reason that previously comfortable life now held very little appeal to him, it was a thought he naturally had not the least intention of pursuing.

Since Trelawney's timely arrival had spared him from being drawn any further into the rescue of that unfortunate woman—for which blessing he was extremely grateful—he learned nothing more of Anjalie's probably outrageous plans for her. He continued to keep a wary eye on his minx of a sister, but had no way of knowing how much or how little she was seeing Miss Cantrell. He himself took good care not to go riding in the park at an early hour when he might expect to find Anjalie there; and if he was a little annoyed at how much this sensible precaution cost him, he was careful to thrust that out of his mind as well.

He was at least aware that Anjalie continued to be seen in his cousin Darcy's company, a fact that made him wonder cynically what she was up to. He did not for one moment believe she had any intention of marrying that enterprising gentleman; but he would have been considerably startled—as would Lady Fernhurst—to discover that the shy Anne, and not Anjalie, was the real attraction. He had very little interest in his heir's affairs, but if asked to venture an opinion on the matter, he would unhesitatingly have advised that expensive profligate against allying himself with a female of only modest beauty and no fortune, so perhaps it was as well he had no inkling of the true state of affairs.

Anjalie, in the meantime, was a somewhat guilty observer of this unexpected romance. Her cousin Anne had shyly blossomed in Mr. Hughendon's company, and he in turn seemed to be flattered by her obvious admiration. Anjalie had no notion what would become of such an unlikely pair, but had little doubt that her aunt—and probably his lordship as well!—would strongly disapprove of such a match. Even she was secretly of the opinion that Anne might do very much better for herself, despite the fact that Darcy was Chance's heir. But since she also believed strongly in a woman's right to choose her own husband, she had no intention of helping to separate even such unlikely lovers merely to suit her aunt's or his lordship's outdated views.

Certainly, Anne seemed never to be shocked—as her more forthright cousin often was—by that enterprising sprig's admittedly erratic way of life. Nor did she seem to see anything in the least unusual in his peculiar and rather elastic views on personal finance. Anjalie herself, with her father's shrewd head for business, might think an engaging manner unlikely to compensate for a lifetime spent in financial uncertainty, almost wholly dependent upon the throw of the dice or the turn of the card or the outcome of some race somewhere, but it was obvious her cousin did not share these views.

Anjalie did venture to ask Anne once if she were not

worried about Darcy's irresponsibility and lack of fortune, but Anne replied simply, "Oh, no, for we are dreadfully poor too, you know! Besides, Mama once told me that half the families in London exceed their income. I know very little about such matters, of course, and I am sure Frederick is at least right that no female has any head for business, but it seems to me it would be nonsensical in me to expect him to give up his way of life just for me."

There was much in this naive speech to startle Anjalie, and she could not resist saying a little dryly, "Frederick is *not* right, for I have quite a head for business, and it is nonsense to say that no female can hope to understand it. But does it not at least bother you that Mr. Hughendon apparently has not a feather to fly with and owes debts all over town?"

"Well, I daresay I would *prefer* it if it were not so, for it must be very uncomfortable for him," said Anne, apparently considering the matter for the first time. She then blushed and added shyly, "But I like him so much better than Mr. Cowling or Lord Maplethorpe. Only I daresay M-Mama will not countenance the match, and Lord Chance, too, will think he could do v-very much better for himself, which of course he c-could. But if *he* cares nothing that we should be as poor as church mice, I am sure I do not."

Anjalie could not dispute any of these statements, for Mr. Cowling was a plump young man who perspired a great deal, and talked of nothing but sport, while Lord Maplethorpe was a widower of some forty years who required a stepmother for his three orphaned children; and it was very true that neither side was likely to welcome such an improvident match. But then Anjalie did not acknowledge their right to interfere in such an outmoded way over what ultimately concerned them so very little, and so continued to provide the unusual lovers with an excuse to see each other, wondering how it would all turn out.

Chapter 14

Anjalie found herself in something of the same predicament regarding Georgy Hughendon. While she continued to think Georgy might do very well in Jamaica, she did not care to directly encourage her to defy her brother—at least until she was on surer ground where young Ludlow was concerned. As with her cousin, she could only adopt a wait-and-see attitude, answering all Georgy's eager questions truthfully, but warning her that the West Indies were not for everyone, and even counseling against too hasty a marriage.

That might have startled Lord Chance very much, had he been privileged to hear it; and it certainly surprised Georgy too, for she cried in disappointment, "Oh, I thought you would be the last person to give me such stodgy advice! Why must I be cautious, when I know I love him, and he loves me?" She added suspiciously, after a moment, "Did Stone make you say that to me?"

Anjalie could not help laughing. They were walking in the park together, for Georgy did not much care for equestrian exercise, and complained besides that her brother's groom spied upon her, and very likely reported all her conversations back to him. "Not in the least!" she reassured her, amused. "How could he make me do anything I didn't wish to?"

"Well, I don't know," said Georgy frankly, "but he generally manages to get his own way, which is why it is so particularly unfair of him to blame me for being just like him! But I hope you don't mean to suggest, dear Miss Cantrell, that you would let your papa have anything to say to whom you married, for that I won't believe."

"Well, if he were *very* much opposed to my choice, I think I must at least listen to him, you know, for I have a great deal of respect for his shrewdness." said Anjalie truthfully. "And under those circumstances I certainly shouldn't rush into anything, for fear he had been able to see something I was for the moment too blinded to realize."

Georgy did not find this advice much to her taste, but thinking of Mr. Trelawney, whom she had met several times by then, she asked curiously, "Do you mean you would never marry without your papa's approval? That sounds dreadfully tame and poor-spirited!" She giggled then, returning to her own more pressing problems. "Besides any man Stone approved of would be bound to be deadly dull, as well as *dismally* respectable!"

Anjalie was obliged to laugh again. "Perhaps, though I suspect your brother is not quite as conventional as you believe him. But to do him credit, you and I are in the same boat—as is your brother!—and when one is lucky enough to possess a fortune, it complicates matters somewhat, you know."

Georgy made a quick face, protesting at that. "That is *exactly* what my brother says! But it is all so odious, and depressing, and almost makes me wish I didn't have a fortune, especially if it means I must be cautious and distrust everyone. I want to have excitement and romance and take risks, not just marry dutifully to please my family and grow old and staid and respectable before I've ever really known I was alive. I thought you of all people would understand that, for you have led such an exciting life. How I envy you!" She sighed.

"Well, I do understand, of course," said Anjalie sympathetically. "But although it sounds very romantic to be married, I'm afraid I have always regarded marriage as an *end* to adventure, rather than the beginning. That's why I have never wished for an early marriage myself, for then the children come, you know, and when that happens even the most romantic man alive tends to grow into a respectable husband. Before you know where you are, you find yourself tied to home and hearth, with children and a household to manage, and very little chance for adventures or excitement."

Georgy looked rather struck by that. "How horrid! But I won't believe that *all* husbands automatically become staid and respectable! I am sure Guy won't, for he is full of gallantry and charm, and he loves me very much, and *not* just because of my fortune, whatever Stone may say."

"Let us hope you are right. But that is sometimes worse," added Anjalie even more thoughtfully. "I fear gallant and charming husbands are sometimes so afraid of becoming dull and domestic that they tend to prove unfaithful, which has often seemed to me to be far worse. *We* are left at home with the babies and the responsibilities, while *they* amuse themselves elsewhere. If parents and guardians would take care to inform their daughters of that danger, instead of ranting and raving and forbidding the banns, I daresay it would do a great deal more good in the long run. Indeed, I have often thought it a great mistake to keep young females so sheltered and naive, especially as they seem to do here, for how else are they to learn of the world?"

Georgy was torn between flattery at being thus treated as an adult, and her even greater dislike of this prediction. "I am sure Guy would never be unfaithful to me," she said staunchly. Then she unexpectedly giggled. "And I'd like to see Stone talk to me so frankly on such a subject, for although lately he has seemed to acknowledge that I am more grown up than usually he can be brought to credit, he still is determined to believe I have not the least sense or knowledge of the world. But is that really why you have never married?" she added curiously.

"Well, in part, I daresay," said Anjalie, her eyes beginning to twinkle. "In fact, if I were you, I would sooner make my brother take me to see rather more of the world than tie myself down to a husband at so young an age! And that is all the advice you are going to get from me, I'm afraid, for of all things I despise people who are forever telling everyone else exactly how they should live their lives. It is certainly none of my business—and very little more of your brother's, come to that."

Lord Chance might not be pleased with that last remark, but in any case she thought she had said enough, for Georgy was looking more than a little thoughtful. And with that his odious lordship would have to be content, for Anjalie had not the least intention of doing his dirty work for him. She had little doubt of his ability to prevent his sister from doing anything that he might consider foolish, and did not wish to alienate Georgy merely to please him. And besides, she had a great deal else to occupy her at the moment.

Lord Sedgeburrow's housekeeper, who called herself Mrs. Milford, had duly been lured out unsuspectingly to meet Anjalie on her half day off by an exchange of notes delivered by an enterprising clerk from her father's London office. She proved to be unexpectedly young, scarcely as old as Anjalie herself, and though she should have been pretty, in a fair English way, was unnaturally pale and painfully thin. She looked, indeed, as if she had not fully recovered from childbirth, and admitted, when pressed, that her infant was not yet three months old. Anjalie, remembering the recent signs of hard physical labor laid over years of neglect that she had seen in Lord Sedgeburrow's house, was more disgusted than ever by such heartless exploitation, and was hard-pressed to curb her tongue on the subject.

As for poor Mrs. Milford, she found it understandably hard at first even to take in the meaning of Anjalie's words. Her recent unfortunate experiences had not prepared her for much hope of meeting even with simple kindness, let alone rescue, and when she was at last convinced that it was not some cruel joke at her expense, she had been almost too overwhelmed even to speak. Anjalie liked her quiet dignity, and was even more impressed that she did not indulge in an emotional outburst, or attempt in any way to justify her previous conduct. Nor did she blame Lord Sedgeburrow, or his dreadful nephew, or even her own parents in casting her out penniless upon the world. She was far more inclined to wonder what she had ever done to deserve such kindness from complete strangers, especially given the shameful nature of her own conduct, and to say so, endlessly.

That Anjalie put an end to, saying quickly, "Let us hear no more of that, if you please! It is little wonder, after falling into the hands of two such despicable creatures, that you should question even normal human kindness, my dear ma'am, and I will admit that England seems to contain more than its share of selfish, judgmental people. But you must not judge everyone by such standards. Indeed, if you do consent to go out to the West Indies, as I hope, I think you will find at least a degree more kindness and compassion than seems to be the case in this great, heartless city."

Contrary to Lord Chance's expectations, Mrs. Milford, when the whole of Anjalie's plan had been related to her, seemed genuinely relieved to be given an opportunity for a fresh start, however drastic a change it might entail. "Oh, yes!" she exclaimed in a low, passionate voice. "To be able to leave this place, so that my daughter might escape the dreadful consequences of my own actions! It is what I have prayed for, only I did not see any hope—but it is too much! I cannot let you do so much for me, ma'am, and pay my fare to the West Indies as well! How can I be so beholden to you, a perfect stranger, when my own—but I do not mean to speak of that. Only, if you will indeed forward me the money, dearest Miss Cantrell, I will promise to work my fingers to the bone once I am out there, and pay you back every penny!"

"Well," said Anjalie cheerfully, relieved to have that hurdle cleared and wishing somewhat basely that Lord Chance might have been there to hear it, "there is not the least need to talk of fares, for it is my papa's ship, after all, and you and one small infant will scarcely take up much room. Adam here will be more than happy to escort you himself, for he will be returning home in a few week's time, you know. And in the meantime, you may live with my friend, Mrs. Tixall, who assures me that not only will she undertake to have you and the baby both fit and well again, but will look upon it as a favor to herself, for she is in indifferent health, and will welcome the company. So that is all settled. Only, I do not wish you to make too hasty a decision, or minimize the changes it will mean for you. You will be going to a new land, you know, and one that is very different from here, and you may find you dislike it very much. If that is so, of course, you may always come back again, but I don't wish to make light of the length of the journey, or how very different your life will be out there."

"You could not say anything more inclined to convince me, ma'am," said Mrs. Milford in a voice that betrayed her conviction. "There is nothing I shall mind leaving here— nothing I will not look back upon with the most profound relief to be leaving behind, and I shall never wish to come back again. Only, it is too much—too kind! And Mr. Trelawney, as well! How can I ever be able to thank you? I am well aware I don't deserve such kindness—such charity."

That too Anjalie brushed aside, of course, saying more practically, "Pooh, it is certainly not charity, for we can always use another useful citizen out there. I do think, however, that you should remove from that dreadful house as soon as may be possible, and Mrs. Tixall assures me you may come at any time. So we have only the immediate details to decide, and how we may best spirit you and your baby away without arousing the suspicions of either Lord Sedgeburrow or that dreadful butler he keeps."

Mrs. Milford actually shuddered. "Oh, he is almost as bad as his master—for they are both evil, evil men! But I confess I don't see how it is to be done. His lordship rings for me twenty times an hour, day or night, to administer his medicines or to see to his comfort, and Cane will not deign to lift a finger. How I am to be able to get away, with the baby and our things, especially the way both of them spy on me, is more than I can see."

Anjalie's eyes began to twinkle. "Good heavens, do not let that trouble you! I feel sure that between us, Adam and I can contrive to defeat that old miser and his butler! We *might*, of course, effect a daring midnight rescue, complete with rope-ladders and secret passwords, and I have a young friend you may someday meet who would be profoundly disappointed in anything less. But it occurs to me that Adam would prefer something a little less dashing."

"Infinitely," said Adam decidedly. "In fact, I see no reason why she may not pack her things and walk out of the house at a respectable hour, and with no need for a romantic rescue at all. He is not her gaoler, after all."

"Yes, but I fear—he is suspicious of me, you see," put in Mrs. Milford apologetically. "I am sorry to be so troublesome, but I do not see how I could set out with the baby and even a small portmanteau, for one or the other of them is bound to see me."

Anjalie's eyes twinkled even more. "Then a midnight rescue it must be after all! No, no, dearest ma'am, pray don't apologize, for it will do Adam the world of good to be forced to take part in anything so dashing for once in his life. In general, you must know, he is far too staid and set in his ways. Indeed, there is another gentleman I am strongly tempted to drag in as well, if only I could hit on a way, and make the whole plot so Machiavellian and complicated as to force them both to abandon their precious dignity!"

"Thank you, but I see no reason why the plan needs to be at all Machiavellian," insisted Adam firmly. "What time do his lordship and the butler retire for the night, ma'am?"

"His lordship goes early to bed," said Mrs. Milford anxiously. "But Cane is prone to sit up late. But then he is also prone to drinking his lordship's port, and getting fuddled almost every night, so perhaps it will not matter."

"Good God, what a household," exclaimed Adam in disgust. "Do you think you could contrive to get out of the house at—let us say eleven, just to be safe—where I shall have a coach waiting for you? If it should prove too difficult, I am sure you need not worry about bringing a portmanteau with you, for I doubt Miss Cantrell will balk at purchasing a few items for you and the baby."

"No, indeed," said Anjalie promptly. "Though I still think, Adam, that you and I ought to contrive to break into the house in masks and with drawn pistols, to distract the household while Mrs. Milford escapes out the back," she insisted mischievously.

"Pay no attention to her, ma'am," said Adam, giving Anjalie a quelling look. "Is eleven late enough, do you think?"

"Oh, yes, I will contrive somehow, if I must drug Cane's port to do it!" said Mrs. Milford resolutely.

That made Anjalie laugh. "What an excellent notion! But if for some reason you find you cannot get out on the appointed day, why, we will simply have to try again, as many times as necessary until we have you safe."

"Oh, I would not for the world put Mr. Trelawney to such trouble!" cried Mrs. Milford, appalled.

"Why not? I keep telling you it will do him the world of good. But it is settled then, and I think we should do it rather sooner than later, don't you? Is tomorrow night too soon? I mean to be there myself, of course, for I may fob my aunt off with some hoaxing tale of Adam taking me to the theater, or some such. And you need not worry, dearest ma'am, for we will wait at least an hour for you, in case some unforeseen obstacle arises, and you cannot get out as early as you planned."

Mrs. Milford cried out against the thought of Miss Cantrell putting herself to so much trouble, but since Anjalie and Adam had agreed between them that she ought to be there, if only to allay any fears the woman might have of their interest and intent, she spoke to deaf ears.

She then again tried to find a way to adequately thank them, but Anjalie put an end to that, saying, "Good God, it is no more than I would do for anyone in the same circumstances, so let us hear no more of that. Besides, I have been looking for many years for a way to get some revenge upon your employer, for you do not know what misery he causes at home. Now I fear it is more than past time you were getting back, if you are not to rouse any suspicions."

That warning was enough. Mrs. Milford hurried away, and even Adam, who had been previously skeptical of the plan to rescue her, said forcefully as soon as she was gone, "Poor woman! I may have had my reservations before, Anjalie, but I tell you now I would happily even break into that old devil's house in order to rescue her!"

Anjalie laughed. "Let us hope it will not be necessary. I do think she will do very well at home, don't you? In fact, once she is well and happy again, she will probably marry very speedily, and no one need be any the wiser about her sad history."

Adam was scrupulously honest, and could not quite condone such deception, even in so good a cause. But he wisely made no comment, and Anjalie, very aware of his scruples, for once forbore to tease him.

And thankfully the rescue came off without a hitch. They were obliged to wait until nearly midnight, and the house had long since been completely dark, before Mrs. Milford at last came hurrying out, breathless and trembling and full of apologies. His lordship had had a bad night, and had twice rung for her to fetch his cordial to him, and Cane had seemed suspicious at her nervousness, so that she had not dared come sooner, and had in fact almost abandoned the whole project, at least for that night.

Once in the warm carriage they had hired for the occasion, however, she began to calm down—though she could not forbear to look fearfully over her shoulder as they drove away. Anjalie took charge of the infant, leaving Adam to allay the housekeeper's fears in his calm way. He spoke so matter-of-factly, and seemed to regard the evening's extraordinary events in so natural a way, that gradually Mrs. Milford began to relax, and even to feel, insensibly, that she had allowed her imagination to run away with her.

Mrs. Tixall, an elderly, motherly woman, had a warm bed and hot milk waiting for her, and made such a fuss over the baby that Anjalie was soon able to leave her protégée in such capable hands with a clear conscience. Her only regret over the whole satisfactory episode was that she had no spy in Lord Sedgeburrow's household so she might learn of his fury when he discovered his loss—and that Lord Chance had not somehow been inveigled into lending his unwilling support. She would have given much to see that disapproving peer forced to lurk in a closed carriage at midnight to effect a clandestine elopement of another man's housekeeper and her three-month-old infant.

Chapter 15

A njalie visited Mrs. Milford several times, and soon had the satisfaction of seeing her begin to look more rested and put on some much needed weight under Mrs. Tixall's warm care. But the poor woman confided to Anjalie that she would never feel truly safe until she had put England behind her, and there was little doubt that she was still highly nervous and could barely be brought to set foot out-of-doors, even in Chelsea, for fear of being recognized.

Anjalie said decidedly to Adam, after one of these visits, "I think the sooner we get her away the better. I had wished her to build up more strength for the voyage, but instead I fear she will merely fret herself unceasingly, undoing all Mrs. Tixall's good work. I've no wish to cut your visit short, for I have so enjoyed having you here, but I begin to think it would be best. The nursemaid I've hired to accompany you assures me she can be ready to go whenever I wish, so it waits only on your own business. And Papa's, of course."

He grinned at this belated addition, but assured her that

he could leave at any time. But he added curiously, "You don't mean to go with us, then? I confess I thought you would be more than eager to leave by now. And your presence on the voyage would do far more for that poor creature's reassurance than my poor efforts."

Anjalie was aware of his eyes on her, but said airily, "Oh, I still have one or two more things to attend to here— not the least of which is that I still have not completed my business with Lord Sedgeburrow—at least the business I came for. Though I certainly am beginning to long for home and to see Papa again."

"What mischief are you brewing that you haven't told me about?" demanded Adam resignedly.

She laughed. "None, on my honor!"

He ignored that to say seriously, "If it has to do with Miss Hughendon, I wish you will not interfere. I have come to admit—reluctantly—that you were right in the case of Mrs. Milford, but let that content you. Miss Hughendon is a very different proposition, and I am not at all sure I don't agree with her brother on this."

"Good God, what perfidy is this?" she demanded in mock anger. "I never thought to hear such heresy on your lips, Adam, let me tell you!" But when he did not even smile at her railery, she added, with a grimace, "Is this merely an attack of your tiresome English upbringing, or do you have some reason I don't know about? Do you perhaps know more of young Ludlow than you have yet told me, for instance?"

"No," he said unhelpfully. "It is simply that Miss Hughendon is very young, and used as well to every comfort and privilege. It is not my place to lecture you, of course. But I think it would be very wrong to interfere or encourage her in any way to defy her brother."

She was a little surprised at his vehemence, but said frankly, "Well, I assure you I don't mean to interfere— though it goes much against the grain not to, I can tell you. She is admittedly very spoilt, but there is a spirit about her and a strength of will that makes me think she could do at least as well at home as Mrs. Milford. *There* I have indeed been a thought high-handed, if you like, for I am sure she has not the least conception of what she is letting herself in for, poor woman! I would own to considerable misgivings on her part if I did not think it so important to get her right away, so that she may start over with a clean slate."

He smiled faintly. "Yes, I agree. But in the case of Miss Hughendon, I hope you are not letting your desire to get the better of her brother influence you too greatly."

She laughed and had the grace to blush a little as well. "Oh, well! I own that he deserves a set-down, but you wrong me if you think I would ever do so at the expense of his sister. Besides, you may be sure he is very well able to prevent her from doing anything foolish, whatever my destructive influence."

He said no more, and the subject was allowed to drop.

Somewhat to Anjalie's surprise, Georgiana knew about Mrs. Milford, for her brother had told her at least part of the story himself. When she learned of the success of the rescue, Georgy expressed a strong desire to meet Mrs. Milford and Mrs. Tixall for herself.

Anjalie found herself torn by this simple request. On the one hand she knew perfectly well that Lord Chance was unlikely to wish his sister to be introduced to either woman, on grounds of class as well as morality; on the other, that was exactly the sort of snobbery she had no patience with. But when she said as much to Georgy, that damsel had merely tossed her head and said, "Oh, pooh! Stone is not so gothic as that! Besides, he told me about them himself, so he can hardly object to my meeting them."

So Anjalie allowed herself to be persuaded, particularly since Mrs. Milford would soon be gone, and Mrs. Tixall lived retired from the world, so that his lordship need have no fear of being burdened by such an unfashionable acquaintance.

During the visit Georgy made a great fuss over the baby, and seemed to take an unexpected liking to Mrs. Tixall, who however much the relict of a merchant she might be, was a warm, motherly sort of woman with excellent sense and a dry humor. Indeed, Georgy confided naively on their drive back from Chelsea, "What a dear little baby! And I liked your friend, Mrs. Tixall. She reminds me of just what a grandmother should be like, and seldom is. Mrs. Milford is very brave too, isn't she? Mama would have a spasm if she knew I had met her, but I don't mean to be guided by such old-fashioned prejudices, and I admired her very much. She is going out to a strange land all alone, and I don't think I ever realized, before today, exactly how much that means. And *she* has no wealth, and no family, or anyone but herself to rely upon! How kind it is of you to help her."

Anjalie had taken that as a good sign that Georgy was at last growing up, but said merely, "Well, Adam is the one to receive your appreciation, for he is going to look after her on the voyage, and most men, I am sure I have no need to tell you, would have shrunk at such a responsibility. As for Mrs. Milford, I think she is a very brave woman, for life has not treated her very kindly. I am glad you do not despise her."

"Despise her? Oh, you mean because she lost her virtue, I suppose? Mama would certainly despise her, and so would most of the people I know," said Georgy thoughtfully. "But I am glad you took me to see her, for after meeting her, how could I despise her, poor thing!"

Anjalie was quite pleased with the progress of her protegée, and wondered what Chance would think of it. It was never possible to predict with him, of course, for at times he could be the most conventional and disapproving of snobs, and at others surprise her, as he had by telling his sister of an affair Anjalie would have wagered almost any sum he would have kept from her.

Anjalie was naturally present in Chelsea to see the travelers off on the first leg of their journey. They were to sail out of Bristol, and Adam meant to convey his charges there by easy stages. If he had qualms about assuming the responsibility for a strange woman and her infant on a difficult voyage of many months, he did not betray them, and Anjalie, fully appreciative of this fact, could not forebear saying with warm affection, "Oh, Adam, you never fail me! Perhaps I should have come with you after all, for I fear I am imposing dreadfully on your good nature!"

"No, why?" he asked in his sensible way. "You have provided an excellent nursemaid, and I don't suppose I shall have much to do with either of them on the voyage."

Anjalie laughed at this eminently male view of the matter. "And if they are all seasick from the moment you lose sight of land?" she teased him.

He grinned. "In that case, you should be glad you did not come, for very likely I shall be longing to wring your neck!"

"What a comfort it has been to have you here the last few weeks, and how I shall miss you! Give Papa all my best love, and Juba too. And *thank you!*"

A rather convulsive hug, and the travelers were off, Mrs. Milford pale and even more quiet than usual, but when questioned rather anxiously by Anjalie, professing no doubts or regrets. It was Mrs. Tixall who wept a little, saying to Anjalie as soon as the coach had turned the corner and was out of sight, "How foolish! You must forgive a sentimental old woman, my dear. It was only that it brought it all back to me, and made me long, just for a moment, that I'd thrown caution to the wind and gone with them!"

"Do you still miss it, dear ma'am?" asked Anjalie curiously.

"Lord, yes, and I daresay I always shall. I remember my own first voyage out there, as if it was yesterday. Newly married I was, and that frightened—! But of course Mr. T. had an ambition to go out there, and I wouldn't have stood in his way for a fortune—which it turns out is what it would have been, for it suited him down to the ground, just as it did your pa, and a fortune was what he soon enough made. I've always been glad to think I had the sense not to carry on and hold him back, just because I was a silly chit of a girl, scared of missing her mama and convinced, as I confess I was at the time, that I could never be happy in such a place! It makes me laugh whenever I look back upon it now."

Anjalie smiled too. "I only hope Mrs. Milford will adjust as well as you did."

"Lord, there's no need to worry of that, m'dear," said Mrs. Tixall comfortably, drying her eyes. "Though I'll miss 'em, and assured her that she'd always have a home with me, if she cared to stay. I never thought she would, mind, for she's too much pride for that, which is an excellent trait to be taking to the colonies, to my way of thinking." She added comfortably, after a moment, "Does that sweet young friend of yours really mean to go out there, as well, m'dear? Or was that just a romantic notion she's took into her head?"

"I don't know," said Anjalie frankly, curious to know what Mrs. Tixall had made of Georgy. "Do you think she would succeed as well? Recollect she comes from a very different background from poor Mrs. Milford, and I daresay has never been obliged to fend for herself in her life."

"There's no predicting, I'm sure," said Mrs. Tixall. "But I confess I liked her, for she's got a merry way about her and wasn't a bit high in the instep, though I can't be just what she meets every day of her life." She chuckled again. "Thankfully I'd never the least desire to figure in society, or pass myself off as any other than what I was, and that's good yeoman stock. Your pa's just the same. I daresay if the husband she's chosen is the right one, a woman could be happy on the moon, so long as he was there," she added placidly. "At least so it was in my case, and I daresay your mama's as well, and if this Miss Hughendon is genuinely in love with her young man, she'll be happy enough, I promise you."

Anjalie sighed. "Yes, there's the rub, isn't it? How do you know he's the right one to make such a sacrifice for?"

Mrs. Tixall watched her shrewdly, with slightly twinkling eyes. "When the right man comes along, a woman knows, my dear," she said with another of her chuckles. "And I'm afraid that's the closest thing to an answer I can give you."

Between her cousin's and Mrs. Milford's affairs, Anjalie had seen less of Georgy lately, and almost nothing of Chance. But she rode out early as usual the next morning, and she saw Lord Chance astride his gray, obviously waiting for her. Her first reaction was surprise, followed by uncomplicated pleasure, for it had been a while since she had enjoyed a good gallop.

Even when she saw that his mouth was set in unusually harsh lines, and his eyes looked as hard as granite, she did not immediately perceive that he was blazingly angry. She merely greeted him teasingly, saying, "I was beginning to fear you had quite washed your hands of me, my lord. Or have you come to scold me for some imagined sin of omission or commission?"

His lips tightened, and his horse, as if driven by a careless spur, started to sidle, and was brought under control with a ruthless hand. "So you *are* still here!" he exclaimed contemptuously. "I doubted you could be, for I thought you must at least wish to see the outcome of your handiwork— if not avoid the consequences here of your unconscionable actions! But then perhaps I should not be surprised after all, for it obviously means nothing to you that you have ruined a young woman's life!"

She gaped at him, thinking only that he must be referring to Mrs. Milford, and at a loss to understand why he should be suddenly so very scathing. But her own temper started to rise, and she retorted, "Let me tell you, my lord, that your sister may accept that tone from you, but I do not! And why you should be so contemptuous now, when you knew very well what I meant to do, has me in something of a puzzle."

Again his gray sidled, as if in tune with his master's savage mood. "Good God, I might have known you possessed nothing even remotely resembling a conscience, ma'am! You don't even trouble to deny it! I may have suspected what you meant to do, but you will no doubt find it ironic to learn that I forced myself to squash my own suspicions, for I had come to think you incapable of such perfidy! Does that make you laugh? And all the time you were planning how best to hoodwink me!"

"Oh, come now, my lord," she said impatiently, not understanding the reason for this tirade and having no intention of allowing him to vent his ill temper on her. "There is surely no need for all these histrionics. There is no question of hoodwinking you, and as for ruining her, that is merely your ill temper speaking. Just because *you* cannot believe anyone could be happy in such a place, does not mean that others share your prejudice. And why you should have the least concern in what Mrs. Milford chooses to do, *or* the least right to dare to come and criticize me, is more than I can understand or grant you, let me tell you!"

His lips tightened still further, if possible, and he shot out, "Mrs. Milford! What the devil is she to the purpose? We are talking of my sister, ma'am! And when you helped her to run away to marry a fortune-hunter, it was the worse day's work you ever did. But then I gather that will hardly keep you awake at night. And the worst of it is, you did it merely to score over me, and it is that I will never forgive you for!"

Chapter 16

All the belligerence that his anger had kindled immediately deflated, and Anjalie exclaimed, appalled, "Your sister!"

"Don't attempt to pretend ignorance, ma'am!" he informed her gratingly. "You have said yourself I must have known what you intended to do, for you made little secret of it!"

But she was scarcely listening to him. "No, no, it is not possible! I have admittedly seen very little of her of late, but I swear she gave no hint to me—when did you find out? What evidence do you have that that is what she has done? I tell you, when I saw her last she had no such intention—in fact, quite the opposite, for I—" Then she broke off, unwillingly remembering the last time she had seen Georgy, when they had gone to see Mrs. Milford, and therefore how very much Anjalie might indeed be to blame.

He saw her hesitation, and sneered at it. "At least you possess some shame if you cannot finish that sentence, Miss Cantrell!" he told her bitterly. "Unfortunately I did not learn of it until the early hours of this morning, and as for evidence, she was obliging enough to leave a letter telling me exactly what her plans were. She has taken passage aboard the same ship carrying that unfortunate woman you no doubt coerced into going out there, and if you expect me to believe that is merely a coincidence, or that it is not one of your father's ships, you apparently believe me an even greater fool than I had yet guessed!"

But Anjalie was still thinking rapidly, trying to assess this new information and make some sense of it. "It is true that she might have learned of the sailing date from me," she said a little guiltily, "for I saw no reason to make a secret of it. But as for the rest—no, no, I still cannot believe it! If nothing else, Adam is escorting Mrs. Milford, and he would never have allowed the *Serafina* to sail with your

sister on board, for you must know that he disapproves
quite as much as you do of my interference in the affair."

"You amaze me, ma'am!" said his lordship sarcastically.
"I had not thought him capable of opposing even the most
outrageous of your actions. But I know well where to place
the blame."

Again her temper rose, and she said crossly, "If you did
it would be better for all concerned, for I warned you how
it would be if you continued to bully your sister and treat
her as a child.'

"So now it is my fault, is it? I might have expected no
better, for you have lost few opportunities to be a thorn in
my flesh. But it is you, ma'am, who filled her head with
romantic rubbish about the West Indies, and encouraged
her to defy me at every turn. We did very well, Miss Cantrell, before you came to interfere in what did not concern
you, and even provide the means for my sister to contract
a marriage guaranteed to make her miserable for the rest
of her life!"

"Oh, this is language more suited to the theater, my
lord," she exclaimed disgustedly. "I thought you had no
taste for Cheltenham tragedies! You know no more than I
whether such a marriage will make her miserable, and I
warn you right now I have no intention of letting you vent
your foul temper on *me,* so don't think it! I am far more
interested in getting to the bottom of what I confess still
makes no sense to me. How came it that you did not learn
of her absence for so many hours? I cannot believe she is
not better guarded, especially when as you maintain you
had every reason to suspect her."

He flushed, and said as if goaded, "Until she met *you,*
ma'am, I had no reason to suppose such an escapade even
remotely possible. If you did not actively plan the whole
with her—which I am very far from yet conceding—at the
very least you conveniently provided her with the name of
a ship going out to Jamaica, and even the time and date
of its departure! As for the rest, I have never attempted to
conceal the fact that my stepmother is as foolish as my
sister is, and believed her when she said she was spending
the day with a friend. I was myself out all last evening, and
consequently only learned of it when I came home in the
early hours of the morning, to be met by all the stages of

hysterics, and the pleasing intelligence that my sister had run off to the West Indies. If my stepmother had had the sense to send for me earlier, I might have been able to go after her, but since I understand the ship was to sail from Bristol at first tide this morning, by that time there was nothing I could do to save my sister from the worst folly of her life."

"And so instead you lost no time in coming to take it out on me!" she exclaimed sarcastically. "Upon my word, you almost deserve what has befallen, for you have mismanaged the whole from the very beginning. I will admit that I may be somewhat to blame, but that scarcely excuses *your* own part in the whole, my lord, for if you had not threatened and tyrannized over her, or increased young Ludlow's romantic appeal by forbidding her even to think of him, none of this would have happened. And if you had had the still better sense to take her out there yourself, as I advised, it would have been even more to the point, and might have spared me a further sample of your ill temper!"

He flushed still darker, and said furiously, "I did not tyrannize over her! I did not even forbid her to think of him, though it obviously lessens your own blame to think so, ma'am! And if we are to talk of ill tempers, you have certainly seldom missed an opportunity to put me in the wrong."

"And you have seldom missed one to misjudge me! But I will tell you once more, and for the last time, my lord, that I had no hand in this elopement, and had I known of it, I would have done what I could to stop it. Believe it or not, as you choose, for it is immaterial to me. What is far more important now is what is to be done next. What do you intend to do?"

"What do you think?" he demanded grimly. "Go after her. If she survives the voyage, which is by no means certain, I can scarcely hope to arrive in time to prevent so disastrous a marriage. But if Ludlow proves to be what I think him, I will have no hesitation in having the marriage put aside. There is very little chance of avoiding a scandal, of course, but thanks to you, that cannot be helped!"

"Yes, that is exactly what I thought you would say! You must naturally do as you think best, and it may help alleviate your conscience somewhat to undertake this extremely foolish and misguided rescue, my lord! But I have told you

Adam is aboard the *Serafina* and may be relied upon to do whatever he can, for he has an absurd respect for conventions which I have not, and will be almost as anxious to restore your sister to you as you are to recover her! If he discovers her presence in time, you may be sure he will turn the *Serafina* around and return her immediately. It may not be possible, but there is still no need for so foolish and quixotic a rescue—which even you admit will be far too late to do any good! Adam may be trusted to do everything in his power to prevent the marriage, as will my father, once they reach Jamaica. Indeed, you would be far better off to stay at home and leave it all to them, and spend the time more usefully examining your own conscience and culpability in the whole!"

"You must forgive me if I find little comfort in relying further upon any members of your family, or have any intention of tolerating any more infernal and unwarranted interference in my own and my sister's affairs! But you are right about one thing at least!" he said bitterly. "It was indeed my fault for ignoring my own better judgment and permitting myself to like you, against all inclination or reason. If I had not made *that* mistake, and so lowered my guard where you were concerned, none of this would indeed have happened."

"And I was mistaken in believing you in any way different than all the other conceited and narrow-minded fools I have met with since coming to England, my lord!" she exclaimed, her eyes very bright. "I once even thought it might do you good to be obliged to go out to the colonies, where the men are still men and title and fortune count for far less than ability and self-sufficiency. But I think now I was indulging in far too much optimism! What's more, I begin to regret now that I *didn't* help your sister to escape from expectations that seem to be based on nothing but pride and worldly advantage, and wholly ignore either her own wishes on the subject, or even her potential happiness. Far from ruining her life, this elopement may well have saved it!"

He bowed, tight-lipped. "If you did indeed refrain in this instance, Miss Cantrell, it must be the first time in your long and outrageous career. From the moment you arrived in this country you have set us all dancing to your impudent piping, and may now go home happy. My sister's reputation is ruined, I must undertake a damnably inconvenient voyage I can ill spare the time for, and my stepmother is free to imagine herself into a decline, all at your bidding. How you must be laughing!"

"Oh, there is no talking to you!" she exclaimed angrily. "You are determined to believe what you want to believe! Make a fool of yourself then and see if I care!"

He bowed again. "We are at least agreed on one thing, ma'am: that there is no good to be derived from continuing this singularly pointless conversation. Indeed, there may be one silver lining to the whole impossible affair, and that is that by the time I return from my ill-fated voyage, with my sister in tow, you will hopefully have made all of England too hot to hold you and returned to wreak havoc on your native colony, and I need never set eyes on you again!"

Without another word he wheeled his horse and rode away, and she was left to stare stormily after him, the hectic color high in her cheeks.

She galloped off the worst of her rage and frustration on Erin, to the imminent danger of assorted nannies and their charges in the park that morning. When she at last pulled up the sweating black her eyes had lost a little of their storminess, and her mind had begun to work again.

For a long time after that she stared sightlessly between her horse's ears, seeing nothing of the tame, peaceful green of the park, but instead a colorful, hot climate that was not tame at all, and where peace meant something very different. It was not until the black began to sidle that she seemed to start and come out of her reverie, for she gathered the reins up and said in annoyance, "Oh, the devil! I am letting that wretched man make me even neglect my horses, and he's not worth it!"

She then gave an unexpected laugh, the mischief back in her eyes once more, and headed back to her aunt's house, for she had a great deal to do and very little time to do it in.

His lordship, in the meantime, had also ridden home in as black a rage as any he could ever remember, and one that was out of all proportion to his natural worry about his sister. Despite Anjalie's denials that morning, he had been convinced from the first moment that she had been behind his sister's elopement, for he did not believe Georgy capable of making all the arrangements on her own. The bitter knowledge that they must have been planning this behind his back for weeks did nothing to help his present mood, and he found he was as angry with himself as he was with Anjalie. She had dared to say that he was as much at fault as she was, and he knew that to be true, for he had allowed his reluctant liking for her to cloud his judgment, and so fatally relaxed his guard, and for that he would never forgive himself—or her!

He had gone to meet Anjalie that morning with no very great expectation of finding her still in England, for he had believed she must have gone with Georgy. At one time he had even convinced himself that his feelings would be considerably relieved if only he could confront her once more and tell her exactly what he thought of her.

But the discovery that she had remained in London had somehow merely fanned the flame of his anger and disgust. To discover that she could, despite all he had come to believe her—and despite his oft stated wishes on the subject—actually stoop to encourage and abet a green girl, gently reared and with almost no experience of the world, to undertake such a journey to marry a man Anjalie herself knew nothing about, was so unconscionable, that it filled him with renewed rage every time he thought of it.

The longed-for confrontation had therefore not relieved his feelings at all, for not only had she brazenly denied any complicity, but even dared to lecture him on his treatment of his sister, and in every way shown herself, by her carelessly destructive actions and middle-class notions, to be exactly what the whole of London had always thought her.

Chance liked to be made a fool of no better than the next man, and probably less; but even that unpalatable fact did not explain why he found himself filled with such a corroding bitterness, or why he rode home, after this highly unsatisfactory interview, in so savage a mood that he jabbed at the gray's mouth in a manner wholly unlike him. He further relieved his feelings by cursing at the groom who came warily to take the gray's bridle from him, and snarling at the footman who let him into the house.

Nor did the Dowager Lady Chance, who in his savage opinion bore a considerable part of the blame by her foolish indulgence and endless megrims, do anything to improve the next few days. She had chosen to enliven the night and much of the morning by a series of hysterical spasms that were as exhausting to the staff as they no doubt were to her, and declared herself convinced from the very first moment that her precious daughter was permanently lost to her. If the ship on so dreadful a voyage did not go down with her, or Georgy didn't die of privation and neglect, which was more than probable, for she had gone without so much as a maid to attend her, she would doubtless be taken off immediately, once she reached that barbaric land, by some deadly fever, or attack of pirates, or probably both.

His lordship, in no mood to exercise patience, and possessing little tolerance at the best of times for his stepmother's megrims, tried in vain to convince her that a respectable female and her child, along with a nursemaid, were on the same voyage, and would hardly abandon Georgy, and that Mr. Trelawney was also fully to be trusted. But since his lordship found himself placed in the untenable position of arguing a position he himself had scathingly dismissed when Anjalie had proposed it, he very soon abandoned all attempts to comfort her and occupied himself instead with the more pressing business arrangements to be made before he could undertake a journey of some months.

Even that proved unexpectedly difficult. His agent found no ship planning immediately to set out bound for Jamaica, though one or two were due soon, and another had just arrived. But the captain of that vessel naturally meant to remain some weeks in port after so long a voyage. Luting reported him a reasonable man, and his lordship had made it clear that money was no object, but the captain of the *MaryAnne* had pointed out with some truth that with the best will in the world, it was scarcely in his power to set out again so soon.

Nor did it help that even if he set off immediately, there was precious little likelihood he would be able to arrive in time to put a stop to what he continued to regard as so disastrous a marriage. Despite his words to Anjalie, he found himself forced to put what little faith he had in Adam Trelawney, for he had formed a good opinion of his sense, if not his taste in matrimonial partners. Whether that mild young man could exert the least control over his strong-willed sister was very doubtful, however. As for the unknown Mr. Cantrell, Anjalie's father, Chance dismissed any influence he might have out of hand, while reserving for himself, if he should ever be so fortunate as to meet him, the opportunity of telling that enterprising gentleman exactly what he thought of his outrageous daughter and his child-rearing principles.

The promise of that might relieve his feelings somewhat, but it was the only thing he found to look foward to. Realistically, the most that could be hoped for was that he might buy young Ludlow off, a necessity which infuriated him even more. It would be impossible to avoid a scandal, and might even entail a rupture between him and his sister, for if Georgy felt strongly enough about Ludlow to run thousands of miles to join him, it was highly doubtful she would be willing to acknowledge her mistake so soon, and return meekly home with her brother.

In short, the foreseeable future, for as far as he could see, looked unrelievedly bleak, and that, too, he owed to Anjalie's unwarranted and unconscionable interference in his life. His anger toward her had not lessened with the passage of days as he had half expected it would, but instead seemed to have steadily increased. What she was feeling herself, or if she cared at all for the mischief she had caused, he naturally had no way of knowing, for the one thing that did not waver was his strong resolution never to see her again.

Luckily for anyone who fell into his orbit during this time, Luting was at last able to report that the captain of the *MaryAnne* had agreed to a considerable sum to curtail his own and his crew's much-needed shore leave, and set sail for home, for the ship was based in Jamaica. His lordship's agent, in desperation and against his lordship's express orders, had felt compelled to reveal at least a part of the reason for this undue haste, and Captain Morton, who admitted that he himself was a father, had in the end been swayed as much by sympathy as the hefty fee that had been promised him.

Chance's first view of the *MaryAnne,* however, lying at anchor in Bristol harbor, was scarcely a favorable one. He would not have believed so small a vessel could make such a long voyage, but since he had never been to sea in his life before, he wisely forbore to say so. At that point he thought he would have gone to sea in a row boat if nothing else had offered, and so he grimly embarked at first light, having arrived in Bristol the night before by post—another novel experience—and put up in a noisy inn that had given him a further prejudice against all things naval.

Fortunately Captain Morton turned out to be a cheerful, sensible man, weather-beaten as to face and rolling as to gait, for he confessed freely that he had spent his entire life at sea, having gone as a cabin boy at the age of eight, and never regretted it. The *MaryAnne* was plainly his pride and joy, and he promised to show his lordship around her, once they were safely embarked. He also lost no time in inviting him to dine at his table that evening, assuring him that though he would find nothing but plain honest fare, it was plentiful, and they would none of them go hungry.

His lordship, who profoundly hoped he would not add seasickness to all his other problems, accepted both invitations, and since he had no desire to spend the interval cooped up in his rather claustrophobic cabin, remained on deck to watch all the bustle, wholly foreign to him, of departure.

He found it more interesting than he would have expected, and mercifully seemed not to suffer more than a slight queasiness as this operation took place. One of the sailors informed him kindly that it would be better once they were in the open sea, and though he found this prognostication extremely unlikely, so it soon proved. He watched the shore gradually disappear, if not without a pang, at least with resignation, and though he had undoubtedly undertaken the journey without enthusiasm, and expected little but discomfort and trouble in the course of it, he was surprised to discover a faint stirring of excitement in him, as if he were off on an adventure and not merely an unpleasant duty.

That first day also passed more rapidly than he had supposed. He found life at sea strange, but not uninteresting, and if he were more at home on horseback or in the hunting field, and feared he would soon become intolerably bored by the cramped quarters and enforced inaction, novelty for the moment still held boredom at bay. He certainly preferred the open deck to the cramped quarters allotted to him, for the *MaryAnne* was Spartan in the extreme, and his cabin scarcely as large as his dressing room at home. The next eight weeks promised to be as uncomfortable as they were tedious, and he thought grimly that that was yet something else to be chalked up to Anjalie's account.

He would be lucky if tedium were the worst he had to suffer, for they were, after all, still at war with France, and summer was the season for hurricanes in the Caribbean, as Captain Morton had informed him with cheerful unconcern. There were also pirates, and shipwreck, and mutinies, and doubtless a dozen other dangers he could not even imagine, for he had as yet scant faith in either Captain Morton or the *MaryAnne*.

But for some reason even these threats failed to alarm him, and he felt again that brief stirring of excitement, as he had on the quay in Bristol. He found himself whistling a little as he changed for dinner—an operation made unexpectedly difficult by the roll of the ship—and if he once more regretted the absence of his valet, since he had seen no need to have that expensive individual kicking his heels in so confined an environment, and wondered if he would ever accustom himself to having the floor rise and fall beneath his feet and the sounds of the wind and the sails and the creaking of timber forever in his ears, he was surprised to discover he felt almost cheerful. At any rate, there was scarcely room for two people in his cramped quarters, and the floor pitched so much they must inevitably be bumping into each other at every turn, a prospect so ludicrous that it almost made him laugh for the first time in a long while.

He was scarcely in the mood to make polite chitchat to the worthy but dull captain, and looked forward to the evening with little enthusiasm, but it seemed preferable to one spent on his own. Besides, he had no wish to appear above his company, and had as well his own comfort and interests very much in his mind. Without his valet, stuck on this tiny vessel for many tedious weeks, he was very much at the mercy of Captain Morton and his crew, and it behooved him to get on that individual's good side as quickly as possible. Nor was he anywhere near the snob Anjalie had accused him of being. His wealth might have bought him a berth on this tub of a ship, but he knew cynically that neither it nor his title would render the coming days any less uncomfortable, or whisk him magically to Jamaica.

Then for the first time it occurred to him to wonder if he had left his valet at home merely to prove a point to Anjalie, that he was fully capable of taking care of himself under even these trying circumstances. The thought infuriated him, for he had no wish to acknowledge she still had the power to disrupt his life to such a degree.

He found the captain's door hospitably open, and he entered to find it much roomier and more luxurious than his own cabin had led him to expect. It occupied the whole of the stern of the ship, with an unexpected expanse of windows, and was furnished comfortably if functionally with a table and chairs, and a large fitted bed. He inspected it curiously, and so did not immediately perceive, in the gathering dusk, that there was someone else already in the room before him.

He frowned, for he had not known there were any other passengers. Then the figure turned and stepped into the light, and he fell instinctively back a step, his expression hardening, even as a jumble of unpleasant emotions overtook him, chief among them shock and outrage.

"You—?" he ejaculated in a voice of loathing. *"What the devil—?"*

Chapter 17

Before Anjalie could answer, however, he had recovered himself, annoyed at that momentary betrayal, and said contemptuously, "But I don't know why I am surprised, after all. Have you come to gloat over your triumph, Miss Cantrell, or have you indeed made London too hot to hold you by now?"

She was looking very becoming in one of her French gowns, but at that her eyes began to sparkle dangerously. "Oh, for God's sake, I thought you would have come out of your sullens by now!" she exclaimed impatiently.

He stiffened still more and retorted icily, "My 'sullens' as you call them, ma'am, would naturally be incomprehensible to you. After all I have had ample evidence that you possess neither conscience nor the least compunction where other people's feelings are concerned."

"Oh, there is no talking to you!"

"That had certainly been my intention," he said with some irony. "It seems you do not agree, however—though if you imagined that by following me you would contrive to convince me—"

Then he broke off, as a new certainty shook him, and after a moment he added with cold fury, "But what a fool I am! It seems your machinations know no bounds, Miss Cantrell, for you have once again managed to set me blindly dancing to your outrageous tune. It is now becoming all too infuriatingly clear to me why this ship was not at first available, and then out of the blue Captain Morton became so very accommodating. Is it owned by your father? But of course it is! I begin to be ashamed of my own naïveté!"

She bit her lip, as angry as he had ever seen her, but there was, perhaps fortunately, time for no more. Captain Morton had entered in his usual bustle, making his bluff apologies for keeping them waiting.

Instantly the two antagonists turned away with studied indifference, she as flushed as his lordship was pale. But it seemed she was more mistress of her emotions than he was, for she recovered almost at once, and began to talk to the captain on some unexceptional subject. His lordship, furious with himself at his own lack of self-control, went to stand at the window with his back to the room.

Captain Morton looked between the pair of them, his eyes twinkling a little, but what conclusions he drew he did not share. In another moment a servant had arrived with the soup, and the awkward moment was glossed over, though it was all Chance could do to prevent himself from storming out and refusing to sit down to dinner with his chief tormentor.

Unfortunately only a moment's reflection showed him the supreme folly of such a gesture. They were apparently trapped together for many weeks on that damned ship, and he could scarcely sulk in his cabin the whole time. Nor had he any intention of giving her so much satisfaction. He bitterly realized that she had once more managed to put him at a disadvantage, and only by the exercise of a super-human will did he force himself to turn and greet the captain as if nothing were wrong.

It appeared they were the only passengers—or at least they were the captain's only guests—and if conversation was somewhat stilted at the beginning, it quickly became clear that Miss Cantrell and Captain Morton were very old friends. They were soon chatting away on a variety of subjects, and although Anjalie's eyes still sparkled a trifle dangerously, and she addressed very few remarks directly to his lordship, she seemed determined to go out of her way to prove how unaffected she was by his presence.

When Chance commented with some sarcasm on their apparent friendship, it was the captain who chuckled. "Oh, aye, my lord, I first made Miss Cantrell's acquaintance when she was but three years of age, if I remember correctly, and naught but a bit of quicksilver. I swear there was never any knowing where she would turn up next. Let me see: that must have been in '95, and I was never nearer to finding myself with a mutiny on my hands, for your lordship must know sailors tend to be a superstitious lot, and having any female on board, let alone a child in arms, is considered by many to be the worst of bad luck. But her pa was the owner, when all was said and done—for the *MaryAnne* was one of his very first ships, and as stout today as she was then, I'm happy to say—and so the crew was obliged to muffle their grumblings. But how it would all turn out I had not a notion. Well! I promise you we'd scarce been at sea two days before she'd got even the most hardened of that crew—and a rascally lot they were, too, as I remember—twisted round her tiny thumb; and the worst villain on board ready to lay down his life merely to amuse her. After that, the only trouble I had was to keep them to their duty, for I swear they'd have spent all their time dancing hornpipes to make her laugh, or carving bits of tomfoolery to bestow upon her. From then on it was considered a high treat to have the owner's daughter on board, and every one of his ships vying for the honor."

His lordship said with even more irony, "It would seem

Miss Cantrell has a way of making her presence felt wherever she goes."

Captain Morton chuckled again. "Oh, aye, though mind you there were many who faulted Ned Cantrell for dragging her with him on board ship, and exposing her to such dangers. But he felt most at home on board a ship, and I daresay saw no reason why his wife and daughter should be any different. Mind you, I'd always a suspicion his poor wife did not care for it as much as he or her daughter did, who was born to it, you might say. But then she'd not many years to endure it, poor lass. But the truth is, Miss Cantrell here could captain any ship in the fleet by now, and I for one would be proud to serve under her!"

"Captain Morton flatters me, I fear," Anjalie said immediately. "But he is my father's ablest captain, and the *Mary-Anne* has always been my father's favorite ship, so we have taken some memorable journeys together." She sighed and added, "How long ago those days seem now! Indeed, the *MaryAnne* is named for my mother."

"Aye, the poor sad lady, and a fitting name for a bonny ship I've always thought it," said Captain Morton. "There's many newer and smarter in the fleet now, out of course, but I've always been proud to be her captain, and never wanted any better."

His lordship's lip curled a little at these revelations, which did nothing to improve either his mood or his situation. He could not begin to guess what game she was now playing, unless it was, as he had first accused her, merely her desire to be present to gloat over him in the hour of her triumph. She had said many times that she would like to see him in Jamaica, and though he did not suppose that even she could have devised the whole plot just to lure him there, at that point there was very little he would put past her. But the knowledge that he was aboard a ship owned by her father, and worse, in any way beholden to either of them for his passage, galled him almost past bearing. Nor had he missed the implication that she was a general favorite of both the captain and crew, and that for pride's sake, if nothing else, he would be obliged to be civil to her, at least in public.

In fact, if it had been possible, he would have demanded to be set down at the nearest port and sought any other means of reaching his destination, however much satisfaction that might give her. But it seemed her triumph over him was complete, for not only would that make him appear ridiculous, but he had already learned that ships heading for the Caribbean were few and far between, and it might be weeks—or even months—before the next one offered.

He was to discover an even more bitter pill was soon to follow. During the course of what seemed to his lordship an interminable meal Captain Morton let slip that the cabin they were dining in was not his own, as Chance had assumed, but Miss Cantrell's. It appeared it was the owner's cabin, always reserved for him, and so naturally occupied by his daughter when she was on board.

His lordship stiffened at this news, and castigated himself for an even greater fool for not having guessed something of the truth. Short of getting up and stalking out, however, there was nothing he could do about it at the moment, though he vowed silently never to set foot in it again, if it meant starving first.

But he should have known by then he would be thwarted even in that. When the dinner was finally at an end, and before he could manage to make good his escape, Captain Morton was called out on some urgent business, leaving the two of them momentarily alone together. Chance took the opportunity of saying bitterly, "Accept my compliments, ma'am, on a most excellent dinner, but believe I would not have accepted the captain's invitation had I known these were your quarters. You may be sure that it will not happen again!"

Anjalie's mood had appeared to soften during the course of the evening, but at that she said scornfully, "Suit yourself, my lord! As far as I am concerned you may starve yourself all the way to the West Indies if you choose! By all means have your valet wait upon you, and insist upon dining in solitary splendor in your cabin if that will make you feel better, for it is no more than I would expect of you, after all."

"I have not brought my valet with me!" he countered furiously. "And since you must be very aware of the size of my cabin, as familiar as you are with this ship, you must realize there is nothing in the least splendid about it. But

I would indeed starve myself rather than endure another meal in your company, or ever set foot in your cabin again!"

She actually had the temerity to laugh. "Good God, this is privation indeed! I thought no Englishman ever dared stir a foot without his valet. I am only surprised you did not insist upon bringing your butler and your cook as well to insure your comfort on such a primitive ship. But understand this, my lord! This is a cargo vessel, and everyone on board has his own duties. I am afraid no one has time to be waiting upon you merely to indulge your vanity! We had dinner in my cabin because it is customary, and the largest, but if you choose to sulk in your own, you are certainly welcome to do so."

He bit his lip, both annoyed and chagrined, and without another word, bowed and left her.

He told himself he might be obliged to endure dinner in her cabin, but vowed to spend as little more time in her company as was humanly possible on board so cramped a ship. At the same time he was damned if he were going to skulk in his own tiny cabin, giving her more excuse to claim he was sulking. He consequently emerged the next morning, after a better night's sleep than he had expected, and proceeded to behave exactly as he would have if she had not been on board, ignoring her presence as much as possible, and coldly acknowledging her if they should happen to meet by accident.

On board so small a ship, that was naturally bound to happen more than he liked. But aside from that one inconvenience, he found life at sea more to his liking than he had ever supposed he would. There was a certain sameness to the days, of course, and he chafed a little under the lack of exercise; but the open-air life appealed to him, and it was all a novel experience, from watching the sailors run nimbly up the rigging, to the tightness and efficiency required aboard ship, to the admirable discipline of her crew. Captain Morton appeared to be an excellent master, and his lads, as he called them, clearly respected him. Nor was there any of the surliness or outright fear his lordship had somehow expected from the many tales of abuse and mutiny he had heard of life at sea. He could not help but remember with wry amusement his stepmother's apparent conviction that her daughter was unlikely to survive the privations of such a voyage, for if the *MaryAnne* were anything to go by, he had little doubt Georgy would be having the time of her life. That he had himself said much the same more than once, and had looked forward to his own voyage with considerable dread was something he now found it more convenient to forget.

Even the food was better than he had expected, if somewhat plain and monotonous. It was possible that life aboard the *MaryAnne* with the owner's daughter on board was scarcely the normal state of affairs aboard all ships, but even with that caveat, Chance was obliged to admit somewhat reluctantly that the owner must be a shrewd and able businessman—however deficient he might be in the rearing of daughters.

His lordship had perforce continued to dine each night in Anjalie's cabin, much against his will, and if he exchanged as few remarks with her as was humanly possible, he grew to have a genuine respect and liking for Captain Morton. And since, contrary to Anjalie's accusations, he was neither a snob nor in the least hard to please, that worthy had probably seldom had a less demanding passenger. Chance had discovered his sea legs early, and found himself curious about everything to do with the ship, and consequently spent most of his time on deck, preferring that to his claustrophobic quarters. He was used to an active life, and was not even above taking off his coat and pitching in on occasion, for he soon discovered that to be hauling in rope, or helping to set the sails was capital exercise. It was only when confronted by Miss Cantrell that he pokered up, and became both haughty and rigidly correct once more.

Even the weather seemed to connive to show him the best of life at sea, for though it was occasionally blustery, Captain Morton assured him that the Atlantic in high summer could be unexpectedly pleasant. That was the season of hurricanes, of course, but the more frequent danger was being becalmed, and Captain Morton told of days and even weeks of such helpless inactivity, sometimes with disastrous results. But the seas continued mild and the wind fortuitous, and the days slipped by more pleasantly than Chance would ever have believed possible. The view of endless sea and sky never varied, of course, but he was shortly to learn that there was enough excitement, and even danger, on board ship to suit the most adventurous. Once while he was on deck, a lad fell overboard from the rigging, and though they hauled in the sails as rapidly as they could, there was no way to do it fast enough, or to distinguish one mile of open sea from the next when they sent a long-boat back to search for him. The rowers were forced to return to report that they had found no trace of him, and after that his lordship was never again lulled into forgetting that sailors risked their lives every time they cast off from shore.

Captain Morton and the crew were also full of tales of deadly shipboard fevers, meat gone bad, even voyages where the sea or wind were so against them they ran out of drinking water, and endured day after day without rain, their lips and tongues blackened and with such terrible thirst that many men were driven to drinking seawater and died in terrible agony. Then there were the adventures on distant and exotic shores, for every sailor had some harrowing tale to tell of murderous heathens or knife fights in taverns, or running afoul of the local populace.

His lordship himself was awakened early one morning, in the second week of the voyage, by what sounded for all the world like a cannon being fired at alarmingly close quarters.

He was not unnaturally startled, but when he looked out of the porthole he could see nothing but the usual endless miles of empty sea. Nor was the shot repeated, making him wonder at first if he could have dreamed it. But there seemed to be an unusual stir on deck, so that he decided to dress and go up and investigate.

By the time he appeared on deck it was to discover, considerably to his astonishment, that the *MaryAnne* was grappled to a French man-of-war, guns bristling from every port, and the French captain was already on board the merchant ship, in close converse with both Captain Morton and Anjalie.

Feeling a little as if he must indeed be dreaming, his lordship joined them in time to hear Anjalie say, in excellent French and as if in amusement, "I fear I do not know what is to be done, *Capitaine* LeFleur. As Captain Morton has told you, the *MaryAnne* carries no cargo this trip. I was in urgent need to return home, and so Captain Morton was obliged to turn her around before she could be loaded."

The French captain was equally polite. In fact throughout the rather fantastic scene, both sides displayed an amity his lordship found incredible, considering the state of war that existed between their two nations. "If you say it, mademoiselle, of course I must believe you," he said gallantly. "And yet, you will confess it is not an easy thing to credit that this entire ship, a merchant vessel, has been commandeered for no other purpose than to deliver one or two passengers. It is of a liberality, a wastefulness even that is hard to believe, especially given the reputation of the English."

Anjalie, who seemed wholly unafraid, actually laughed. "I very much fear my father will share that opinion, *mon capitaine.* But pray search the ship if you like."

The French captain bowed with great urbanity, and smilingly gave the orders, contriving as he did so to convey both his admiration for Anjalie and his complete disbelief of her story. As the French sailors carried out a diligent search of the *MaryAnne,* he remained on board and maintained a gentle flow of compliments; even going so far, when his men turned up nothing, of shrugging and apologizing, and gallantly making Anjalie a present of a dozen bottles of cognac.

When the French captain had at last bowed himself off to return to his own ship, Chance could not help remarking somewhat incredulously, "Good God! Are you often boarded by the French, Captain Morton?"

The captain chuckled, evidently also hugely entertained by the whole. "Nay, lad, not often, for if we'd had a cargo to be seized, I'd naturally have done my best to avoid them."

"Would you give fight against a fully armed French man-of-war, merely to protect your cargo?" he inquired curiously.

"Aye, well, it depends," said the captain, his eyes twinkling. He had long since abandoned all formality with his noble passenger, and treated him now much as he did his crew—or Anjalie, for that matter. "The owner is far from appreciating the loss of an entire cargo, though it's unavoidable at times, of course, especially with this foolish war. It eats into the profits, you see, and to outfit a ship of this kind for such a voyage certainly don't come cheap. Ned Cantrell is a reasonable man, mind you, but a captain who allows himself to be boarded too often is apt to find himself looking for new employment."

"And how do you avoid it?" inquired Chance, rather fascinated despite himself.

"Oh, there's ways and ways. I don't say I haven't exchanged shots with a French ship now and again, in the course of a long career—aye, and successfully, too. But in general, if it comes down to a set battle, we're badly outgunned, o' course. It's best to outrun them if you can, and usually that's easy enough to do, for Frenchies ain't good sailors, as a rule. Too punctilious, I daresay, to bustle about. On this occasion, however, it seemed safe enough to let ourselves be boarded and searched, for it may confuse them the next time they meet one of our fleet."

"I see. And what prevented him from seizing the ship and holding Miss Cantrell and myself for good measure?" he inquired, still merely curious. "They might have made a tidy sum in ransom."

It was Anjalie who answered this time. "The French are usually far too gallant for that," she assured him in amusement. "No Frenchman would dare to appear so unchivalrous before a lady, which is why I came up on deck. Besides, more practically, they would have had to get the *MaryAnne* safely to a French port, which without a cargo would have been far more trouble than she is worth."

Lord Chance stiffened, both because he had forgotten for a fatal moment that he was not speaking to her, and at this reminder of their lack of cargo. Once Captain Morton had been called away, he said in a lowered voice, but with hostilities fully resumed, "The French captain is right, Miss Cantrell! Such liberality and wastefulness on a merchant ship scarcely argues sound business practices, I fear. But then I am sure you had not the least hesitation in commandeering this ship and crew merely to suit your whim, and such trifling considerations as your father's profit and Captain Morton's as well—for I understand he gets paid a share of the profits—are wholly beneath you."

She had been laughing the moment before, but at that her own face stiffened. "You needn't worry, my lord!" she said disdainfully. "Captain Morton and the crew will be fully compensated for their loss. And don't forget you would still be kicking your heels in London waiting for a ship if it were not for my whim, as you call it."

"I would have preferred even that to being forced to be obliged to you in any way, ma'am," he retorted unpleasantly. "Nor, after this episode, can I help wondering what might happen to the ship my sister is on, along with that poor unfortunate woman you bullied into traveling with her child, if they should be similarly boarded. Presumably they *do* carry a cargo—unless, of course, you commandeered that ship as well, in an attempt to get my sister away before I could discover your plans!"

But after a moment she merely shrugged. "The *Serafina* does indeed carry a cargo, but I assure you your sister is perfectly safe. English ships are not boarded as often as you seem to imagine, my lord. If they were, my father could scarcely make a profit, and that is, after all, the main point in the exercise, as you so correctly point out. But I am fully aware that you care not a groat for my father's profit, and mean merely to be disagreeable—as usual!"

"You also once reassured me, ma'am, that a voyage to the West Indies was scarcely more dangerous than a drive to the country, as I recall. Your reassurances might carry more weight if I had not just been rudely awakened by the sound of cannon being fired across our bows, and had my baggage searched by French sailors," he returned even more nastily.

She unexpectedly laughed. "I have a great deal more faith in your sister than you apparently do, my lord. If they should indeed be boarded, I suspect she will enjoy it immensely. At any rate, you are forgetting that Adam is on board, and is wholly to be relied upon."

"I have not forgotten it, but I fear I place a great deal less faith in Trelawney than you seem to, ma'am. I do, however, sincerely pity him with all my heart, for he will scarcely have his soul to call his own—if he does now— once he is married to you. I hope your father's fortune will succeed in recompensing him for a life spent dancing to your bidding, but you will forgive me if I take leave to doubt it!"

"Once he is—?" she repeated, then abruptly broke off

and closed her lips tightly over what else she had been going to say, her eye beginning to sparkle dangerously once more. "I thank you for the compliment, my lord! But I think you will find Adam would be surprised at your pity, for we are most sincerely attached to each other. Besides, your sarcasm would seem to be somewhat misplaced since you obviously desire the same sort of practical marriage for your sister."

"If so, you have successfully shown me the error of my ways!" he returned savagely, and put an end to the conversation by moving away from her at once.

Chapter 18

Anjalie, disgusted with this latest example of his ill humor, had never been closer to regretting having persuaded Captain Morton to agree to an early return. She had done so because there was just enough truth in his lordship's accusations about his sister to make her feel guilty, and because she had, of a sudden, had more than enough of England and wanted to go home herself. But Chance's determination to hold on to his anger and blame her for his present predicament put her out of all patience with him.

She had at least been proved right about one matter, however, though by then it gave her little pleasure to acknowledge it. She had once predicted that Lord Chance would be the better for being thrust out of his protected world, and she was obliged to admit she had been more prescient even than she had realized.

While avoiding her as much as was humanly possible on so small a ship, and behaving with cold formality whenever they were obliged to meet, it both gratified and annoyed her to see that he had quickly become a general favorite with everyone else. Captain Morton, usually the shrewdest of men, spoke highly of him, and had long since adopted a fatherly attitude toward him, and even the crew, quick to sense and resent condescension, clearly respected him. She was even obliged to admit that he was a wholly different creature with them. Gone was the stiff formality, even the cynicism and quick impatience that so often had marked his behavior in London, and she had seen him laugh more in the weeks on board than in all the time she had known him. It would all have been most promising, if he had not annoyed her so much with his continued blame and resentment toward herself.

She had stayed out of his way as much as possible, thinking that in time he would come out of his sullens. But he showed no signs of doing so, and she was fast concluding that he was deliberately fanning his resentment toward her.

Otherwise, even his appearance had altered for the better. He spent so many hours on deck that his face had taken on a healthy bronze color, and she had once or twice happened upon him when he had removed his coat and waistcoat and rolled up his shirtsleeves to reveal surprisingly muscular forearms, as he helped the crew to haul in the sails. On these occasions he looked quite human, and she would temporarily forget the rift that lay between them, amused to see him laughing and so well entertained.

But then he would look up and see her, and the laughter would die from his face, to be instantly replaced by the cold mask she so much disliked. It was sometimes all she could do to prevent herself from slapping him.

Like his lordship, however, Anjalie stubbornly refused to skulk in her cabin just to please him; and since life on board ship was inevitably confined, and they met every night at dinner, they were both often put to ridiculous shifts to avoid each other. It would have been amusing if it hadn't been so infuriating.

But at least they made excellent time, and had encountered remarkably good weather. She was far too experienced a traveler to expect it to last, however, and knew quite as well as Captain Morton that it was the season for hurricanes in the Caribbean. So she was not in the least surprised when the weather turned squally even as they approached warmer waters.

She had never minded storms, and one particularly blustery day went up on deck, seeking solitude and finding the wild weather in perfect sympathy with her present mood.

The *MaryAnne* bucked in heavy seas, the wind tore through the rigging, and spray and an occasional wave, higher than the rest, made the footing dangerously slippery. But wrapped in a heavy boat cloak, and with the knowledge that the sea spray in her face was warm now, and no longer icy, it was impossible for her to remain tamely in her cabin. She could even almost fancy that the wind that whipped her cloak so wildly about her, and made it impossible for her to keep her hood up, so that her hair was soon blown into a damp tangle, had a faint, familiar tang of blossom to it.

She certainly did not expect to find anyone else above decks in such weather, and stood at the railing for some time—or clung to it, rather, to prevent herself from being blown overboard. It was easy to forget that she was not the only creature alive in the tempest, so that the sound of a door being slammed behind her was an unwelcome intrusion. She involuntarily turned, to see Lord Chance stagger out, equally braced against the wind. His own cloak bellowed out behind him, and he had not yet seen her, for he had his head down, struggling against the wind as against a physical presence.

Then he caught sight of her, and instantly his face stiffened. She shrugged and turned away, refusing to allow him to spoil the moment for her, and fully expecting him to withdraw in a huff and leave her to welcome solitude.

He would undoubtedly have done so, but at that precise moment a more than usually strong wave caught them. The *MaryAnne*'s deck heaved violently, and perhaps because of that brief distraction, Anjalie found her grip on the railing slip as she was unexpectedly thrown off balance. Whether she would actually have fallen and been washed overboard—which seemed all too likely—she was never to know, however, for Chance reacted unexpectedly quickly, and with a strength she had not known he possessed. She was scarcely aware of her danger before she found herself caught in an iron grip, and dragged roughly to safety.

For a moment he held her tightly against him, so that she was half blinded; and the strength of his arms around her, added to the danger she had so narrowly missed, made her heart pound unnaturally loudly in her own ears, almost drowning out the screech of the wind. She was aware of the smell of his wet cloak pressed so closely to her face, and the beat of his own heart, beneath her ear, almost as rapid as her own, so that it was difficult to distinguish one from the other. Still his arms did not immediately loosen their stranglehold, and she was vaguely conscious of pain— and would indeed find bruises later.

She managed at last to raise her face from his wet coat, aware her hair was streaming untidily around her, and her face dripping. He seemed to tower over her, his own face unnaturally grim, his hair blown almost as wildly as her own was, and both soaked through by then. Still he did not let her go, but his arms seemed to tighten even more, so that she began to entertain serious fears that her ribs would crack under the pressure.

She tried to say so, but the wind snatched her voice and it did not reach even her own ears. Certainly he gave no sign of having heard, nor did he release his hold. It was impossible to tell, by the frozen immobility of his face, whether he was regretting having saved her, and might yet dislike her so much he would undo his work and throw her bodily overboard, but she knew no fear of him, but stood in his grip, only her heightened color betraying her.

The storm and her recent narrow escape merely heightened her own mood, and she laughed up at him fearlessly. She had somehow managed to free an arm, and whether this movement and her laughter spurred him at last to renewed fury, or whether he were driven by the same impulse of the storm she was never to know. At any rate as if against his will he bent his head and kissed her savagely.

For a moment Anjalie was too taken by surprise to react. She knew the genteel ladies of his world would undoubtedly faint, or give way to hysterics under so brutal an assault. She thought fleetingly that genteel ladies must miss a great deal; and then compelled by some of the same forces that no doubt drove him, threw her one free arm up about his neck and began hungrily to kiss him back.

He tightened his grip until she was sure one or two ribs must indeed be broken, and kissed her as if he were bent on punishing her for everything he had laid at her door.

But at least he had at last abandoned the cold formality that she had so much resented.

And certainly her impression that he was very much a man despite his birth and upbringing was more than amply borne out. She could taste the salt spray on his lips, as he could no doubt on hers, and the potent combination of wind, the sea, and pent-up emotions found more than adequate physical outlet in her as well. She was clinging to him for reasons that had nothing to do with the heaving decks, and aware that for all her wide adventures she had never experienced anything remotely like that before. The irony that it had taken a supercivilized Englishman to make her feel as if she had fully come alive for the first time did not escape her.

What might have been the eventual outcome she was unfortunately never to know. The ship took an even more violent lurch, and they were drenched with a wall of icy water, a most effective counter to passion. Their lips were torn apart as they gasped at the shock, and they clung together of necessity by then, staggering to keep their footing. Anjalie could only be grateful for his superior strength, for he managed somehow to keep them both upright. She clung to him, near laughter at this most unromantic conclusion to the overwrought scene that had gone before, and shouted into his ear, "The storm's worsening! We'd better go in or be swept overboard!"

He nodded, transformed in an instant from what? Lover? Avenger? She hardly knew, except that for those brief few moments he had been as blind to everything but his own passion as she had been. His black hair was plastered to his head, water streamed off his harsh countenance, and he held her still clamped to him with an arm of iron, as he braced himself against the force of the wind, but there was nothing any longer in the least loverlike about his grip. Together they staggered toward the door, but Anjalie had no illusions that it was his strength alone that saved them. The wind was strengthening every minute, and it had begun to rain heavily, the sheets of water joining with the wind and the lash of the sea to reduce visibility to only a few yards. After some effort Chance finally succeeded in reaching the door and pulling it open, and together they literally tumbled down the steps, and stood gasping and panting at the bottom of them in the sudden comparative calm. The absurd circumstances, the wet climax to that pent-up scene, the ridiculousness of their puny quarrels in the face of the monumental natural struggle going on all around them, which was tossing the *MaryAnne* as if she were no more than flotsam, were ultimately Anjalie's undoing. She began to laugh helplessly, knowing that in his present mood he was unlikely to share her mirth, but instead to take it as a deadly insult.

He did stiffen, but then said in a more natural voice than any she had yet heard from him since they had left England, "What an abominable girl you are! You do like to live dangerously, don't you?"

She said cheerfully, "Oh we were never in much danger—thanks, I'll admit, to you! I might certainly have been blown overboard if you hadn't happened to be there, so you may preen yourself on having saved my life, if you like. I'm only surprised you didn't take that way of being rid of me once and for all."

He was regarding her rather as he used to, as if she were some rara avis he had never seen before. She knew her hair to be streaming wetly down her back and clinging untidily to her face, her boat cloak and the gown underneath it alike soaked, every inch of her streaming with wet as he was. But vanity had never been one of her besetting sins.

At last, he said dryly, "I congratulate you on your remarkable fortitude, Miss Cantrell."

She was even more amused. "Good God! Were you expecting me to collapse in terror now that all danger is past? I'm sorry to disappoint you, but I am neither the villain of your recent imaginings, nor a heroine now, simply because I don't fall apart in the face of a little danger."

He stiffened a little, but then merely shrugged. "I must confess your definition of danger is scarcely mine, but unless you are equally immune to contracting a cold from standing around in drenched garments, I would recommend that we both get out of our wet things as soon as possible. By the by, do you still expect me to believe this is no more than a tropical storm, as you and Captain Morton have been at such pains to assure me?"

She was obliged to laugh. "If so, I own it is a particularly strong one. But I have complete faith in both Captain Morton and the *MaryAnne,* so you need not give yourself up for lost just yet, my lord."

"On the contrary, I begin to think I was lost the moment I met you, Miss Cantrell!" he retorted even more dryly, and turned away to his own cabin.

Chapter 19

Whether Lord Chance would have reverted to his former resentment, or some thaw had indeed set in, Anjalie had little time to discover, for by the time they had both changed out of their wet things, it had become apparently that they were indeed in for a blow. The wind continued to increase, and howled around the corners of the ship like some soul in torment; the rain came down in torrents, and it was impossible to tell where the sky left off and the angry sea began. There was nothing to be seen but water from any vantage point, and the ship bucked and tossed under the onslaught as if it had been no more than a toy. It was difficult to stand, and movement was almost impossible, at least without lurching from one wall to another, like a drunken sailor totally out of control.

Anjalie, an excellent sailor, knew from long experience that the only thing to be done was to sit it out, for one was even inclined to be tossed violently out of bed. It was not long before Captain Morton, soaking wet himself, came to confirm rather grimly that they were in for a regular gale. "Hopefully we'll not catch the brunt of it, for to my mind that's still south of here. But there's no denying storms can be as capricious as a fickle maid, as you well know, lass," he said forthrightly. "Happen the *MaryAnne* will weather her, for she's withstood many a one before this, but there's never any saying, of course."

Lord Chance must have heard his voice, for it was necessary almost to shout even below deck in order to be heard over the wind. He reappeared, changed and dried, and staggered rather than walked to Anjalie's door to hear the tail end of this. If there was some slight constraint between them, he did not look at her, and the unusual circumstances undoubtedly did much to make that scene out in the storm seem irrelevant for the moment.

"It is a hurricane, then?" he inquired with what Anjalie was obliged to admit was admirable sangfroid.

Captain Morton looked to see how the information might be taken, for one never knew with a landlubber. But his lordship looked perfectly calm, and the news must come out sooner or later. "Oh, aye, my lord," he acknowledged, "though I was just telling the lass here that we would seem to have caught the fringes only, thank God!"

"If so, I hope to God we don't catch any more! May I ask what makes you think that?" demanded his lordship politely.

Captain Morton actually laughed. "If we were taking the brunt of a hurricane, lad, we'd scarcely be standing here talking about it! We'd be manning the longboats and uttering our last prayers, for there's no ship built that can survive a full-blown hurricane, not without divine intervention, that is. Miss Cantrell knows that well enough, for she's survived a fair few. They can toss bigger ships than this about as if they were twigs, and break up anything in their paths."

"Yes, but I *have* survived a fair few, as Captain Morton says," said Anjalie cheerfully, "and I don't doubt he's lived through considerably more, so there's no need to be unduly alarmed."

His lordship did look at her then, with considerable irony in his glance. "I have yet to discover what *would* succeed in alarming you, Miss Cantrell, and begin to hope I never will. Exactly what are our chances, Captain? You need not be afraid of telling me the truth, for I believe I am not likely to panic, if that is what you fear."

Captain Morton gave him another assessing look, and then chuckled. "Aye, so I can see, my lord. But there's no need for panic just yet. The *MaryAnne* may be old, but she's as water-tight as any I've ever sailed, and with luck we'll successfully ride it out. For the moment I would suggest you get what rest you can, both of you," he added bluntly, "for it's best to be prepared, and there may be precious little to be had later."

His lordship, who was obliged to hold onto the doorsill

with both hands, and shift his weight to prevent being thrown off his feet, managed to resist the acid retort that sprang to his lips at this suggestion. "I begin to see why sailors sleep in hammocks," was all he said. "But at the moment sleep is the farthest thing from my mind. Is there anything I can do to help?"

"Nay, lad, not unless you're half mermaid," said the captain, his eyes twinkling as if aware of the unspoken comment. "With a storm such as this there's very little that anyone can do but hold on tight to whatever's handy. One good thing is we're not many days out from Jamaica now, and with any luck the storm will deliver us to our destination as neatly as if we had planned the whole."

When his lordship looked even more skeptical, Anjalie said in some amusement, "The trade winds are extremely strong for the West Indies, and even without our sails, the chances are that they will take us there fairly accurately."

"Aye, lad, don't write us off just yet. Put your faith in the *MaryAnne,* as I do. Now I must be off, for there's still much to be done."

He was gone on the words, and Lord Chance was left to look at Anjalie, an unwilling question in his eyes. "Was that for my benefit, or was he serious?" he demanded. "I own I am astonished the ship has managed to survive thus far, for it sounds as if all the hounds of hell were let loose out there."

She laughed. "Of course he was serious. Captain Morton is one of the best skippers there is, and though I daresay he would sugarcoat the news for many passengers, he must see you are unlikely to fall into a panic."

He shrugged. "If we are to drown there seems very little I can do about it, and though I would prefer not to end my days in a watery grave, I will be damned if I'm going to be outshone by you, Miss Cantrell," he told her bluntly. "By the by, what are the odds the *Serafina* is facing this same storm?"

She said unconcernedly, "Oh, I am convinced they must have reached Jamaica sometime ago, my lord. If not, they should be near enough to some port to take shelter."

He shrugged again, since there was clearly nothing he could do about it, and after a moment he left her to stagger back to his own cabin. Anjalie was obliged to admit he was taking the whole better than she had expected. While not wishing to overrate this achievement, she had seen a great many seemingly brave and stalwart men succumb to panic and behave in extremely unbecoming—not to mention dangerous—ways.

She did attempt to follow Captain Morton's advice and get what sleep she could, for she knew as well as he did that under these circumstances disaster could strike in an instant. It was pointless to try to go to bed, for even propped round by pillows, you were in constant danger of being thrown out. Instead she contented herself with wedging herself into a large chair, and had at least fallen into an uneasy sleep when she was abruptly and rudely jerked awake again by some noise loud enough even to penetrate over the endless howl of the wind.

For a moment she didn't know what it could have been; then another loud cracking sound, as of timber, brought her to her feet, for she knew that ominous sound. In the interests of safety she had not dared to leave a lantern burning, and so staggered to her door, feeling her way in the pitch dark. She found it at last, more by instinct than sight, and wrenched it open, to discover a light already in the passage before her. A moment later she realized that it was Lord Chance, also still fully dressed and holding a lantern. He said sharply, at sight of her, "What was that? I swear I heard a great crack!"

She was hesitant to alarm him any further, and so said only, "I think—" Then her quick ears heard another door being slammed with great violence, and she turned, seeing Captain Morton making his way toward them against the increased pitching of the ship. He too held a storm lantern, and had evidently been up on deck, for he was dripping water with every step as he came. He saw his two passengers standing in the hall, but spoke only to Anjalie, telling her bluntly, "The mainmast's come down, lass, as you no doubt heard. I've no need to tell you what that means, for the *MaryAnne*'s likely to be naught but kindling by morning. I may have to order everyone into the longboats, and I'm warning you now, lass, that I'll have no mutiny aboard one of *my* ships."

"What do you mean to do?" she demanded suspiciously.

He shrugged. "I'll not abandon the old girl until I'm convinced she's headed for the bottom," he said even more bluntly. "I'll keep one or two lads with me, enough to get her home if we *should* turn out to be lucky. If not, I'll abandon her in time, never you fear."

"If you're staying, so am I," she said stubbornly.

"Aye, that's what I feared you'd say, but that you will not, lassie, not while I'm still captain of this ship," Captain Morton said gruffly. He cast a narrow glance at his lordship, who had so far been silent, and added, "My lord, likely I'll have my hands full keeping this old girl afloat even for so long as it will take to get everyone off, so I'm charging you directly with seeing the lass here does as she's bid! It occurs to me you'll stand no nonsense, whereas she'd likely talk any of my crew round her thumb before the cat could lick her ear."

"Very well," responded his lordship calmly. "If you order Miss Cantrell to the longboats, I give you my word she will go—though I don't doubt it will be the first time in her life she's ever been forced to obey anyone's command but her own. But I confess in my ignorance I am somewhat of Miss Cantrell's mind. If even this ship is likely to be broken up by the storm, what good are longboats likely to do us? Surely we'll be tossed around and capsized before we can even get them safely launched?"

Anjalie was still bridling at his earlier words, but she explained briefly, "The size of the *MaryAnne* makes her more vulnerable, not less, and without her mainmast, even were she to remain afloat it would be next to impossible to get her home. But I will do as I please, I thank you both, and am not to be discussed and disposed of as if I were a piece of cargo!"

"Understand this, Miss Cantrell!" retorted his lordship somewhat grimly. "You have baited and insulted me in every way possible; you have dragged me on this damned voyage, and interfered unconscionably in my life by encouraging my sister to flaunt me, and it will give me a great deal of satisfaction to get at least a little of my own back again. You will do precisely as the captain says, if I have to carry you kicking and screaming to the boat and toss you in myself! Have I made myself perfectly clear?"

She cast him a dagger glance, but Captain Morton chuckled. He was looking tired and disheveled, and had scarcely slept in two days, but he said appreciatively, "Aye, lad, I'd somehow guessed I might rely upon you in this instance. Pack up what few things you care to salvage, both of you, for it's more than likely what's left behind will be at the bottom of the sea by morning. There's no immediate danger of our sinking, I believe, and it may turn out we won't have to abandon ship after all. But there's little point in not taking all necessary precautions, I always say."

Anjalie hesitated, and then capitulated, though she informed his lordship frigidly that if she consented to abandon ship, it would be in obedience to Captain Morton's orders, not his own threats.

"Your vanity and reputation for bravery are both safe, ma'am, for I did not suppose otherwise!" retorted his lordship. "Indeed, I will readily concede that you far outstrip anything in the way of courage that *I* can boast, for I seem to recall you once assured me that to undertake a sea voyage was not in the least dangerous!"

Her lips quivered betrayingly, but she said severely, "Don't be ridiculous! I assure you that in all my years of sailing I have never once been forced to abandon ship. This is—this is quite out of the ordinary."

"I wonder why that does not reassure me? But remember what I said, Miss Cantrell, for I meant every word of it." He then turned on his heel and returned to his cabin, presumably to pack up his belongings.

It occurred to Anjalie, watching him critically, that despite his words he did not look to be in the least afraid. Apart from his threats—and he would soon learn his mistake if he thought to bully her!—he had seemed to take the whole in his stride. She wondered rather mischievously what he would make of it if they were indeed forced to take to the longboats.

And it soon became likely that they would. Without a cargo they were at even worse risk—a fact she had taken care not to pass on to his lordship—for it would have provided them with ballast, and stabilized them against the fury of the wind. As it was they were tossed around almost as easily as one of the longboats would be, and from the sounds Anjalie began to fear that the *MaryAnne* would literally shake herself apart from the pressure long before she could sink.

So Captain Morton seemed to feel as well, for he returned within the hour with the news that the old girl was not equal to so great a storm, and at her last death throes. "She's busting her struts, and beginning to take on water in a dozen places, and I fear it's only a matter of time now," he reported grimly. "My lord, I'll rely upon you to do as you promised. Lass, inform your father I'll stay with her as long as I can, but I fear there's little enough hope. I've ordered the entire crew to the longboats, and you'd best make your way as well as possible. I'll wish you good luck and Godspeed now, for you can scarce hear your own voice over the shriek of the wind once we're above decks. Don't forget there'll be a dozen stout lads in your boat to see you come to no harm, and to row you to the nearest port when the time comes."

There seemed little more to be said. Anjalie tried to expostulate with the captain, but he merely chuckled tiredly. "I've no intention of going down with my ship, lass. I'm not that noble—or that chuckleheaded. But I've an affection for the old girl, and I'll stay with her to the last. Now no more argument. If I were to lose his only daughter I *would* have some explaining to do to your father, and it's not an excuse I relish being called upon to make! I don't doubt we'll all meet safely again in Jamaica before too long, and raise a noggin to the old girl's memory."

He gave a bear hug to Anjalie and shook his lordship warmly by the hand, and in the face of his calm and cheerful manner it was impossible for either of them to behave otherwise. She stole a glance at his lordship's face, which looked grim but unafraid. He saw her look and shrugged, but said merely, "Well, Miss Cantrell, I must confess I am at somewhat of a loss to understand your fondness for sea travel."

She was forced to smile, and at least privately acknowledged that much must be forgiven a man who retained a cool head in an emergency, and could even still make jokes.

This momentary softening on her part was of brief duration, however, for he was soon to incur her wrath once more. The descent into the longboats was not easy even in the best of weather, for the smaller boat was lowered into the water and held there by grappling hooks and long oars while passengers must negotiate a slippery ladder over the side. When both boats were pitching wildly, and the wind was also doing its best to pluck one off, it was likely to be ten times worse. Even to get to the longboats in such a storm was not easy, for it was necessary to cross the heaving deck first; and in that blinding rain, where visibility was almost nil, it was difficult even to determine directions.

To guard against that danger, a rope was tied around their waists to prevent anyone from being swept overboard from the outset. Another rope was strung tightly from the door to the ship's rail, so that one might pull oneself hand over hand along it as a further precaution.

When the time came, however, Lord Chance took one look at the pitching and rainwashed deck and to her fury chose to take matters into his own hands. Without a word he picked Anjalie up and tossed her bodily over his shoulder. She was naturally outraged by this cavalier treatment, but unfortunately the wind snatched away her protests, and she was not fool enough to struggle with him in such conditions. Soaked, blinded, and in a rage, not to mention breathless and bruised by his ungentle hold upon her, it was in this ignoble fashion that she was carried across the deck, fuming. Nor did he put her down when he reached the rail, but instead negotiated the tricky ladder with her still over his shoulder, like nothing so much as a sack of flour.

Once successfully in the longboat he dumped, rather than set her down, and turned back to help the sailor who was coming after them. That close to the water they had almost no protection from the rain or the wind, and she could do no more than huddle into her cloak, which provided very little protection. She was therefore unaware of the danger until it was too late. One moment the longboat was held grappled to the side of the *MaryAnne,* while a sailor nimbly followed them down the ladder, and Chance stood precariously below ready to receive him.

The next a particularly large wave struck them, driving the two vessels apart, and Chance was thrown off his feet to tumble heavily to the bottom of the boat. The sailor was left clinging dangerously to the side of the *MaryAnne,* while those above tried desperately to prevent the straining longboat from breaking completely away. The next moment the longboat, with only Anjalie and Chance on board, was lifted and tossed away as if she had been no more than a cockleshell, and a fast widening expanse of black and empty sea yawned between them.

Chapter 20

Within seconds the longboat was a hundred yards away from the *MaryAnne,* though they could still see her storm lanterns and hear a few faint shouts in the wind. In a few seconds more even those were gone, and there was nothing but the howl of the wind and the lashing rain and the reality of a pitifully small boat that seemed even more appallingly puny in all that black, storm-wracked ocean.

Anjalie was still crouched in the stern, but Chance had grimly managed to get to his knees again, still straining futilely to catch a glimpse of the *MaryAnne.* Blankly he told himself that the chances of their surviving such a storm in so small a boat had never been high, even with a dozen stout lads to man the oars. But to be separated from the rest of the crew and stranded on their own, in that impossibly small boat, made it seem much worse. Deaf and almost blinded by the slashing rain, he continued to think foolishly for some time that Captain Morton must surely send one of the other longboats after them, or else they would soon catch sight of the rest of the crew, put to sea in their wake. But the waves were so high and the night so black that he could see almost nothing, no matter how many times he dashed the water out of his eyes, and so shouted somewhat helplessly to his huddling companion, *"Now what? Shouldn't we try to get back?"*

Anjalie had the hood of her boat cloak pulled up so that he could not see even the pale oval of her face, but if he had thought to find her driven into panic at last, or indulging in vapors or hysterics—in short, any of the things any other female of his acquaintance would have done under similar circumstances—he was once more doomed to disappointment. He had to strain to hear her voice against the wind, but he might have known her comment would be imminently practical. "No use! We'd never make it. But I'd suggest you get down, my lord, unless you wish to be washed overboard!"

Her unnatural calm in what he considered so catastrophic a situation annoyed him, but he had already become aware of the truth of her words for himself, and so had no choice but to join her in the stern with rather more speed than dignity. In the lee of the steep sides of the boat there was at least some relief from the wind, although by then he was convinced there was no part of him that was dry. He said sarcastically in her ear, still having to shout to be heard, "Well, Miss Cantrell? Do you still maintain this is the only way to travel, and there is not the least cause for alarm? What do you propose we do now?"

"Try to get some rest, my lord!" she retorted. "There is nothing to do but ride out the storm, and I fear it is going to be a very long night."

He did not know whether she were truly insensible to the danger, or merely bent on showing him up. He was cold and wet, and fully expected every minute to be sent to the bottom of the sea, and the thought of sleep had never been further from his mind. But the necessity of shouting his reply against the wind—in which a good deal of the sarcasm would undoubtedly be lost—not to mention the futility of trying to argue with her at all when they were both facing an almost certain watery grave, made him decide in the end to leave his withering reply unuttered. Instead he turned his attention to the more pressing problem of making them both as comfortable as possible—though that seemed scarcely to be hoped for under the present circumstances.

But by dint of using his own boat cloak as a sort of tent, he was at least able to protect them from the worst of the driving rain. But that slight improvement was almost immediately overshadowed in his own mind by the near panic he felt at being thus blinded. His common sense told him there was nothing to see, and that even if there were, she was right: he was wholly powerless to do anything to prevent whatever might come. But the unpleasant sensation of feeling himself blindly tossed about by forces that seemed both incredibly powerful and oddly malevolent, as if deliberately bent on their destruction, was not easily overcome by such logic. He had never before doubted his own courage, but he felt wholly out of his element, as a fish must do out of water, and vowed that if by some miracle he should survive this night, he would never again venture to tempt the natural order of things. At the moment even life on a deserted island seemed infinitely preferable to ever putting to sea again.

To his added annoyance, Anjalie betrayed none of his own panic, and merely arranged herself more comfortably and seemed prepared to follow her own advice.

This determined sangfroid, far from impressing him, merely made him long to throttle her. For his own part he had not the smallest hope of surviving the night, for if their tiny cockleshell of a boat was not broken up by the force of the wind and waves—which seemed only a matter of time—the immense waves would soon inundate them, or else they would be capsized as easily as a child's paper boat in the bath. At the moment it scarcely seemed to matter which was to be their ultimate fate, for any would be more than sufficient for the purpose. But of the three he was inclined to think they would capsize first, for it was impossible to believe they could long remain upright. The long-boat, capable of holding perhaps a dozen men, was flung about as if it had been no larger than a walnut shell, eddied and tossed at the complete mercy of the wind and the waves.

He thought he was already resigned to the worst, but he was soon to discover that he was mistaken. From the first day at sea he had remained thankfully free of any tendency to seasickness, even during the present storm; but he was rapidly discovering that the relative size of the two boats was likely to prove key. Aside from the pitching and tossing they were presently enduring, the boat would willy-nilly climb one huge wave, seemingly the height of the tallest building in London, only to plummet like a lead weight at its peak. Chance's sense of balance was outraged by movement he was convinced no human was meant to withstand, and the smothering darkness of his cloak only made matters infinitely worse. He soon began to fear he would add the final indignity of being wretchedly seasick to all the rest.

For some reason that seemed to be the last straw. He

knew it was ludicrous to worry about so small a matter when he was surely facing his last moments on earth, but he was damned if he was going to so disgrace himself, especially when his companion—and a mere woman!—seemed wholly immune to either terror or nausea. In fact, it soon became his chief object to defeat her, at least on that one minor point. So fiercely did he concentrate on overcoming the revolt of his own stomach that he was mercifully aware of very little else for some time.

It also helped, of course, to lay the blame squarely where it belonged, for there was no doubt that Anjalie was the author of all his troubles. *She* had dared to encourage his sister to defy him, *she* had taken delight in tormenting and enraging him from the moment of their first meeting, *she* had cut up his peace, and made him seriously doubt his own intent and convictions; and most unforgivable of all, it was she who had gotten him on that damned ship—no doubt with this very end in mind!—when he had had not the least intention or desire of ever undertaking such a journey. She was outrageous, ill-bred, brazen, badly behaved, and every inch a vulgar nabob's daughter—all the things he had accused her of in London. If during the weeks of the voyage he had been aware of a fatal softening in his attitude toward her—as witness that dangerous kiss—that was thankfully all over with. If by some miracle he were to survive his present ordeal he would determinedly put her out of his thoughts once and for all, and thankfully return to his safe, even humdrum life.

In the meantime, he was somewhere in the Caribbean Ocean, in a tiny boat in the middle of a hurricane waiting to be drowned, and finding even that a welcome promise of relief from his present extremis. It was even very little comfort to him that she was bound to perish with him, since she undoubtedly deserved her fate, and he with her, for being such a damnable fool as to allow himself to be caught in her toils. In fact, he could not decide which of them he was more angry at, her or himself; and for some time this quite unimportant point consumed him even to the point of forgetting his stomach.

Contrary to all his expectations, in the end he did sleep, for there is only so much the mind can cope with, and his own violently swinging emotions contributed at least as

much as the storm to his ultimate exhaustion. He woke
hours—or days—later, to a sense of immense peace, and
so bright a light beating against his closed eyelids that he
instinctively put up a hand to shield them from its intensity.

His first vague thought was that he must be dead. He
had never really believed much in an afterlife, but it
seemed that upon that point too as upon so many others,
he must have been mistaken. Nothing else could explain
the dazzling power of the light that almost blinded him, or
the extreme peace and contentment he felt; and when he
at last lazily opened his eyes, the intensity of the blue that
filled his vision. But that was as nothing to the celestial
light, concentrated overhead, which generated a warmth
that penetrated to his very bones when it seemed he had
been cold and wet for as long as he could remember. He
was being rocked gently too, which no doubt contributed
to his present feeling of utter content and weightlessness,
and even the air was perfumed, more heavenly than anything he had ever known before. If this was indeed death
he could not imagine why he had resisted it for so long.

Convinced that he was dead, and in some sort of heaven,
he lay there in that dreamy state for a ridiculously long
time before the truth at last began to dawn on him that by
some miracle they had been preserved from almost certain
drowning, and that the storm must be over. He was still in
the longboat, which explained the rocking he had been
aware of, the same waves that had previously threatened
every moment to swamp them now grown as gentle as a
cradle. The celestial light was the sun, enormous overhead,
and far brighter and hotter than any he had ever seen before; and the heavenly blue was the sky and sea, which was
all that was to be seen in any direction, and of so intense
a color that it seemed to bear no relation to sky or sea as
he knew them.

He was still aware of an immense feeling of well-being
and lassitude, so that the ramifications of these discoveries
did not immediately strike him. Only gradually did he become aware of a weight on one shoulder, and discovered
that Anjalie was sleeping trustingly against him, her lashes
on her cheeks like a child's, and her hair a burnished mahogany tangle in the sun. She looked remarkably beautiful,
especially given all that they had been through, and did not

immediately stir. He had no idea how much time might have elapsed, but an exploratory hand told him that he badly needed a shave. In addition his eyes felt bloodshot, and his tongue and head both were amazingly fuzzy, as if he had drunk too much the night before.

He also became belatedly aware of a sharp pain in his middle which set up other, far less pleasant memories. But a moment's analysis was enough to reassure him that it was not nausea this time, thank God, but merely acute hunger, a fact that rather surprised him. There had been many hours, during their ordeal, when he had been convinced he would never want to eat again even if he survived, which at the time had seemed extremely unlikely.

However that might be, he was certainly hungry now. He must have stirred, or tightened his arm unconsciously, for Anjalie's long lashes unexpectedly stirred, then lifted. Then she smiled up at him, betraying no more self-consciousness than if she woke every morning with her head on his shoulder, and her arm across his chest. Chance for some reason discovered he was even dizzier than he had previously supposed. Despite his recent resolutions and all he had endured at her hands, he could not prevent himself from smiling involuntarily back at her.

She seemed to be almost as disoriented as he had been, for she said huskily, "Oh, hullo! I thought I was dreaming, but you are here."

Acutely aware of this new danger, for they were God knew where, stranded together for God knew how long, Chance forced himself to sit up, and said briskly, "Good morning! We would seem to have survived the storm, against every expectation. But whether that will prove to be a blessing is still very much open to question."

She blinked at this deliberate dash of cold water, and sat up herself, instinctively putting her hands up to her hair as if to try to restore some order to it. But at least she sounded more like herself when she said with a touch of impatience, "What an ungrateful creature you are! Of course it is a good thing! Where are we, by the by—or have you even troubled to try to find out?"

"I fear you must hold me excused, for I confess one patch of ocean looks very much like another to me," he pointed out acidly. "As for being better off, I see little preference between drowning and being stranded helplessly on the open sea to die of hunger and thirst. But I have no doubt you are going to point out to me all the advantages of the one over the other, so I will save my breath."

She gave an exclamation of annoyance, as he had intended that she should, and fully threw off that dangerous languor, apparently once more complete mistress of herself. "Oh, I wash my hands of you! We are not going to die of thirst or hunger, and we are not in the least helpless!" She stretched quite unself-consciously—and if she felt anything like he did, her back was aching from sleeping in such a contorted position, and her neck exceedingly stiff—then knelt on the floorboards to shield her eyes with her hand against the glare of the sun and water to search the horizon for all the world as if she expected instantly to spot land.

He somewhat skeptically followed her example, but could see nothing but endlessly blue sea and sky in whichever direction he gazed. Both were admittedly of a more incredible blue than any he had ever seen before, but he discovered he was in no particular mood for appreciating beauty at the moment, and so he merely watched with resignation to see what conclusion she would come to and what outrageous statement she would next utter.

He need not have feared being disappointed. After a considerable time she sat back and said with considerable satisfaction, "Well, we are at least in the Caribbean, that much is certain. With any luck we should strike one or another of the islands before very long, for we were no more than a few days out when the storm hit, and the trade winds are unlikely to fail us."

He could not resist observing somewhat witheringly, "If I am ungrateful, Miss Cantrell, you are the most annoyingly optimistic female of my acquaintance! I am, admittedly, wholly ignorant of these—or any!—waters, but I am finding it difficult to place as much faith in these trade winds of yours as you so obviously do! It seems to me it would take a miracle far greater than the one we have already experienced if we should conveniently, and wholly without any active participation on our part, strike what seems to my no-doubt insular European way of thinking a small handful of incredibly tiny islands in a very large ocean. In fact, what seems far more likely is that we might drift for days or even weeks without ever catching a single glimpse of land, for if there is an ounce of honesty in you—which I am beginning to doubt!—you will admit you have no more notion of where we are than I do!''

"I may not know where we are, my lord," she retorted, "but I would scorn to give up as easily as you do! Even you must be able to determine that we are traveling west, particularly since both the current and the winds in the Caribbean always set strongly in that direction. If nothing else, we must sooner or later hit the coast of Central America, but I am reckoning we will not be forced to drift so far. We might, of course, hit Cuba or Hispaniola, which would be somewhat inconvenient, since they are both occupied by the French at present. But I would be willing to wager you any sum you cared to name that we will be driven straight to Jamaica, for I think we would have hit one or the other of the two before now if we were going to. Remember, without a clue where he was going Columbus found a number of the islands in the Caribbean, including Jamaica, not by sheer luck, as you seem to imagine, but because the wind and current are so strong in their direction."

He could only shake his head at so much stubborn refusal to ever admit herself at a loss, but it seemed pointless to argue. He still felt, besides, an odd sort of detachment, as if, having survived the storm against all odds and his own expectations, and even having for a brief moment already imagined himself dead, he seemed beyond any further shock or fear.

"Anyway, what matters at the moment is that I'm starving to death," she added more practically, which was a sentiment he found himself in so much agreement with that he abandoned for the moment any further attempt to bring her to a sense of their still highly precarious situation.

The emergency stores proved less than satisfactory, however. There were several kegs of water, which he was very glad to see, but the food proved to be little more than hardtack, a sort of hard biscuit that might keep starvation at bay—just—but to Chance's mind was almost unchewable and wholly unsatisfactory as a means of alleviating hunger. It seemed churlish to say so, however, and so after slaking

their considerable thirst, they both sat determinedly trying
to chew the dreadful stuff. Anjalie, catching his eyes and
correctly reading his unspoken thoughts, said somewhat defiantly, "You need not sit there looking at me like that! At
least it will keep us from starving."

His lips twitched, despite himself. "Whereas you, ma'am,
having spent the better part of your life at sea, no doubt
find it delicious—or at least have every intention of trying
to convince me that you do!"

She too laughed somewhat reluctantly. "At least it is better than sitting here like two bristling cats, trying to stare
one another out of countenance. Or sulking, just as you
have done since we left England! Besides, I warned you
that you might someday find yourself in a situation where
your title and wealth would be of very little use to you,
and now we see exactly how well you are able to cope."

"I am not sulking," he returned witheringly. "In fact,
considering all the provocation I have had to endure, I
think I am behaving with remarkable restraint. As for my
wealth and title—which you have delighted in throwing up
at me from the moment of our first meeting—I would almost suspect you of being in deliberate league with my
cousin Darcy, for I fully expect never to see either again."

Conversation naturally did not flourish after that, and
since they were still exhausted, both slept some more—
though this time at opposite ends of the boat. His lordship
was at first extremely grateful for the warmth of the sun,
which had soon dried his clothes completely, but he soon
began to realize that he was indeed in the tropics, for after
a while the heat seemed scarcely to be preferred over the
previous cold. His companion seemed to suffer less in that
regard than he did—and besides, her clothes were a great
deal lighter in weight than his own—and from all outward
appearances was soon asleep again. Chance shrugged, and
thankfully shed his coat and waistcoat. Neither, after having
been soaked with seawater and then slept in, could scarcely
have been said to do him credit in the end anyway and it
seemed senseless to cling to convention at such a moment.

He would like to have discarded his shirt as well, but
was obliged to resist the temptation since he rightly feared
that a bad case of sunburn would add little to his present
comfort—and no doubt merely confirm her in her obviously

low opinion of his adequacy to cope in a crisis. It was yet
another natural advantage Anjalie must be said to have
over him, for her skin, though it had lost a little of its tan
during her weeks in London, was far more used to the sun
than his own, and seemed already to have taken on a honey
tone that he envied.

When he woke again, the light had softened and turned
golden, indicating that evening was near, though it was still
astonishingly warm. He was even more fuzzy-headed than
before, as if the heat had addled his brains. He stirred and
yawned, and saw that Anjalie was seated on one of the
benches in the stern, again gazing into the distance, her hand
shielding her eyes from the glare on the water. Her profile
was turned toward him, her hair a fiery halo around her head,
and he was again obliged to own, however unwillingly, that
she was indeed a magnificent creature. She had shown no
panic, no fear, scarcely even any shock at the plight they
presently found themselves in, let alone any maidenly alarm
at finding herself stranded alone on a tiny boat with a man.
For all she knew they might be stuck together on that
damned tiny boat for days or even weeks, but she had yet
to betray any awareness of what that might entail. His lordship, himself acutely aware of it, could not decide if she
were merely wholly lacking in normal feminine modesty,
or else deliberately intent upon minimizing the danger.

On the other hand, she might irritate him almost past
bearing with her unceasing optimism, but he was obliged
to ruefully own that he did not like to think what the experience would have been like with any other member of her
sex. His stepmother, for instance, or even his sister Georgy
would have progressed rapidly through all the normal feminine stages of tears, hysteria, and vapors, and would not
only have blamed him for the whole, and demanded instant
rescue, but rendered what he still believed to be his last
days on earth so hideous that he was inclined to think he
would soon consider drowning a welcome relief.

Even on the thought Anjalie seemed to become aware
that he was awake, for without turning her head, she announced with considerable satisfaction in her voice, "I told
you we would strike land soon, and I was right. What's
more, unless I'm very much mistaken, it is Jamaica, exactly
as I foretold!"

He could scarcely believe she could be serious, but was up on the instant, his headache forgotten, and intently scanning the horizon in the direction she was looking, straining his eyes against the glare of the setting sun and its reflection off the sea until they watered. At first he could distinguish nothing in the hazy distance, and was inclined to think that she had imagined whatever it was she had thought she'd seen. But then gradually, as his eyes adjusted to the still dazzling light, he too could just make out a misty image in the distance, which appeared to him to be no more than a line of darker blue against the endless horizon to the south.

He impatiently dashed his hand across his eyes to clear them, and tried again, hoping against hope that she might be right, but fearful of disappointment. "I do see something," he conceded at last. "But whether it's land or not, or merely a mirage, I have not the least notion—and nor I strongly suspect do you. At the very least you might tell me how, at this distance and in this light, you can be convinced it's one particular island amongst so many?"

"I swear if a three-course dinner appeared before you right now, you would demand proof that it was real before you would eat it!" she retorted, still shielding her eyes with her hand. "It may very well not be Jamaica, but at the moment any land will do as far as I am concerned."

"For once I am perfectly willing to defer to your supposed superior knowledge, Miss Cantrell," he told her dryly. "Though if you possessed anything like a conscience, you would not dare to talk to me of food at this moment!" He strained his eyes again in the direction she was looking, but could not lay claim to the knowledge behind her own, and so could only ask skeptically, "And you still maintain this precious current of yours will take us right to it?"

She spared him a bright, impatient glance. "No, it will take us straight past and on to Central America, unless we exert ourselves a little! We shall have to row, but that is far preferable to sitting here idly with nothing to do but complain."

He wisely let that pass. "And what then? Assuming for the moment that it is Jamaica—though I confess I am having some trouble in swallowing that—do you tell me we have only to walk up on land and knock at the nearest cottage door and our ordeal will be over?"

This time there was no mistaking the annoyance in her

glance. "This is the West Indies, my lord, not England! What's more, if I am right and it is Jamaica, this is the north shore, which is largely unsettled. Depending upon where we are able to put in, there are only a few isolated plantations; but with any luck, two or three days' walk should find us some help."

He could only gaze speechlessly at her, thinking that not even she could actually be proposing to walk for two or three days before they could hope to encounter civilization. He knew, from one or two abortive walking expeditions with his sister, that the majority of her sex could scarcely walk a mile or two without complaining that their shoes pinched, and they were tired, and end by refusing to go another step. But after a moment he wisely let that pass as well.

As if aware of his skepticism, she added with callous cheerfulness, "Always assuming we don't run into any runaway slaves, or even buccaneers, of course, and assuming it *is* Jamaica, and not one of the French-held islands."

He knew she meant merely to further annoy him, but it was so entirely of a piece with all that had gone before that he couldn't help it. He threw back his head and somewhat helplessly began to laugh.

Chapter 21

Anjalie looked a little taken aback at this unexpected response, but as he continued to laugh, she began to look amused herself. When he was at last able to speak, he gasped out, "Don't mind me! It seems that having already given myself up for lost, I find nothing has the power to surprise me any longer! Let us row ashore by all means, and if we do not end up as French prisoners of war, we must hope we are not murdered by pirates. Are you sure there are not any cannibals on some of the more remote islands as well? At the moment nothing would seem too fantastic for me to believe."

"I've never heard of any, but I am glad to see you have recovered your sense of humor, at least, my lord," she told him carelessly. "You will find it will serve you far better than forever imagining the worst."

"Oh, I still fully expect the worst, Miss Cantrell!" he retorted, still inclined toward inappropriate mirth. "But I find that almost continual alarm has deadened me to any fresh disaster, as one cannot be wetter than wet. In fact, my heart is still firmly set upon there being cannibals at the very least, and I warn you I shan't easily be satisfied with less."

He was less pleased, however, when he discovered she intended to man the oars with him. "I am fully aware that you have set me down, along with the rest of the effete English you so much despise, as being wholly useless in any emergency," he told her with some asperity. "But I assure you I have been rowing from a child, and might at least be trusted to do the brute work."

"And I have warned you that we are in the New World now, my lord, and no longer bound by such outmoded notions," she countered immediately. "If you have been rowing since a child, so have I, and to much more effect, I'll wager. Besides, you've no notion how strong these currents can be! If this *is* Jamaica, there is a reason the north shore is largely unsettled, for aside from the current, there are no natural harbors, and the trade winds blow almost incessantly. I suspect it will take all our combined effort to put in at all, let alone where we want to. Columbus may have managed to land somewhere along here, but that was undoubtedly through necessity, not choice, and since then most ships have preferred to put in on the leeward side of the island."

After a moment's strong debate with himself, Chance forbore to inquire how she could possibly know where they wanted to put in, since she had not the least notion where they were. But since he had again perforce to bow to her superior knowledge—and had every reason to know how stubborn she was by then, he had to give in.

He was soon obliged to admit—if only to himself—that she was undoubtedly right, for both the wind and the current seemed to be set strongly against them. The hazy blue line on the horizon remained stubbornly elusive, still scarcely indistinguishable from the brilliance of sea and sky.

Even if it were an island, he began to fear that they would be swept straight past it, despite their backbreaking labor.

Anjalie was also annoyingly right that rowing in that extreme heat, and against both current and wind, was scarcely comparable to rowing on a calm English lake. He was soon sweating freely, his hands beginning to blister, and the effect of such heavy exercise on an already hollowly empty stomach scarcely added to his comfort. He stole a glance at Anjalie, refusing to believe she could be any more immune to these particular ills than he was, and was further annoyed to discover she was setting to with a will, and showed no particular signs of discomfort.

But when he paused to wipe the sweat out of his eyes, he discovered that at least the misty mirage they were making for seemed to be drawing nearer. He shipped his oars and looked again, and remarked blandly, "I begin almost to hope that it *will* turn out to be one of the French-held islands, for the French must feed even their prisoners fairly well, and after so much exercise I find I am hungrier than ever."

She too shipped her oars and took a welcome breather. She did not look as hot as he felt, and had matched him stroke for stroke, a fact that had done nothing to add to his already sorely deflated vanity. But she was breathing rather fast, and the unruly tendrils around her face were again damp. But she retorted with unimpaired spirit, "I fear you are far more likely to find yourself foraging for roots in the bush than dining with the French, my lord, for *I* am becoming increasingly convinced that this is indeed Jamaica, exactly as I predicted. But perhaps it is as good a time as any to warn you that if you are expecting me to assume responsibility for feeding us, I fear you are doomed to be disappointed. You must be very aware by now that I possess few womanly attributes, and cooking certainly does not happen to be among them."

The heat must be making him lightheaded, for he found that amusing as well. "Good God, what is this?" he demanded with mock astonishment. "I had begun to believe there was nothing you could not do, ma'am. But if it is indeed Jamaica, surely the pirates—I beg your pardon! Buccaneers!—or even the runaway slaves that we will undoubtedly fall afoul of, will feel themselves compelled to feed us before they ultimately slit our throats. On second thought, although I shall clearly be murdered without compunction, for I cannot conceive of what use I could be to anyone, I suspect you have very little to fear, ma'am. You will soon be ruling over either with a rod of iron, as I am convinced you have been doing with your father's empire since the age of three!"

She laughed. "Much as I hate to destroy your illusions, my lord, I fear times are grown sadly flat, even in the West Indies. Far from murdering us, any of the three including the French would be perfectly delighted to ransom us back to my father for a handsome profit. As for feeding us, I suspect you would find many of the native recipes scarcely to your taste, though I grew up on them and like them very well. But at least the buccaneers are reputed to be confirmed hedonists, and I shouldn't be surprised to discover they have made a point of capturing one or two French cooks for themselves, so at least you need not abandon all hope yet."

"Then let us at once determine to be captured by pirates, for I have developed a considerable ambition to meet one of these brigands for myself," he returned promptly. "I refuse to believe they are not bloodthirsty villains, with patches over their eyes and cutlasses in their belts, and a thousand dark secrets in their souls!"

She smiled again at this nonsense. "I fear it is a reputation carefully fostered by them to further their own ends, which I suspect have always been far more mercenary than bloodthirsty. Nor do I have the least intention of being captured by anyone. Papa would never let me live it down, besides considering it a great waste of his money merely to rescue me from the consequences of my own folly!"

He looked at her with renewed interest. "Perhaps all unconsciously you paint a most fascinating portrait of your father, Miss Cantrell, not to mention life in the colonies. Everything that has happened to me in the last month or more is so fantastic I can still scarcely believe it, and yet you have taken it all very much in your stride."

"Oh, we are not nearly so set in our ways here, my lord! We may not have cannibals, and the threat of attack by pirates or Maroons has grown sadly less, but life is still far

from tame and we seldom know from one day to the next
exactly what will happen, as you do in England."

He smiled, though he was still watching her oddly. "At
least I can well believe that your father has taught you to
take care of yourself. But that he has better uses for his
money I take leave to doubt. It is more than obvious that
he dotes upon you."

"He may dote upon me, but he would certainly expect
me not to be so stupid as to allow myself to be captured
and held for ransom!" she retorted. "But I don't know
about you, but I would like to reach shore long before
dark!"

He laughed again, amused despite himself at so much
stubborn optimism, but obediently unshipped his oars.
After half an hour more he was heartily sick of his labors,
but becoming more and more convinced that it was indeed
land they were making for. The hazy blue line had become
much more distinct, and after another hour of muscle-
cracking effort, when he paused again to catch his breath,
he could clearly make out a line of dazzling white sand and
greener jungle, both of which were unbroken for as far as
the eye could see.

Greatly heartened, he ignored his rumbling stomach and
his raw hands, and redoubled his efforts. What he could see
of the island was amazingly beautiful, but at the moment he
was far more concerned with the fact that in such lush
surroundings there must at least be food. His notions of
tropical islands were sketchy, but he supposed that fruits
must grow abundantly, and certainly where there was vegetation there must also be animals. The thought made his
stomach give a more painful squeeze than ever; and he
glanced again at his companion and saw that she too was
watching the shoreline, and looking justifiably satisfied.

Even so, Chance was not convinced they were yet out of
danger. He instinctively preferred land over water, but
there was no sign of civilization: no ships or boats of any
kind at anchor, and no buildings, of any size, to break up
that lush green landscape. He had never seen anything so
empty before, or, prior to this absurd voyage and its consequences, scarce spent an hour away from civilization. The
island seemed of considerable size, for the unbroken shore
stretched without end in either direction for as far as the

eye could see, but he couldn't help thinking of *Robinson Crusoe*. He glanced again at Anjalie, who seemed untroubled by similar fears, and made an effort to banish these thoughts, and went back to his rowing.

By the time they had at last battled their way into the line of surf, and once again shipped their oars for a much-needed rest, his muscles were burning from the strain, his hands were bleeding freely from the unaccustomed rubbing of the oars, his stomach was so empty by then it felt hollow, and he had never been so exhausted in his life before. He again stole a glance at his companion, and saw that Anjalie was looking equally exhausted, her face alarmingly pale, her chest heaving as it sought to draw air into her labored lungs, and her eyes closed in the first sign of weakness he had ever seen in her.

He had longed for the day he would see her obliged to own herself human like the rest of them, but he discovered it was far less satisfying than he had anticipated. In fact, he had a powerful urge to take her into his arms and comfort her as he would have done Georgy when she was a little girl—a feeling that he had certainly never thought to associate with Miss Cantrell, and a dangerous emotion he would do as well to overcome.

He forced himself with some effort to avert his gaze from her drawn face and exhausted posture, and examine the shore that was by then so tantalizingly near. However eager he was to reach land, its desolation made him begin to wonder uneasily if they would not be wiser to keep to the boat until they found some signs of civilization. He thought he would indeed at that point even welcome the sight of a pirate or a runaway slave, for he was not convinced that to be set down on that empty shore was much preferable to being stranded on the equally empty ocean.

He reluctantly ventured to say as much, but he might have known he could have saved himself the trouble. Anjalie straightened immediately, as if to deny even that brief moment's weakness, and said promptly, "On the contrary, *I* am increasingly convinced I know exactly where we are! And if I am right, not only are the waters more dangerous either to the east or the west of here, but we could not have done better if we had planned it ourselves. Unless I am much mistaken, we're in Discovery Bay, the exact place Columbus himself first put in."

He scarcely knew whether by then to deplore or admire her determination never to own herself beaten, and after striving with himself, merely demanded somewhat dryly, "And on what do you base this extraordinary conviction?"

She cast him an impatient look. "I have been here several times, and when you stop to consider, it is really not so very surprising as you seem to think. What's more, Columbus and his men managed to survive here for more than a year, living off the land—though that is one circumstance I have not the least intention of emulating! We are no very great distance from my—I mean from my father's coffee plantation in the Blue Mountains, which you can see yourself in the distance if you would take the trouble to look."

He could, indeed, see a line of mountains in the far distance, but found the sight less reassuring than she obviously intended. He judged them to be every bit of fifty miles or more away as the crow flies—and they were unfortunately neither of them crows. In addition, they were close enough by then for him to see that the line of green that she called bush, but seemed to him a veritable jungle, looked densely impenetrable. If he had before found it hard to believe that she was seriously proposing to walk such a distance, now that he had seen the conditions they must make their way through, he was even more skeptical.

"We are indeed fortunate, then," he said with even more dryness. "But I just venture to ask—would it not be better to sail entirely around the island, and put in on the south side, where you tell me most of the settlements are to be found?"

He had fully expected the glance of scorn she cast him. "Since we have no sail, you would far prefer to walk all those miles than attempt to row them, my lord, little though you may now believe it."

Since after his recent experiences there was scarcely anything he would like less, he meekly made no further protest, even when they had at last battled through the surf and were close enough to shore for him to jump out and drag the boat the rest of the way, and she unhesitatingly jumped overboard with him before he could guess at her intention.

The water was milky warm, after the first cold shock, and the surf surprisingly strong, so that after his first instinctive annoyance, he was again obliged to own that she was right. The longboat, however small and frail it might have seemed in the middle of a vast ocean in a hurricane, proved to be extremely heavy and cumbersome, and it was necessary to drag it up on the sand to the point where it was safe from being pulled back out again by the outgoing tide, in case they might need it later. It required their combined strength to maneuver its weight against the powerful suck of the tide, and if her palms were anything like his own, the salt water stung like the devil, and the bite of the rope was scarcely bearable. She never flinched, however, but stood shoulder to shoulder with him, both soaked to the skin once more—which Chance had to own was a welcome relief from his previous overheated condition—and braced against the slap of the surf to keep from being pulled under themselves, as they strained together on the rope.

Once she lost her footing and almost fell, and he grabbed her instinctively, feeling the heat of her body as a shock through the flimsy barrier of her dress. She glanced up and thanked him breathlessly, then righted herself and turned back to her task. He recovered his wits more slowly, ruefully thinking that Adam and Eve in the Garden of Eden could scarcely have been more alone, and that the ordeal before him was likely to be even greater than he had imagined.

If she was at all aware of similar misgivings, she gave no sign of it. When they had at last dragged the boat far enough up on shore to be safe from the tide, they collapsed onto the warm sand, wholly spent. She closed her eyes and lay unself-consciously in the hot sun, seemingly equally unaware of how revealingly her wet dress clung to her. After that first glance Chance quickly averted his gaze, aware that his own shirt was plastered to his skin, and his boots were full of water. He was so thankful to have dry land under him again, however, that he ruefully closed his eyes and followed her example, too exhausted to worry about larger issues for the moment.

When he had regained his breath, he sat up and emptied his boots, even more ruefully regarding the wreck of his expensive hessians, and buckskin breeches. Aside from a hot meal, he discovered he longed for nothing so much as a shave and a hot bath and a change into fresh clothes, and once more thought fleetingly of his valet, whose services he had never fully appreciated until now.

The thought of the comfortable life he had left behind him in England seemed curiously alien to him, however, as if it belonged to someone else. It seemed that he had been cold, wet, and hungry for most of his life—when he was not hot and sweating with exertion—and had been bedraggled for so long that he could scarcely remember anything different. He had a change of clothes in his portmanteau, but since it seemed safe to assume that the rest of his belongings were now at the bottom of the sea, they represented the sum total of the wardrobe he had left to him, and as such had best be hoarded in case they ever reached civilization again.

He remembered the few other things he had packed in the moments before they abandoned ship, which included all his money, as well as his gold watch and ivory-backed brushes, a pair of serviceable pistols, and the few other things he had thought too valuable to lose, but they, too, seemed to belong to another life. It would have been far more to the purpose if he had brought instead what food he could lay his hands upon, and abandoned his money to the bottom of the sea without a backward glance. At least he had thought to put in a couple of bottles of burgundy, and one of brandy for medicinal purposes, a fact he remembered now with silent thanksgiving.

He shrugged and lay back again as Anjalie was doing, linking his hands behind his head and staring up at the blue of the sky, now streaked with vivid pinks and oranges as the sun began to set. The heat, which had been so unpleasant while they were rowing, was now once more very welcome, and would no doubt soon dry his clothes on his body as it had done before. Other than that, and the empty state of his stomach, he discovered that he felt amazingly unlike himself, as if he could not possibly be lying on an empty shore, with no food and very little water, and no way of knowing what the immediate future might bring.

For a long time he lay there, trying to analyze the strange and wholly unexpected sense of detachment he felt. It might merely be, as he had told Anjalie, that already having given himself up for lost, nothing much had the power to alarm him any further. But that scarcely explained why he felt almost carefree and oddly irresponsible. It was a novel feeling, for accustomed from an early age to the weight of his many responsibilities, and assuming the guardianship of his young sister when he himself had scarcely reached adulthood, it seemed that he had never once questioned what he owed to his name and his numerous dependents, or whether he enjoyed his exalted position and all the responsibilities that came with it.

Now, his responsibilities left behind, along with his title and privileged existence, he found himself curiously unconcerned—even lighthearted. His sister, on whose concern he had launched this whole mad enterprise, was wholly out of his reach. In fact, it amazed him to realize that he had scarcely given her a thought in their present ordeal. For all he knew, she might have been caught in the same storm and be dead by now, or already married to her ne'er-do-well; but in either case there was nothing he could do about it.

In reality, he acknowledged for the first time that probably there had never been much he could have done. He was no longer even sure that this whole mad journey had been prompted by his desire to save his sister from an improvident marriage as much as by his own pride—and his resentment against Anjalie. It even seemed possible that Anjalie—damn her!—had been right from the start when she insisted that his objections to his sister's marriage had always been more about his own prejudices and expectations than any concern for his sister's happiness.

But somehow even that realization failed to shock him, as it might once have done. He supposed if he ever reached civilization again, he would be left with little choice but to give his consent to the marriage, and settle at least part of his sister's fortune upon her, but he discovered he could view even that annoying necessity with surprising equanimity. He was not so far gone that he could yet believe the marriage an equal one, or that she would not live to regret her choice. But for some reason it seemed far less important to him than it had done a mere six weeks ago.

He lay thinking about that, and made an even more

shocking discovery. Despite all that had happened, despite all that he had endured; despite the coming days, which promised to be at least as uncomfortable and even dangerous as those that had just passed; he was unable to convince himself that he wished it all undone. He might even now be back in his safe and predictable life, not lying exhausted and disheveled and starving on a deserted beach somewhere in the Caribbean, with not the least idea of what unpleasant surprises tomorrow might bring. But if he could somehow have magically wafted himself back to England at that moment, he realized he would not do it. He had an even stronger suspicion that he did not know himself any longer. It seemed he had changed so much in a few short weeks—perhaps even a few short days—that there might never be any going back again to the man he used to be.

If so, he had no need to look for the author of this transformation. He turned his head lazily to regard Anjalie where she still lay in the sun. Despite their being stranded together like Adam and Eve on a deserted island, and despite his newfound sense of irresponsibility, nothing had really changed between them. Whatever might be his present feelings toward her—and they were extremely mixed at the moment, to say the least—he must never let himself forget that their worlds ultimately lay too far apart ever to be bridged.

That firmly decided, it occurred to him belatedly that her very lack of awareness of any danger as she lay unselfconsciously beside him in the hot sand, showed him clearly that however much his feelings toward her might reluctantly have changed, hers had obviously not undergone a similar transformation. His vanity, already badly battered during the past few days, was even more piqued. Pursued all his life for the sake of his money, he had finally found a female who cared not a jot for either his money or his title, and the devil was in it he didn't even know whether she liked him or not. She had certainly said once, long ago, that she did—if only against her will; but a great many events had intervened since then, and it might no longer be true. And when he considered the way he had treated her, not to mention her own scarcely disguised scorn for his inadequacies during their present predicament, she might by now dislike him very much indeed.

That scarcely mattered, of course, for he assured himself firmly that he had just enough sanity left to refrain from committing that one final folly. He might be grateful to her at the moment, and possess enough justice to acknowledge her undoubted virtues, but it went no further than that. Trelawney was welcome to her!

Probably his present, not unpleasant feeling of unreality would disappear in time—assuming he was not murdered by pirates or escaped slaves first!—and he would recover from this current rather novel sensation of scarcely knowing himself. And if she seriously meant to march them overland for mile after weary mile on the morrow, as seemed all too probable, the chances were all too high that he would quickly come to hate her as much as he now reluctantly admired her.

Until then, however, it seemed he had abandoned himself to his fate, and he did not wholly dislike the feeling. For the first time in his life he had not the slightest idea what tomorrow would bring—except that it would be outrageous, and probably damnably uncomfortable! Either he was suffering from some temporary insanity brought on by fear and discomfort, and would soon enough recover; or else he had indeed undergone some fundamental change, in which case he was in uncharted territory—both literally and figuratively. In his present mood he was not even in any particular hurry to find out which.

Chapter 22

Anjalie, wholly unaware of these thoughts, sat up at that point and said briskly, "It will be dusk soon. We'd better get going."

Chance opened one eye to regard her warily. "Going? Going where, for God's sake?"

"I regret that we are most unlikely to be rescued here, my lord, lazing on the beach," she pointed out sarcastically.

He sat up with extreme reluctance. "You still persist in this fantastic notion that out of all the islands in this part of the ocean, you know exactly which one we have been set down on and even which bay we are in?"

"I do, and it is not nearly so fantastic as you suppose. But even if I am wrong, do you have a better plan?" she countered.

"If it means walking fifty miles as the crow flies, probably through impenetrable country and almost certainly, if I understand you correctly, up a mountain, I would find almost anything preferable," he told her frankly. "And if that is your 'plan,' I see no need to set out tonight, since as you so accurately point out it will be dusk all too soon and we are both of us tired and hungry already."

"Well, your dinner is hardly likely to walk up out of the ocean and present itself on a silver platter for you," she said even more scathingly. "I am sorry to be the one to break it to you, my lord, but if you haven't realized it already in the last few days, you have left your safe and privileged life far behind, in a busybody attempt to control your young sister's life, and there are no servants here at your every beck and call. Nor will your title put anything in your belly! If you want to be rescued, you will have to do it yourself."

"If we are to talk of safe and privileged lives, Miss Cantrell," he retorted, "don't trouble trying to convince me you have spent many—if any!—nights sleeping rough on the beach, or been forced to tramp miles on your own, for I frankly won't believe you. Your father, however unusual he may be, plainly worships the ground you walk on, and you order your Adam around as if he were your personal lapdog."

"Don't compare me with yourself, my lord, for I daresay I can boast many more nights spent out in the open than you can. Before you came on this trip I seriously doubt you ever spent a night without your valet and your groom and I don't know how many others besides to pave the way for you and cater to your every whim."

"If you dare to throw my privileged life in my teeth again, Miss Cantrell, I don't know what I'll do to you, but it will be something terrible, I promise," he told her calmly. "My first and only voyage to date has ended in the ship going to the bottom of the sea, since which I have endured endless days being tossed in a cockleshell boat in a hurri-

cane, suffering from both acute terror and nausea—and of
the two I still am frankly undecided which was worst!—and
firmly convinced that every moment was my last. Now I
find myself stranded on an unknown and probably perilous
island with the prospect of tramping fifty miles or more
with very little reliance on reaching civilization at the end
of them. Add to that the fact that I am sore and exhausted,
and so hungry I am reduced to looking upon even hardtack
as a high treat, and you will perhaps see why I have every
right to be somewhat aggrieved.''

"*I* didn't make you come tearing after your sister in this
highly quixotic way!'' she repeated indignantly. "As for
being tired and hungry, so am I, but I would scorn to sit
around merely bemoaning the fact. And I fear you will
be a great deal hungrier still if you don't bestir yourself,
my lord!''

He sighed. "I have put up with a great deal from you,
Miss Cantrell, but if you call me 'my lord' again in that
odiously condescending way, I warn you I will not be responsible for my actions. I don't give a damn for my title,
and since I have a fairly good idea what I must look like by
now, it must seem a little threadbare by now, even to you.''

Anjalie, looking him over critically, was obliged to own
the truth of that, at least. He might almost have been taken
for a buccaneer himself by then, for he had sensibly abandoned his coat and waistcoat alike long since, and had
opened his shirt almost to the waist and rolled up his
sleeves. His buckskins were sea-stained, his boots scratched,
and he was unshaven and unkempt, but she thought he
looked younger and much more human. "On the contrary,''
she said truthfully. "At least you look like a man, now, and
not merely an *Englishman.*''

Unexpectedly he gave the attractive shout of laughter
that so transformed him. "And I am well aware that worse
you could not say of anyone! Let us hope we are not
stranded together for too many days, Miss Cantrell, for I
strongly suspect we will end by murdering each other.'' He
looked her over in turn as frankly as she had done him
and added wickedly, "Allow me to return the compliment.
My sister assures me that it is now the height of fashion
for women to damp their petticoats in order to attain just
such a charming affect as you have achieved so naturally.

In fact, I confess I never realized until I saw you in your native land how truly red your hair is."

She did blush then, but merely said crossly, "I am well aware that was meant to discomfit me, but I have no time to worry about such unimportant matters at the moment. We can stay here endlessly bickering, in which case we will undoubtedly starve to death, or we can put ourselves to a little exertion, and might even achieve a bath tonight, as well as a meal, both of which I admit are my own main concerns at the moment."

He abandoned his teasing on the instant. "Good God! You can't be serious? Do you tell me we are actually close to some house or other? Why didn't you say so at once?"

She quickly burst that particular bubble. "No, I told you the north shore is pretty much unoccupied, except for a few scattered sugar plantations. But if I am right about where I think we are, there is fresh water to be had not too many miles from here. We may camp there for the night."

He was disappointed, but when she reminded him, in the tone an adult might use to a rather dim child, that where there was fresh water there was bound to be wildlife, he said no more, but rose at once, reaching down a hand to help her up as well. She hesitated, then accepted his hand, visibly wincing as she did so.

He frowned and retained her hand even when she had reached her feet. She tried to pull it away, but he took her other hand as well and grimly turned both over.

For a long moment he said nothing. Then he raised his eyes to her face. "You are a damned little fool, aren't you?"

She shrugged and retorted, "Don't pretend that yours are any different, my lord! I consider it a small enough price to pay for our present good fortune."

His lips tightened with annoyance. "I keep changing my mind, Miss Cantrell, whether you are a heroine or the most annoying female of my acquaintance," he told her truthfully. "These will have to be seen to before we go anywhere. I have some ointment in my cloak bag."

She winced a little under his treatment, for her palms were raw where blisters had formed and then broken under the unaccustomed work; but she informed him indifferently that saltwater was a surprisingly good cure for such minor ailments. He shook his head, but allowed her to return the favor by anointing his own hurts.

After that they packed up what they were to take with them. His lordship was strongly loath to leave behind the several small barrels of drinking water the longboat had contained, but Anjalie assured him that the island was riddled with fresh water, especially in the mountains where they were bound. She seemed scornful when he insisted upon carrying his portmanteau, but ultimately gave in on that point, merely warning him that he was likely to grow extremely weary of the burden.

He, in turn, looked startled when she ruthlessly ransacked her own small trunk and wrapped what few articles she meant to take in a shawl. He would have insisted upon carrying her bundle as well as his own, but she merely laughed and tied it round her shoulders as she said the slaves did. When they were at last ready to go, he could not prevent himself from casting a last, rueful look at the boat pulled up high onshore out of the reach of the tide. "Why do I feel as if I will regret this, when just a few hours ago I had not the least wish ever to set eyes on another boat again?" he remarked. "Never mind. *En avant,* Miss Cantrell. It seems I am placing my life wholly in your hands—and I have an even stronger feeling I shall soon live to regret that!"

Since Anjalie judged it best to make their way along the beach, the going was necessarily rough. They were both soon breathing heavily, but since she was uncertain of the distance they must travel, and knew how brief the twilight was in the tropics, she did not abate the brisk pace she had set.

And at least Chance made no complaint. She thought mischievously that if she had attempted to devise a plan to test him she could hardly have succeeded better. He seemed to have abandoned his resentment of her for the moment, and even seemed to have lapsed into an unanticipated and uncharacteristic bout of frivolity, which did him no particular disservice in her critical eyes. Nor had he yet lost his head or lashed out at her, as most other Englishmen in similar circumstances would have done. She did not delude herself that he would ever have chosen such an ordeal, or would remain long in Jamaica once they were rescued, but she was not sorry to have this opportunity of discovering if her impressions of him were correct. Raised in the tropics, the bush held no terror for her, and in fact had there been a house within a few miles of where they were, she thought she would have been faced with a considerable dilemma. She had no particular desire to put an early end to so promising an adventure

Perhaps luckily she was not faced with that dilemma, so she walked steadily on, ignoring her own achingly hollow stomach. They stuck wherever possible to the higher packed sand, which made walking easier, but also made it necessary to follow the meandering shoreline, which lengthened the distance they must cover considerably. Chance ventured once to point this fact out to her; but when she told him frankly that without a path the going would be far worse inland, he took a long look at the impenetrable wall of green that lined the shore, no doubt thinking of his own tame country, and made no further protest.

But mostly, to his credit, he matched her stride for stride, and showed no immediate signs of flagging. Once he caught her assessing glance, and said ironically, "You've made your opinion of me more than clear, Miss Cantrell, but you forget that I am a country man, born and bred. I assure you I walk a good deal further than this when I am out shooting. In fact, if you wish to reach this place of yours before dark I would suggest we pick up the pace a trifle."

Amused, she did so, wondering if he could really be as pot-valiant as he seemed, or was merely trying to annoy her. Shooting in England, as she well knew, tended to be a tame affair that usually involved gamekeepers, bearers, and loaders, and half a dozen stalwart servants known as beaters, whose job it was to put up the game to provide their masters with an easy shot. She decided that if his lordship remained in Jamaica any length of time—which seemed unlikely—she would have to have Adam take him shooting, colonial-style, which sometimes meant days out in the bush, and far more elusive game than he could ever be used to.

It was still very warm, so that despite his attempts to put her to the blush her gown and hair had quickly dried, as she had known they would. But she was soon perspiring freely, so that the unruly tendrils of hair about her face were damp again. He too had great patches of sweat on his shirt, and there was a fine sheen on his skin, which had darkened considerably since they had left England, she noticed admiringly.

After an hour of increasingly hard trudging, she had begun to fear she had miscalculated after all. She was increasingly convinced this was indeed Jamaica, but for some miles she had been faced with the dilemma of deciding how, and at what point to call a halt. There was perhaps an hour of light left to them, and the walking was too treacherous to try to make their way in the dark. Her own preoccupation with a bath, to wash the sticky salt out of her hair and skin and change clothes, was still strong, but if they were to have anything to eat besides the hardtack Chance disliked so much, they must have some daylight still left to them when they at last made camp.

In the end they came upon the spot she had been making for quite unexpectedly. She had deliberately not warned him what to expect, so that it was all the more startling when they rounded one last long wearisome curve of shore that had taken them many unnecessary steps to cover. The land to their right had been steadily rising, but the roar of the tide had effectively covered any further sound of rushing water, so that the falls burst upon them both with a dramatic effect. The water fell from a considerable height to a series of lesser drops, only to tumble the last twenty feet in a spectacular show of noise and foam to finally feed into the sea.

He stopped as she did, wholly astonished. "Good God!" he said. "Is *this* what you were making for? Then I take it all back, Miss Cantrell. It was well worth the walk."

She tried not to show that she was pleased with this response. "The water comes straight down from the mountains, and could not be colder or purer. We used to come here now and then when I was a child, and I thought I could not be mistaken, though I began to fear I had miscalculated how far to the west we had landed."

They both slaked their considerable thirst, drinking from their cupped hands, not minding that they were splashed by the icy water in the process. His lordship, taking in the idyllic setting, and her unmistakable look of satisfaction, began to laugh again. "Very well, ma'am, I will concede that you were right after all: this clearly is Jamaica, and what's more, it is exceedingly beautiful. A man would have to be hardened indeed to find fault with such a paradise."

He again eyed the icy falls, and added in amusement, "But if this is the bath you promised, it will be a cold one! Under the circumstances I can, with very little reluctance, chivalrously offer you the first chance at it. And if you really plan to strip down and stand under that icy spray, you are more intrepid even than I thought! I confess I may content myself with a good wash and a shave. But I will leave you now to your sylvan ablutions and see if I can't fulfill my half of the bargain by finding us some dinner."

She wondered if he would manage to find some game, but since she was by no means so squeamish as he was, only waited till he had gone to strip down, and bathe and wash her hair under the admittedly frigid stream. It was a wonderful relief after the heat of the day and their exertions, and it was only with reluctance that she finally emerged to put on her one fresh dress and comb out her tangled hair. The twilight was falling rapidly by then, and she wasted little time after that in gathering what driftwood she could to build a fire. She was sitting before this, finishing drying her hair, when the hunter at last returned.

The combined sounds of rushing tide and falls managed to disguise his approach, so that he startled her by stepping out of the twilight without warning to remark in amusement, "You look like a mermaid—or do I mean dryad?—sitting there by the fire weaving your toils. But I have no intention of asking what mischief you are next plotting, for I am convinced I would much rather not know."

She turned to regard him, noticing with approval that he had not returned empty-handed. She had earlier heard several shots in the distance, and it pleased her to see that he was capable of fulfilling his side of the bargain.

As he saw the direction of her glance, he raised his trophies, saying ruefully, "I have no idea what they are, but they look vaguely like rabbit, and I confess I am hungry enough to eat almost anything at this point."

"They are conies, which is a distant relative of the rabbit, I suppose, and are considered quite tasty," she told him in amusement. "What's more, they are far wilier than the fat and complacent English rabbits, so you must be a very fair shot."

"Of course they would be. But you mustn't risk spoiling me by such unaccustomed praise, ma'am," he protested in mock humility. "Besides, by now I feel reasonably certain that you were merely throwing me a sop and are probably at least as good a shot as I am."

"I can shoot," she conceded, "but I confess I don't like to shoot harmless animals, especially merely for sport. And I told you the truth that I have not the least talent for the more domestic virtues, so if you expect me to clean or cook those things, you are in for a disappointment."

He laughed. "Can you be human after all? Very well, I will engage to see to our dinner. It seems the least I can do, since so far I am of about as much practical use in our present adventure as you have always suspected me of being. I am even ready to brave the falls, for after such Herculean labors I feel more in need of a bath than ever. And in case you did not recognize it, Miss Cantrell, that was a hint to make yourself scarce."

They ate in unusual amity, both tired out and too hungry to talk much. The meal, after the hardtack, was ambrosial, for the conies tasted wonderful grilled over an open fire, and Anjalie had provided yams and plantains, as well as a pineapple, foraged while Chance was bathing and shaving. He still looked surprisingly unlike himself, even clean-shaven once more, and she had never seen him so relaxed and carefree.

Since he produced a couple of bottles of burgundy and one of brandy from his portmanteau, their meal even took on an unexpected elegance. She laughed when she saw them, and said teasingly, "I might have known you would not willingly abandon every luxury, but if you carried those bottles all that way, you are entitled to some reward."

He grinned companionably at her. "I only wish I had had the foresight to bring champagne, for I think a celebration is definitely in order. I never would have believed twenty-four hours ago that I would still be alive, let alone so comfortable."

So they drank a very expensive burgundy with their makeshift meal, and if he thought the yams and plantains, baked in the coals, decidedly odd, they both enjoyed the pineapple very much, eating it with their fingers and letting the sticky juice run down their faces.

At last they sat back, replete, and Chance said lazily, "I take it all back, Miss Cantrell. I begin to think this is indeed paradise. No cares, no responsibilities, nothing to do but eat—and that seems easy enough with fruits and wildlife wherever you turn—and sleep. No need even for any shelter, for the night is almost as warm as the day, and you were right that it is all incredibly beautiful. Only look at those stars! Is this what makes colonists abandon their homes for the lure of the untamed wilderness? This sense of going back into the Garden of Eden before the fall?"

She said in amusement, "Loath as I am to introduce a note of reality, my lord, even my partiality doesn't blind me to the truth. It may seem like paradise at the moment, but I fear you are forgetting such trifling inconveniences as hurricanes and earthquakes, pestilence and disease. But the appeal of an unspoilt land is admittedly strong—and the temptation to pit your wits and strength against every obstacle even stronger. Some come only to exploit, of course, and there is always the danger of turning paradise into a copy of what was left behind. But for the most part you must see for yourself by now that life is not safe or tame here, however beautiful. And that is the real lure, I think, for people like my father who are bored with the tame restrictions of your world, and come here to escape civilization more than anything else."

"And you plainly expect me to be immune to that lure. But this is a moment out of time, and I refuse for once to quarrel with you. But speaking of paradise, are there any serpents in this particular one? At the moment I've surprisingly few complaints, but it is as well to be forewarned."

She laughed. "I daresay there are a few poisonous snakes, but the most you might have to worry about is a wild boar or two, and they seldom come down onto the beach. Mosquitoes are our biggest threat, but on the north shore the wind always blows so strongly, especially so near the sea, that you should not be too troubled by them. Of course it may rain, for the summer months are given to sudden showers, but I don't see a cloud in the sky."

He too looked up at the sky, the stars seeming so close

he could almost reach up and touch them. "I refuse to believe it will rain on such a night," he insisted lazily. "Besides, I have been so wet the last few days that a tropical rain in this warmth hardly seems to matter. But confess, now: have you ever actually slept on the beach yourself?"

"When I was a little girl, Papa would sometimes let me. I told you I have hardly led the sheltered life you are used to, my lord."

"So it begins to appear, and in this idyllic setting I can finally begin to understand why. Tell me about your childhood."

He sounded genuinely interested, so she told him about the early years, many of them indeed idyllic, when she rode wherever she wished on her pony, often escaping from the black servant delegated to watch out over her at all times, or went adventuring with her father. "That was after Mama died, of course, for she could not quite rid herself of all English prejudices, and feared I was growing up to be a complete hoyden—which I was, of course."

"Perhaps the sacrifice she made was not as great as I have always thought it. But I take it you would never follow her example and give up your home and family for the man you loved?" he inquired curiously.

"Never," she answered firmly. "This is my home, and I love it here. You saw for yourself how out of place I was in England. I'm not sorry that I went, for it was interesting to see where my parents came from, but I could never live there permanently." She added as if deliberately, "Any more than you could live here, my lord."

"On the contrary, I begin to think I could live here very well indeed, for I am not nearly as immune to its attractions as you seem to think."

When she made no answer, he added mockingly, "Never mind! I would suggest we get some sleep for tomorrow promises to be a long one. You may retire to your chaste patch of sand on that side of the fire, Miss Cantrell, and I will retire to mine on this, thus observing the proper conventions."

But after they had settled down, his voice came again, from out of the darkness. "By the way, I don't know whether you keep bringing up the differences between us to convince me, or to convince yourself. But you may yet find yourself required to eat your words, as I have had to eat so many of mine lately.

When she still made no answer, he laughed and added ironically, "Sweet dreams, ma'am! I don't know about you, but I feel as if I could sleep for a week, so that not even my spoilt upbringing will keep me awake tonight."

Chapter 23

His lordship found it more natural than he would have thought possible to sleep in the open, the sound of the surf in his ears. He woke at last to brilliant sunlight, to find Anjalie already up before him, looking energetic and even surprisingly neat.

He had watched with interest the evening before as she braided her hair down her back; and he saw with some surprise that she was barefoot now, both of which made her look younger and far more vulnerable—an impression he knew well was a misleading one. She also looked happier and more carefree than he had ever seen her, and he was forced to acknowledge that she was indeed back in her own element.

He yawned and stretched, very aware of his own wrinkled clothes and again-unshaven jaw. He was also astonishingly hungry, when he seldom ate breakfast at home.

As if aware of it, she said cheerfully, "So you're finally awake! I hope you like clams, my lord, for that, along with fruit, is what we are having for breakfast. We'll save what's left of last night's meal for later, for there will be little time to stop during the day if we hope to reach my home by nightfall."

So they broke their fast with fruit and clams, which she had energetically dug that morning and baked in the fire, a simple meal that for some reason tasted better to Chance than the most gourmet dish prepared for him by his exorbitantly expensive French chef at home. All that was lacking was coffee, but Anjalie promised him, again in the consoling tone of an adult to a rather fractious child, that when they reached her home in the mountains he would taste coffee like he had never tasted it before.

Chance, giving himself up to the absurd situation he found himself in, discovered he was in no great hurry to reach her home, even after a grueling day and a night spent in the open. The odd feeling of detachment had not left him, and he was even aware of a disinclination to leave so idyllic a setting. Since food and fresh water were so plentiful, it occurred to him they might benefit from spending a few days there to rest up.

But when he said as much, she laughed. "It is tempting, I know, but you forget that everyone must think us dead. And you still have to rescue your sister, which is why you came in the first place."

Even this mention of his sister failed to move him as it would once have done. "My sister," he told her a trifle grimly, "with the help of your friend Trelawney and probably even that wretched woman you bullied into coming out here, is undoubtedly already married, as you must be very well aware."

"Nonsense!" she retorted. "If I know Adam, the last thing he would do would be to help your sister to an impractical marriage."

"Do you know Adam?" he inquired rather dryly.

But she was immune to his sarcasm. "Of course I do! I have known him since I was ten."

"That is exactly what I meant," he pointed out even more dryly. When she made no answer, he added curiously, "Which reminds me that from one cause or another, I never asked how you managed to be ready to leave England so quickly. What did you do with your horse, for instance?"

"Oh, Erin!" she said on a sigh. "How I wish I had him here now. He is to be shipped over later, of course, and under the circumstances, I suppose I must be glad I didn't try to bring him with me. As for the rest, it was no great problem to pack my trunks and say good-bye to my aunt and my cousins."

"I imagine they were extremely relieved to be rid of you," he remarked in amusement. "And did you take an equally touching farewell from my cousin, after having encouraged him all those weeks to sit in your pocket? Or was that done merely to annoy me, as I long suspected?"

She began to look mischievous. "I doubt his heart was broken by my departure."

"On the contrary, from what I hear he practically haunted your aunt's house and I never before knew him to—oh, my God!" He broke off and regarded her with sudden suspicion. "Was he—is it possible he was dangling after your *eldest cousin* instead? What was her name? The shy one?"

"Anne," she supplied, watching him with the mischief still very pronounced in her face, but volunteering no more.

"I can see the truth in your face. Tell me, Miss Cantrell, do you make unsuitable matches wherever you go, or did you do it merely to get back at me?" he demanded disagreeably.

"Merely to get back at you, of course!" she retorted at once.

"In that case, I'm sorry to disappoint you, but I care not a jot whom Darcy marries," he informed her calmly. "Though I rather suspect your aunt and your cousin Frederick may not be nearly so tolerant! I have not the least notion why Darcy should choose to shackle himself to a timid little mouse with neither wealth nor any great beauty to recommend her, but it is nothing to do with me, I thank God!"

She was surprised, but said at once, "I consider my cousin has far the worst of the bargain, as a matter of fact, for your cousin has nothing to recommend him but being heir to a title he will never occupy."

He began to look amused. "Oh, I don't know. He came devilish close in the past few days, you must admit. In fact, I wouldn't be at all surprised if this were not all some elaborate plot to do away with me merely to help your cousin."

"If so, my lord, I would take very great care how you provoked me!"

"An unnecessary warning!" he retorted. "I go in constant fear whenever you are near, ma'am."

She merely laughed, and they set off soon after. It was already getting hot, and once they entered the bush, as she called it, it became a great deal hotter. In fact, his worst fears were soon realized, for the going was extremely rough, and he could find no signs that any other human had ever been there before them. They followed no trail, and at far too many places had to literally force their way through the lush vegetation, which caught at their clothes and hair, and greatly hindered their progress.

He was soon liberally scratched, and grimly regarded her in her flimsy gown. "You'd better let me go first" he told her. "Do you tell me it will be like this the entire way?"

She halted to wipe her face and say with some impatience, "Did you think we had only to stroll down some primrose-lined path, my lord? I warned you the going was likely to be rough. But at least it will be cooler once we reach the mountains. Besides, with any luck—but I shan't tell you that, yet, for I may not be able to find it, and then you will have gotten your hopes up to no purpose."

He found little enough comfort in her words, for he thought the mountains still many days' hard trek away— and to add to their difficulties, once in the bush the trees were so thick that they could no longer see more than a few feet ahead of them. It seemed extremely unlikely to him that without a compass and more distinguishing features than he had yet discovered in that tropical wilderness, finding anything was akin to trying to find a needle in a haystack. But that opinion he wisely kept to himself.

Away from the sea it was also breathlessly still, and even though they were thankfully out of the sun, the humid heat made it increasingly difficult for him to catch his breath. In addition, Anjalie's warning the night before was soon shown to be unpleasantly accurate, for without the stiff wind that seemed always to blow onshore, mosquitoes rapidly became a considerable nuisance.

Even so, it was all exceedingly beautiful—an incredible green that almost hurt the eyes, and every tree, vine, or bush seemed to be covered in flowers: huge, colorful, and incredibly exotic, and which emitted heavy scents that clung to their clothes when they brushed past them. And then there were the birds, largely invisible and falling briefly silent as they made their way through, only to break out again louder than ever a moment later. Sometimes a great cloud of them, small and extremely colorful, and unlike any birds he had ever seen before, would start up at their approach, squawking and protesting, until the air seemed almost alive with them.

The first time it happened he was not unnaturally startled. "Those are parakeets," Anjalie informed him in amusement. "They are amazingly noisy, and some plantation owners think them impossible pests, but I've always liked them. A few people have caught and tamed one as a pet, but it always seems a shame to me to place them in a cage."

He agreed, thinking the sparrows and thrushes of home incredibly dull by comparison. She as yet showed no signs of flagging, and if she was tired or feeling the heat herself, she certainly did not confess to it. She was more used to it than he was, of course, and he was still burdened with his cloak bag—though he was rapidly coming to begrudge its unwieldy weight—while she had only her bundle, tied crosswise across her back. It left her hands free for pushing branches out of the way and for slapping at mosquitoes, both of which actions were constantly necessary. He noticed with concern that she had several long angry scratches on her bare arms, and some thorn or other had torn the shoulder of her gown, leaving an ugly red weal on her tender flesh. But he knew better than to comment upon either fact, or expect her to slow their torturous progress.

They had been walking for several hours when without warning they came upon a clearing which held a primitively constructed structure. It was so wholly unexpected in that empty wilderness that Chance halted in utter astonishment, glancing at Anjalie's face for enlightenment. It bore considerable triumph, which Chance was bound to own was justified.

"I hoped I might be able to find this," she said in answer to his glance. "It's a sugar plantation and boiling house, though an extremely primitive one. In fact it's owned by Lord Sedgeburrow, which explains why it is so far out in the middle of nowhere. He—or rather his overseer—has little desire for anyone to see the wretched condition the slaves are kept in, and I warn you that you are likely to be extremely shocked and disgusted. *I* am hardly popular with Jacobson, for obvious reasons, but he is a little afraid of my father, I think, and may be persuaded to lend us a couple of horses. No other consideration would make me have dealings with him."

The building, he saw on closer inspection, was little more than a thatched roof on poles, with a dirt floor and vast copper tins in rows down the open sides. He had been aware for some time of a strange sweet smell, and now he recognized it as emanating from the coppers, presumably sugar cane being boiled down into sugar. He was interested despite himself, and glad of a break from walking, but he saw with deepening revulsion that the tubs were indeed being tended by sticklike figures, many of them nearly naked, and all of them looking perilously close to starvation.

They were the first slaves Chance had seen, in fact, and they were hardly a recommendation for the institution. Their eyes looked dully out of skull-like heads, startlingly yellowish white against their dark skins, and their emaciated limbs seemed scarcely sturdy enough to hold their frames up, let alone perform any hard physical labor. If they were in turn surprised to see two Europeans appear out of the bush without warning they did not reveal it, but went on with tending the coppers.

Anjalie said under her breath, "Not all slaves are in such bad shape as this, but all Lord Sedgeburrow cares about is profit. His overseer, Jacobson, is infamous for working his slaves until they drop. He pockets what he saves from not feeding and housing them decently, which is yet another reason he runs his operation so far from civilization. Even in Jamaica people are starting to complain about such inhumane treatment. Do you see now why I tried to buy him out?"

He had no time to answer, for one of the scarcely human creatures detached himself from the others, and shuffled forward. Anjalie said again under her breath, "He will be the headman, to whom they all look for guidance, just as in their villages back home."

Chance could see little difference between him and the other scarecrows, for he ducked his head in deference, and did not once raise his eyes from the ground as he reluctantly approached them.

Anjalie said something to him in a pidgin that Chance could not understand, and after a moment he answered sullenly back. Anjalie explained for Chance's benefit, "He says the overseer is drunk and passed out in his hut, and the only horses they have are workhorses, which he daren't literally for his life let us have."

Chance asked curiously, "If the overseer is drunk, why on earth don't they run away and join the others you have told me so much about? What did you call them—Maroons?"

"Because even they would turn them in for the bounty," she said in disgust. "For their own protection they have had to make peace with the colonists, and signed a treaty promising to give up any runaways they find in return for a reward."

"Good God! Could they not set up their own villages, then? The land seems bountiful enough and surely it would be an easy matter to disappear into the interior?"

She cast him a look of profound pity. "They use dogs to track them, which the poor creatures are understandably terrified of."

He absorbed that, looking again at the desperately thin figures. "Why do they look so starved? In this lush country, where fruit and meat are to be had for the taking, it seems incredible."

She shrugged. "They are not allowed to have weapons of any sort, for obvious reasons. Even to take a piece of fruit from a tree might earn them a beating. They are deliberately kept half starved, for that keeps them docile, and it is cheaper to buy a new slave to replace any who may actually die than it would be to maintain them decently."

After a moment he said merely, "Well, what is to be done? Shall we try to sober this Jacobson up and demand his permission to borrow some horses?"

"No, for I've no wish to deal with him! Have you any money?" she demanded unexpectedly.

He was surprised at the request, but said automatically, "Yes, of course. But what good is money out in the middle of nowhere like this?"

"We shall arrange to 'buy' two horses from Jacobson, and leave the money for him. The horses belong to Lord Sedgeburrow, of course, and it is extremely unlikely he will pass the sum on to his master, but at least he may not punish the headman for letting us have them." She went into a lengthy discussion in the same pidgin with the black man, who kept his eyes down the whole time and did not seem to be either agreeing or disagreeing with her.

The deal, however, in the end seemed to be struck, and Chance handed over the agreed-upon amount. Throughout the headman had not lifted his eyes and Anjalie explained for Chance's benefit," They learn never to look a European directly in the face, for they can be beaten for that as well."

Even so, the others, who had clearly been listening to the entire exchange, slowly had begun to draw nearer. Chance saw that some of those minding the huge vats were very young children, and Anjalie again explained, "Only the weak—the elderly and very young—will work here, for anyone stronger will be used out in the cane fields." She smiled and spoke cheerfully to the others, in the strange language, but received no smiles of acknowledgments in return. One very young child, with the emaciated frame and big belly of advanced starvation, sucked his fist and stared solemnly at them, but his mother jerked him abruptly behind her back, out of sight.

Anjalie said abruptly, "Let them have whatever leftover food we have. It will scarcely go round, but it will still be more meat than they have seen in a month."

He willingly did so, ignoring the rumblings in his own belly. So much unaccustomed exertion had made him unnaturally hungry, and he remembered rather ruefully that he had even nourished naive hopes, when he first saw the clearing, of being offered a decent meal. Now he acknowledged that had the overseer been sober, he would not have sat down to a meal with him knowing the condition of the poor wretches outside the door.

The food seemed pitiably meager to be shared amongst so many, but it quickly disappeared into the rags they called clothes, instead of being devoured upon the spot, as he had half expected. Anjalie held out a piece of meat invitingly to the small child who had earlier stared at them, and at her urging he shyly came from behind his mother, snatched it, and then ran away, as if he feared even then she would take it back again.

Chance said abruptly, "Find out how drunk the overseer is! If he is drunk enough, I can get more game for them to eat while you rest."

She said regretfully, "It's too risky. Were he to waken and find them with any meat, he would whip them and hang the headman, fearing they had somehow found and secreted a weapon. One of the pitfalls of slavery, especially when you treat them as badly as this, is the justifiable fear that they will one day rise up against you—and don't forget that the Maroons are a constant reminder of how often it has happened in the past. But I'm sure they've long ago learned how to snare a certain amount of game."

He had to rely upon her judgment, but before anything more could be said, there was a curse behind them, and a coarse voice demanded drunkenly, *"What the hell do ye think ye're doin'?"*

Chapter 24

They both wheeled fast, and the natives faded back to their jobs, eyes still cast down and the whites even more prominent from fear.

Anjalie looked the newcomer over, and made little attempt to hide the contempt in her voice. "Hello, Jacobson! It is I, as you see."

Jacobson was unshaven and extremely unkempt, and smelled sourly of rum. He was also swaying drunk, and dangerous with it. He was a massive, black-haired bully at the best of times, and reportedly spent so much of his time in the bush that he was scarcely civilized any longer, but Anjalie had never seen him drunk before. He carried a pistol in one unsteady hand, which he did not lower even at her words, and his very unsteadiness did not lessen, but rather increased the danger.

It seemed to take a considerable time before her words penetrated through to his fuddled brain, but then he said thickly, and with a pronounced sneer in his voice, "I'll be damned! Miss Cantrell, is it? Well . . . well . . . well . . . Don' tell me ye're jes' payin' me a nice, friendly little visit, ma'am, for as I recall, ye couldn't wait to wipe the dirt of this place off yer feet the last time ye was 'ere."

She hesitated, then said reluctantly, "We were forced to abandon ship in the hurricane, and managed to make it to

shore not too far from here. This is Lord Chance, by the
way. We came to borrow or buy some horses from you, for
we have a great many miles still to cover."

He seemed to find that exquisitely humorous. He went
off into a paroxysm of drunken laughter, slapping one knee
and almost losing his balance in the process, and waving
his pistol about in an extremely dangerous manner that had
the blacks cowering fearfully. "Well, well, well!" he said
again, still cackling drunkenly. "The boots on t'other leg
now, is it? Taken down a peg or two, ain't ye, from the
last time ye and that pa o' yourn was 'ere, lookin' down
yer nose at me and makin' demands?"

He next took in Chance's disheveled appearance, and
seemed to derive even more amusement from that. "*Lord*
Chance, did ye say? Better 'n better! Well, Miss Cantrell,
you and 'is *lordship* 'ere can jes' whistle for a pair of 'orses,
and walk all those wearisome miles through the bush if it
kills ye, which it well may, for ye'll git no favors from me.
Thinkin' yersel's better'n anybody else, and puttin' on airs!
Well, le's see how far that 'll take ye in the jungle, on foot!
From the looks of it ye've already 'ad quite a time of it,
and I'm guessin' 'is *lordship* 'ere is about as much use to
ye as a flea on a cur."

A new idea seemed to strike him, for he added sugges-
tively, "But o'course, if ye'd care to make some *private*
arrangement, like, ma'am, ye might find me more accom-
modatin'. Maybe ye're tired o' these overbred dandies and
would prefer a real man for a change?" He looked her
over in a way that was extremely insulting, taking in her
tangled hair and the torn shoulder of her gown. "Ye're too
damned bossy fer my taste, and I likes my wimmin to *be*
wimmin, but it's bin months since I seen me a white one,
and I dessay I ain't too particular by now—"

He never got to finish the sentence. His lordship, seeming
to move like lightning, hit him with an extremely powerful
right to the jaw. Jacobson, taken wholly off guard, and his
reactions slowed by alcohol, only belatedly got off a shot
which exploded with a deafening crash, causing most of the
blacks to throw themselves to the earth in terror. He then
crashed heavily backward, and lay sprawled unconscious in
the dirt, breathing stertorously, and with a blackening
bruise beginning to show on his lower jaw.

Anjalie, who had not even squeaked when Jacobson's pistol had gone off, was regarding his lordship with new respect. He was calmly shaking out his right hand as if it hurt him, and she saw that the knuckles were grazed and bleeding slightly. While not supposing it required any particular heroism to knock out a drunken bully, she liked the speed and efficiency in which it had been done, and knew that Jacobson, though drunk, was immensely strong and had something of a reputation as a fighter. She had not previously seen Chance in such a light, though she remembered now that Adam had once speculated that he would peel to advantage.

He returned her regard a little mockingly, still nursing his knuckles. "I don't care for the way your friend negotiates. Let's take what horses we need and get out of here."

"Willingly! Do you box?" she asked curiously.

"Yes, Miss Innocent, I do!" he retorted. "Don't bother to tell me that you didn't believe me capable of knocking a man down, because I am well aware of it. And since he was three parts drunk and weaving on his feet with it, you need not do much violence to your feelings. In his present condition I daresay these miserable wretches could have succeeded in flooring him."

She was obliged to laugh. "Perhaps, but I am not so unimpressed as you might think. He is a notorious bully and has a local reputation for being a considerable brawler. But let us by all means get out of here."

The headman, with a great deal more willingness than he had shown before, helped them to saddle up two horses. The ugly, half-starved brutes he produced, with dirty tack and, of course, no sidesaddle for Anjalie, gave both of them pause, but they were certainly in no position to be too picky. Even mules would have been preferable to walking, but Chance said uneasily, "Good God! You will be saddlesore before ever we've gone a mile. Can't he find something else?"

"You must have seen by now that not a penny that could go into Jacobson's own pocket will have been wasted, and no doubt these poor animals, dreadful as they are, are treated considerably better than the slaves," retorted Anjalie. "But don't waste your concern on me, my lord! I only wish I were wearing breeches, for when I am in the interior

I often ride astride. Never mind! I will engage for it not to fall off, even with my annoying skirts. Besides, I can't exactly see these poor miserable bundle of bones running away with us, can you?"

He was obliged to stifle his doubt, and reluctantly threw her up into the saddle of the handsomer of the two animals, whose frame was not quite so angular as the other, and whose sides showed a fraction fatter. She managed to get her knee efficiently over the pommel, and pronounced herself excellently suited.

Chance made no reply to this patent exaggeration, but once astride his own allotted brute, hesitated, and then asked somewhat helplessly, "Is there nothing more we can do for these people? Will he blame them for the horses when he regains consciousness?"

"Probably," she returned shortly. "It does nothing to help these poor wretches, but the days of slavery are numbered, even in Jamaica. Most of the planters remain convinced they cannot run their plantations without it, but I have wholly disproved that with my coffee plantation. England has already outlawed the trade, as you well know, and though so far there are plenty of ways around the embargo, there are enough humane souls, both here and in England, that I firmly believe the practice will be wholly abolished within my lifetime. But that is small consolation to these poor devils."

He shrugged, and since they both thought it best not to wait until Jacobson regained consciousness, they thanked the headman again and took their leave.

Chance was soon to discover that his own nag possessed a mouth as hard as iron, and a plodding amble that was so uncomfortable it almost made walking seem preferable. But at least he could rid himself of his cloak bag, whose weight and cumbersome bulk he had long since wearied of, and although they scarcely made better time, for neither brute would quicken at all, at least the horses took the main brunt of forcing their way through the close brush, which spared them a certain amount of cuts and scratches.

Once they had left the sugar plantation behind, Chance glanced again at Anjalie to see how she was faring. Her own rasher of wind scarcely looked suitable for plowing the fields, but even mounted on such a bag of bones, and with no sidesaddle, she still took the shine out of any other female rider he had ever seen. He shook his head, and inquired somewhat dryly of her, "I must suppose that after you helped his housekeeper to run away, Lord Sedgeburrow will be less inclined than ever to sell to you. But do you mean to give up on that particular notion?"

"Not at all! I hope he has no particular reason to connect me with poor Mrs. Milford, but if Adam cannot convince him to sell to me, the next time he is in England, I shall find someone else to act as a go-between."

"I see you have at least dropped the polite fiction that your father has anything to do with the affair. But I might be able to help once I have returned to England. And if he does not agree to sell to me voluntarily, after having seen these poor wretches I confess I will not hesitate to find other means to—persuade him, if necessary."

"Thank you! Any means you can bring to bear on him would be greatly appreciated. But short of kidnapping him and dragging him out here to see for himself the misery he causes, I fear nothing is likely to help."

He began to laugh, the unexpected sound startling another cloud of birds to take wing, squawking and protesting. "Don't try to tell me you're not fully capable of doing exactly that, Miss Cantrell, for I warn you I wouldn't believe you."

She grinned reluctantly at his amusement and little more was said for some time. Both were eager to make up for lost time, and put such a dreadful place behind them as quickly as possible. His lordship, his unwilling admiration for Anjalie growing almost hourly, stole a glance now and then at her face, wondering if she could possibly be as unaffected by their ordeal as she pretended. The going was still extremely rough, even with the horses, and once they lost sight of the sea he himself was totally lost. For all he really knew they might be going around in circles. Even so, he could not deny that there were certain aspects about their present adventure that he was enjoying very much.

Even the episode with Jacobson, unpleasant as it had been, had not been without its satisfaction. So far he feared he had merely reinforced the weak opinion she already had of him, and he still had little choice but to meekly follow where she led. Her view of him as an effete Englishman incapable of proving himself in such an uncivilized world unfortunately seemed all too accurate—a fact that annoyed him more than it no doubt should have.

When they began to leave the sea behind and climb into the interior, at least it began to grow slightly cooler. They had neither of them had anything to eat since breakfast, and Chance's stomach was beginning to rumble again by then. But he felt as she did that the more ground they covered the better, and so did his best to ignore his growing hunger. They stopped once or twice for a rest and a drink of tepid water, and luckily fruit was plentiful. She had directed him once to gather a few coconuts, which she promised him were delicious and had their own water stored in them besides. But mostly they pressed on, soon too hot and tired even to bother to talk.

He had no way of assessing how much time had passed, and he had no real belief that they would reach civilization before nightfall. The thick junglelike growth mercifully shielded them from the full glare of the sun, but it seemed to him they had been plodding along for a great many weary hours. More, they had begun to climb in earnest by then, which made the going even more treacherous.

It was then, as they climbed a particularly steep grade, that they unexpectedly flushed a pair of brightly colored, raucously screeching birds who flew up out of the brush and straight at them. The iron-mouthed, bony-rumped commoner that Anjalie was precariously perched upon, without a sidesaddle, reared in sudden fright. Even so, ordinarily Anjalie would have been more than capable of controlling him. But that iron mouth, coupled with the steep grade and her lack of sidesaddle, were her undoing. Before Chance could reach her, hampered as he was himself by the steepness of the narrow path, and his own mount's intractability, the clumsy brute had overbalanced and crashed heavily backward. Anjalie, her knee hooked round the pommel, and no doubt hampered by her skirts as well, did what she could to save herself, but she perforce fell heavily with him.

Chance was out of the saddle in an instant, and had reached her almost as quickly, but to his extreme alarm she lay ominously still where she had fallen.

She looked pale, and was sprawled uncomfortably on the steep trail, but he dared not move her. At least she was breathing, and when he found the pulse in her neck, it was beating strongly. He could not tell if she were merely stunned or unconscious, but when he called her name in an imperative voice, he thought her eyelids fluttered slightly. Considerably relieved, he called to her again, and was even more relieved when after a moment she slowly opened her eyes.

She stared vaguely up at him, as if dazed, but seemed to have all her senses, for she demanded weakly, "Good God, what happened?"

"Your horse came down with you," he told her curtly. "Don't try to move just yet."

She stirred, ignoring this command, and said with the beginnings of disbelief, "Did you say *I fell?*"

He was even more relieved at these returning signs of normalcy. "No, I said your horse came down with you, the clumsy brute," he said calmly. "And for once in your life do as you're bid. We don't know what damage you may have done."

He was rapidly feeling her arms and legs as he spoke, but predictably she again ignored him and tried to sit up. She made it only halfway, however, before giving a strangled cry and falling back again.

He regarded her with rapidly reawakening alarm. "What is it?" he demanded grimly, "You may as well tell me, because I can see from your face that it's bad."

She had closed her eyes again, and lay somewhat rigidly, but she said through gritted teeth, as if the words were forced out of her, "If you must know, I—would seem to have—broken—my wrist! *Hell and the devil confound it!* Of all the stupid—clumsy—" She abruptly clipped off the words and turned her head away, shielding her eyes from the sun and his scrutiny with her right hand, the other lying awkwardly where she had fallen.

Chapter 25

He wasn't even tempted to smile at these most unlady
like words, and could only stare down at her, appalled
Her left wrist was indeed already badly swollen and begin
ning to show considerable bruising. There were no bones
protruding through the skin, or obvious signs of dislocation
but that seemed cold comfort to him. He made no attempt
to examine it, but said even more grimly, "I have very little
experience of such things, but I'm afraid you may be right."

She swore again, then clipped out, "Then you will—just
have to set it. Are the—horses lamed? You'd—best go
and—see, for then we—would be—in the suds."

He was uncertain whether to admire or deplore such
foolhardy courage, for he privately considered that it could
scarcely have been worse. He knew absolutely nothing
about setting bones, and even ignoring that considerable
obstacle, he did not see how she could possibly ride on
over that impossible country on the back of a brute whose
every clumsy step must mean agony to her.

There seemed to be no point in revealing these misgiv
ings to her, however. He therefore made her as comfort
able as he could, putting his rolled cloak under her head
before he went reluctantly to secure the two horses. She
was right: however much he might bitterly blame them for
the present catastrophe, they would need them more than
ever if they were ever to get out of there. He ran his hand
over the legs of the clumsy nag who had started it all, by
now unconcernedly cropping vegetation, but he seemed to
have emerged unscathed. He tied the reins of both nags to
a handy bush and then went about his grim preparations
First he purloined a spare petticoat from Anjalie's bundle
without apology, on the theory that when—or rather if—
they ever reached civilization again, she would have an en
tire wardrobe to fall back on, whereas he now possessed
scarcely more than the clothes he stood up in.

Then he went to find a pair of suitably straight sticks

and cut them to the length he calculated he would need. He was dreading the coming ordeal probably even more than she was, but when he went reluctantly back to kneel beside Anjalie, she lay with her arm over her face and her eyes closed, the pain in that unguarded moment clearly to be seen on her face. His own courage almost failed him, but she opened her eyes then and looked straight up at him and said weakly, "Don't—look so alarmed. It is only— a broken wrist, after all, and I promise—not to yell and scream, or faint dead away, if—that is what you fear."

He refrained from saying that on the whole he would prefer it if she did faint, for it would make it easier on both of them. "No, that's not what I fear," he said even more dryly. "Here, drink this."

She might be in considerable pain, but she had lost little of her spirit. "What is it?" she demanded crossly. "If it's brandy, I don't want it. I'm not likely to—die of a broken wrist, and the longer you put it off—the harder it's—going to be."

"I didn't ask whether you wanted it or not," he told her bluntly. "However sure you may be of your own courage, Miss Cantrell, mine is likely to be severely tested in the next few minutes. Now open your mouth!"

She looked rather as if a pet dog had just turned on her, and despite their present predicament he almost laughed. But then she surprised him by abruptly capitulating.

He took full advantage of this unwonted docility, lifting her head and ruthlessly tilting a considerable quantity of brandy down her throat before she could voice any further objections. She choked a little, then lay back weakly, her eyes again closed and her good arm covering her face from his view. He took a deep breath, and then made himself go about his grim task.

It would have been hard to say which of them suffered the most under his undoubtedly inept ministrations. He knew enough to know it was necessary to get the ends of the broken bone again aligned or it would never heal properly, but the swelling hampered him in this seemingly simple task. Throughout it all she lay rigidly, her head turned away, and her right hand clenched tightly against the pain, and did not once cry out. He knew he must be hurting her abominably, and was soon sweating in a way that had nothing to do with the heat of the day.

He half hoped she would faint, but knew by the continued rigidity of her body and the raggedness of her breathing that she was still conscious—a circumstance that certainly did not help his task any. By the time he had at last straightened the broken bone to his satisfaction, then splinted the wrist and wrapped it as tightly as he dared, he suspected he was the one in need of brandy.

"It's over, thank God, so you may abandon your heroics, Miss Cantrell!" he told her rather harshly. "It may surprise you to know, I wouldn't have thought the worse of you for crying out when you were hurt."

She opened her eyes to look up at him and said pantingly, "You should know by now—that I am—far more likely to swear!"

He could not resist smiling down at her. "Swear then by all means. You may madden and infuriate and thwart me at every turn, but at least I have long since given up being shocked by anything you may do, Miss Cantrell. Now try and get some rest, for I must leave you briefly. I mean to get us something to eat while you are resting, for we will need food if we are indeed to go on."

It was not the whole truth, but he thought it would be time enough to clear the next hurdle when he could no longer keep it from her. It was doubtful, anyway, that she fully understood his words, for she merely closed her eyes again wearily, a deep frown of pain between her brows. He hoped she might drift off to sleep, and so reluctantly rose and left her.

His preparations, fortunately, did not take as long as he had feared. When at last he came to her again and knelt beside her, she seemed thankfully to have fallen into a light doze. He wouldn't have awakened her, but she stirred at his presence and slowly opened her eyes.

For a moment she seemed not to recognize him, then her vision cleared, and she drew a sharp breath as if with pain. "Oh, it's you," she said in a slightly slurred tone. "Is it time to go?'

He smiled down at her again, not wholly sorry for this opportunity to get a little of his own back again and informed her with unwonted gentleness, "I am sorry to be

bliged to break it to you, Miss Cantrell, but we are not
oing any further today. There is a place I have found not
o distant from here that is comparatively level and even
as a spring, and we are going to camp there for the night."

That brought her more fully to her senses. "Nonsense!"
he said more sharply. "Do you think I—cannot sit a horse
st because I've broken my wrist?"

"I'm sure you would make the attempt, if it killed you,"
e told her with exceeding frankness. "But I have no inten-
ion of allowing you to martyr yourself. And you needn't
lare, or think to run roughshod over me any longer, as
ou have been doing ever since we left the ship. You have
ragged me all over this damnable island, and enjoyed
ourself very much in doing it, and I have voiced no com-
laint, but I regret to inform you, Miss Cantrell, that the
ables have now turned. We are certainly not going on
oday, and I am even doubtful about tomorrow. If you are
ot wholly exhausted by my alarmingly inexpert ministra-
ions, I confess I am, and I suspect I shall need at least a
lay to recuperate from my ordeal."

It was too much to expect she would not put up an argument. She made a spirited attempt to convince him that
he was fully capable of riding any number of miles through
lifficult terrain with a broken wrist, or a broken leg for
hat matter. But in the end even she seemed to realize that
he was at a disadvantage, lying awkwardly on the ground
nd in so much pain that the least movement jarred her
njured wrist almost unbearably. The brandy no doubt
lelped as well—a fact that he had been strongly counting
n—for she seemed increasingly heavy-eyed, and her argu-
nent began to lack conviction.

When he grew tired of such willful folly, he interrupted
er without apology. "Oh, enough, ma'am!" he said impa-
iently. "I have never doubted your courage, if that is what
ou fear; but you are wasting your breath, and what is
vorse, exhausting yourself to no purpose in this senseless
argument. I have made up my mind. The first thing to be
lone is to move you to the campsite I have found, and I
uspect that alone will try your courage as thoroughtly as
ven you could wish. And if that thought does not suffi-
iently daunt you, remember that you are dependent upon

me now for your simplest needs, and it would be as we
for you to remember the fact!"

She said in an exhausted voice. "It seems you are of
sudden full of a great deal of—resolution my lord, most c
it unwarranted. But—very well. I will—concede the poir
to you for today. But don't forget you have not—the leas
experience of the tropics and if you think that you can—

"What I think," he interrupted again without compunc
tion, "is that if you hope to prevail on me tomorrow, yo
would do as well to save your strength now. I don't knov
whether you perpetuate the myth you have concocte
about me to convince me, or merely yourself, but in eithe
case I have grown extremely tired of it. Admittedly I hav
no experience of the tropics, but I am at least more capabl
than someone who can barely draw a breath without cryin
out from pain. And if I cannot succeed in taking over th
responsibility for our survival in this extremis, then I de
serve every hard word you have ever said about me. Nov
I am going to carry you some few hundred yards—and tr
if you can to get through *that* ordeal before you boast an
more to me of your stamina."

Without further ado he knelt beside her, and carefull
placing her injured wrist across her body, picked her u
easily. For all her strength of will, he was surprised to fin
her unexpectedly light; and as he had suspected, after th
first moment it took every ounce of that will for the reall
formidable task of keeping herself from fainting dead awa}
so that she had no breath left for protest.

He had no very great distance to cover, but she was rigi
with pain by the time he laid her carefully down on th
piled-up bed of greenery he had prepared for her, an
wrapped one of the boat cloaks around her. She seeme
by then to have lost all will to complain, and instead la
with her eyes closed, looking wholly exhausted. But h
should have known she would still manage to have the las
word. Just as he was about to withdraw and leave her t
sleep, she said bitterly, without troubling to open her eye:
"You may have won for now—my lord!—but the—argu
ment is very far from— being over. If I—were you, I
would—enjoy your brief victory while you can!"

He laughed, and raising her sound hand to his lips, kisse
it before he rose and left her.

She slept fitfully for what remained of the day, though she seemed restless, and once or twice moaned in her sleep. He himself performed a number of small tasks, including fetching the rest of their stuff, providing for the worthless horses, and building a small fire against the coming night.

She seemed to have accepted the inevitable for the moment, but short of hog-tying her he had little hope of being able to keep her quiet for one more day, however unfit she might be to travel on the morrow. On the other hand, he was anxious to get her to a doctor, for he mistrusted his own handiwork. All in all, the next day promised to be fraught with difficulty, and his former carefree mood had certainly abandoned him with a vengeance. He tried not to think what he would do if she became seriously ill, or unable to lead them. But he could not deny that there was a certain satisfaction in knowing that she was reliant upon him for a change.

Soon after the tropical dusk had fallen she roused and said sharply into the darkness, "Who's there—?"

He rose and went to her immediately. "It's only me," he said reassuringly. "How do you feel—or is that a foolish question?"

When she made no answer, he added dryly, "Of course it is. Never mind. Are you hungry?"

"Hungry?" She sounded groggy and unlike herself, as if the word had no meaning to her. He frowned and put his hand on her forehead, fearing to discover she had developed a fever. He was relieved to find it cool enough, and even more relieved when she pushed it away, muttering pettishly, "Don't treat me like an invalid! And don't dare to gloat over my downfall. This is merely a—temporary setback, I assure you."

"You're welcome," he retorted with some irony. "But don't think to take your spleen out on me, my girl. You should know by now I will give as good as I get. Whether you're hungry or not, you must eat something, for you've scarcely had anything all day. I managed to get a brace of some bird or another, and though my culinary skills still leave a great deal to be desired, I myself was so hungry I was in little mood to be choosy."

"Oh, go to the devil!" she snapped, sounding more like herself.

But when he brought some of the meat to her, and warned her that unless she were sensible and tried to eat they would certainly not be stirring a step on the morrow, she made a show of trying to do so, though in truth she got very little down. But that seemed to exhaust her sufficiently that she soon went back to sleep again.

They both passed a fitful night, not helped by the fact that it rained a little toward dawn. It seemed to be no more than a brief tropical storm, and scarcely even cooled the temperature down any, for it remained amazingly warm, even for the altitude. They were to some extent sheltered by the trees from the worst of the rain, and thankfully Anjalie did not awaken, helped by the fact he had pulled the boat cloak wholly over her for protection almost as soon as the first drops began to fall.

His lordship, who had thus far spent an even less restful night than his patient, abandoned any further attempt to sleep at that point; and once the brief rain was over, rebuilt the fire and sat over it until morning, a prey to his own thoughts, many of them exceedingly unwelcome.

Shortly after first light she roused. Chance thought she looked pale and heavy-eyed, and far from well, but he was not surprised when she defiantly pronounced herself perfectly able to travel. But since he did not think another night spent in the open would be at all beneficial, he blandly pretended to accept her assurances.

"But only if you agree to eat something first," he warned her. "And if I should decide for any reason that you are unfit to go on, do not think you will bully or browbeat me into continuing, my girl. You may be used to twisting your father and Trelawney round your thumb, but I warned you that the reins of government have changed hands, and for once in your life you will do as you're bid. Is that clear?"

She did not even deign to reply to that, but at least she did eat more of the leftover meat than she had managed to choke down the night before, and drank thirstily from the wine bottle he had filled with ice-cold water from the springs. He knew nothing of tropical fevers, and watched her warily, fearing she might be vulnerable in her weakened state—especially after the night's rain. But he knew better than to voice such a thought aloud, or try again to feel her forehead.

He did, however, insist upon fashioning a sling for her with the remains of her torn-up petticoat, adjusting it so that her arm was held close to her body and would be jolted as little as possible. Whether she could endure a day's hard riding was open to doubt, but there seemed little to be gained by remaining there and he was increasingly anxious to get her to civilization.

When the time came, he lifted her into the saddle as gently as he could, and thereafter kept an extremely worried eye on her. She in turn sat stubbornly erect, and whenever she caught his eyes upon her took care to hide whatever discomfort she might be feeling—a fact that did not increase his pleasure in the day any. She didn't succeed in fooling him that it was anything other than an ordeal that grew increasingly more difficult as the hours passed, and the only good thing to be said was that she soon lacked even the energy to take her bad temper out on him.

He thought her a stubborn little fool, and the bravest female he had ever known, and almost called a halt a dozen times. But his own anxiety to get her home, coupled with her stubborn refusal to confess to the least weakness, always kept him silent in the end.

In the beginning she had still insisted upon assuming charge of their journey. His lordship had by then managed to find his bearings, and knew that they were making always to the southeast—though they were far too often forced to go considerably out of their way, whenever the way grew too steep or they came up against some obstacle that the horses found too difficult to cross.

As the day wore on, though, and it obviously required all of Anjalie's energy merely to remain upright in the saddle, he began to take over more and more of the decision-making. He had a fair sense of direction, and continued to lead them, wherever possible, in the same general direction, but her weariness caused him to slow their already snail-like progress even further. In the meantime he refused to think what the consequences would be if he got them wholly lost in such an empty wilderness, which was a fate that seemed all too unpleasantly likely.

He told himself that the island was not very large, and if worse came to worse, they would end up on the protected southern shore, where most of the population lived. But another glance at her set, pale face warned him that Anjalie was almost at the end of her tether. They had stopped only briefly for lunch, which she made no pretense of eating, and a brief rest, and toward the end of that long, extremely wearing day he began to think seriously of calling a halt once more.

They would have to stop soon anyway, for the sun had long since begun to sink toward the west—at least reassuring him that they were still traveling in the right direction. Anjalie had been silent for some hours, and only managed to stay in the saddle through instinct and sheer stubborn determination. But she had begun to sway, her face so white he was growing seriously alarmed.

It was at this extremely opportune point that they crested one last rise, and to his immense relief he saw a very different terrain laid out before them. Even to his inexperienced eyes it looked unmistakably cultivated, and though he had naturally never seen a coffee plantation in his life before, and had vaguely imagined the beans grew on trees, not bushes; it seemed very likely that that was what was growing before him in such neat rows.

Chapter 26

The next moment a very small black child appeared as if out of nowhere to gape at them. He had several fingers in his mouth, and wore next to nothing, but bore little other resemblance to the scarecrows Chance had seen the day before. He was plump and curious, and stared at them unblinkingly for a long moment, then abruptly took to his heels, beginning to shout something at the top of his lungs.

Chance followed more slowly, Anjalie's mount docilely behind him, as it had been for some hours. He trusted the child was leading them toward the house, and wondered belatedly if there was likely to be anyone there who spoke anything but the pidgin he had heard spoken so far, and which was totally incomprehensible to him. Anjalie seemed scarcely aware of what had happened, and might well be past translating by then. But the most important thing was to get her into a decent bed and have her broken wrist looked to by someone more knowledgeable than himself.

In a few minutes Chance caught sight of a large house, painted a dazzling white and built on a rise, with deep screened verandas on all sides—both no doubt designed to help deal with the heat, which even at that elevation and that late in the day was considerable. Tropical flowers rioted everywhere, and he found the whole oddly attractive, though unlike anything he had ever seen before. Flowering vines climbed even the side of the house itself; and behind were to be seen a number of outbuildings, as well as a row of well-built palm-roofed huts.

At first there was no sign of any other human habitation, but the child had obviously penetrated into the house by then, for in another moment a tall, spare black woman came quickly out of the house and stood shading her eyes against the glare of the westering sun. She was dressed in colorful garb, and held herself with an oddly regal grace, and bore even less resemblance to the wretches he had seen the day before.

For a long moment she stood there immovable, which belatedly reminded Chance of what they must both look like by then. He was certainly unshaven and bedraggled, and Anjalie was no better, so that it was little wonder if the woman scarcely recognized them.

Then Anjalie apparently roused sufficiently to realize where they were, for in the next moment she had given a little cry, and before he could begin to guess at her intention, had tumbled from the saddle, despite her hurt wrist, and was running toward the tall figure. "Juba!" she cried joyfully. "Oh, *Juba!*"

Chance watched somewhat ruefully as the figure on the porch started toward her and Anjalie was enfolded tightly in the black arms. After that neither of them said anything for a very long time and he knew himself to be wholly forgotten.

Juba was the first to raise her eyes, though she did not release her tight hold on her former nursling. Chance had dismounted by then, and was watching this touching reunion with an odd smile on his face. She in turn studied him curiously and more than a little critically, her eyes beginning to twinkle a little as she took in the ragged and unshaven creature before her.

"You must be the English *milord* I have heard so much about," she remarked in perfect English, but with a surprisingly strong French accent. "I confess, you do not look exactly like what I had expected. But *Dieu soit béni,* you have brought *la petite* back to us."

His smile involuntarily grew, for he liked what he had seen of her so far. But he said frankly, "If you know anything at all of your *petite,* ma'am, you must know that the boot is very much on the other leg. And if you are relieved to see us, you cannot know how relieved I am to see *you!*"

Anjalie had lifted her head by then, and surreptitiously wiped her damp cheeks, before saying in some confusion, "But I don't understand. What are you doing here, Juba? And where's Papa?"

Juba replied with a composure Chance was to learn was seldom lost. "In Port Royal, awaiting word of your safety, *petite*—unless, of course, he has already set sail to go in search of you, for he was threatening to do so when I came away. You know well *le bon papa* will never trust anyone but himself, especially on so important a matter."

Both Anjalie and his lordship stared at her. "To go in search of me?" Anjalie repeated in bewilderment. "Do you mean he already knows the *MaryAnne* was lost?"

"Of a certainty, but the *MaryAnne* was not lost," said Juba even more surprisingly. "After you and *Monsieur le vicomte* here were swept away, *Capitaine* Morton was able to bring her limping into port, though with such heavy news to bear, or so he thought, that he confessed he almost wished he had drowned rather than face your father. Everyone naturally assumed that you must be lost, *tous les deux,* but that would never do for *le bon papa.* And it appears that he was right," she added dryly.

"Good God!" said Anjalie blankly. "But what are you doing here?"

"To wait for you, of course. *Capitaine* Morton assured him the *MaryAnne* was not so many days out from Jamaica when the hurricane struck, and that you might make it safely to land. After that, *le bon papa* naturally insisted ᵇbornly that he would trust to the trade winds to do the and guessed you might come here."

Chance couldn't help it. It was so ludicrous, and so exactly what he might have expected of her father, that he burst out laughing.

Both Anjalie and Juba stared at him as if he had taken leave of his senses, which made him laugh all the harder. He remembered Anjalie had once told him that Juba was the closest thing she possessed to a mother, and he could see now that it was true. It was more than obvious that an uncommonly strong bond existed between the tall black woman, so alien to anything he had himself ever known before, and her white former nursling, who had revived in her presence as a flower does to water. Anjalie was still alarmingly pale, and he suspected she would have fallen without Juba's strong arms around her, but she looked happier and more content than he had ever seen her.

Juba seemed to agree with him about her precarious state, however, for after another shrewd glance at Anjalie's face, she said merely, "But there will be time enough for all these questions and explanations. Now I think you would be much better in your bed, *p'tite*. And I think, *hein?* it would be best if *Monsieur Le Vicomte* carried you there," she added practically, "for you do not look as if you could manage on your own."

"With the greatest pleasure on earth, ma'am!" said his lordship promptly, and swept Anjalie up at once into his arms. She protested indignantly that she had no need to be carried, and had no intention of retiring to bed until she had been told all that had happened. But Chance noted with interest that the remarkable Juba seemed to be the first person he had so far been privileged to meet whom Anjalie actually obeyed, for she submitted in the end more docilely than he would have believed possible.

The house was equally a revelation to him: cool and airy, with softly polished mahogany floors left bare for coolness, a minimum of furniture, and deeply shuttered windows to keep out the sun's glare while admitting both air and light. He carried Anjalie up a broad flight of uncarpeted stairs in Juba's wake, to a bedchamber on the first floor like the rest of the house, with a four-poster bed made out of some light, exotic wood, and sheer mosquito netting drawn all around it.

He had by then formed a good enough opinion of Juba

to count her a formidable ally, and so said bluntly as he deposited his burden, "She needs a doctor to attend to her, ma'am! She suffered a bad fall, and has broken her wrist, and while I set it as best I could, I regret I know next to nothing of such matters. Today's ride cannot have helped, let alone a night spent in the open. If she does not end in a high fever I will own myself very much surprised."

"Good God, I don't need a doctor!" exclaimed Anjalie scornfully, evidently fast recovering her spirits. "Do you really imagine me so fragile and helpless as to contract a fever from no more than a night spent in the open? Juba knows me better!"

And for once even Juba failed him. She looked to be quietly amused by this spirited interchange, but said somewhat apologetically, "I regret, *milord,* a *medecin* could not be fetched in under a day or two, for he would have to come all the way from Kingston. Besides, it is true enough that *la petite* is seldom ill."

"Then I beg you will at least take a look at her wrist, ma'am, for I place little reliance on my own handiwork," he said even more grimly. "She has been assuring *me* all day that she is perfectly well, when she could hardly remain erect in the saddle. But I am delighted to leave her in your capable hands. Perhaps *you* will be able to talk some sense into her."

Juba looked between them, her eyes twinkling once more. "I fear, *m'sieur,* that you have not had an easy time of it," she said in some amusement.

He grinned involuntarily back at her. "Your talent for understatement is remarkable, ma'am. But I confess it— had its moments. Try if you can convince her to stay in bed for a few days and rest."

"Don't discuss me as if I were not here!" Anjalie protested furiously. "And I have not the least intention of spending so much as a day in bed, for I have every intention of leaving tomorrow for Kingston to see Papa."

His lordship and the black woman exchanged resigned glances, but it was Juba who said pacifically, "*Quant à ça,* word has already been sent that you are safe, *p'tite;* and as
myself, I fully expect to see *le bon papa* here by first
omorrow. He is every bit as foolish as you are, de-
's age, and will certainly waste little time in riding

ventre à terre to see for himself that you are safe. And now I will venture to prescribe for *Monsieur le Vicomte* as well. A hot bath and a shave, *hein?* and then a good meal, for I confess you do not at all resemble the English *milord* I was expecting."

Chance rubbed his chin rather ruefully. "And *I* confess I have been dreaming of very little else for days, ma'am. But I have grown so used to my current disgraceful condition that I scarcely even notice it any longer. And at least if the *MaryAnne* is not at the bottom of the sea, there is some hope I may eventually be reunited with the rest of my baggage, which is more than I had dared hope for."

"Thus averting a tragedy!" put in Anjalie flippantly. "You will find, Juba, that his appearance is the only thing an Englishman cares about."

"I also find, *hélas,* that none of it would seem to have rubbed off on you," Juba told her with mock severity. "I hoped you might return from so sophisticated a city having learned at long last to be a lady; but instead you are the same *petite sauvage* as ever. I fear *Monsieur le Vicomte* must be very much shocked."

"You needn't worry, Juba," retorted Anjalie, "for he knew me for a savage the moment he first set eyes on me, and has thus been spared any consequent disillusionment. For my part, though I am well aware that he cannot wait to put this ordeal behind him, I consider that a few days in the tropics, forced to fend for himself without his valet and his butler and I know not what besides, has done him a world of good!"

Juba again looked between them with her disconcertingly shrewd eyes. "I see as well that your sojourn in England has failed to soften your tongue, *p'tite,* which I confess is an even greater pity."

"No, no, I am relieved enough to see her so much restored to her usual self, ma'am, that I assure you I do not regard it," his lordship told her in amusement. "Now I will take you up on that promise of a bath, and leave her to your expert ministrations."

He bowed, then unexpectedly possessed himself of Anjalie's hand and added softly, for her ears alone, "I can see I leave you in good hands, Miss Cantrell. But you are mistaken about one thing: contrary to your expectations, there is much about our recent ordeal that I—enjoyed very much indeed." He then again raised her hand to his lips and kissed it, a disturbing light in his eyes. The next moment he was gone.

After a luxurious hot bath and a shave, during which as much as could be done to brush and press his clothes and polish his boots was accomplished by a highly efficient staff of beaming blacks, his lordship was able to present himself to Juba in a slightly more civilized guise.

He also discovered he was to get his French meal after all. Juba had prepared it herself, and stood behind his chair in the correct manner, refusing his invitation to join him, while he was served. He ate ravenously, complimenting her and assuring her that she would be in much demand as a cook in England, which seemed to amuse her.

She had earlier assured him in her calm way that she had examined the broken wrist of her former nursling, and found it much inflamed, for which she had applied some concoction of her own, and replaced his makeshift splint with something rather less makeshift, all of which her charge had borne with fortitude. She was now sleeping, urged thereto both by the exhausting ordeal she had endured, and the lavish use of laudanum her nurse had had no hesitation in giving her.

"Thank God for that—though I must confess I'm surprised she consented to take any," he said rather ruefully. "I fear you must be shocked to have her returned to you in so desperate a case, ma'am."

But he was to find that Juba, like her charge, took the shipwreck and all that had followed very much in her stride. "If I were to tell you of the desperate straits she has gotten herself into—and out of again—and even the bones I have set for her, you would be surprised, *m'sieur.*" She deftly refilled his wineglass, and directed one of the servants to offer him more veal. "Even as a child she was always into mischief, and never happy unless she was risking her neck. Many's the time I warned *le bon papa* that he ought to turn her into a proper young *demoiselle,* but he never would listen to me."

"Yes, I have understood from things Miss Cantrell let drop that he is a—most unusual father," Chance remarked, unable to keep a slight edge out of his voice.

If she heard it, she gave no sign. "Of a certainty. He said that if she was to be part of the New World, he would not have her corseted and confined, in mind or body, and concerned with nothing but her mirror," she said placidly.

He laughed. "She is certainly not that," he agreed. He found himself curious about the history of so enigmatic a figure. Juba gave every sign of being educated, and certainly possessed a great deal of dignity, and was unlike anything he had expected.

"In fact, Miss Cantrell is the most unusual woman I have ever encountered," he added truthfully. "I doubt, however, that I would have the—fortitude to follow her father's example where my own daughter was concerned. What is he like? I confess I have come to be extremely curious about the progenitor of so remarkable a female."

Juba shrugged. "Very shrewd. And very little different, *quant à ça,* from the boy who first ran away to sea. But do not mistake, *milord,* for he dotes upon *la petite,* and she him." She added, as if in warning, "If one is to embrace the daughter, he must of necessity embrace the *papa* as well, *enfin.*"

"That I had also gathered," he said dryly, and wondered how much more the shrewd Juba had already guessed.

Chance spent the first comfortable night he could remember in what seemed like weeks, and slept exceedingly soundly. In the morning, over a huge breakfast, Juba again gave him reassuring tidings of the invalid, saying that *la petite* had passed a comfortable night and was now extremely cross and demanding to be allowed out of bed, which she assured his lordship were excellent signs.

He was halfway through the meal when sounds of an arrival reached him. A loud voice was heard flinging an impatient question, then there was an even louder exclamation at the answer, so that Chance was prepared when a few minutes later the senior Cantrell strode unannounced into the breakfast parlor.

His lordship slowly rose, and the two men eyed each other for a long moment, not without a certain natural hostility. For his part Chance found Anjalie's father unremarkable at first glance: not quite as tall as he was himself, and with rich living beginning to add a paunch. There was no immediately discernible resemblance to his daughter, for his hair was grizzled and his complexion deeply weather-bitten from his years at sea, and his dress both careless and somewhat old-fashioned. It was only in the lively intelligence in the eyes that Chance could trace a likeness to Anjalie, or guess that this was one of the richest men in the West Indies, who had started with nothing and built up his fortune by his own native shrewdness and hard work.

He had no idea what Cantrell saw in turn, but it was the latter whose eyes began to twinkle, and who abruptly thrust out his hand, saying with a pronounced north-country burr, "So you're the lad who's been plaguing the life out of my daughter!"

His lordship grasped the rather horny hand, but corrected him dryly. "No, sir. I am the man whose life your daughter has turned upside down, in her own inimitable way, so that I suspect it will never be the same again!"

Far from being insulted, Ned Cantrell threw back his head and gave a great roar of laughter. "Aye, led you a merry dance, did she, lad? I thought she would!" he said, not without considerable satisfaction.

Chapter 27

Chance regarded him with rising hostility, thinking his unconcern where his daughter's safety was involved was bordering on the inexcusable. "Oh, no, whatever gave you that idea, sir?" he inquired sarcastically. "She has merely encouraged my sister to defy me and make a disastrous marriage, dragged me halfway round the world when I had not the least intention or desire ever to travel to this benighted place, caused me to be shipwrecked and washed up on a tropical island, only to endure heat and mosquitoes and exhaustion, all of which she herself treated as the merest commonplace. I confess I expected a little less complaisance from her father, however. But at the very least it has inspired me with a strong curiosity to meet you, sir!"

The twinkle had grown more pronounced. "Aye, and *I'd* a strong curiosity to meet you, my lord," retorted the other bluntly. "But you're out if you expected me to believe my daughter drowned, as the rest of those fools did! I hope I taught her to take care of herself better than that. Nor you won't find her swooning away at the least little thing, for she's no delicate English miss, I thank God!"

"The least little—" After a considerable struggle with himself Chance merely said thinly, "I can only admire your fortitude, sir, even if I cannot share it."

"Nay, she's been in tougher corners than this before, lad," said her father with cheerful unconcern. "I'll warrant *she* wasn't panicked! Brought you both out safely as well, which to my way of thinking should make you devilish glad I brought her up the way I did."

"At the small cost of a broken wrist—but I have no doubt you will regard that slight inconvenience as lightly as she did herself," Chance agreed, taking little trouble by then to disguise the edge to his voice. "I can only repeat, sir: I admire your fortitude."

Cantrell laughed again, and tossed off the glass of dark rum he had gone to pour out for himself. "Ah, nothing like rum to buck a man up!" he said appreciatively. "Happen you should try it yourself, lad, for I can see you're as blue as megrim. In fact, something begins to tell me you don't like me overmuch."

"I wonder what could have given you that idea, sir?" inquired his lordship even more sarcastically.

But Cantrell seemed more amused than affronted. "Nay, lad, it's no use coming the lord over me," he said frankly, "for happen my daughter will have told you I've no great use for the aristocracy. Nor I've no intention of staying to bandy words with you, for despite what you may think, I'm sufficiently concerned about my daughter to ride half the night and the devil of a long way to see her. If you're so set on picking a quarrel with me, it'll have to wait, and happen you won't find me so unaccommodating then, either!"

He poured himself out another glass of rum and tossed it off, then went out in his leisurely way to see his daughter.

Chance had finished his breakfast and gone out onto the screened veranda when Cantrell at last reappeared some half an hour later. The lurking twinkle in his eyes was even more pronounced, and he said without preamble, "I'm

sorry to disappoint you, lad, but happen if you're still wishful of picking a quarrel with me you'll be wasting your
breath! It appears I'm something in your debt, for my
daughter tells me—most reluctantly, mind!—that it was you
who got her safe back after she was hurt. Put her in a
terrible temper, it has, for she's no more liking for being
beholden than I have. Still, Ned Cantrell don't forget a
favor, so if you're still framing to break squares with me—
as I can see you are!—go ahead. I've a broad enough
back."

"But then I've no great liking for forlorn hopes!" retorted his lordship disagreeably. "As for being beholden to
me, neither of you need regard that, for I was merely returning the favor. Your daughter certainly saved my life
more than once during our—ordeal."

"Aye, I'll be bound she did." Cantrell chuckled. "But
that reminds me that I've a bit of news for you, my lord,
which in all the bustle I clean forgot! It's about your sister,
and not likely to put you in any better frame of mind, for
from all I've heard from my daughter, and indeed what I
can see for myself, you look to be a proud, stiff-necked
sort of man. But since I've no use for roundaboutation I'll
tell you straight out that—"

"My sister is married!" interrupted his lordship grimly.
"You're right, I *don't* like it. But the news hardly comes
as a shock to me by now."

"Nay, lad, you're out there, for she's not married," said
Cantrell, with another of his disconcerting twinkles.
"Though whether you'll think the whole of my news any
more to your liking I can't yet tell, having not had enough
time yet to take your measure."

"I thought, like your daughter, it was enough to know I
was an aristocrat to take all the measure you needed!"
retorted his lordship. "But did you say my sister is *not
married?*" he repeated incredulously, the words only then
penetrating.

Cantrell chuckled. "That's right. At the moment she's
installed in my house in Kingston, and the devil's own time
I had in dissuading her from coming with me, once she'd
heard you were safe. Mighty worried about you she's been,
and blaming herself something chronic, though precious little good that would do, and so you may be sure I told her.

In fact, I don't hesitate to tell you, my lord, I've taken a rare shine to that young sister of yours, despite her aristocratic background, for I'm not quite such a snob as you seem to think me."

Chance's brows had suddenly met in a heavy frown, and he was regarding his host intently. "If we are not to quarrel, it would be as well if I didn't tell you what I think of you, sir," he said frankly. "But I confess your news does indeed come as a considerable surprise to me. Do I take it I owe this sudden about-face to you?"

"Nay, lad, which by your bristles I guess will come as even more welcome news! Happen you owe it to yourself, in a roundabout manner o' speaking. That and the long sea voyage, which gave her time to think, which is what I've always found sea travel good for myself. Took to life aboard ship, according to that boy of mine, as if she'd been born to it like my own lass was, and apparently never enjoyed herself more."

Chance was still frowning. "Are you seriously telling me that on this precious sea voyage my sister came to realize her mistake?" he demanded incredulously.

Cantrell chuckled again. "Aye, she's apparently discovered she mistook her own heart exactly as you told her she had. But before you go running away with congratulating yourself on your narrow escape, my lord, you'd best hear the rest, for I suspect you won't like it! Seems she's instead fallen head over top in love with that lad of mine, and he with her. Happen you'll consider that little improvement, but if so, I'll tell you to your head, that I'll think even less of you for it. He may not be as well-born as she, with a fine title to his name and a long line of blue-blooded relations at his back, but you'd have to go a long way to find so promising and steady a lad as Adam Trelawney, or one with a better future, come to that. He's a wealthy man already in his own right, though you mightn't think it to look at him, and will take over my business when I'm put to bed with a shovel. You may think that little enough to boast about, given the aristocratic contempt for anything to do with vulgar trade. But I can promise you there are plenty who know exactly what that's worth, and will be inclined to consider your sister the lucky one in the bargain!"

Chance was wholly astonished, though not for the reasons Cantrell imagined. *"Going to marry Trelawney—?"* he repeated, and then demanded abruptly, "Good God, sir have you told your daughter this?"

"Aye, just now," replied Cantrell, still watching him with that disconcerting twinkle in his eyes. "Happen she be trayed considerably less surprise than you have, though which leads me to my own conclusions."

Chance's expression hardened. "At this point I would put nothing past her, but if I thought for one moment that you were right, sir, I would wring her neck! You're a man who likes the word with no bark on it, so I will tell you frankly that a more unprincipled, badly brought-up, infuriating female I have yet to find! In fact, there is a great deal I have stored up to say to you on the subject, but it appears it will have to wait, for I've a more pressing matter to deal with at the moment."

Cantrell showed no particular resentment at this slur upon his abilities as a father. He merely inquired curiously "Eh, lad, what are you meaning to do?"

"See your daughter, sir! And if I find she did indeed have this scheme in mind from the start, I *will* wring her neck!"

Cantrell merely laughed and made no objection. Chance without further apology, abruptly left him to take the stairs two at a time to Anjalie's room.

He entered without ceremony, and after only the most cursory of knocks, to find her out of bed, in defiance of her nurse's orders. She was still in her nightdress and wrapper, both of some floating material trimmed lavishly with lace, with her mahogany hair streaming down her back and her injured arm in a rather more professional-looking sling. She still looked pale and unexpectedly fragile, however which fact brought him up short as perhaps nothing else could have.

There seemed to be nothing fragile about her temper however, for at sight of him she said disagreeably, "If you have come to blame me for this latest development, you are wasting your breath, my lord, and so I warn you!"

His expression again hardened, and he rather deliberately shut the door and leaned his shoulders against it. "Does Juba know you're out of bed?" he demanded, and then before she could answer, reverted to his original purpose. "And let me warn *you,* my girl, that if you mean to take your damnable temper out on me, you are also wasting your breath! Instead, tell me the truth—if you are capable of such a thing! Did you dare to throw my sister and Trelawney together, as your father suspects? Answer me!"

"You needn't look daggers at me!" she countered at once. "I may have had my suspicions, at least on Adam's part, but they were no more than that. But I couldn't be more delighted at the news, for they will deal charmingly together, however little *you* may think it! I realize it does not suit your exaggerated sense of your own importance to have such a connection with vulgar trade, but I warn you you will be doing the worst deed of your life if you try to interfere this time! What's more, if you drag her back to England against her will, I believe she will only run away again! You should have learned from your last disastrous attempt to run your sister's life that she has the right to choose her own husband, and not have one foisted on her merely to suit *your* pride and consequence!"

He ignored that to search her face closely. "And what of you and Trelawney?" he demanded "Did you ever have the least intention of marrying him, or was that merely another of your lies, designed to goad me past bearing?"

He was glad to see she at least had the grace to blush a little, though she said defiantly, "It was you who jumped to the conclusion that I meant to marry him, no doubt for reasons of your own, my lord! I merely chose not to disillusion you on the point. I love Adam dearly, but we are like brother and sister, and he is the last husband for me—as I am the last wife for him. He will suit your sister very well, and I am delighted for them both. As a matter of fact, I have not the least intention of ever marrying, for I have yet to meet any man who could offer me anything more than I have already. Now if you are quite finished, my lord, I would suggest you—"

"Have you, my girl?" he interrupted without apology, his eyes kindling. *"Have you?"* And without warning he swiftly covered the brief steps between them and pulled her ruthlessly into his arms, regardless of her broken wrist, to kiss her with considerable violence.

Apparently outraged by this treatment, Anjalie did not give in without a struggle. But hampered, as she was, by her injured wrist and generally weakened state, Chance merely laughed at her feeble attempts to free herself. Instead, his arms tightened around her still more, and he kissed her again, wholly ignoring her furious protests.

When he lifted his head the second time, he had the satisfaction of knowing he had managed to silence her, however briefly. She was breathless and clinging to him, her one good arm thrown around his neck as if for support, but he might have known it was only a temporary victory. "Let me go—damn you!" she insisted weakly. "I warned you not to try to take your bad temper out on me!"

He looked down into her pale face, and said truthfully, "If I let you go, you will only fall down. And from now on I intend to kiss you whenever I like, you little termagant! You have made all of us dance to your outrageous piping, from Darcy and that meek little cousin of yours, to that poor female and her infant whom you all but shanghaied, and now I find even my sister and that poor devil, Trelawney, have not escaped your toils! And that is to say nothing of what I myself have endured at your hands! I told your father I was coming up to strangle you, and the only thing that still has any power to amaze me is that someone has not done it long since. In fact, I came perilously close on more than one occasion recently!"

She had lowered her deceptive lashes again, but now she lifted them and said swiftly, "I am not your sister, and you will not succeed in bullying and browbeating me, my lord, so don't think it! What's more, you are in *my* house and *my* country now, and neither your title nor your wealth will avail you here."

"I thought it would not be long before we were back to that! Though how you can still dare to throw either of those into my face, after all that I have endured, merely shows how little conscience you possess!" He took another look at her white face, and without apology picked her up bodily and carried her to a convenient sofa, where he sat down with her on his lap and firmly held her there against her protests. "Will you marry me, outrageous, badly behaved, impossible girl that you are?" he demanded.

She ceased struggling, but pretended to be profoundly shocked. "Good God! Do you expect me to be flattered, my lord? I care not a jot for your title, and have not the least need of your fortune, so there is nothing to induce

me to endure your vile temper. Besides, have you forgotten
that I refuse to live in England, and you would never consent to live here?"

"I could live here very happily for the rest of my life,"
he retorted, "for I have never enjoyed myself so much as
in the past few days, as you would have seen for yourself
if you had not been so busy fighting me at every turn, my
love. But you are at least right that I have responsibilities
in England, as you do here. I therefore suggest that we find
an acceptable compromise and divide our time between the
two. I am even prepared to brave the sea again if you can
manage to endure the overcrowded conditions and snobbery of England."

The mischief was very pronounced in her eyes by then,
but still she would not admit defeat. "Surely you don't expect me to believe you have fallen in love with me!" she
argued. "You don't believe in love, remember? And besides, I thought I had plagued your life out and you could
not wait to be rid of me? Don't forget I have encouraged
your sister to defy you, dragged you all this way, shipwrecked you, forced you to exert yourself in a manner
wholly unbefitting your dignity, deprived you of—"

"If you dare to mention my valet again, I will not be
answerable for the consequences," he warned her, and shut
her up by the simple expedient of kissing her again, very
thoroughly.

This time when he raised his head he had the satisfaction
of seeing her with a glow at the back of her eyes, behind
the laughter, that he had never seen there before. But she
murmured wickedly, "I told you the New World would improve you beyond all reckoning, my lord! You are beginning to seem quite human, in fact. But aren't you forgetting
your sister? How can you forbid her to make an unequal
marriage when you yourself make an even more disastrous one?"

His arms tightened still more, and he dropped a swift
kiss on her hair. "If you don't take care, you will find out
exactly how human I am! As for my sister, I will confess
that her affairs have long since begun to pall on me. She
may marry your Adam with my blessing—in fact, he has
all my sympathy, for he looked to be a sensible fellow and
no doubt little guesses what he is letting himself in for.

And I suspect you knew from the beginning that my feelings toward you were—extremely mixed, to say the least. But I have certainly never been bored. You were also right—damn you!—when you told me the New World was just the antidote I needed for too much civilization, little though I may have believed it. You forced me for the first time in my life to cope on my own, without the trappings of my title and fortune to buffer me from the world, and for that I will always be grateful to you. But I have a strong suspicion you meant to marry me almost from the moment we met. Didn't you? Confess, vile and outrageous baggage that you are!"

Her eyes were full of all the old devilry by then. "I will only admit that the first time I met you I thought you might be the type to do very well here, despite your blue blood and your dictatorial ways. But that was before I got to know you better! Afterward you disliked me so amazingly, and were so unreasonable about your sister—let alone blaming me for her actions in that odious way, that I very soon changed my mind about you. It wasn't until we were shipwrecked together, and you forgot your precious dignity at last, that I began to think I might have been right after all, and there was some hope for you."

"That at least surprises me," he said ruefully. "Was it when I was vilely seasick that you changed your extremely unflattering opinion of me, or when I let you lead me around like a Tantony pig?"

She laughed. "Oh, you didn't do so ill, my lord—for an Englishman!" she retorted. "You are admittedly spoilt, and annoyingly pessimistic, but all in all you endured it far better than I had any right to suspect you would."

He dropped another quick kiss on her hair, then stiffened as a new idea occurred to him. "Oh, my God! You wouldn't—even you could not have actually *dared* to contrive the whole just to test me, you outrageous, unprincipled—hot-at-hand—" Words almost failed him. "I will confess I first had my suspicions when I heard that the *MaryAnne* had managed to limp home after all, but I refused to believe that even you could be so wholly without human compunction. And if I thought for one minute that you were responsible for the entire ordeal, merely so you could prove a point, I would—I would—"

She once more hid the laughter in her eyes, but then lifted them again almost immediately to demand in turn, "You would what? Murder me?"

Instead of answering, he kissed her again, very thoroughly. When they both had recovered their breath he said simply, "Have I told you yet that I adore you, unscrupulous jade that you are?"

She laughed, thinking she would scarcely have recognized him for the same man she had met in London all those months ago. But she said provocatively, "No, no, you know you cannot *seriously* wish to marry a West Indian nabob's daughter! You may be grateful to me now, but if I were so foolish as to accept your offer, how do I know you wouldn't soon come to regret it, and blame me for it?"

"Anjalie, my love, shut up!" he told her patiently. "It has amused you from the beginning to think you know me so well, and like nothing better than to put words and feelings into my mouth, but the truth is you know next to nothing about me. You little fool, have you never wondered where the name Chance came from?"

She looked surprised, and wrinkled her brow a little at that. "Good God, what does that have to do with anything? I assumed it was the name of your home."

"It is the name of my home, but to put it bluntly, my naive little love, my not-too-distant origins are scarcely more respectable than your own. My great grandfather was by all accounts a consummate rogue and ne'er-do-well whose roots were every bit as plebeian as your father's. He was shipped off to India at a very young age, the only difference being that he seems not to have been quite so enterprising as your father, and certainly did not return with a fortune. No doubt he would have died in much-deserved obscurity had he not also been a confirmed gamester, and subsequently won the estate as a result of a drunken wager at dice. He renamed it to honor the occasion, and still later, when he seems to have settled down somewhat, took the same for his title—which incidentally was purchased at a time when the royal exchequers were particularly impoverished, and not achieved through any distinguished service to the Crown."

She was laughing outright by then, but asked suspiciously, "Why did you never tell me this before? How do I know you're not just making it up now to get your way?"

"Ask Georgy if you don't believe me! And it seems I inherited more from him than I knew, for the truth is I have been bored my entire life, with nothing to do but manage my estates and cope with my young sister's antics. Which reminds me that after all the time we spent together, in such extremely close intimacy, you scarcely have any choice but to marry me, for I will not believe that even in the West Indies the proprieties can be so little regarded. In fact, we should be married almost at once, if only to make an honest woman of you again; and I know exactly where we shall spend our honeymoon. On the beach by the waterfall where we spent our first night together."

"What? I thought you could scarcely wait to be back in civilization again?" she teased him. "Besides, if we are to talk of the proprieties, my lord, it is certainly most improper for you to be in my bedchamber when I am wearing nothing but my nightgown and wrapper!"

"Even more reason why you should marry me immediately," he countered, then added wickedly, "And I have seen you in far less, if it comes to that."

When she looked puzzled he added, "Your dress, after having jumped into the sea, was scarcely decent, my intrepid little love, but I don't even mean that. If you *will* insist upon taking baths in waterfalls, you deserve all you get! Why else do you think I want to spend our honeymoon there?"

She gasped. "Of all the—and you dare to call *me* outrageous and unprincipled!'

Then she somewhat spoiled her effect by adding provocatively, "Besides, how do you know I didn't return the favor, my lord?"

His eyes alight, he would have kissed her again, but she held him off—though she could not resist putting her good hand up caressingly to one tanned cheek. "If I do consent to marry you, aren't you afraid that you will never be master in your own home, especially after all the hard names you have called me?"

His response left her weaker than ever. When she could at last manage to speak again, she protested breathlessly.

"Careful! Papa and Juba are apt to come in at any minute to see whether you have murdered me."

"I may yet! Especially since you haven't confessed that you love me and meant to have me from the start, thorn in my flesh as you are!"

She laughed up into his eyes, no longer troubling to hide the passion in her own. "I don't love you! If I agree to marry you it will merely be to stop you from persecuting your poor sister! No, no, I'm serious! Papa and Juba *will* be up here soon enough! Stone—! I begin to think you will do even better here than I had thought, for you are clearly no gentleman—!"